SUICIDE WATCH

BY CHRIS RELLIM

For information, or to order additional copies, please contact:

Beacon Publishing Group
P.O. Box 41573 Charleston, S.C. 29423
800.817.8480 | beaconpublishinggroup.com

Publishers catalog available by request.

ISBN-13: 978–1–949472–23-3

ISBN-10: 1–949472–23-3

Published in 2022. New York, NY 10001.

First Edition. Printed in the USA.

Dedication

This novel is dedicated to my brother, Derrick John Miller. Rest in paradise, brother. One day, we shall reunite.

The characters in this novel are not intended to reflect any person—living or deceased. Any similarities contained herein are purely coincidental.

A PANDEMIC

CHAPTER 1

1

Was he dead or just playing possum?

The Chesterville police officer approached the lifeless body sprawled across the grass of the baseball field with caution. The six-foot stout officer with gelled tar-black hair slicked back—much like an Italian mobster—kept his hand positioned near his gun—you know, just in case—as he snailed his way to the muscular-built teenaged John Doe.

The full moon against the backdrop of the pitch-black night sky resembled something straight out of a horror movie. The officer, oddly enough, loved the feeling someone was creeping up right behind him. An adrenaline-rush junkie.

"Hey, buddy?" the officer said, lightly tapping the shoulder of the person with the toe of his spit-shined shoe. "You alive?"

And the John Doe was indeed alive—confirmed by his mumbling—but disoriented. He rubbed both his eyes and smacked his lips a few times. Then he removed the shoelaces wrapped around his neck, all the while keeping his eyes closed.

"It's nearly four in the morning," the officer said. "Your ass should be at home in bed. What's your name?"

"Johns, sir. Derrick Johns," he mumbled, eyes still closed.

"Do you require medical assistance? Are you injured at all?"

"No. I'm fine."

"You keep mumbling, son. I can't understand a goddamn word you're saying. I can make more sense out of what Ozzy Osbourne sputters out of his mouth more so I can yours."

"Rude fucker." He patted the ground, hoping to stumble upon his glasses.

The officer turned his head to the radio clasped on his shoulder and called for an ambulance and used the code *ten-forty-four* followed by the word *attempted*. A ten-forty-four meant suicide.

When Derrick started to stand, the officer ordered him to stay on the ground and wait for medical assistance, and he complied. Seconds later he was unconscious. Paramedics arrived a few minutes later.

He would never know just how close to death he had gotten.

2

Three nurses positioned at different areas—nearly equidistant from one another—around the horseshoe-shaped nurse's station released a faint scream when Bruce stumbled to the counter demanding to know what room his son—Derrick Johns—was located. Once he had his answer, he thanked the nurse who looked up the information and apologized to all three of them once again for startling them before racing to the end of the hallway and making a right to get to Derrick's room.

Meanwhile, one of the nurses couldn't help but comment on Bruce's physique and status: short, slender, and single—based on his naked ring finger. Her favorite feature on Bruce was his pruned brown chevron mustache.

When Bruce stepped into the hospital room, a doctor and a nurse stood facing each other on opposite sides of the bed. An

IV bag hanging from a metallic hook on a stand dripped fluid at periodic intervals—roughly every six seconds. *Drip...drip...drip...* A heart machine beeped every ten seconds. *Beep......beep......beep......* Sometimes the two occurrences would sync up together.

"Good morning. I'm Thomas Ivy—Chief Psychiatrist," the five-foot-two heavyset doctor said. "This is Nurse Galarza. And you are?"

Looking like a baseball bobblehead as he slurred his words, Bruce said: "I'm Bruce Johns, I'm his uncle—I mean dad. Sorry. What can you tell me about his condition?"

"He's stable, and he'll make a full recovery," Thomas said. *This guy has been drinking. The stink of alcohol alone...*

Nurse Galarza double-checked Derrick's IV flow and stepped out of the room while Bruce and Thomas continued to talk.

"That's...good...news," Bruce stammered. "Does anyone know how this happened?" he asked, staring at Derrick.

Thomas clicked his tongue. "No, I'm sorry. We tried to ask him, but he seemed to be in some sort of stupor." He pulled down the bandage coiled around Derrick's neck. "ER physicians treated him for abrasions to his neck though. The officer responding to the scene postulated it was an attempted suicide."

With heavy-footed steps, Bruce walked to a seat in a chair positioned against the wall to the left of Derrick's bed, plopped into it, and covered his mouth. It was as though a wrecking ball had hit his stomach, though Dr. Ivy thought Bruce was about to vomit, as drunkards tend to do.

Now Bruce's hand was over his heart as he inhaled and exhaled a few times.

Thomas cleared his throat. "I can understand this must be hard for you to hear, but I must ask you some additional questions."

Bruce nodded. "I'll answer anything I can."

"Has Derrick ever exhibited signs of suicidal ideation?"

"No. Never." He wiped drool from his chin.

"He's never threatened to kill himself—overtly or covertly?"

Another two beeps sounded from the heart machine before Bruce mustered up the courage to respond. During the interim period, Bruce contemplated what he should do: lie or tell the truth. Thomas was a mental health professional there to help Derrick, to improve his well-being. Surely, Bruce could tell Thomas the unfiltered truth. Couldn't he? Perhaps the bigger question was *would* he.

Bruce glanced at his iWatch. "Around two in the morning Derrick and I had a huge fight."

"So that was four hours ago."

"No, not this morning. The day before." Thomas nodded and Bruce continued. "He said some things, then I said some things. One thing led to another, and the fight culminated with Derrick storming off to his room shouting: I wish I were dead. I'm going to kill myself."

A keen observer and a perceptive reader of people's body language, Thomas could tell by Bruce's rocking motions as he sat in the chair and shared the pertinent—yet painful—information that Derrick spoke out of anger and frustration—as most teenagers tend to do, especially teenage males with their undeveloped pre-frontal cortex—and didn't have any intention of killing himself. Thomas had seen thousands upon thousands of these cookie-cutter cases over his twenty-two years of experience.

"There appears to be a side effect from Derrick's attempted suicide," Thomas said.

"What's that?" Bruce asked, concerned.

"This machine right here—"

"EEG machine. I work on those all the time."

Thomas nodded. "Very good. Very *very* good. Yes, this an EEG machine. I trust you know what it does?"

"Yes—measures the electrical activity of the brain. Why?"

"Good. Very good. Very *very* good," Thomas said. He was proud of his pupil. "Nothing serious. Every so often there will be a huge spike in the readings, but then they return to normal a second or two later. This sort of anomaly should correct itself over time."

Bruce started to nod off as Thomas spoke. Thomas snapped his fingers near Bruce's ear and demanded he pay attention. After Thomas repeated himself about the bizarre EEG activity in Derrick's brain, he asked Bruce if he needed to call a cab or someone to pick him up.

"I had my neighbor Scott drive me here," Bruce slurred, bobbing his head. "I'm fine."

Teenagers often say things they don't mean, and Derrick's proclamation to kill himself was no exception—an idle threat. The question that perplexed Thomas was why did his idle threat morph into an active one then?

3

As part of standard protocol, Derrick was required to spend a minimum of twenty-four hours under around-the-clock supervision, also known as suicide watch. He was transported from Room 19 in the Emergency Ward to Room 2412 within the Behavioral Assessment Unit, or BAU for short.

The BAU had strict visiting hours, and Bruce wasn't even permitted to accompany Derrick when he was transferred from the ER to the BAU—at least not without the presiding psychiatrist's permission, and that was Thomas, who refused Bruce any additional contact with Derrick until further notice.

It was eight-twenty-seven when Derrick woke up and found himself in a small room with only a bed, an overbed table, and a chair. An orderly wearing green scrubs and booties was sitting in the chair with his legs crossed staring at Derrick as if he were some obscure exhibit in an art gallery.

"Where am I?" Derrick asked.

"St. Catherine's Hospital," the orderly replied in a British accent, never taking his eyes off Derrick.

"Why am I here?" *What's with his bug eyes?*

"Maybe you could tell me that."

"I have no idea."

"I don't know all of the details," the orderly said. "All I do know is right now you are under intense observation to ensure you don't harm yourself or others. Dr. Ivy will be able to tell you more."

"Dr. Ivy? What's his first name? Poison?"

The orderly never broke character even though he found Derrick's remark about Dr. Ivy's name mildly funny (but more so corny). What made the remark funny was Derrick's confidence in telling the joke coupled with his facial mannerism.

Though the door was open, someone knocked on it before entering. Another hospital staff worker walked towards Derrick and placed a plate covered with a silver top onto the overbed table and pushed the table so that it now was in front of Derrick. "Enjoy," the staff worker said before exiting the room.

When the cover was lifted, a smokescreen of steam rose, as if performing a magic trick, from the food: scrambled eggs, sausage links, and wheat toast.

"How am I supposed to eat this?" Derrick asked, perplexed. "I didn't get any silverware."

"Your hands. We don't provide silverware to those under suicide watch," the orderly replied.

I'll let this slop cool. "Suicide watch? There's a mistake. I'm not suicidal. Where's my cellphone? Can I call my dead—I mean dad?"

A voice spoke from within Derrick's mind.

(Dead is exactly how you should be. I'll fix that soon enough.)

Derrick violently shook his head, then smacked his forehead. He had never heard a voice like before in his mind, and it made his blood run cold. He repeated his question to the orderly again.

"You'll have to ask Dr. Ivy that. He should be in to speak with you soon."

At this point, Derrick wasn't sure if his Dad even knew where he was, but presumed the Chesterville cop who found him would have contacted his dad, Bruce. The last thing he wanted to do was worry him.

While waiting for Dr. Ivy to make his grand entrance, Derrick wolfed down the breakfast as if he had been stranded on an island without food for days. Within a few minutes, only some toast crumbs remained on the plate, and shortly after, those were gone, too. He had tilted the plate at an oblique angle and lightly tapped the plate so as to let the crumbs fall into the palm of his hand.

He asked for seconds, but his request was denied. The sensation of a surge of electricity zapped into Derrick's brain and the plate flew across the room like a Frisbee.

"I didn't touch the plate," Derrick said. "It did that on its own. Must be a ghost."

The orderly smirked. "Yeah, that's it. The ghost did it." He picked up the plate and placed it in the trash can. "Is your hissy fit over now?"

Derrick carried his empty juice cup to the garbage can and dropped it inside of it. The remark the orderly made incited Derrick.

As the orderly sauntered back to his seat, another surge of electricity radiated through Derrick's brain and a second—two at most—the garbage can tipped over and skid across the room, stopping outside of it in the hallway.

"Let me guess," the orderly said. "The ghost?"

Derrick nodded, then turned around to fetch the garbage can from the hallway. The orderly directed Derrick to stop and informed Derrick he wasn't to leave the room or his sight.

"Honestly, Der-dick—I mean Derrick. Sorry about that. But, seriously. Why do you have to throw stuff about? If you really want seconds, I'll get you seconds. You don't have to have a toddler-like temper tantrum."

But it wasn't Derrick's fault.

Derrick cleaned his glasses using his bed sheet and placed his glasses back onto his face. Then he laid on the floor and started to do some sit-ups.

There wasn't much else to do while waiting for Dr. Ivy. The room had no TV or radio, and Derrick's cellphone was in a safe located at the nurse's station within the BAU. To kill time, he did some stretches and calisthenics. He hoped soon he'd be able to leave and return to his sanctuary: his weight room, where he often spent part of the day strength training. If not in the weight room, then he was often in his bedroom, at his desk, studying.

4

Thomas sat in the break room of the BAU with an uncapped Pepsi bottle about one-quarter of the way full and a nearly-spent pastrami on rye on a paper plate in front of him.

A stream of wispy smoke from his cigarette resting in the ash tray traveled towards the ceiling. He picked his cigarette up—Insignia was his brand—took two more puffs, and then extinguished it.

In the break room—mounted to a wall—was a twenty-six-inch flat screen TV, and on it was the eleven o'clock news. A meteorologist stood in front of a zoomed-in map of Northwest Indiana. "…a heat advisory is in effect until four this afternoon. And here's your five-day forecast."

Thomas didn't give two shits about the weather as he spent most of his waking days indoors anyhow. Hell—sometimes he even slept on the couch in his office.

A news anchor opened with a statement that caught Thomas' ear: "A Chesterville man is dead, found in Miller Park with an apparently self-inflicted gunshot wound. His name: Jordan Hosland. The twenty-six year-old man had plans to marry in two days and start a new career as an electrical engineer the following week. He recently graduated from Purdue University Northwest with his master's in engineering. The motive for the suicide is unknown at this time."

When the news segment ended, Thomas remarked: "Coward." He lit another cigarette and took delight in the first drag. His mouth—now a locomotive chimney—spewed a thick cloud of smoke. "Couldn't handle the impending pressures of adult life, could you?"

A sports anchor began his segment and Thomas cleared his plate—just like his mommy encouraged (and forced) him to do growing up, and this likely a major reason for his out-of-control obesity. He finished off his Pepsi, then waddled to the soda machine for another one. He swiped his bank card and tapped his foot as he stared at the word AUTHORIZING on the card reader display.

A different news anchor interrupted the sports anchor: "I'm sorry to interrupt you, but we have some breaking news. A woman reportedly threw herself in front of an Amtrak train about fifteen minutes ago. Jenny O'Hara—CBS field reporter—is on the scene. Jenny."

The screen split to reveal both Jenny and the anchor who introduced her. A tall, thin-figured woman wearing a hip-hugging dress that stopped slightly above her ankles clutching a microphone in one hand and a stenopad in the other said: "Yes, Mark, that's correct. The woman hasn't been identified as of yet, but what we do know—according to passenger interviews—is the woman jumped in front of this Amtrak train as it passed traveling at over sixty miles per hour. This is a developing story and as details become available to us, we'll pass those on to our viewers."

"What the hell?" Thomas whispered.

5

Bruce called off of work from Porter Memorial Hospital where he was employed as a medical equipment technician. He knew he should eat something—if only for sustenance—but he lacked the energy to get his keister out of the chair and fix himself something. A bowl of fruit on top of a centerpiece doily-like placemat had a banana sticking out from the edge. Its peel had spots of brown unevenly distributed all around it, which reminded him of the lesions his grandfather had on his face and neck a few years back.

He reached for the banana, but chose the pear instead. While he was biting into the flesh of the fruit, someone rang the doorbell. Bruce glanced at his iWatch. The time was close to one in the afternoon. He wasn't expecting anyone.

When he opened the door, a short, petite woman with shoulder-length frizzy hair stepped into his house and hugged him.

It was Gayle—his ex-girlfriend. "How are you holding up?" she asked.

What the hell is she doing here? he thought, lightly patting her on the back. "I've been better, but at least Derrick is making a full recovery," he said. *Too bad he didn't die—I mean I'm glad he didn't die.*

"What happened?"

"Nobody at the hospital has been able to give me answers, and the officer who responded to the call only told me he arrived to the scene and found Derrick on the ground in the outfield near the fence."

Gayle's eyes widened. "Did someone attack him?"

"The responding officer believed he tried to end his life by using his shoelaces." She covered her mouth with both hands. He continued. "And he was treated for abrasions to his neck. His brain doesn't have any damage, but sometimes the electrical activity within it spikes. Derrick's psychiatrist told me his brain should make a full recovery over time."

As he stood to make a pot of tea, Gayle asked: "Where is Derrick now?"

Bruce opened the cupboard door and pulled a box of Lipton Organic Black Tea. He yanked three tea bags and neatly arranged them in an overlapping spiral-shaped configuration. As he filled the carafe with tap water, he turned to her and said: "He's at the BAU in St. Catherine's. I'm waiting for a call from the psychiatrist. I hope Derrick gets released today."

"Do you know what I'm going to do for you?" Gayle asked.

Leave? "I have no idea."

"I'm going to fix you a nice meal. You look drained, dehydrated, and decrepit."

"I don't want any food. I ate a pear on my way to the door." He pulled the partially-eaten pear out of his pocket and displayed it like a trophy. "I'm fine. I can't think of eating or drinking or anything else. All that is on my mind right now is Derrick." *That fat ass Dr. Ivy better not pry too much into Derrick's psyche.*

In spite of his pleas, she denied all of them and got to work preparing him a meal. He sat at the kitchen table—waiting for the tea to finish brewing—as she chopped up some onion, tomato, and green pepper. He already knew what she was preparing: a vegetable omelet. It was the only meal she knew how to prepare without it tasting like something off of the bottom of a hamster's cage.

When the coffee maker gurgled three times, it meant it had finished digesting the tea—almost like burping after eating a big meal. Before he could stand completely up, she was already pouring him a cup. He sat back down.

"How much sugar do you want?" she asked.

"I can do that," he replied.

"No. I'll do it. Now how many? Two? Three?"

He dropped his head, and his chin nearly hit his chest. He said nothing; instead, he raised his hand with two fingers pointing skyward.

She fixed his tea just the way he liked it and set the cup in front of him. He thanked her with a nod and smile and she returned to the stove to finish cooking the omelet.

"I can't fathom Derrick doing such a thing," Gayle said. "It's not like him."

"I don't know how I'm to act around him after this. It's my job to correct him when he does something wrong, but he's overly sensitive. I just wish things didn't get too out of control two days ago."

"Are you saying the last interaction between the two of you was a fight?"

"Yes. He stormed out of the room shouting he'd kill himself. He stomped up three or four stairs, then stopped dead in his tracks."

"Why?"

"I don't know. It was almost as if he was looking at someone standing on the stairs, like someone was speaking to him. He stood there for maybe a minute or so, then intently stared at his wrist with bug eyes."

Gayle fumbled the spatula. "Jesus. Do you think he was thinking about slitting his wrists?" she asked, rinsing the spatula off in the sink.

His voice trembled and eventually trailed off when he said: "I didn't then, but I do now. Maybe he chose to…"

She placed a hand on his shoulder. "It's okay. You can tell me."

"It's too hard to say," he said, dropping his head onto the table. He took a breath. "Maybe he didn't do anything to his wrists because he wanted to spare me the horror and gore of the aftermath."

She scooped a pile of eggs out of the copper-coated skillet and dumped them onto a plate. "Please. Eat something."

"You don't listen, you know that! I said I wasn't hungry!" He picked the plate up and threw across the room. The plate smacked the wall and shattered into several pieces. Remnants of the omelet slid down the wall, though some of it stayed put.

She walked over to the busted plate and started to clean the mess up. He left the kitchen and locked himself in his bedroom where he cried into a pillow before tiring himself out and falling asleep.

Gayle, however, wasn't buying his drama. She knew a faker when one showed him or herself to her.

6

When Thomas entered Derrick's room, he was finishing another set of push-ups, counting them out as he did each one. Thomas signaled to the orderly—a female this time—to leave the room, and once she did, he took the seat in which she once sat.

"...98, 99, 100," Derrick said.

Thomas lightly clapped. "Bravo. Good. Very good. Very very *very* good. I'm Dr. Ivy, but you can call me Thomas. I'm not all that big on titles anyway. And what's your name?"

"You're a doctor, but you can't read? My name is at the top of your legal pad. I can see it from here even without my glasses."

"I see you've got moxie. That can be a useful attribute when used properly. Will you please introduce yourself to me? Pretend I don't know anything about you."

This goofy-ass goober. Jabba the Hut-looking— With a hint of sarcasm, Derrick said: "I'm Derrick. Nice to meet you."

"That's better," Thomas said, shaking Derrick's hand. "Nice to meet you, too. I'm here to help you."

"How can you help me?"

"I can help you help yourself."

"I'd really like call my Dad and have him pick me up."

"He's been here already, but you're not going anywhere until I'm convinced you're not a threat to yourself or others."

With a hard stare, Derrick said: "Fine. I'll play your game. I'm not going to hurt anyone. I'm not going to hurt myself. There. Can I go now?"

The inhuman voice he heard a few times during his stay in the BAU crept into his brain again.

(Oh, you are so wrong about that, Der-dick-less! You will eventually kill yourself. You should be dead. Soon, you will be dead.)

Thomas shook his head with smirk. "If only it were that simple." He his arm extended outward to his side. "Please get comfortable."

The veins in Derrick's neck popped out and his chest heaved. Part of him wanted to sock the doctor square in the nose, then make a break for the door.

But he didn't. He sat on the bed.

"Talk to me about the baseball field," Thomas said. He clicked his pen and pressed it to his pad.

Derrick removed his glasses to clean them. "I don't remember how I got there."

"Do you go there often?"

"I pass by it on my way to my girlfriend's house, but I've rarely been on the property."

"But you have been at the baseball field in the past?"

"Yes. My girlfriend and I sometimes would sneak in the dugout and…talk." *I hated it when she tries to get me to have sex with her. It's not the right time. When he get married will be the right time.*

He said that to Dr. Ivy with a sort of boastful confidence, hoping to impress the doctor. But the reality was Derrick was gun-shy when it came to intimacy. Eventually, Danielle stopped trying to get him to do sexual things with her.

Thomas asked: "Why do you keep staring at your wrist?"

"I don't know."

Thomas clicked his pen and leaned forward. "Are you thinking of doing something to your wrist?"

"No," Derrick said, confused. "What do you mean?"

Thomas didn't supply any clarification. He changed the subject, asking Derrick to provide details about his last night at the baseball field.

Derrick gawked at the back of his wrist while he caressed it with his thumb. His other fingers were coiled around his arm. "What do you remember about the baseball field?"

"An overweight cop is the last thing I remember before waking up in the hospital."

Thomas leaned back in his chair, clicked his pen, and scribbled some notes on the pad. Occasionally he'd look over the top rim of his glasses at Derrick, cock his head slightly, then look back down at his pad and write some more.

"Can I call my dad now?" Derrick asked, tapping his foot on the floor.

"In due time. What's the last memory you can recall before the baseball field?"

"Lying awake in my bed, staring up at a poster of Robin Williams, thinking about my girlfriend."

"Oh? And what is about your girlfriend you were thinking about?"

"How she is my one and only. I want to marry her."

He lit up like the morning sun when he talked about his girlfriend, Danielle, and Thomas made a note of this on his legal pad. Thomas asked more questions. What are your career goals? How are you doing in school academic-wise? What makes you happy? And a host of others. It was all white noise to Derrick, but he was a good sport and played ball.

"Let's return to some other people in your life," Thomas said. "Tell me about your mother."

"Nothing to tell. I want nothing to do with her. I'd prefer not to talk about her either. She hurt my dad really bad."

"Physical kind of hurt?"

"No, emotionally. I don't know though—maybe physical, too. My dad's lips seemed to be hermetically sealed when it comes to the topic of my mom."

"I see... Interesting..." Thomas cleared his throat. "Do you hate your mother?"

Derrick spent several seconds pondering the good doctor's question. It was a question he never asked himself. Up to this point he had resented his mom mainly because his dad did. Now he had to decide for himself if he truly hated her. He told Thomas he would give that more thought before answering that question and Thomas commended him for not taking the matter lightly.

"Given our session today, I'm still puzzled," Thomas admitted.

"About what?"

"Why you wanted to kill yourself. Why you tried to kill yourself."

"But that's just it. I *never* wanted to kill myself, and I *never* tried to kill myself... I want to live... I've *always* wanted to live."

7

After taking forty winks following his temper tantrum, Bruce woke up to morning wood but sawed it down to size by emptying his bladder. He exited his bathroom and stepped into the living room. His bare feet turned to ice when he stepped from the carpeted living room onto the hardwood floor in the kitchen.

Gayle was gone, but she did fix him a fresh omelet, which she left for him on the stove. He flipped the lid off the skillet and—using his hands—tore the omelet and placed some of it in his mouth.

After releasing an expletive when he checked his missed calls and saw he hadn't yet received a call from the BAU at St. Catherine's, he attempted to call Gayle, but she didn't answer. He sent her a quick text message apologizing for his explosive behavior. He wouldn't be surprised if she never spoke to him again after his outburst.

He stood in the living room, replaying in his mind the fight he and Derrick had two nights ago. Some of the things he said, he wished he could take back, but it was too late for that. What's done was done, and that was that.

Bruce plunked down on the couch and called St. Catherine's, wanting to speak to someone in the BAU. "Damn automated menus," he mumbled. "I'd like to talk to a human." He pushed zero, hoping he'd be redirected to a live person.

But he wasn't. The automated voice started all over again with the menu options. Press 1 for emergency, press 2 for urgent care, press 3 for cardiology… He grit his teeth and listened, but after option four still didn't match what he was looking for, he chose four and asked the person to redirect him to the nurse's station at the BAU, and the nurse in pediatrics who answered his call did just that.

"BAU. St. Catherine's. This is Deborah," a woman said.

"Yes, good afternoon. My name is Bruce Johns. I'd like an update on my nephew, Derrick Johns. He was admitted there earlier this morning around five."

"Just a moment."

A click sounded followed by elevator music, a jazz tune, and it was surprisingly catchy. Bruce found himself humming and whistling to bits and pieces of it. An avid jazz enthusiast, he had several records, cassette tapes, and CDs stored away in his closet. The records were handed down from his grandfather to him after his passing. Bruce sometimes played the records on his grandfather's old phonograph machine, which was in his bedroom. Bruce was grateful his music collection survived the fire at his parent's house when he was a teenager in college.

His favorite jazz artists included Duke Ellington and Glenn Miller, but there were others, also. He regretted not pursuing music as a course of study. His primary instrument was trumpet, and he was offered a scholarship to attend Jacobs School of Music at Indiana University, but he ultimately decided a career in music was too cutthroat—a live hand-to-mouth field unless one taught in the schools or managed to make it big and acquire enough gigs to survive. The life of a starving artist didn't interest him at all, so he opted to attend Commonwealth College in Valparaiso, graduating with an associate's degree in biomedical technology.

"Mr. Johns," Thomas said. "Sorry to keep you waiting. What can I do for you?"

"I'd like to know what's going on with my son," Bruce said, massaging his temples. "Can I come and get him? Can I talk to him?"

"I understand you're frustrated. This is a difficult situation, no doubt. I'm drilling down deep into Derrick's subconscious to ascertain why he tried to kill himself even though he didn't display any of the usual signs of someone who is likely suicidal."

"Usual signs? Like what?"

"A feeling of hopelessness, panic attacks, social isolation, just to name a few. It's not making sense, but he may be dissembling."

Bruce released an exasperated sigh. "What's that mean?"

"I'm saying he may be concealing his true feelings, fearing additional confinement."

"If he told you he had thoughts of killing himself in the past, would you keep there longer?"

"Possibly."

"But if he doesn't tell you, you're still keeping him there, right?"

"Just for a while longer. I need to be assured he's not going to harm himself or someone else."

"I'd like to come and pick him up. He's not suicidal, he's never been suicidal. He may have said after our argument he wanted to kill himself, but we all say things we don't mean, and I know he didn't mean that."

"But the evidence shows he *did* try to commit suicide, and within a short period of time after the argument the two of you had."

Bruce cleared his throat. "What are you planning to do?"

"Continue to establish a rapport with him. Once a certain level of trust is established, I'll ask more personal questions."

"When do you think he'll be able to come home?"

"He'll be here another day for sure, but it could be more."

Bruce clenched his fist. "Can I talk to him?"

"Sure. Hang on."

Same elevator music as before. They played it on a loop. While the music played, Bruce turned on the TV and muted it. CNN was the network on the TV, and the image on the TV was shot from a helicopter. A man stood on the ledge of a highrise in Chicago. Bruce turned on the closed captioning. "…according to coworkers, he told them today his time is limited and he has no choice but to end his life. You can see he keeps mouthing something over and over, and to me, it looks like he's saying: *Today I die. Only minutes left now…* He's checking his arm again, something he's done repeatedly…"

"Mr. Johns?" Thomas said.

"Yes?"

"I'm sorry, but Derrick is asleep right now. When he awakes, I'll have him phone you at once."

Once the call ended, Bruce unmuted the TV and changed the channel. He wasn't interested in watching a man swan dive off of a highrise roof. He already struggled to get over a news segment where a man fleeing from police ditched his vehicle, ran through a deserted field, stopped, and shot himself in the head. Though the footage was aired with a five-second delay, the man's suicide was broadcasted.

8

Aaron Egarton was a fifteen-year-old boy who was struggling to figure out who he was, what his purpose in life was. He was going to be a sophomore at Chesterville High School—along with Derrick, who lived next door—but was already behind in credits. He was about a foot shorter than Derrick, gaunt, and had a head of blond hair that ran about a half inch past his shoulders.

Aaron's father—Scott—was a maintenance worker for Chesterville Petroleum Company—also known as CPC. His mother, Karen, was a dental hygienist, but took maternity leave after she had Emily—now four months old. Brandon was Aaron's younger brother and he and Aaron often exchanged playful banter with each other.

The sound of Scott screaming Karen's name nearly put her into an early grave. She lunged out of bed and ran to the sound of his voice. She rushed into Emily's room and her blood ran cold when she saw Scott's ear pressed against Emily's chest.

"Her heartbeat is weak!" he screamed.

"I'll call 911!" she said.

She rushed out of Emily's room and back into hers, fighting to keep herself focused. It took every fiber of her being not to fall to the floor and bawl.

An ambulance arrived to the house about three minutes after the call was placed to 911.

9

(Wake up and kill yourself!)

When Derrick opened his eyes, he glanced around the room. The only person he saw was the orderly—a different one this time—assigned to his suicide watch.

"Did you just tell me to wake up?" Derrick asked.

"No. I haven't said a word," the orderly said.

Derrick intentionally left the 'kill yourself' part out for fear of prolonging his stay. He wondered if the orderly was lying. Part of him rationalized the voice he heard as the orderly testing him, trying to gauge to what degree Derrick's suicidal ideation was at, so the orderly could report it back to Thomas.

"Okay, then," Derrick said, sheepishly. *That voice again. What the hell is that about?*

"Something wrong? Hearing voices now?"

Derrick released a prolonged chuckle.

The inhuman voice spoke again.

(Let's see how much you're laughing when you're dead!)

"It must have been in my mind, part of a dream. The only good thing about the fact I was dreaming is it means I was in deep sleep."

"Beats me, man. My background isn't in psychology; it's in English. I'm only doing this job because it's all I could get."

"Oh. Sorry to hear that."

After a brief yawn, Derrick's head hit his pillow and a few moments later he fell back asleep.

10

Watching CNN in the break room, Thomas puffed on a cigarette and nibbled at an egg salad sandwich he purchased from the hospital cafeteria.

After the commercial break ended, well-respected and reputable news anchor Corrine Ostercamp started her segment with a sobering announcement.

"Many scholars who study mental health are concerned about the recent spike in suicides," she said. "According to Dr. Ryan Unger—a professor of clinical psychology at Harvard—reports around the globe there was been a six percent increase in suicides over the past week, the largest of which is accounted for by the USA followed by China—or as Donald Trump says—Gyna. Joining us now is Dr. Unger to…"

"Good grief," Thomas muttered. "That's alarming. That's very, *very* alarming indeed."

Though he desired to watch the rest of the news segment, he had to get back to his office. Paperwork was mounting and his superiors were riding his ass like mechanical bull to get it done.

CHAPTER 2

1

Sitting in a booth at the Chesterville Burger King on Indian Boundary Road, Andrew and Codi both scarfed down their Double Whopper with cheese, but Andrew won the competition. It was a game they played—oftentimes with Derrick—in which they would start eating at the same time and see who would finish their burger first. The winner got his next meal at Burger King paid for by the rest of the participants in the game.

While waiting for Derrick to respond to his multitude of texts asking him why he didn't show up to eat with them—just as they had done every Tuesday at the same time—Andrew piddled around on his phone for a few minutes. Texting. Tweeting. Instant messaging. A CNN notification banner popped down on his phone, which he clicked on, and directed him to an article. "Shit, dude," he said. "A plane crashed into a mountain. Flight 5952."

When Codi finished slurping his soda, he said: "Accidents happen."

"You're right. They do. Still. It's a shame all those people on board are likely dead."

Andrew scrolled and read through some of the comments people posted underneath the article. "A few people think it was an unrecoverable stall."

"What the hell does that mean?"

"An aerodynamic stall is where there isn't sufficient airflow over the wings. Without proper airflow, the plane falls out of the sky."

Codi's eyes widened. "What might cause the plane to stall?"

"Low airspeed. Ice formation on the wings."

Now Codi's interest was primed and he searched for the plane crash Andrew mentioned. Codi was more of an auditory learner, so he chose to find news coverage clips through YouTube. One clip suggested the plane veered off-course and traveled for several miles before it disappeared from radar. The pilots didn't reply to radio transmissions from air traffic control.

"How is it both pilots wouldn't respond to ATC?" Codi asked. "Is it possible they wanted to crash the plane?."

"Maybe. Perhaps the two pilots were gay lovers who wanted to enter the afterlife together in a unique way."

With a wide-eyed stare, Codi gave Andrew a piece of his mind. "Man, that's not funny. Three-hundred-and-four people were on that plane."

"You're right. Bad joke."

"It's one thing if two people want to off themselves in some sick Romeo-and-Juliet manner, but to take over three-hundred people with you is unfathomable."

Andrew stood with his beverage container in hand and grabbed Codi's, then walked to the pop dispenser and refilled both their drinks. When he returned, Codi was on the phone talking to Bruce. Andrew sipped his Mountain Dew and pissed away some more time on his phone—as most teenagers tend to do.

A little boy screamed bloody murder in the play area of the Burger King, which was in an adjacent room separated from the main dining area with a glass wall and door. Andrew turned around. The little boy's mom had a firm grasp on his arm. The boy was four years old with blond hair and blue eyes, and slightly shorter than average.

The boy screamed and cried as he flailed his arms and feet around while lying on the floor, making the mother's task of getting the boy's shoes on all the more difficult. "I don't wanna go home! I wanna play! I wanna stay and play!"

"Dylan! That's enough. Mommy has to go home, shower, and go to work," the mother said, her heart breaking from her son's wails and cries.

"Just kill me! Kill me now!" the little boy with short black hair screamed. "I wanna die! I'm gonna kill myself with Daddy's rifle!"

But a second or two later, his ear-piercing pleas and screams abruptly died almost instantaneously. Total peace. No crying. No screaming. No yelling. He stared pensively at the ceiling. He glanced at his wrist, then a tear streamed out of both eyes in unison. His life in that moment was forever changed.

With the drama at a standstill, Andrew turned back around and sipped some more of his soda. Shortly after, Codi ended his call and said: "Derrick is in the hospital."

"Why? What happened?" Andrew asked, genuinely concerned.

"Bruce was tight-lipped about what happened, but he assured me Derrick was alright and would likely be home later today."

"No wonder he hasn't been replying to my texts."

"Bruce said he'd have Derrick call or text me once he's out of the hospital."

"Why don't we just go to the hospital and visit him? Do you know what hospital he's at?"

Now Dylan and his mother—Heather—walked out of the playroom and passed Andrew and Codi. Dylan was rubbing his eye with a closed fist (right hand) while staring at the back of his left arm.

"Have a better day, Dylan," Andrew said, smiling.

"That was nice of him to say," Dylan's mom said, stopping. "What do you say?"

"Thank you," Dylan whispered, almost inaudible.

Andrew texted Derrick's girlfriend—Danielle Alemendez— news about Derrick while Codi threw away the trash and placed the tray in the return.

2

Derrick finished another set of fifty sit-ups and wiped the sweat from his forehead. Thomas walked into his room and the orderly in the room exited.

"Can I go home now?" Derrick asked. "I think I've proven I'm not a threat to anyone, including myself."

"Soon," Thomas replied, his tone dry.

"What is it I need to say for me to get paroled?"

"I'm sorry you equate your time here as a prison sentence," Thomas said. "Your mental well-being is of utmost concern to me."

(You want to be released? Kill yourself! It's the ultimate release! Soon—very soon—your soul will be mine.)

Derrick dropped to the floor and started to crank out push-ups. His chiseled arms were that of a gorilla. When he exercised, he was more apt to ignore the growly, gruff voice.

While silently counting his push-ups, he pondered whether he should share with Thomas the auditory hallucinations he'd been experiencing.

"You like exercise, don't you?" Thomas asked.

"I do," Derrick replied, grunting. *You should try some, tub-a-lub.*

"It's good for the body and the mind. Do you want to tell me about the argument you and your dad had approximately two days ago?"

"We didn't have an argument."

"Please think hard. Try to remember."

Derrick closed his eyes for several seconds as he continued to crank out push-ups, but he was unable to recall any argument he had with his dad. Thomas moved his questioning to Derrik's dad.

"He's been good to me. He stepped up to the plate and took care of me in after my mom discarded him and me like a bubble gum wrapper," Derrick said. "I'm lucky to have him in my life."

"Can you share some details about that?"

"From what my dad told me a few years ago, my mom abandoned me. Under the ruse she'd be back after she went to the store to get diapers and food for me, she left and never returned."

Thomas nodded. "And how did you react when it became apparent she likely wasn't coming back?"

Derrick sneered. "I danced a jig and high-fived my dad," he snapped. He took a breath. "How do you think I reacted? I probably screamed and cried. I loved my mom." *Then again, I don't remember her though.*

Exactly. Derrick assumed he loved his mother, but he couldn't say he did with absolute certainty.

"Go on," Thomas said, scribbling on his legal pad.

"My dad and I accepted it and we moved on."

Thomas scribbled some more notes down on his notepad, but then it abruptly flew from his hand, striking the wall across the room. He removed his glasses, stunned and shaken.

"I'm sorry," Derrick said. "I think I did that."

"You ripped the pad from my hand?" Thomas asked. "I thought it was a ghost."

"I don't think so. Watch this."

Derrick stood and stared at the pad for a few seconds. Then the pad became airborne and struck Thomas in the chest, but not hard. Thomas picked the pad up off the floor and sat in the chair again. Then he held his glasses up towards the lights of the ceiling before placing them back on his nose.

"I apologize again," Derrick said. "I haven't quite learned yet how to control this energy. Why do I have this ability all of a sudden?"

Thomas swallowed hard and took a deep breath. "It could be when you attempted to commit suicide—"

"I never tried to kill myself!" Derrick asserted.

Thomas' glasses flew off his face and skidded across the floor. He picked them up and placed them back on his face. Derrick plunked down on his bed and placed his face into his hands.

"I'm sorry," Derrick said. "I wish you would stop accusing me of trying to kill myself."

"Okay, fine," Thomas said. "Let's just say for argument sake, you did. I'm trying to explain why you might have this telekinesis power all of a sudden."

Derrick nodded.

"The brain is a remarkable organ full of untapped potential. Perhaps when the laces were constricting blood flow to the brain and then all of sudden were loosened, a rapid flow of blood enter one of those untapped regions of the brain. This overstimulated that part of the brain and now you have this telekinesis ability."

"Am I going to be in confinement forever now?" Derrick asked.

"No, of course not, but we will want to learn controlling your anger impulses, because if you really lose your cool, someone could be seriously injured or killed."

"How long will I have this ability? In all honestly, I don't want it."

"I don't know. It could be a day or it could be forever. If you don't want to hone the ability, we can do some exercises to suppress it, but first let's take a break and get back to the topic of your mom. Have you ever thought above finding your mom and establishing a relationship with her?

Derrick thought for a moment or two. "A few times, but my dad doesn't think it is a good idea. He gets angry when I bring up the idea. Besides, he's probably right. She doesn't give two shits about me. If she did, she would be fighting tooth and nail to see me."

Thomas nodded. "Has your dad ever hurt you?"

Derrick closed his eyes. After about ten seconds, he said: "No, not that I remember. But one time—about ten years ago—he made me think he was going to shoot me though. He pointed his rifle at me."

Thomas scratched the back of his wrist. His damn rosacea was acting up again. "Why did he do that?" he asked.

"He and I argued about a microscope I wanted. One thing led to another. He basically said I was dead weight and he wanted me dead. He grabbed me by the arm, threw me onto his bed while at the same time kicking his door closed. He reached under his bed while holding me down and brandished his rifle. He cocked it and pointed it at my chest. I blacked out at that point. The next thing I remember is waking up in my own bed. He nor I discussed the argument. We acted as though it never happened."

"Do you resent your dad at all?"

"Not really. He can be controlling sometimes, treating me like the bitch of the house, like his personal Kunta Kinte. I cook his meals, clean his house, and the like. Other than that though he lets me do as I please."

"Do you love your dad?"

"I do."

"I'm intrigued though. How is it you can remember all of these details about your dad and the rifle but you can't remember trying to kill yourself?"

"I *didn't* try to kill myself."

Fortunately, this time no objects became airborne.

Thomas removed his glasses and exhaled onto the lenses, and Derrick took this opportunity to do the same.

After Thomas wiped them down with a Kleenex, he placed his glasses back onto the bridge of his nose.

Derrick hit the pavement and cranked out twenty push-ups. Upon finishing those, he stood and once again wiped his face with the towel while sitting on his bed. He downed a glass of water out of a Styrofoam cup, wishing he was at home where we had essentially a limitless supply of Dasani—his favorite brand of water.

"Your dad called today," Thomas said. "I think you should have a chance to talk to him."

"I'd like that very much."

"Follow me, please."

And to Thomas' office they went, which was not far from Derrick's room within the BAU. Hang a right once outside Derrick's door, walk down to the end of the hall—which was about three doors down—make a left into the adjacent hallway. Thomas' office was the second room on the right.

Thomas' U-shaped executive-style desk had several neat stacks of papers on it, some stacks only a few sheets and others equivalent to two reams of printer paper.

The first thing Thomas did when he entered his office was scurry to the mini-fridge and take out a Twix bar—one of many. Twix bars, cans of Pepsi—which he preferred to the bottles, and a few weight-loss candy bars, one protein bar, and shakes were the contents of his mini-fridge. He offered Derrick a Twix, but Derrick declined the temptation—only because he didn't like too much sugar in his diet nor empty calories; he was more of a fruit-flavored-chewy-or-hard-candy guy. He did ask Thomas if he could have the protein bar, which Thomas obliged.

"You can sit at my desk and talk to your dad," Thomas said, "but first let me talk to him. I'll be brief."

"Fine by me." Derrick unfurled the wrapper of the protein bar and bit into it.

Thomas dialed Bruce's number. Bruce answered right away. "Can I pick him up now?" Bruce said without so much as offering a hello first.

"In due time. I wanted to let you know Derrick and I are making progress. As promised, I told you I would have him call you after he awoke. I'm a man of my word. Here he is."

"Wait, Thomas," Bruce said, his tone frantic. "I'd appreciate it if you wouldn't dig too deep into Derrick's memories. He's had to ensure some traumatic experiences that he's since gotten over—or repressed might be the technical term. I don't want him to have to relive those painful memories again."

"My utmost priority is doing what is best for my patients. Here's Derrick."

Thomas passed the phone to Derrick and then unwrapped his Twix bar. He ate his Twix bar in a unique way: first he bit off the caramel layer, then he ate the cookie layer.

"Dad? Why do I have to stay here?" Derrick asked. "I'm not going to kill myself or you. I'm not going to hurt anyone. Please will you do something to get me out of here? This place is going to drive me into an early grave."

"Is Thomas still in the room with you?"

"Yes."

"Well don't be saying stuff like that in front of him. That's just what he needs to hear to keep you in confinement."

"Sorry."

"It's alright. I know you don't like it there, but soon you'll be home. And believe me: I want you home just as much as you want to come home, if not more so. By the way, Codi called me earlier. I told him you were in the hospital, but I didn't go beyond that as far as details are concerned."

"You can tell them the truth if you want."

But he wouldn't. In fact, the less people who knew about Derrick's attempted suicide, the better. He didn't want the publicity nor the stigmata attached to those who attempt suicide, let alone those who actually commit it.

"Something else I wanted to tell you. I'm sorry about our tiff earlier this week. I didn't mean some of the things I said to you."

Derrick scratched his head, then ran his fingers through his thick sandy blond hair—front to back. "What argument? I don't remember us having an argument."

Bruce didn't believe Derrick, but he didn't push the matter. If anything, Bruce hoped any recollection of the fracas they had that sent Derrick in a fit of rage—so much so that he had been declaring he wanted to kill himself—was nonexistent.

Thomas opened his mini-fridge and pulled out two more Twix bars. He placed one in his shirt pocket and the other he opened and gave the same treatment to this one as the one he ate before as he stretched out on the three-seater couch.

Bruce and Derrick spoke for a few more minutes. Derrick asked Thomas when visiting hours were to which Bruce responded Monday through Friday three to six; Saturdays, one to four; and now visiting hours on Sunday.

"I'll be there at three to see you," Bruce said. "I'll bring you some clothes."

"You don't need to do that. I'm taken care of with clothes here."

"Hang in there, champ. Love you."

"Love you, too. See you at three."

"Hey, Dad? Before we say goodbye, will you tell me what mom's name is? Maybe a little about her?"

A heaving sigh gusted into Derrick's ear; he could almost feel the air from it. An eternal brief period of time passed before Bruce responded.

"Why do you want to know that? Is doctor-fat-fuck-Freud bringing her up? Fuck that bitch-slut-whore mother of yours!"

The sound of glass crashing to the floor tricked into Derrick's ear through his phone.

"Jesus Christ!" Bruce shouted. When Derrick asked his dad what happened, Bruce said: "A handful of plates flew out of the cabinet. It was like the cupboard puked. There's been all sorts of crazy stuff happening around here."

Derrick grimaced when the sound of Bruce swallowing something emanated through the speaker. Bruce was drinking his favorite booze: Jim Beam.

"What crazy stuff has been happening?" Derrick asked.

With slurred speech, Bruce said: "Well, this morning I woke up and all of the cabinets in the kitchen were opened. Then I found my cellphone hidden in your bedroom on your bed inside the pillowcase. Then I saw this blackish mass, but I don't remember if that was in my dream or in real life."

"Why don't you drink it off?"

"Way ahead of you, son."

Dumbass, Derrick thought. *I was being sarcastic.* "Will you tell me mom's name, please?"

"You're lying to me. That Humpty-Dumpty doctor of yours is filling your head with thoughts about your mother, isn't he?"

Chewing with his mouth wide open, Derrick said: "No, Dad. I'd like to know more about her. That's all."

As Thomas yanked a hair out of his nose with his fingers, with his other hand he snapped his fingers at Derrick and reminded him how disgusting it is to chew with one's mouth open.

At about the same time Thomas pointed out Derrick's faux pas, Bruce said: "Heidi, I think. No—wait—that was a different woman I dated. Tabitha—that was her name—I know that because—shit. That's not right either. Her name was Catrina." *Dead bitch she is to me. That bitch is dead to me, and she needs to be dead to you, too.*

After the call, Derrick picked up a picture that rested on Thomas' desk—a picture of people Derrick presumed was Thomas' family. In it was Thomas, a woman, and two children— two girls. "Goddamn that's too much estrogen. A boy and girl would be better. Is this your wife and children?"

"Firstly, please don't use bad language in my presence. Secondly, yes—well, ex-wife. Soon-to-be ex-wife. We're separated, but not legally divorced as of yet."

"Sorry to hear that. Not a lot of marriages last these days, do they, Tommy-boy?"

"Please don't call me Tommy-boy. Address me as Thomas or Dr. Ivy—one or the other."

"Sorry. How old are your children?"

Thomas slightly lowered his glasses on his nose and looked over the top of them. Then he slid them upward with his pointer finger. He cleared his throat. "Nine and seven." *Who's the patient and who's the therapist here?* "Alright. Come on. Up. Let's go back to your room."

"Chillax, *hombre*. I'm sure you know it's important to establish a connection with your patients. I'm opening that door."

Checkmate, Thomas thought. "You're quite right," he said. "But I need to get some things done so please take a seat over there on the couch and let me sit at my desk. We can chitter-chatter while I complete some bureaucratic paperwork nobody is going to read anyway."

"Fine."

Derrick stood and walked towards the couch. Along the way, he passed a bust of Freud. He couldn't resist to practice some Three-Stooges slapstick on it. He gave it a Moe-poke (peace fingers—one in each of the bust's eyes) and smacked it across the face, then sat on the couch.

With steeple fingers, Thomas observed this playful behavior. He grabbed his legal pad and jotted down a few notes. Derrick flexed his arm and smiled with delight at his bulging biceps.

"Do you play any sports?" Thomas asked.

"I played in Pee-Wee football when I was eight or so. I don't care all much for sports. I prefer to spend my time strength training and learning."

"Would you like to take up a new sport, perhaps something you haven't tried before?"

"No," Derrick said, his tone emphatic. "I'm too busy preparing for SATs and reading and researching aeronautics. What are your kids' names?"

"Nicole and Ashlee."

Shuffling through one of the heftier stacks of papers, Thomas located the document he needed, flipped through it, then placed on top of the pile from which he pulled it. He then proceeded to ask Derrick about Bruce's alcoholism and if it had a negative effect on him.

3

Dylan was asleep on the couch and his mother—Heather—was in the bathroom applying the finishing touches of make-up to her flawless-complected face. No signs of blackheads. Large pores. Frown lines. Her face was that of a mall-store mannequin.

The TV from her bedroom was airing The Price is Right, and it was at the stage of the game where the big jackpot is presented and the two remaining contestants bid. She guessed right along with them. She hoped one day she'd be a contestant on the show and have the chance to win big for her and her son.

Three knocks on the door woke Dylan who instantly started crying. Heather rushed to the front door and invited Stacey—Dylan's babysitter—inside.

"Baby, why do you keep staring at the back of your wrist?" Heather asked.

Now Dylan furiously scratched at his wrist while crying. Heather and Stacey glanced at each other, then Heather picked Dylan up and whisked him away to the bathroom. She set him down on the toilet seat. He still fervently rubbed and scratched at his wrist in frustration.

"Tell mommy what's wrong, baby," Heather said.

"Is there something I can do to help?" Stacey asked.

"I don't know," Heather admitted. "I don't think so." A few seconds later, she said: "Maybe get the Calamine lotion and cotton balls out of the hallway closet."

Stacy nodded and made herself scarce to accomplish the task. As she receded, the floor of the house vibrated.

Heather presumed Dylan may have an onset of poison oak since he was playing in the woods with his dad—Mike—near their house a few days ago. Mike took his eyes off Dylan for a few seconds to lit and savor a smoke, and during that time, Dylan wandered off of the trail when he saw a ball trapped within some vegetation.

With the back of his wrist facing his mom, he said: "Look, mommy. Do you see it?" He wiped tears away from eyes with his other hand.

"See what, baby? I don't see anything on your wrist except scratch marks, blood, and redness."

Now he wailed. "He was right. You wouldn't be able to see it."

"Who? What he? Did someone do something to you?"

"I can't tell you. If I tell you…" Dylan said. He wrapped his arms around his mother's neck and gripped her breathlessly. He sniffled. "I can't say."

And Dylan wasn't putting on an act. He couldn't tell, for if he did, he risked certain death, as was clearly told to him.

Stacey stepped into the bathroom with the Calamine lotion and a bag of cotton balls. She uncapped the bottle, turned it upside-down onto one of the cotton balls, and handed the cotton ball to Heather, who then gently blotted Dylan's rash-colored wrist. As she did this, Dylan's frown turned into a smile, as if something ugly and frightening had been destroyed.

When she stopped, Dylan looked at the back of his wrist and smiled once again. But a second—two at the most—later—his face dropped. "I can still see it," he said, sobbing. "It's still there… It's not going to go away unless I…"

"What's not going to go away? Who is he? You said something about a he earlier," Heather said.

Not a word uttered from Dylan.

"You've got to tell me, baby," Heather pleaded. "I'm not mad at you, but I do need you tell me. I want to be able to help you, so please tell me."

"I can't, mommy," he whispered. "I'm sorry."

Heather embraced Dylan for several seconds before she glanced at her cellphone and announced she had to leave for work. She carried Dylan into the living room and set him on the sofa. Stacey followed closely behind like a carriage attached to a horse.

On the TV was one of Dylan's favorite cartoons: Kody Kapow. Dylan himself was in martial arts classes, and it was this cartoon that inspired his interest in it. But Dylan had no interest in watching cartoons. He covered his face with his Jets blanket. His arm stuck upward from within the blanket—as if he was staring at the back of it.

"Dylan?" Heather whispered. "Do you want to tell me now?"

"I can't, mommy, but don't worry. I'll fix it," he replied, his voice strange and its tone matter-of-fact.

Heather stood and walked towards the front door. Dylan stayed silent during their conversation.

"Do you think he should go to the hospital?" Stacey asked. She regretted asking the question, but felt it was the right thing to do.

"I don't know what they could do for him, but I would like to know who he meant when Dylan said *he*," Heather said. "I wish I could stay home with him, but I can't. I need the money."

"He?" Stacey asked, perplexed.

"Yeah. There were these two kids at the Burger King, but I didn't hear them say anything to him that was mean or threatening."

"Maybe one of the kids in the playland thingy at Burger King said something mean to him or grabbed his wrist—or one of the parents did."

"That's a good point. I hadn't thought of that."

But Stacey's conjecture was false. No kid at the Burger King playland did anything harmful to Dylan's wrist nor did any adult there.

Heather eyed her cellphone. "I got to get going. Mike will be home around five tonight. Please text me with updates on Dylan. I'll call a few times, also."

"Will do," Stacey said.

"Bye bye, my angel baby," Heather said to Dylan. "I'll see you when I got home from work tonight. Mommy loves you."

"Love you, mommy," he whispered, and it was nearly inaudible because he was almost asleep, and this gave Heather peace of mind to leave for work—knowing Dylan would be asleep soon.

Heather hopped into her silver Hyundai Santa Fe, started its engine, and backed out of the multi-fissured driveway, stopping before the ass end of her vehicle stuck out into the street. Stacey stood at the front door waiting for Heather to either pull forward and stay home or continue to back out of the driveway and head to work.

Once Heather drove off, Stacey sat on the couch next to Dylan's feet, but didn't bother him. She pulled out her cellphone and caught up on some reading for one of her summer college courses.

4

To keep his mind occupied, Bruce performed a spring cleaning—which he intended to do every March but never did—of the main level of the house. The living room. Kitchen. Bathroom. The couch was like a collection plate on Christmas. He rounded up enough change to be able to purchase a two-for-six deal at Burger King—Derrick's favorite fast-food restaurant.

His iWatch beeped several times, alerting him it was two-thirty, and he needed to hightail it if he was going to make it the BAU by three sharp for visiting hours.

He changed out of his robe and dingy T-shirt—one of several Gayle tried to convince him to throw away, but didn't. She told him if they ever lived together, his T-shirts would be one of the first things she'd pitch. She purchased him new T-shirts, which he wore, but he liked his yellow stained T-shirts, too.

He stepped into his attached one-car garage and backed up his silver 2015 Lexus ES300 so it was now in the driveway. He kept the engine running while he exited his vehicle to check the mail.

Bruce's next-door neighbor—Scott—was watering his grass. "Good afternoon, Bruce," Scott said.

"How are you?" Bruce asked. Today was a light drinking day so far, so his speech wasn't slurred. He opened the mailbox, pulled out the mountain-high stack of envelopes, and closed lid, which made a clank sound.

"Trying not to murder my son."

"Oh, now. What happened now?" *I've been there.*

"As my boy Aaron likes to say: same shit, different smell. The kid steals money, does drugs, drinks, steals my tools and pawns them. Last night, I was reviewing my finances."

"Yeah? Can you finally retire?"

"No, but I did discover Aaron wrote himself a five-hundred-dollar check to himself and cashed it."

All the accusations Scott made about his son Aaron were true. Aaron did struggle with drugs and alcohol, and had for the past four years—ever since Scott's mom suddenly died. He did steal his dad's tools and pawn them for money to purchase his drugs. And, finally, he did write the check and cash it, but it wasn't for drugs. It was for something else, something special for his dad, which Aaron hoped would silence his dad's nagging and berating once and for all.

"Sorry to hear about that. Maybe he needs to go back into treatment," Bruce said.

Scott scoffed at the notion. "I don't think treatment will work. He has to want to fix himself in order for treatment to work. I may just need to throw him out of the house."

"He's sixteen, Scott. He's the same age as Derrick. Don't throw him out."

"Why not? Maybe that's what needs to happen. He's a wounded bird, no doubt, but he needs to see I'm not going to be able to fix his broken wings all the time."

Scott shut off the water to the hose and turned the crank to reel the hose back onto the storage wheel.

A spot-rusted black Ford Taurus pulled into Scott's driveway and the driver honked twice. Aaron galumphed out the front door towards the car.

"Hey! Where do you think you're going?" Scott asked, his tone agitated.

"Out," Aaron replied, continuing to walk to his friend's car. He was a lanky kid, standing six-one and one-hundred-forty pounds. He had shoulder-length brown hair. Bruce referred to him as the new Fabio.

"Get back here. You're grounded, remember?" Scott bellowed.

But Aaron refused. He sat in his friend's car and the two of them drove away. Two honks sounded as the car shifted from reverse to drive, which to Scott added insult to injury. He erroneously thought Aaron's friend—Kyle—beeped, but it was actually Aaron who sounded the horn, and much to Kyle's chagrin, who fiercely admonished Aaron for it as they drove away.

"That kid doesn't listen for shit," Scott lamented.

"I'm sorry you're having a rough time with Aaron," Bruce said. "Derrick's in the hospital. I'm on—"

"What? Is he okay?"

"He's fine. I'm on my way to visit him right now."

"What happened?"

"He injured his wrist. His friend Codi drove him to the hospital."

Scott nodded. "With all the weightlifting he does, I'm not surprised."

"Hopefully Aaron straightens himself out. He and Derrick used to be such good friends."

"I think I'm gonna change the locks on the doors. Give that kid a rude awakening."

Bruce rolled his eyes, but his back was turned to Scott. He opened his car door, but before getting into his vehicle, he turned around to face Scott, who was now lighting a cigarette. He wanted to give him some advice, but decided to keep it to himself. Besides, he had more pressing issues on his mind.

He backed out of his driveway and drove away, honking twice and waving as he passed Scott's house. Scott waved back as Bruce passed, gradually rotating his wrist and lowering all but one finger.

5

Andrew and Codi pulled into the hospital parking lot of St. Catherine's and sashayed to the front desk. When the representative looked up Derrick's name, no results were returned. Andrew asked he try again, but the same thing happened. No results. Codi thanked the lady for her time and walked to the vending machine area adjacent to the front lobby.

"Why would Bruce lie to us?" Codi asked. He shoved some coinage into one of the vending machines.

"Maybe Derrick already left," Andrew suggested. "Or maybe you're mistaken as to the which hospital Bruce said."

"No, it's not that. Bruce specifically said this hospital."

"Well, maybe he was mistaken then. Why don't you call him?"

Standing in front of the candy-and-chip vending machine, Andrew swiped one of the gift cards he received for his birthday last week and chose a bag of Cool Ranch Doritos. Codi called Bruce, but the phone rang until it was sent to voicemail.

The two of them sat at a table within the vending machine area, devouring their snacks while they both dawdled on their cellphones. Codi updated his Facebook status and Andrew took some pictures of himself with the mannequin doctor behind him and uploaded them to SnapChat.

Codi's cellphone chimed the opening tune to Bruno Mars' *That's What I Like*. His face turned flush and he claimed his phone had been changing settings uncommanded, but Andrew didn't swallow what Andrew was feeding him. The caller was Bruce. Codi took the call.

"Sorry I missed your call," Bruce said. "What's up?"

"Hey. Not much. Andrew and I popped in at St. Catherine's to visit Derrick, but we're being told there is no record of him here."

"What?" Bruce shrieked. "No, that can't be right. He's there."

Now, Bruce wasn't at all pleased Andrew and Codi were at the hospital nosing around for Derrick. He wanted the visiting hours all to himself. He also didn't want Derrick's friends to find out the real reason Derrick was there.

Codi took a swig from his Pepsi bottle, then said: "We can ask again, if you want."

"No. That's okay. I'm on my way up there," Bruce asserted. "I'll sort it out. I'll have Derrick call you and Andrew later."

"But since we're already here, can't we see Derrick before we go?"

"To be frank, I'd rather *I* visit with Derrick today and find out what's what. If he's released, you guys can come over to the house and visit him, but if he's staying another night, you can visit him at the hospital tomorrow. Understand?"

And Codi agreed.

6

"What are you doing?" Stacey demanded to know. When she started to speak, Dylan shuddered. His back was turned to her, standing on a white step stool in front of his dad's glass gun cabinet located in his parents' bedroom.

"I… I was gonna clean Daddy's shotgun," Dylan said. He peeked at the back of his left wrist.

"I don't think so, little man," Stacey said. "You can do that when your Daddy gets home, but for now I need you to stay in my sight. Okay?"

Stacey picked Dylan off of the step stool and set him on the ground. He started to run out of the room, but Stacey ordered him to halt, which he did. She removed the keys that were sticking out of the gun cabinet's lock and placed them in her pocket.

Dylan's bottom lip jutted outward and his shoulders heaved up and down. "You ruined my surprise for Daddy," he said.

"I'm sorry, but no kid should be fooling around with weapons—loaded or not," Stacey said.

At once, his eyes widened and his itty-bity Adam's apple moved when he swallowed. His hands trembled.

Out of the blue, Dylan shouted: "Quit saying tick-tock! And quit calling me Killin' Dylan!"

Stacey spun around. "What's wrong? I never said any of those things." A few seconds later, she asked: "What are you staring at?" She was genuinely worried about his well-being.

"Nothing," he replied, sheepishly.

"You sure you don't want to tell me."

He didn't vocalize an answer, but he did nod—just barely though. *I can't tell you anyway*, he thought. *I can't tell anyone.*

"Come on into the kitchen. I'll make you something to eat.

Dragging his feet, he eventually made his way into the kitchen where Stacey already was—standing at the table smearing some peanut butter on a slice of bread. Dylan climbed atop one of the four chairs situated around the circular dark-stained table and rocked back and forth with his eyes fixated on the placemat in front of him.

Stacey smacked the peanut-buttered slice of bread on top of the jelly-smeared bread, plopped the sandwich onto a plate, and set it in front of Dylan, whose rocking never ceased.

"Aren't you going to eat?" she asked.

He didn't answer. He blinked once, but she didn't think he was communicating anything by that.

She turned his left arm to view the back of it. The Calamine lotion was still there. Had it have rubbed off, she would have applied another helping of it onto his wrist.

"You can't see it, can you?" he asked.

"See what?" she asked.

"I got my answer. Forget it. I'm doomed."

She placed her hands on his shoulders to stop him from rocking, but she felt the force of him trying to move forward. She gripped his shoulders tighter. Tears streamed down his face. She picked him up off of the chair and carted him off to the living room where she laid Dylan onto the couch. He immediately slithered his body into a fetal position and covered himself with his blanket.

Before planting her voluminous tukus on the couch, she switched the channel of the TV from cartoons to CNBC. The headline at the bottom of the screen read: CHICAGO MAN JUMPS FROM HIGHRISE, DIES. Not interested in such a grisly topic, she changed the channel to Channel 444—another one of Chesterville's local news stations. The headline read: TRUMP RESIGNS, PLEADS INSANITY DUE TO OVERWORK.

Stacey released a loud guffaw, akin to a hyena. Dylan shuddered, but she helped him fall back asleep by rubbing his back while with her other hand she texted Heather to provide her with an update. Heather replied back a few minutes later. She texted: *If you need to, do what I do sometimes and slip some cough syrup in his Juicy Juice. He'll stay asleep for hours.*

Unwilling to offend Heather by insisting that her suggestion was wrong—and also potentially dangerous, she simply replied: *Okay. Thanks.*

Channel 444 ended their nationwide coverage segment and switched to local news, but Stacey wasn't interested in that story either. The headline read: MAN KILLS WIFE, KIDS; THEN SELF.

But something compelled her to listen to it anyway. The reporter said: "A Chesterville man ended his life tonight, but not before strangling his wife and shooting his four children—ages 12, 10, 7, and 10 months—multiple times in the back of the head with an AR-15. David Lewis is at the scene with more details. David."

The screen split to show David along with the news anchor who introduced him. "Connie, thank you. Yes, a tragic story of a loving father turned murderer. The father—Erick Waterfield—a clinical psychologist specializing in children who practiced privately and twice-recipient of Father-of-the-Year Award murdered his entire family before walking onto his front yard, placing the AR-15—the same one he used to maim his children's skulls, which instantly killed them—slid a metal bar between the trigger and guard, placed his chin on top of the barrel, and jumped onto the bar as if the AR-15 were a pogo stick."

The screen cut to an elderly woman who spoke into a microphone held in front of her. Her name was Delores Stritz—according to the information at the bottom of the screen. She was one of the Waterfield's neighbors. She said: "I was outside watering my garden when I heard gunshots next door. I ran inside and called the police. I stepped outside to wait for them, and that's when Erick walked outside and…did what he felt he had to do."

"Were there any signs at all he was planning to harm his family?" David asked Delores.

"Not-uh. None whatsoever," she replied.

"Did he say anything before he ended his life?"

"Yes, and it sends a chill up my spine every time I think about it."

"What did he say?"

"I can still hear his voice." She covered her mouth. "Oh, my."

David stood silent with the patience of a monk holding the microphone in front of Delores' mouth. Delores' eyes turned to buckets of water.

"I'll avenge you in the spiritual realm, (beep), were his last words." The expletive—fucker—she said was censored.

To whom was the now-no-longer-living Erick referring? Debt collectors? His wife's secret lover—if she had one? A deranged patient who killed himself and taunted Erick into madness? Who?

7

After being nearly run over by a motorist driving like a maniac in the parking lot, Bruce entered through the automatic doors of St. Catherine's and approached the front counter, though nobody was there, which struck him as odd. Moments later, a woman walked behind the counter and asked how she could help him. He stated his business and asked what room Derrick was in, but she found no record of Derrick—just as Codi was told, and as Codi had relayed to Bruce.

Undeterred, Bruce demanded the representative check again, which she did, but again her computer found no record of Derrick. If Bruce had any atherosclerosis in his veins before, the plaque was likely flowing through his veins now, because his blood was boiling.

He demanded to speak to a supervisor and the representative promptly called one who arrived at the front desk within a few minutes—no more than five tops. The supervisor did a search for Derrick's name, but she, too, was unable to find any record of a Derrick Johns.

"I'm about to call the police," Bruce said, his tone caustic. "I spoke to my nephew on the phone earlier today. He told me visiting hours were from three to six. He's in the BAU."

"Now I know why no record of him is turning up," the supervisor said.

"Why?"

"His records likely are blocked from the public directory given where he is."

"I want to see my nephew. Where is the BAU?"

"Hang on. Let me call up there for you."

And she did. The BAU cleared Bruce to come up and see Derrick. The supervisor escorted Bruce to an elevator not accessible to the general public. When they entered the elevator—a freight elevator—she pressed the button marked 4 and up they went. As the elevator's wheels and pulleys squeaked during the ascent, Bruce apologized for his brusque attitude, which the supervisor accepted but insisted she would have been madder than a hippo with a hernia had it have been her in the same situation.

When the elevator doors squeaked opened, Bruce thanked her as he stepped out and proceeded to follow the signs leading to the BAU. When he reached the main doors to the BAU, he pushed a switch to alert the front desk worker he was at the main doors.

"Can I help you?" she asked.

"I'm here to see Derrick Johns. I'm his legal guardian."

"Come on in."

He checked his watch and swore at himself. It was now ten after three. He was late.

"Please sign in," the front desk worker asked.

"Fine," he said.

"And I'll need your driver's license or state ID."

Though he didn't like to relinquish his ID, he did. Had he not, he wouldn't have been permitted to see Derrick. Access denied.

After she processed Bruce, she asked him to put his arm out, and he did. She wrapped a visitor band around his wrist and provided him instructions as to how to get to the visiting area. He had to walk out the main doors of the BAU, turn left, buzz for the elevator, and go to the fifth floor.

He followed her directions. Once off the elevator, stepped into the visiting room where he was greeted by a security guard. "Please sign in," the guard said. He handed Bruce a clipboard with a pen connected to some purple yarn which was looped and tied through the clip. After Bruce signed in, the guard said: "You can have a seat wherever. He'll be here shortly."

The room had two sofas and three tables with four chairs around each. Near the back wall were two recliners with a small coffee table in between them. Bruce took in one of the recliners and heaved a sigh.

"This is your first time here, isn't it?" the guard asked.

"It is."

"It's tough, I know, but the thing you don't want to do is show any sadness or disapproval."

"I agree. Try to stay positive," Bruce replied.

"That's right." The guard dispensed some eye drops into his eyes. "I had to go through this with my son a few years back. It's nothing to be ashamed of, you know. We all go through struggles, some worse than others."

Bruce offered no spoken reply, but he did nod. About a minute later—two tops—Derrick walked in and Bruce's heart sunk to his feet. As a knee-jerk reaction, he nearly covered his mouth in shock and surprise at Derrick, who was not wearing any of his own clothes. No Aeropostale. No Tommy Hilfiger. No Abercrombie & Fitch. Instead, Derrick wore what could only be described as a green prison uniform with the letters BAU in black located on the right side—about two inches below the shoulder.

Bruce and Derrick relished in a hug—something they hadn't done in a long while. Not because they disliked each other. It was simply something that had faded over the years as happens with most relationships between father and son.

The hug lasted for about a minute and then they both sat. Bruce couldn't get his mind past the fact Derrick was in prison garb, but he made no mention of this to Derrick.

Derrick's eyes filled with tears. "I'm sorry for all this."

"Stop it," Bruce insisted. "Would you please just stop it? There's nothing to be sorry about."

"I still don't understand why I'm here," Derrick said. He took his glasses off and dried his eyes with his shirt. "I have no memory of even walking to the baseball field. I do know this: I'm not suicidal. I want to come home."

"Don't worry, champ. I'm confident you'll be out of here soon."

"I hope so."

"I want to apologize for the argument we had a couple of days ago."

Derrick squinted his eyes. "I don't remember any argument though."

This ungodly voice spoke from within Derrick's mind once again.

(Are you going to kill yourself? Or do I have to find ways to encourage you to do it? Here's an idea. Kill Bruce, then yourself. Fuck that evil fucker. Actually, don't kill Bruce. He still has some more work to do.)

Bruce nodded. "That's okay. But if you do end up remembering it, know I am sorry, okay?" *I hope he doesn't remember. It's better that way.*

"It must not have been an important argument if I don't remember it. There is something else I wanted to discuss with you."

"And what's that?"

But Derrick didn't answer right away. It seemed to be a damned-if-you-do-damned-if-you-don't situation. There was the possibility Bruce wouldn't give a damn he was in a public place and fly into a tirade—just as he had done the last time Derrick revealed his intentions. On the other hand, if he didn't explode, Derrick feared Bruce would resent Derrick for springing the bombshell on him around other people, including BAU personnel and a security guard, even though they weren't in earshot.

After about fifteen seconds elapsed, Bruce encouraged Derrick to speak his mind, promising him he didn't need to fear reprisal.

"Just tell me," Bruce said. "I'm sure it's not as bad as you're thinking it is."

"I would like to find my mom and give her a second chance," Derrick said.

All the muscles in Bruce's face tensed up and his eyes compressed. After he took in and released a deep breath, he said: "Why do you want to bother with her? She ditched us, remember?"

"She's my mom. And, who knows. Maybe her reasons for absconding are good. Maybe she feared she would be a crappy wife or an even crappier mom. I'd like to hear her reasons, confront her about what she did, and try and start a relationship with her."

Bruce folded his arms. "I don't think that's a good idea. And what makes you so sure she wants anything to do with you anyway?"

The inhuman voice crept in again: *(Hey, Der-dick! Now's your chance, boy-o! Grab the security guard's gun and pistol-*

whip your so-called dad into submission! Then blow that massive brain of yours outside the back of your fucking skull!)

Derrick fervently rubbed his forehead with an open hand. "I think she deserves—"

"I tell you what," Bruce sneered, his tone dark. "If you think she's so great, you go ahead, you find her, and then you move in with her." Heads shifted in Bruce's direction. "After all these years I've taken care of you without her help I'd think you'd want nothing to do with her, but do what you got to do." He stood.

"Dad, will you please lower your voice?" Derrick asked, standing.

(Silence him good, Der-dickless! You're dead anyway. Kill him, then yourself! It's your destiny! You belong to me! You don't know how lucky you are to be alive! Enjoy it while it lasts!)

Ignore the voice, Derrick thought. *Ignore it.*

(I'm unstoppable. I'm invincible. In that valley I'm the shadow of death. You can't escape me. One way or the other, I'll have your soul and then I'll torture along with the others!)

"Why do you keep making that face?" Bruce asked. "Is something unscrewed in your brain?"

Derrick swallowed hard. "What do you mean? What face?" *Maybe I did try to kill myself and the lack of oxygen has caused brain damage. Now I'm hearing voices.*

(And before, too. Just kill yourself like you were supposed to do. Remember?)

"Your eyes widen, your jaw opens slightly, your fingers tremble. It's like you see a ghost or something."

Derrick laughed. "I'm sorry. I'm not *seeing* anything. I'll try to… Please sit down, Dad. Let's not fight. We'll talk about anything but mom."

And Bruce did sit. They talked for another hour about miscellaneous topics with the focus on Derrick. His weightlifting progress and goals, registering him for school, courses he might be interested in taking this school year, and some new clothes he wanted.

Before Bruce left, he and Thomas talked about Derrick and a projected release date. Thomas anticipated one more day, already convinced Derrick wasn't suicidal, but wanted to prolong it a bit longer before pulling the trigger.

8

Stacey's phone vibrated a few times before she woke up from her catnap. The caller was Mike—Dylan's dad. He called to let her know he was asked to work four hours of overtime and if she was able to stay longer before he agreed to work the additional time, which she was.

With a trembling voice, she provided Mike with an update about Dylan and shared with him Dylan's bizarre behavior. The desire to clean the guns in his dad's cabinet, the obsession with his left wrist, and the fixation on the meat cleaver in the wood block on the kitchen counter.

For sure, he was just as alarmed at Dylan's behavior as she was, and he offered to forgo the overtime in order to get home, even though the family was hurting financially—even with both parents working—and needed the money.

She insisted Dylan would be okay for a few more hours in her care. He assured her Dylan was likely pushing boundaries and shouldn't worry too much about Dylan's behavior. He offered to come home if she felt it necessary, but she allayed his fears and convinced him everything would be fine. Besides, she knew how much the family needed the extra income simply to make ends meet.

"Can I talk to Dylan before my break ends?" Mike asked.

"Sure. He's right—" She looked to her left, but Dylan wasn't on the couch. "Hang on. I think he's in the bathroom. I hear water running."

She opened the bathroom door and as she entered the bathroom, her mind simultaneously entered a state of temporary bewilderment. Dylan was slouched outside the tub with his left arm submerged in scalding hot bath water, though he didn't show any signs of physical pain.

"Dylan. Your dad is on the phone," she said. She placed the phone to his ear.

"Hi, Daddy," Dylan said. "I don't wanna die."

"Son, why are you talking like that?"

"He's making me do it, Daddy."

"Who is?"

Dylan's lip curled and tears dripped from his face into the bath water, causing a ripple effect. "Why is this happening to me, Daddy?"

"What do you mean? Tell me."

"But I can't." He pulled his submerged arm out of the bath water and gazed at the back of his wrist. "It won't stop."

Out of the blue, Dylan shouted: "I'm not a crybaby!"

Stacey pulled the back and Dylan drowned his arm in the bath water once again.

"I don't know what to do with him," Stacey admitted. "He keeps talking to nobody."

Dylan sighed. "I told you. I'm talking to the shadow man."

"He'll be okay. He's had a rough time adjusting to me returning to work," Mike told Stacey.

And this was true to an extent. Mike did recently start a new job after being laid off for six straight weeks when the auto parts factory abruptly closed.

9

The short, portly man tightly coiled the four-hundred-foot quarter-inch chain around his legs and secured it with a Master padlock. With a singular smack on top of his left wrist, the handcuff snapped closed. He tightened to the point it was digging into his skin. He gazed at his left wrist and recognized time was of the essence.

He pulled out his wallet—a trifold— from his right pants pocket and thumbed through the picture container, reminiscing about the memories created over the years. Holidays. Birthday parties. And thinking about the ones he'd miss. Graduations. Weddings. Birth of grandchildren.

"I never meant for any of this to happen," he said to nobody. He pulled off his wedding band, but then slipped it back onto his ring finger. He placed his trifold onto the pier.

A brief period of tranquility washed over him as he ignored all sounds except the that of the waves crashing along the shore and against the pier on which he stood. Soon—very soon—he wouldn't hear *any* sound.

He laid down on the pier and looked down at the water. He secured the other handcuff to his wrist behind his back and rolled off the pier. A resounding splash sound was created when his body smacked the water's surface. Now he sank and never resurfaced, the lake now his grave.

10

After grabbing a Twix bar from his mini-fridge, Thomas plopped in his chair, unwrapped it, and started to gnaw on the caramel side of one of the two bars while reading an eBook on his Kindle reader. A colleague of his—a professor of psychiatry at Indiana University Chesterville—was the author, and the topic of the book centered on dissociative identity disorder.

As he pushed the cookie portion of the bar he bit it, almost like a carriage in a typewriter.

His cellphone vibrated as it jangled a jingle. It was his older daughter, Nicole, who preferred to be called Nikki. Without hesitation, he answered the call. "How's Daddy's big girl?"

"Fine, Daddy. I miss you."

"I miss you, too, my princess. How was your violin audition today?"

"I nailed it. My new teacher assigned me an etude by Paganini."

Thomas opened his mini-fridge and pulled out a can of Pepsi. He pulled up on the tab, opening the can, but some Pepsi boiled over the rim onto his Kindle reader. He nearly swore, but stopped himself before it could get out of his mouth.

Next week, Thomas was driving to South Carolina to pick up his two daughters. They would spend the next seven weeks at his house before being flown back to their home to start the new school year.

"Hey, daddy," Nikki said. "Remember Mr. Goines?"

"Yes, I do. He's your next-door neighbor."

"Not anymore."

"He moved?"

"Yeah. He's probably burning in a fiery hell right now."

"Whoa there, Nikki. I don't like that talk."

An audible swallow trickled through the speaker of Thomas' cellphone.

"Sorry, but Mr. Goines blew his face clear off of his shoulders about an hour ago."

"What?"

"Yeah. It's true. He shouted he was tired of being sick with the cancer eating away at his insides."

This was true. Mr. Goines for the last three years had a terminal cancer. Initially, he accepted treatment, which helped, but the last nine months the cancer proliferated at an alarming rate. For the past two weeks, things worsened, and he often proclaimed he wanted to kill himself, be euthanized, or simply die.

"Well… I'm sorry to hear that. He must have been in a lot of pain or had a low quality of life for him to do a thing like that."

"Ashlee and I were outside in the backyard playing when we heard the shot and saw the blast from his house. His brains smacked against his bedroom window."

"Okay, princess, I don't need the play-by-play of Mr. Goines' exit from the living." He took a quick swig of Pepsi. "Speaking of Ashlee, where is she?"

"She's still in her room, crying."

"Sad about Mr. Goines? Is that why?"

They talked for a few more minutes about some summer activity ideas they would do together during her and Ashlee's stay. Walk to the Lakeshore, play some miniature golf, go to the fair, visit the pier, among other ideas.

Sharon's voice trickled into Thomas' ear.

"Wrap it up, Nikki," Sharon said.

"But, Mommy—"

"Don't but Mommy me. Now five more minutes and that is it. That call is long distance and it is costing money."

That was a lie. Sharon recently switched to a new phone service provider: Ooma. Long distance was free. She was threatened by the children becoming closer to their dad, so she did whatever she could to limit their contact with him and went out of her way to vilify him.

Thomas and Nikki talked for another five minutes and said their goodbyes. He asked her to put her mother on the phone. "What do you want?"

"You know what, Sharon. I think I'm going to buy the kids their own cellphone, so this way you don't have to worry about your bill getting inflated because they're talking to their dad."

"Do what you got to do," she replied.

"I will, and I wasn't asking for your permission either. And, something else. If Dalente so much as pulls a hair out of either of my little girl's scalp, I'll personally fly down there and facestomp him."

"You're making a big deal out of nothing, and Nikki was disrespectful."

"I don't care how disrespectful she was, and I'll tell you something else. I don't think Nikki was in the wrong. Dalente shouldn't be putting his hands on my chil—"

"Our," she interjected.

"Right. *Our* children. You need to tell him to keep his hands off of my—our children."

"It was a tap, Tom. A light tap."

"I don't believe that. This is me being nice. He touches one of the children again, I kill him."

"You know what? Sometimes I wish I were dead. I can't seem to make anyone happy. I stick up for Dalente, you and the kids get angry at me. I stick up for the kids, Dalente gets mad at me. I sometimes wanna throw myself in front of a speeding locomotive, sometimes I wanna down a bunch of pills and never wake up again." Now she shouted: "Sometimes I want to kill myself! You hear me! I want to kill myself!"

"You say you're thinking about killing yourself, you've got my attention." After a few seconds of silence, Thomas said: "Sharon? Are you there?… Sharon?"

But she wasn't. Thomas presumed she had hung up on him—business as usual. He nibbled away the caramel off of his second bar in the Twix package while reading more of his colleague's book.

11

Once again, Stacey dozed off on the couch while watching Dr. Phil. Dylan was nowhere in sight. She lunged off the couch and checked the kitchen first, since the light was on, thinking he might be pouring himself some more juice.

But he wasn't there. Her heart leaped into her throat when she noticed one of the kitchen chairs pressed against the kitchen counter—the same counter on which the knives block rested. On the wall in back of the knives block was a nail—the nail on which the meat cleaver usually hung.

But the meat cleaver wasn't there. Stacey shouted Dylan's name as she ran to his bedroom, but his door was locked. She shoulder-opened the door and what greeted her eyes caused her heart to skip several beats.

She grabbed Dylan's arm before he could bring the meat cleaver down onto his left arm. Just below his wrist was a linear impression, and this was formed by the meat cleaver initially resting on it—and from Dylan applying some pressure, wanting to get a sense of how the cleaver would feel as it sliced through his skin like a Samurai sword through a sheet of crepe paper.

As tears streamed out of her eyes, she grasped Dylan in her arms. "What is wrong?"

"I can't tell you," Dylan answered. *I'm not being a crybaby, you asshole!*

"Is it your wrist?"

Dylan nodded.

"What's wrong with it?"

"I can't say." His voice was faint, almost inaudible.

"Why can't you tell me?"

"If I do, the bad man will kill me."

Stacey lightly gasped, experiencing difficulty with what Dylan had just uttered. She believed Dylan was losing his mind—

and, at best, he was making things up for attention, as his dad suggested to her.

But then there was the meat cleaver incident that caused her to pause and give greater consideration to the situation. Had he been beckoning for attention, he would have tried to amputate his hand in front of her. But he didn't. He was in his room—alone. And had Stacey intervened a few seconds later than when she did, an even more horrific sight would have greeted her upon entering his room.

She picked Dylan up and walked to the hallway bathroom. She dropped the lid shut on the commode and set Dylan on it. The Calamine lotion was still sitting on the sink from earlier. She ripped off some toilet paper off of the roll, folded it, poured some Calamine lotion onto it, and dabbed Dylan's left wrist. She shuddered at the thought of what he nearly did to himself.

"Does your wrist feel better now or does it still itch?" Stacey asked him.

"It never was itchy," Dylan said.

"Does it burn?"

"No." He raised his left arm in front of his face as if flexing his muscle. He stared pensive at the back of his left wrist as he pouted. "Why won't it go away?"

"Does it sting? Does it hurt?"

"No."

"Then what?"

He placed a finger to his chin and paused before saying: "I can't say. He'll kill me if I do. Then I'll be sentenced to eternal purgatory."

Stacey was beside herself. *What average four-year-old know words such as eternal and purgatory, and can use them articulately*, she wondered. She presumed someone had to have said those words to him. But, if so, who?

"Who will kill you?" Before Dylan could answer, she continued. "Let me guess. You can't tell me that either."

He shook his head.

She picked Dylan up off of the toilet and brought him into the living room. Dr. Phil was over.

The seven o'clock news was on, and airing was a segment about a woman named Geraldine Primrose, who was set to retire from her position as a city bus driver. At her retirement party in an upscale, ritzy hotel within a banquet room, she danced with her boyfriend, mingled with guests, entertaining them with witty stories and life-lesson anecdotes. Ah, yes, she was the life of the party, and also the murderer of it—and herself.

After delivering her retirement speech to the crowd of two-hundred or so people, she was handed a cake server to cut her piece—which was the first piece—of the sheet cake. The shiny stainless-steel server had serrated edges, which did the deed and made her dead, slicing her jugular when she placed the cake server to her neck and rapidly dragged it across her neck multiple times in a seesaw pattern. Right to left to right to left… The teeth of the serrated cake knife did one hell of a maim job to her neck, which looked as though she'd been attacked by a rabid wild animal in the Amazon.

Blood squirted from her neck like a pulsating sprinkler, hitting the cake and guests. Spilled milk is nothing to cry over, but blood is. She died within forty-five seconds.

The news anchor reported Geraldine had big plans for her future. She and her boyfriend were supposed to go on their cruise next week and she was hired two days prior to work at Chesterville High School as a hall monitor three days a week. She had plans to visit her grandchildren in Maine, New York, and Missouri after she and her boyfriend returned from their cruise. None of her friends could understand why she would abruptly take her own life, and in such a horrific manner, too.

"How are you feeling?" Stacey asked.

Dylan was staring at his left wrist. "Not so good." Then he responded to nobody. He shouted: "I dare you to fix me dead and proper!

"Enough is enough. I'm taking you to urgent care to have your wrist examined."

"Do you think the doctor can help me? Do you think he can figure out what is wrong with me without me telling him and make it is go away?"

"I hope so."

Stacey placed a quick call to Heather and informed her she would drive Dylan to urgent care to have his wrist examined. Heather thanked Stacey for taking such care of Dylan while she was at work, and she also relayed to her the insurance information should be on file at the Chesterville Clinic.

Not wanting to alarm Heather at work, Stacey guarded the meat-cleaver incident like a well-kept secret, and for the time being, she'd take it to her grave if she perished between now and when Heather returned home from work.

Moments after Stacey piddled and changed her pad, she and Dylan were out the door, on their way to the clinic.

12

As Derrick slept peacefully in his bed of the BAU, the voice that seemingly enjoyed encouraging him to kill himself spoke from within his mind again.

(I can't believe you managed to escape me. Your lucky your dad saved you. I'll be hunting his ass down, and when I reach him, I'll destroy him.)

Derrick slightly gasped and opened his eyes. He looked around the room but nobody was there, except for another orderly, assigned to suicide watch.

He sat up in his bed and greeted the orderly, but she didn't have any interest in talking. She gave a slight nod and then resumed filing her nails.

After swallowing a swig of water, he laid back down in bed with a pensive expression on his face. *This voice I'm hearing must be a manifestation from the attempted suicide. I can't keep lying to myself. The evidence indicates I tried to kill myself, and now I've got brain damage from it. That's why I hear this voice in my head.*

Derrick learned how to have a greater deal of control over his telekinesis abilities most time, though sometimes, when angrily provoked, a burst of energy would release from him, and this would cause objects to fly across the room.

13

Andrew pulled up in front of Danielle's house and pumped the horn several times as if giving someone unresponsive chest compressions. She stepped out of the house and sashayed down the walkway leading to the sidewalk. She was all legs and no chest. Though she had no stuff in the front, she had plenty of junk in the trunk. Her satin-like black hair was in a ponytail, and she was wearing a pair of black Aeropostale shorts and a T-shirt with an inscription on the front of it that read: I'M WITH STUPID. A large hand underneath the inscription with a closed fist except for its pointer finger pointed to the left.

She was Derrick's love, and he hers—to those on the outside, though not her first, unlike him. They met approximately two years ago as freshman students at Chesterville High School. They had the same English class, which was fourth period with Mrs. Capodagli. On the first day of class, Mrs. Capodagli instructed the class to partner up with a classmate and interview them—then switch roles—before introducing the person interviewed to the class.

She had moved from Kentucky to Indiana when her dad, Marco, was hired to work at US Steel as a millwright. Her mom Azalea was a loan officer who worked at one of the Chesterville's Chase bank. The one she worked at was located near the Burger King where Derrick and Danielle—along with his friends—often hung out together after school and on the weekends.

When she closed the door to the car, Andrew gave her a slight smile—unsure what else to do. She broke down and placed her face in her hands. He put his arm around her and assured her Derrick was fine and there was nothing to worry about, even though he was unsure himself.

"I don't understand why Bruce won't tell us what happened," she said, sniffling. "I'm worried about Derrick."

"I have a suspicion Derrick overexerted himself trying to lift weights or something and he's trying to help Derrick save face," Andrew contended.

"Save face? What is there to save face about with straining a muscle from exercising? That doesn't make sense."

"Derrick has always been tough, he has always wanted people to see him as strong—not just physically—but emotionally. He may have injured himself severely... You're right. That doesn't make sense. Sorry."

She opened her compact purse and pulled out some tissues from a plastic wrapped stack of tissues. She blew her nose and placed the wadded-up used tissue into her purse. Then she pulled out a Jolly Rancher, unwrapped it, and placed it into her mouth.

"Where would you like to go?" Andrew asked.

"I'd like to go to the hospital and see Derrick," she said.

"Visiting hours are over, and besides, Bruce told me we could visit Derrick on Monday if he was still in the hospital."

"Please take me to the hospital. I need to see him."

"We're not going to be able to see him. We'll be thrown out by security, and that's if we can even get inside the proper ward. Let's go get some ribs from Applebee's."

"You asked me where I wanted to go. I told you." She gave him a cold stare.

He wanted to argue with her, but he could tell by the look in her eyes she wasn't going to cave. Rather than continue to argue and upset her further, he shoved the gear shifter into drive and applied some gas. As he drove away, he pondered whether he should drive to the Applebee's and risk a confrontation or drive her to hospital.

In order to stall, he stopped at the BP on Indian Boundary Road to pump some gas into his tank, which was already three-quarters of the way full before he pulled into the gas station.

On the gas pump was a digital screen. After he selected his gas grade, a C-SPAN news segment aired on the screen. The news anchor said: "A six-year-old child was found dead in his bedroom earlier this morning. Timothy Garrison's mother discovered her son deceased at his desk, apparently from a drug overdose…"

"Jesus," Andrew whispered. The gas handle clicked, but he paid no mind. His attention was on the news segment.

"…an empty pill bottle, the boy's dad's alprazolam. Even more chilling was what was on the boy's computer screen: a YouTube video of a Momo Challenge. Details about that specific video have not been released to us at this time, but for viewers who aren't aware, the Momo challenge is where a doll—named Momo—entices people to commit suicide, and—"

The digital screen switched off the news. Now displaying was a question for Andrew to answer: Do you want a receipt? He selected NO, replaced the gas nozzle, and walked over to the passenger side of his car. Danielle's head was slumped against the window. He knocked on it a couple of times.

"Asshole! Jerk!" she shrieked. "You scared me half to death."

He cackled like a little boy being tickled by someone with long nails. When he regained his composure, he asked: "I'm going inside to get something to drink. You want something?"

"Frappuccino. Vanilla. Thanks."

"Anything else?"

"No, thanks." She took her glasses out of their case and slipped them onto her nose.

"You're sure you want to go to the hospital?"

"Positive. I feel lifeless without Derrick. I feel like shit because I'm not there by his side to help him through whatever pain he may be going through."

Andrew gave a slight nod, turned around, and walked into the gas station. He grabbed a few Frappuccinos and a bag of Cheetos, then headed for the counter.

During their exchange, the radio host read some sound-bites of news around the Chicagoland-Northwest Indiana areas, and the one airing discussed a man who died from a cinder block falling onto his face, crushing his skull. Apparently, the man created an apparatus that dropped the cinder block onto his face. The apparatus was like a table with a trap door—much like gallows have—such that when a button was pushed, the doors swung open, releasing the cinder block.

Standing outside the passenger side, Andrew handed Danielle her Frappuccino. He opened the bag of Cheetos and placed them on top the roof of the car. He offered Danielle some, but she declined.

The radio played Rascal Flatts' *Why*. Danielle initially turned the volume of the radio up and listened to the first stanza of the song, but then she grunted and abruptly turned the radio off.

"What was that about?" Andrew asked.

"I can't listen to that song," she said. "It brings up a painful memory."

"Do you want to talk about it?"

"No."

He respected her wishes and didn't push her to spill her guts. He munched on some more Cheetos before closing the bag, hopping in the car, and starting the engine. His belly and gas tank full, he turned out of the gas station and headed for the hospital.

14

After lighting a cigarette and taking a puff, Scott popped a squat on the couch and turned on the TV to ESPN SportsCenter to watch highlights on the baseball game between the Cubs and the Mariners he missed earlier in the day while at work.

While watching and listening to the announcers' commentary about the piss-poor performance of the Cubs, Scott tried to finish the Sudoku puzzle he started a few days ago. He began playing Sudoku about a year ago and was hooked ever since. The puzzles he attempted to solve were of immense difficulty, but he embraced the challenge.

His wife—Karen—entered the living room from the hallway, holding their youngest child, Emily—who was only four-months old.

"I thought we agreed you wouldn't smoke in the house anymore," Karen said.

"It's one cigarette. Give me a break," he said. *Besides, it's my house. I pay for all the stuff here. The house is all I have left. It's the only thing that cares about me anymore.*

"The secondhand smoke is harmful to the children, Scott. Please go smoke outside."

"No, I'm trying to relax. I worked a hard day today." He opened one of the living room windows to vent the smoke as a compromise.

"We've got the air conditioning on," she said. "Shut the window."

Scott quickly finished off his cigarette and shut the window. He acknowledged Karen had a good point. NIPSCO—their utilities provider—squeezed enough damn money out of them from one month to the next. Highway robbery. Extortion. A stick-up. These were terms Scott often used in tandem with NIPSCO in the same sentence.

Karen exited the kitchen holding a bottle for Emily. She parked herself on the couch—the opposite end from Scott and stabbed the nipple's bottle into Emily's mouth. Emily lightly moaned as she relished the milky nourishment, pumped from Karen's ample-sized breast earlier that day.

"Aaron hasn't come home yet, has he?" she asked.

"Nope. And as far as I'm concerned that little bastard can never return," he responded.

"Scott. He's not a little bastard, he's your son, and you shouldn't say such things, no matter how angry you are at him."

"Look at all the hell he's put us through. Doing drugs. Smoking pot. Stealing from me, you, and indirectly, his baby sister. That's not right."

"He's acting out."

"From what? He's got two loving parents, a roof over his head, clothes—designer clothes, I might add—on his back, food, a room with a view, a computer, a laptop, a cellphone. Stupid fucking me. He has it so rough. I should call CPS right now."

"Scott! Your language!"

"What? I said it in English."

Karen did a mocking, sarcastic laugh and Scott forced himself not to snicker as he so often did when she called him out on his bullshit. She would often say to him: You think you're so funny, but yeah—you're really not.

He stood and sat next to Karen as she continued to feed Emily. He kissed Karen on her cheek and then Emily. *If only it were us four and we didn't have that rotten lowlife son of ours life would be perfect, and maybe I'll get lucky and he'll be wiped away from the face of the Earth,* he thought, but then he silently admonished himself for thinking such a thought.

Once Emily was fed, she fell asleep shortly after and Karen placed her in her bouncy chair and then slumped on the couch. "Will you put on the news, please?"

"I'm watching SportsCenter right now, damn it," he snapped. "Can it wait?"

"Scott! Stop swearing around the baby! I don't want her first word spoken to be a bad one," Karen snapped back—even fiercer than him.

"You need to lighten up. She's going to hear those words eventually."

"I don't care. I don't like it."

"I can't watch TV. I can't smoke. I can't curse. Tell me. What can I do in my house?

She folded her arms and turned away from him. "You can turn on the news and we can watch it together."

He clenched his teeth. If he were a dragon, smoke would have billowed from his nostrils. He took a breath, which released the angry energy coursing through his body. He picked the remote off the end table and switched on the news.

She smiled at him.

"There you go, your excellency," he said.

Again, she mocked a laugh, which made him titter, though only slightly.

The news program was airing footage from a crash site. The headline at the bottom of the screen read: BLACK BOXES

LOCATED; NTSB TO DC TO REVIEW THEM. This plane crash was continued coverage of the one Andrew and Codi learned about while at the Burger King where Dylan screamed bloody murder.

When the news anchor relayed how many people were aboard the downed aircraft, she covered her mouth and said: "All those people. My god."

"That's the way it goes. Every now and again the Almighty likes to swat a plane out of the sky. It's how he gets his jollies, I think."

"Not funny. Three-hundred-and-four people died in an instant. Three-hundred-and-four families forever changed. This isn't something to crack wise about, and if you do it again, I'm gonna crack your skull with your ash tray."

Of course, she was speaking in jest, and Scott knew she would never hurt him nor would he her. They had an interesting dynamic, one that flew into the face of what most would consider a normal relationship, but they didn't care. They loved what they had together and wouldn't have it any other way.

Now they both focused their attention on the former NTSB investigator and now current aviation expert for the CBS network. His name was Jon Fitch. When the news anchor asked Jon why the pilots didn't respond to ATC, he said: "It's possible they were too busy trying to gain control of the aircraft. Another possibility is they were both incapacitated."

The front door opened and Aaron walked through it followed by three of his friends—Ricardo, Shawn, and Tyler—and they were all clamoring and laughing. Scott lunged off the couch and held out his arms like an arm soaring through the sky upon leaving the ground, blocking Aaron and his friends from walking beyond the threshold of the living room.

"What's your problem, Dad?" Aaron asked. "You are baseball referee all of a sudden? Safe!"

But Scott wasn't amused at Derrick's verbal judo. He grinded his teeth, and Aaron picked up on this, because when Scott grinded his teeth, his bottom jaw moved laterally.

"Come on, guys," Aaron said. "My dad is playing around."

Scott placed a hand on Derrick's chest, stopping him from traveling. "No, I'm not," he said.

"What the fuck is your problem?"

"What's my problem? I'll tell you what my problem is. You're grounded. That's my problem. And you better watch your mouth." And to his cackling friends: "You all need to leave. He's grounded—and now for even longer. I'm sorry. You got to go."

"Dad! This is such bullshit! Why am I grounded?" Aaron demanded to know.

"Don't act like you don't know, but if you want to play that game, I'll tell you for the one-millionth-and-one time. Because you stole money from me—again. Because you were caught doing drugs in the house—again. Because you don't help around here. Enough is enough," Scott said.

Aaron's friends listened to reason and left the premises without further incident. Scott stepped into the kitchen to fix himself a snack. He didn't know what he wanted though. All he knew is he was hungry and just about anything sounded good to eat. Without skipping a beat, Aaron followed after his dad.

"I can't believe you," Aaron said to his dad.

"And I can't believe *you*," Scott replied.

"What do you mean by that?"

As Scott sliced some tomatoes, he said: "Your mother and I tell you you're grounded, you leave the house. You come home and try to bring your friends inside like it's party time. Then you want to pop off at the mouth, challenge me, and use bad language. Now you're grounded for an additional two weeks on top of the additional two weeks I added for you violating your initial grounding."

"Another four weeks? That's not fair! God, you're an asshole sometimes!"

"You better watch yourself," Scott sneered. He seasoned with tomato slices with salt, pepper, and olive oil.

"Go to hell!"

"I'm in hell!"

The baby started to cry as Aaron stormed off to his room upstairs while Scott placed some of the tomato slices on pieces of wheat bread to make two sandwiches.

Karen entered the kitchen with Emily's derriere resting on her arm and her face on Karen's shoulder.

"Hungry?" Scott asked Karen.

"I guess so," Emily replied. She bounced Emily using her arm as she sat on a swivel stool at the bar counter in the kitchen. She lightly snickered as she watched Scott cut into another tomato. "I remember when we were so poor tomato sandwiches were all we would eat."

"It has a certain elegant simplicity to it, *n'est pas*?"

She snickered. "*Oui, oui.*"

He sliced her sandwich along the diagonal of the bread and then once more before handing her the plate. He then kissed Emily on her forehead once again before eating his sandwich.

15

The waiting room was packed with multitudinous shades and flavors of sick people, and the sounds emanating were just as varied. Coughs, sneezes, wretches, moans, groans, and the like clashed together, creating a strident symphony.

In front of Stacey was a table with a landfill of books and magazines strewn across it. She pushed a few of the objects on the table around, hoping to find something she could read. Nothing caught her eye, so she grabbed a magazine willy-nilly. She opened it up to a random page and began thumbing through the pages, one at a time after perusing them. Before she turned each page, she stuck her tongue out like a bird in a cuckoo clock and ran her thumb along it.

Dylan was staring at the back of his arm with pensiveness as he toddled in the chair next to Stacey. He was fixated on his wrist.

"I hope the doctor will see us soon," Stacey said.

"Me, too. Time stands still for no one, and for me it's closer to running out each passing second," he replied.

Some people sitting in the row of chairs across from Stacey and Dylan looked up from their phones with an expression of bewilderment at Dylan's remark.

A shadow figure appeared in front of Dylan—the same shadow figure Bruce had seen—and spoke to him. Although Dylan could see this shadow figure, nobody else could.

"That's right, Killin' Dylan!" the shadow figure said. "I'm going to savor killing you if you don't take care of it yourself!"

"Leave me alone!" Dylan screamed. Now the symphonic sounds of sickness ceased and all eyes were on Dylan. Stacey placed both hands on his shoulders.

The shadow figure responded. "Then do it already! Stop fighting it! You can't beat this. There's only one way out: death."

"No! I don't wanna do it!" he replied.

"Who are you talking to?" Stacey asked. "There's nobody saying anything to you."

"Fine," the shadow figure said. "Don't kill yourself. But when the sand runs out of the hourglass, I will. See you on the other side really soon."

Dylan covered his mouth and gawked at the back of his wrist. He said to Stacey: "I can't tell you that." Then he cried, still staring at the back of his wrist. "It keeps going down, and it doesn't stop. It will never stop unless I…"

"Unless you what?" Stacey asked. "Tell me."

His head slumped to his chest as drops of saline from his eyes fell onto his leg. "I can't say. Time is running out though."

Stacey did the only thing she could think of, and that was coil her arms around Dylan.

A few moments later, a woman wearing scrubs exited out of a door. "Myers?"

A man wearing a surgical mask raised his hand, stood, and walked to her, coughing along the way.

Stacey muttered an expletive, upset it wasn't Dylan's turn to see a doctor yet.

"Does your wrist itch or hurt?" Stacey asked.

"No," Dylan replied.

"That's good."

"I want the doctor to cut it off though."

"Why? You just said—"

A different nurse opened the same door Myers went through and said: "Railford, Dylan."

Stacey stood at once, picked up Dylan, and walked to the nurse. The nurse walked them to a room. The door was labeled EXAM ROOM 2. Once inside, Stacey set Dylan on the ribbon of tissue paper that extended down the center of the examining table. She took a seat against a wall near the door of the examining room.

The nurse scanned over Dylan's electronic medical file, then she read the form Stacey filled out, which detailed why Dylan needed to be seen by a physician.

The nurse introduced herself as Carol—though her name tag displayed CAROLINE—and cautiously reached her hand out to inspect Dylan's wrist, and he willingly let her. She examined the entire circumference of it. She held Dylan's arm and rapidly jerked it up and down so the hand bobbled at the wrist.

Carol dropped her well-sculpted gluteus onto a wheeled chair and pushed herself towards the computer that was on the wall across from the examining table. She typed in a few notes into Dylan's electronic file. Then she took Dylan's blood pressure and temperature and noted the results in his e-file. She told them both the doctor would be in shortly.

Dylan released an exasperated sigh. "She couldn't see it."

"See what?" Stacey asked, curious to know.

In a resigned tone, Dylan said: "It's hopeless."

The shadow figure appeared before Dylan's eyes once again. He screamed before the shadow figure spoke.

The shadow figure said: "Bingo, buckaroo! You're going to die one way or the other—either by your own hand or mine. Only one person managed to escape my clutches—thanks to that sword-wielding menace—and I'm going to fix that mistake, rest assured. I'll kill the one who stabbed me, and I'll get the soul that's rightfully mine back, too."

About four minutes later, the door swung open and a man wearing blue scrubs and white tennis shoes—which were unblemished—stepped inside, ducking before entering to avoid busting his forehead on the top of the door jam. He was as tall and thin as a flagpole. Dangling from his neck like piece of jewelry was a stethoscope.

The physician introduced himself as Dr. Randall Garrison, but he insisted they call him Randy. After some brief chatter about nothing, Randy got down to business and inspected Dylan's wrist. Randy took a step back from Dylan and stood clutching his elbow with one hand while his other hand served as a chin rest. "Hmmmm… No signs of damage. No bruising. No contusions."

Dylan held out his arm with his knuckles pointing to the floor and he pointed to the back of his wrist, but nothing jumped out at Randy.

"Do you feel any pain or discomfort in your wrist?" Randy asked.

"No," Dylan replied, "but something is wrong with it."

"Alright. Tell me," Randy replied.

Dylan closed his eyes. "I can't. If I do…bad things will happen to me."

Randy became concerned Dylan may be the victim of child abuse, but didn't tip his hand about that accusation just yet. "I can't find anything wrong with it by looking at your wrist, squirt."

Tapping her foot on the floor, Stacey sharply exhaled. "Well, something is wrong with his wrist."

"I think we need to do some X-rays," Randy said. "That will give us a better glimpse as to what is going on with it."

"Will you be able to see what's wrong with my wrist that way?" Dylan asked.

"It's possible, little fella. The X-ray will permit me to see things I can't see with my own eyes, squirt," Randy said. "I'll be able to see into your wrist."

Stacey rolled her eyes. *How many nicknames is this dufus going to pull out of his trick bag?* she thought.

A slight smile formed on Dylan's face. "And then you can fix it?"

"Yes, indeedy, big guy," Randy said. "A nurse will take you to the X-ray room momentarily. Once we get the results, we can make a diagnosis and focus on treatment and predict prognosis."

Dylan gestured for Randy to come closer to him, which he did, and then Dylan pointed to Randy, who promptly removed his stethoscope and handed it to Dylan. As he placed the eartips of the stethoscope in his ears and the diaphragm of it on his wrist, his eyes widened and the blood in his face seeped to his feet. Dylan removed the eartips and handed the binaural to Randy while keeping his hand atop the bell. Randy placed the eartips in his ears—after wiping them down with a wet nap—and listened for a few seconds, but Randy's face stayed still as stone. He shook his head and admitted he couldn't detect any abnormal sound. Dylan slammed both fists on the examining bed, and Randy took note of this, concluding if there was something physically wrong with Dylan's wrist, he likely would not have pounded the table the way he did. Still, though, to be sure, an X-ray was ordered. Randy wanted to take no chances, especially if child abuse was still a possibility.

After the X-ray results were available, he returned to the examining room where Dylan and Stacey were waiting. Randy knocked before entering, walked over to the computer, and queued up the X-rays. He took a step back from the computer's monitor with an elbow in one hand and the other hand caressing his chin. "Hmmm… Interesting."

"What is?" Stacey asked. "Did you find something? Is it a chipped bone? A fractured wrist? What?"

But the X-ray results offered no additional clues as to what was wrong with Dylan's wrist. This frustrated the hell out of Stacey. The one place she figured would have answers for her had none. She insisted to Randy something had to be wrong with Dylan's wrist.

Randy asked Stacey to accompany him into the hallway for a few moments to chat.

"I think Dylan's conviction his wrist is injured may be a manifestation in his mind," Randy said. "Stated another way—"

"He's faking and he's full of shit?" Stacey asked.

"Not exactly. It may be psychosomatic."

"Look, doc, I barely made it through the eighth grade and I dropped out of school in my first semester of my freshman year. Let's drop all the fancy book learnins and cut to the chase."

"In Dylan's mind, his wrist is injured or damaged. He believes that. He's not faking per se, but he's not in tune with reality."

"What would cause that?"

"Stress, usually. Has he had any major events happen recently? A family member or pet pass away?"

"His dad resumed work. They are extremely close, and spent hours and hours together while his dad was laid off."

"I see. That could influence an impressionable fella's mind. It's like a death in the family—a figurative death."

In a sharp tone, she said: "What do you recommend his dad do then? His dad can't quit work to be at home. He's got to make a living, you know."

What a snooty, snotty biatch, he thought. He wanted to end the conversation right then and there. He didn't appreciate Stacey's attitude. All he was trying to do was help offer possible explanations for Dylan's behavior.

Before Randy could break away, Stacey apologized and asked in a more polite manner for some solutions.

"Have Dylan's dad call in a few times during his shirt and specifically speak to Dylan. Maybe give Dylan a WiFi-enabled cellphone so he can text his dad whenever he wants. If possible, maybe a few times a week, Dylan and his dad can eat lunch together during his dad's lunch break."

They entered the examining room. Dylan was curled up in a fetal position staring at his left wrist. Stacey told him it was time to go, but he didn't want to leave, insisting he felt safe in the examining room, seemingly isolated from the outside world.

"Your dad is going to be home soon," she said. "And your mom, too. Don't you want to see them?"

"I do, but they can come visit me here," he replied.

The shadow figure appeared again and said: "You're safe nowhere, boy-o. In this room alone, I see at least a half dozen ways

I could squeeze the life out of you, much like remnant toothpaste at the bottom of a tube."

"Fuck off! Leave me alone! Let me live!" Dylan screamed. "Get this off my wrist!"

"We can't stay here, Dylan. Now let's go," Stacey said. She didn't realize he wasn't talking to her. She also interpreted his let me live remark to mean let him live his life the way he wanted.

"I don't wanna go home," Dylan cowered.

Randy glanced at his watch. He didn't want to be rude, but there were other patients waiting to be seen and he needed to get the sniveling, short-tempered Dylan out of the examining room.

Once again, she told Dylan they needed to go. He sat up on the examining room table and stared at the back of his wrist. "Why can't they see it? Why can't anyone but me see it?"

"See it? See what?" Randy asked.

After a few seconds of hesitation, Dylan said: "I can't say. The shadow will kill me if I do." He once again summoned Randy closer to him by gesturing his hand. He pulled the stethoscope off of Randy's neck, placed the eartips in his ears, and set the diaphragm to the back of his left wrist. After a few seconds, he handed Randy the binaural and said: "Listen carefully. Do you hear anything? Is it ticking or beeping?"

And Randy did. He listened for a few seconds, but heard nothing. Dylan grabbed the binaural back and listened himself, then he handed it back to Randy, who listened once again.

But he couldn't hear anything. Stacey thanked the doctor for his time and she and Dylan left the hospital, stopping for ice cream along the way, though Dylan wanted none.

16

Convinced Derrick was no longer a threat to himself or others, Thomas granted him access to his cellphone. Unfortunately, it was dead, but one of the nurses in the BAU allowed him the use of her charger. More worried about the hospital's liability if Derrick *did* harm himself or others, Thomas insisted Derrick's phone charge in an outlet near the orderly assigned to supervise Derrick as a preventive measure. Thomas feared Derrick could use the phone charging cable as a ligature.

Another chair was brought in so Derrick could sit across from the orderly and use his phone while it continued to charge.

The phone started to charge and Derrick made himself comfortable in the chair, waiting patiently for the phone to accumulate enough juice to power on.

The room was a depressing sight, so depressing in fact it was a wonder nobody committed suicide in it. Drab walls. No windows. Just a room with a bed and two chairs. One would think there would be rich, colorful paintings on the walls—or at the least, inspirational sayings to encourage people to value and cherish life.

"Did Thomas tell you yet?" the orderly—Tina—asked.

"Tell me what?" Derrick replied.

"You're going to be here another week."

"What?" Derrick said, lunging to his feet.

Tina chuckled. "Relax. I'm joking. You're leaving on Monday, but pretend to act surprised when he tells you. I wasn't supposed to tell you, but I thought he already did."

"Really? Then why did you ask me?"

"Whatever," she replied, smiling.

Now Derrick's phone powered up and a deluge of texts and other message notifications poured in like a steady stream. He didn't wait for all them to trickle in before he unlocked his phone. He immediately texted Danielle. He texted to her: *I miss you, baby. I'll be back at home on Monday.*

She texted back: *I love you, too, baby. I can't wait to see you. What happened?*

It's a long story, he replied via text to her right away.

Tell me. Andrew and I were on our way to see you, but he convinced me to not risk being removed from the property for trespassing. Codi wanted me to tell you he wished he could have seen you before leaving for Missouri.

Derrick took a candid photo of himself and penned a brief message with his finger onto the picture before he sent it to Danielle.

After receiving the picture, she texted: *Awww, babe. I love you, too.* Then she called him. When he answered, she asked: "What happened?"

"Allegedly, I committed suicide," he replied.

"You mean allegedly you *attempted* suicide."

"Always correcting me."

And this was one constant source of contention between he and Danielle. She seemed to get a kick out of proving him wrong and correcting him.

"You're right," Danielle said. "I'm sorry."

"No, you're right," Derrick responded. "Obviously I didn't commit suicide."

"So, what happened? How did you attempt suicide?"

"I was found at the community baseball field near the outfield fence. From what the loony psychiatrist—Dr. Jabba the Hut—told me, I tried to asphyxiate myself."

Danielle gasped. "I wish you would have let me drive you home. I hate myself for not chasing after you when you stormed out of my house on Saturday."

Now Derrick racked his brain, trying to remember being at Danielle's house, but he couldn't. When he opened the drawer pertaining to the past Saturday from the file cabinet in his brain, a few sheets of paper flew out of it—but they were blank.

She tried to massage some feeling into his brain by spouting out a litany of events that happened that night between them. They ordered a pizza, watched some movies, play wrestled, talked, among some other things—and it was these other things that led to Derrick storming out of her house.

"I'm sorry. I don't remember any of that," he said.

"Do you remember the argument we had before you stormed out of the house?" she asked.

A brief period of silence passed. "No, I don't. Why don't you tell me what the argument was about?"

"Throughout the evening your behavior was odd at times. I called you out on it, but you've never been good at sharing your feelings. You retreated into your shell like a scared turtle trying to escape a certain death. You didn't want to tell me. I pushed too hard and you stormed out of the living room. Do you remember now?"

But Derrick didn't have any recollection of the argument in question. Though he couldn't remember specific events, he had some sense of the passage of time, and he believed what she told him, but he was frustrated he couldn't remember for himself. It was if someone had taken White-Out and redacted a large block of time from his brain.

He wanted to remember, he tried to remember. The struggle to remember started to frustrate him just as much as being unable to remember. He wondered if Thomas might be able to help him regain his lost memories. He also was curious as to why such a large block of time would be forgotten.

He was searching for reasons why his memory failed to store the events transpiring from Thursday evening through waking up in the hospital. The first explanation that entered his mind grabbed him by the face and shook him. He feared his brain was deteriorating, thinking he had some sort of degenerative disease.

"That doesn't make sense," Danielle said. "If it were a degenerative disease, you'd probably have other memory lapses."

"You did it again. Corrected me."

"I'm trying to help you. Will park your pride to curb and listen to me?"

He chided himself for acting like such a dick towards her, and he apologized. For the next ten minutes, she asked him a serious of questions whose answers would be difficult to forget. His birthday. His address. Her birthday. Her address. The high school they attended together. The first time they met. He rattled off the answers to these questions, and this helped Derrick accept his brain wasn't suffering from a disease.

"Maybe I was abducted by aliens," he said. "I bet they're going to come back for me and take me away."

Now Danielle was hysterical with laughter. "Maybe Mrs. Givens and you will be aboard the same spacecraft."

Mrs. Givens was their Algebra 2 teacher last school year. She alienated her students by announcing to them at least twice a week the aliens would be landing in her backyard to take her away again. It was next to impossible for any of the students to take her seriously.

"It's nice to hear you laugh. I live to hear you laugh," Derrick said.

"I can't wait to see you Monday. One more day," Danielle said.

"Yep, and it can't come soon enough."

After the call with Danielle ended, he called his dad. They talked for several minutes. Bruce mentioned their house might now be haunted, and this peaked Derrick's interest.

"We may have a ghost in the house?" Derrick asked. "What's it look like?"

"Like a silhouette," Bruce responded.

"Has it said anything?"

"Not a word. It's a mute, I think. I don't think it even has a mouth. Like I said—it's nothing but a translucently dark mass shaped like a human."

Derrick stifled his laughter, convinced Bruce was drunk once again. *How ironic,* Derrick thought. *I'm hearing voices; he's seeing spirits.*

"Dad? What was mom's name again?" Derrick asked.

"Why do you want to bring her up again? I thought you and I put this to bed," Bruce shot back. About three seconds later, he said: "Her name was…Deborah."

"Again her name changes. The last time I asked you for her name you said it was Adelaide. And before that, Erika. And before that, Delilah. I don't know what to believe anymore with you."

Bruce sighed. "I don't want you to get hurt again. Who cares about her? She up and left us. You need to keep that at the forefront of your brain."

But I want to meet her. "Can we look at some old pictures of you, her, and me together?"

"You just don't know when to quit, do you? Now you're being cruel. You know all the photographs I had of us as a family were destroyed in the house fire."

"House fire? What house fire?" *Why is he muttering?*

"I guess I never told you about that and for good reason. Anyhow, all of the pictures were destroyed in a house fire. I told you once, I'll tell you again. If you want to forge a relationship with your mother who abandoned you, go ahead and move in with her."

Derrick sighed. "Dad, don't start, okay? I'm not trying to get you angry. I'll talk to you later. Let's both get some sleep."

"Good night," Bruce said. Then the line went dead.

17

The black box—specifically the cockpit voice recorder—was cut open using what resembled a bone saw. Now one of the investigators located the memory card onto which the data was stored and loaded it into the computer.

The lead investigator—Bob Feith—placed his headphones on and instructed the investigator who loaded the memory card to start playing the recording.

The first twenty-five minutes of the recording consisted of standard pilot talk. Their route. Configuring the plane for takeoff. Communication between air traffic control. Takeoff.

Once the plane reached cruising altitude, the pilots amiably chatted back and forth in between maintaining communication with ATC and monitoring the flight instruments.

At approximately seventy minutes into the flight, the first officer—Hans Schroeder—said: "If you want to use the restroom, now is your chance."

"Agreed," the captain replied.

The sound of a door unlocking and opening was picked up by the CVR, presumably the captain leaving the flight deck. Moments later, ATC attempted to communicate with the first officer, but he didn't respond.

"Flight 5952, please maintain flight level three-six-zero," the air traffic controller said a second time.

But the plane continued to descend. Passengers could be heard screaming in the background. The captain—Peter Kinderheitz—entered in the code to unlock the cockpit door, but it didn't work. After repeated attempts to enter his code failed, he knocked on the door and identified himself, but the co-pilot did not grant him entry into the cockpit.

"Please let me in!" Peter shouted as he relentlessly pounded on the door.

But Hans didn't open the door nor did he respond.

Now the sound of an object striking the cockpit door could be heard on the CVR. Bob wrote the word *ax* on his legal pad. Passengers continued to scream. Air traffic control attempted two more times to establish communication with Flight 5952, but Hans never answered.

Maybe Hans was incapacitated, Bob thought. *But why didn't the captain's code work to gain reentry into the cockpit?*

The final two minutes of the CVR recording provided Bob with ironclad proof the first officer wasn't incapacitated at all. The first officer breathed normally as the Ground Proximity Warning System announced: "Too low, terrain. Pull up. Too low, terrain. Pull up."

The CVR went dead after the sound of a booming impact played.

"It's unthinkable," Bob said. "The first officer intentionally crashed the plane into the mountain, killing himself and murdering another three-hundred-and one people… But why would he do it?"

The members of the team assigned to investigate the crash tossed out several ideas before digging up as much information on the first officer at their disposal.

18

As Scott passed the upstairs hallway bathroom, Aaron was brushing his teeth, standing in front of the sink. Though the door was partially open, Scott knocked on it twice before pushing all the way open.

Aaron offered a nod as a way to acknowledge his dad's presence as the toothpaste-spit foam slid off his chin into the basin.

Scott sat on the edge of the bathtub and stared into the mirror at Aaron, who had a mouthful of water and was swishing it about in his mouth. A torrent of liquid spat out of Aaron's mouth.

"Need something?" Aaron asked. He pulled out two disposable flossers from the bag that rested on top of the wooden shelf to the right of the mirror Scott had installed last year.

"I thought I'd apologize if I was a little hard on you earlier," Scott said.

"It's history."

"Look, Aaron, I'm trying to do my job as a dad to the best of my ability. I'm not grounding you to be a mean guy or make your life miserable maliciously."

Aaron nodded as he flossed his teeth. "Uh-huh."

"Do you want to tell me what you bought with the money you stole from my checking account?"

"Stuff."

Scott nodded his head with a sort of cynicism only he could do. It wasn't a nod of agreement, but one of sarcasm.

"What kind of stuff?" Scott asked, his tone biting.

"I don't know," Aaron said shrugging his shoulders. "Stuff."

Scott shook his head. "Drugs."

"Not drugs. I didn't buy drugs."

"Can I search your room right now then?"

"You probably already did," Aaron sneered.

Before saying another word, Scott took a few breaths and let Aaron finish flossing his teeth. He reminded himself his intention to talk to Aaron in the bathroom wasn't to start another war with him, but to hopefully establish some common ground and start to repair their damaged relationship.

After Aaron finished flossing his teeth, he squirted some Old Spice Face Wash Cleanser into the palm of his hand and then rubbed it with his other hand before applying the blue soapy foam onto his face.

"Are you just going to sit there and watch me wash myself? It's a little creepy," Aaron admitted.

"It's my house. I'll sit wherever I want to sit," Scott retorted, his tone sharp and bitter. *Idiot! Not a good move if you're trying to mend broken fences!* "I'm sorry, son. I didn't mean—"

"Don't, Dad. You've done this a thousand times over in the past. You say something mean or hurtful, then apologize right after. At this point, your apologies are tantamount to the dog shit on my shoe."

"So I shouldn't say I'm sorry anymore? Is that it?"

"No, I'm saying you should try to think before you act or speak."

"Says the thief."

"Man, screw you! I needed the money!"

"Get a job and get you some money then. Don't be stealing from me and your mother. And if you're not willing to get a job, then at least ask one of us if you need some money."

Aaron turned around and cocked his fist back, but Scott stood and got into his face, taunting him to throw the first punch. For sure, Aaron wanted to hurt his dad, and severely, too. Standing there with his dad no less than six inches from his face, Aaron had flashbacks to the times his dad would leave the house, come back with a bag containing a bottle of booze, sit at the kitchen table, and drink himself into a drunken oblivion—all the while shouting insults to Karen. After his brain marinated in booze for some time, his rants turned from verbal to physical. When Karen would try to reason with him, he would push her—and hard, too. One time Scott pushed Karen with such force into a wall, her head bled from the impact, and this was a memory Aaron wish he could forget.

In a flash, Aaron's mind shifted from the verbal and physical abuse his dad inflicted on his mom to the verbal and physical abuse he endured from his dad as a child, and these went beyond beatings with a belt. Aaron commanded his mind to think about something else, anything, and fortunately it did. At this same instant, Aaron—with his face still covered in soap—lowered his cocked fist, walked past his dad praying he wouldn't hit him, and exited the bathroom.

When Aaron reached the first floor, he scurried into the bathroom and washed his face. As he pat-dried (rather than rubbed) his face, his mind wandered. "Sometimes I wish I were dead," he muttered.

Three loud pounds on the door nearly induced Aaron to soil his boxers—not briefs—he liked his junk loosey-goosey. He opened the door and peeked his head out, looking left and then right, but nobody was around. A second later—two at the most— tittering from the closet across the bathroom smacked Aaron's ear as if an insect had crashed into it.

"You little shit stain," Aaron said, mildly agitated. "You nearly gave me a heart attack."

"You're a big shit stain," a young boy's voice from the closet replied, chuckling afterwards.

"Come out of there before the ghost inside throws you out."

"I'm not scared." The little boy—Aaron's younger brother—named Brandon—stepped out of the closet. He was a tiny tot, standing about three feet tall. He had ginger-colored hair, unlike Aaron, who had brown hair.

"Why don't you sleep in there, then, Opie?" Aaron asked.

"Stop calling me Opie, meth head. You know I don't like that," Brandon said.

Aaron and Brandon walked into the kitchen together. Brandon perched himself on one of the chairs at the bar counter while Aaron opened the refrigerator and pulled out a plastic box of tomatoes. Aaron asked Brandon if he wanted a sandwich, and he did.

While Aaron cut some tomato slices, Brandon pulled out a Juicy Juice box from the refrigerator and returned to his seat. As Aaron cut into another tomato, Brandon pictured it as a beating heart, and as the juice and seeds from the tomato seeped out of it onto the cutting board, he envisioned it as blood.

Out of nowhere, Brandon asked: "Have you ever thought about killing someone?"

"What? No."

"Liar."

Aaron squirted some mayonnaise onto a brioche bun. "Why are you asking such a question?"

Brandon shrugged his shoulders. "I saw another Freddy Krueger movie. It got me thinking about killing. I wonder, what would it be like to kill someone?"

"You need to stop watching those horror movies if it's getting you to think about killing people." He placed a paper towel in front of Brandon and dropped the tomato sandwich onto it. When it hit the paper towel, a thud sound was produced. "Eat. It'll take your mind off of killing people."

Brandon complied and bit into the tomato-brioche sandwich. And then another. Meanwhile, Aaron prepared himself a sandwich, but on a croissant with sour cream and chive cream cheese in lieu of mayonnaise.

As Aaron bit into his sandwich, Brandon asked: "Have you thought about killing yourself?"

"What is with you and these questions about murdering people and committing suicide?"

"Forget it. I shouldn't have said anything."

The stigmata of suicide and suicidal ideation, and Aaron was all too familiar with it, but not because he was suicidal. The past school year for his health class—the unit on mental health—

each student was assigned a topic on which to research and present findings to the class, which counted as one-third of their final exam grade. He chose suicide as a broad topic, though his narrowed focus was teen suicide.

Not wanting Brandon to feel like had done something wrong as questions about suicide, Aaron opened up to Brandon. He said: "A few times, but only for a few seconds. Have you ever thought of committing suicide?"

"Yeah. A few times. The kids who tease me at school or the Boys and Girls Club sometimes make me want to kill myself."

Brandon's face had three prominent one-inch scars on his left cheek, which were the result of being ejected through a windshield in a car accident two years ago. His peers called him all sorts of names: Scarface. Freak show. Alien. Ugly Mugly—or to boot—Fugly Ugly Mugly Muggle.

"Don't let them steal your joy. That's what my counselor—Ms. DeAcosta—tells me."

"Yeah. I'll try. I hate it that the instructor lets the kids do it though. He doesn't say anything to them."

"Did you tell dad?"

"I did. All he said to do was suck it up and be a man. He told me I need to learn how to deal with assholes." Brandon bit into his sandwich and chewed slowly.

Aaron finished the last remnant of his sandwich. As he chewed, he asked: "What about mom?"

"She said she would talk to the instructor, but I really want to slice those kids up like an Easter ham."

"That's not a good idea. Do you want me to do something? I'll cave their skulls in with a baseball bat. I'll give them an aluminum shampoo."

Brandon chuckled as he always did when Aaron threatened violence on the bullies who picked on his little brother.

They finished their food and then went to Brandon's bedroom to play some Fortnite together.

19

While Thomas was dead asleep in bed, his cellphone vibrated several times on the chiffonier next to his bed before crashing onto the hardwood floor, which ultimately was what woke him up.

Thomas glanced at his alarm clock. The time was two-sixteen. The cellphone stopped vibrating for six seconds before starting again. He snagged it off the floor. The display screen read: Sharon (aka BFH). *What the hell does that crazy bitch want?* he thought. Uninterested in finding out, he pressed the DECLINE button on the screen, placed his phone back on the chiffonier, and plopped his head on the pillow—during which time his cellphone vibrated once again. The caller ID indicated the caller was Sharon. *Idiot!* he thought. *She could be calling because something happened to one of the children! Answer it!*

"Hello?" he asked. His voice was lethargic.

"Dad! Thank god you answered! Something is wrong with mom!" Nikki said.

"Like how?"

"She's acting strange."

"You mean stranger than normal?"

"Yeah. I guess. She keeps screaming at nobody."

Thomas asked for more details, and Nikki flooded his brain with shocking information like an uncapped fire hydrant. She said her mom shouted obscenities to nobody such as: fuck yourself; you can't control me; I won't go down without a fight.

Nikki also divulged to her dad she peeked into her mother's bedroom where she witnessed her mom tying a noose using a bed sheet. Then Nikki added she observed her mom lasso her neck with the noose before sliding the knot of the makeshift rope towards it, tightening the noose. Finally, Nikki revealed her mom would sometimes pull out the gun she kept in a drawer next to her bed and aim at herself in the mirror.

"When she pointed the—" Thomas started to ask but was interrupted by Sharon shouting: "I'll kill you, you fucker!" After a brief pause, Thomas said: "Wow. She's a firecracker tonight."

"I'm scared. She's never acted this loony before," Nikki said. "What should I do?"

The only suggestion he had was for Nikki to give the phone to her mom and he would talk to her. Nikki complied and brought the phone to her mom.

"It's for you," Nikki said.

"What are you doing with my phone? Why are you out of bed?" Sharon asked.

"Please, mom—just talk," Nikki urged.

And Sharon did, albeit reluctantly. Thomas tried to get to the bottom of what had her panties all in a bunch, but her lips were like a hermetically-sealed safe.

"You're scaring the children with your random rants and nutty behavior," Thomas said.

"The children," she said. Now she started to sob. "I'm going to miss them."

Thomas sighed. "They'll be back the week before school starts." He lit a cigarette.

He thought she was referring to the children leaving her house to travel to his per the visitation agreement handed down by the divorce court. She wanted the children all to herself. If she could, she'd completely cut Thomas out their lives.

20

The time was one-thirty-seven in the morning according to Derrick's cellphone. Derrick responded to the barrage of messages

Danielle had sent him throughout the numerous times she woke up in the middle of the night, unable to fall asleep for long periods of time, worried about Derrick.

After he sent his dad a brief message, he placed the cellphone back on the overbed table and soon fell asleep.

"Are you okay?" the orderly supervising Derrick asked.

After a brief hesitation—two or three seconds—Derrick replied. "Yes. Thank you. I'm fine."

"Bad dream?"

"Kind of."

The orderly—Jeff—a Mr. Clean lookalike suggested Derrick share the details of his dreams. Now, he made this suggestion not necessarily because he was interested in helping Derrick feel better or engage in some sort of Freudian dream analysis, but merely to pass the time and fill the dead air.

Too shaken to fall back asleep, Derrick agreed to share the contents of the dream after he used the bathroom. While Derrick piddled in the pot, relieving his bloated bladder, Jeff piddled on his cellphone, playing a game of Solitaire.

Walking out of the bathroom and entering the main area of the bedroom, Derrick said: "There was this shadow man in my dream—or nightmare, more like." He sat in the chair across from Jeff.

"Shadow man, huh?" Jeff asked, his tone stoic.

"Well, I presume it was a he. I guess it could be a woman in a hoodie. It had a humanoid shape, but no definitive facial features. Nothing more than an opaque silhouette, yet more than that at the same time. It was three-dimensional, but somewhat see-through."

"And what happened? Did he say anything?"

"No. Not a syllable, let alone a word."

"What did he do?"

"He stood in front of me, staring at me, Staring *through* me, even though it had no eyes."

Jeffrey altered his voice, shrouding it with a spooky tone. "They're coming to get you, Barbara."

"Who's Barbara?" Derrick asked.

Jeffrey explained he was quoting a line from *Night of the Living Dead*. He was a classic horror movie buff, and often spent his non-working hours stuffing his face with over-buttered-and-salted popcorn while watching black and white horror movies. *Dracula, Nosferatu: A Symphony of Horror, Freaks, The House on Haunted Hill,* and *Eyes Without a Face* were his favorites, and each time he watched them it was like the first time.

Unlike Jeffrey, Derrick didn't care much for horror movies. He was more into action and drama.

"As the shadow man stood in front of me, I soon felt some force pull me back against a fence."

Derrick had an epiphany. He now knew why he was experiencing such strange things.

"Then what happened?"

"When my body hit the fence, I woke up, so I don't know what would have happened to me had the dream progressed."

"Any idea what the dream means?"

"No."

"Have you had the dream before?"

Derrick shook his head. "It's the first time I've had this dream, and hopefully the last."

They chatted for another few minutes before Thomas walked into the room and greeted both of them. Derrick was much more cordial this time, standing and extending his hand for Thomas to shake.

"You're here at a strange hour," Jeffrey admitted. "Did something happen to one of our patients?"

"No. I just couldn't sleep, so I thought I'd make myself useful," Thomas replied.

"Trouble sleeping? Why is that?" Derrick asked.

"Personal reasons. Family issues," Thomas said. He pulled out a bottle of Aleve, popped two in his mouth, and swallowed. "My wife is going bat-shit crazy. I may have to leave for a few days to travel to Georgia. I'm worried about her, but more so my kids being exposed to her erratic behavior."

"I'm sorry to hear that," Derrick said. *At least your kids have a relationship with their mom. I need to find out who my mom is.* "I hope things get better." *I'm going to find out who she is. I hope I can locate her.*

"Me, too," Thomas said. He exited the room.

Feeling as though he could fall back asleep, Derrick climbed into bed, closed his eyes, and soon entered REM sleep, during which time he dreamed about himself and Danielle graduating from high school and leaving Chesterville for good to attend college together and start the next chapter of their lives together. Later during his sleep, he dreamed about reuniting with his mother.

21

As Derrick was lying on the couch in Thomas' office, Thomas asked him to discuss whatever was on his mind. At first, it was difficult for Derrick to talk about much of anything, so Thomas offered him prompting questions, which helped. Some questioned included: What are some of the problems in your life from your viewpoint? How would you describe your affect right now? What would make you feel happier?

The question about being happier prompted Derrick to talk for what seemed like hours. He talked about his desire to attend an Ivy League college to become a biochemist. He shared with Thomas his hope Danielle would eventually marry him and they would have a family together. He also expressed his ambition to be a centurion.

But now Thomas wanted to get to talking about what he believed Derrick needed to confront, and that was the night he was at the baseball field, attempting to exit from the physical world.

Using a string with a metal ball affixed at the end of it as a pendulum, Thomas encouraged Derrick to focus on the ball and to clear his mind of any distractions. Yes—Thomas was attempting to hypnotize Derrick.

"When I snap my fingers, you will stand like a solider at attention," Thomas said. He snapped his fingers. "Excellent!" Then he said: "When I snap my fingers again, you will lay back down on the couch like a dead fish out of water."

And Derrick did just that.

With Derrick under the spell, Thomas asked: "What happened at the baseball field?"

"The Pumbra—this shadow man—tried to kill me."

"The what-a?"

"Right."

"Tell me about the baseball field. Why did you try to kill yourself at the baseball field?"

Derrick closed his eyes. "I remember the shoelaces being lifted off the ground and wrapped around my neck, but nobody was there but me."

Thomas scribbled some notes down on his pad as Derrick spoke, somewhat confused as to what Derrick was even talking about.

"The laces looped around my neck and fence, strangling me," Derrick said. "Kind of like somebody was behind me trying to strangle me. I remember gasping for air. I remember almost passing out, too."

"What happened next?"

"All at once, the pressure around my neck ceased, and I fell to the ground. Then I blacked out."

"So, you didn't want to go through with killing yourself then, right? You decided you wanted to live instead of die. Am I right?"

Derrick shook his head. "But I didn't try and kill myself. Someone else tried to kill me."

Thomas was convinced Derrick tried to kill himself, but was dissembling from admitting so. He jotted down a few more notes.

"Do you remember the most recent argument you and your dad had?"

Again, Derrick closed his eyes, but didn't speak for several seconds. Thomas armed his writing hand to jot down more notes just as soon as Derrick started talking.

But for some reason or another, Derrick drew a blank. This was fine with Thomas. He moved on to one more topic he wanted to discuss: Derrick's mother.

"I want you to think back to the last memory of your mother you have," Thomas said.

Nearly fifteen seconds passed. "I remember being in a van with her and another guy—I don't know who. Then a bad accident happened. I went through the windshield."

"Wow. How old do you see yourself in that memory?"

Derrick shrugged his shoulders. "I was in a car seat, so maybe one or two."

Thomas removed his glasses, nodded, and jotted down some notes. Derrick closed his eyes and nearly fell asleep.

"Very, *very* good, Derrick," Thomas said.

"Great," Derrick replied with a flat affect.

"Tell me—in your view—why did you want to kill yourself?"

"I *never* tried to kill myself. I've told you this. It was somebody from behind me who tried to kill me. It doesn't make sense for me to want to kill myself. I try to do everything I can to prolong my life. I eat right. I exercise. I don't drink soda. I hope to live to be at least one-hundred."

Thomas raised his eyebrows. "But didn't you tell me you and your friends… Andrew and Codi meet at the Burger King and wolf down Double Whoppers?"

"Yeah. So?"

"It's a little contradictory, don't you think? I mean you claim you want to live to be at least one-hundred, but then eat garbage."

"It's one day a week, maybe two at the most, and I exercise so much and eat healthy so often that I cancel those one or two Double Whoppers out, so I'm not worried about it."

"Great."

Then he brought Derrick out of the hypnotic trance.

22

When Mike stepped through his front door after driving home from working numerous hours of overtime, his jaw dropped at the sight of Heather pinning Dylan to the ground as he screamed and flailed. Next to the two of them was an electric knife, rarely used more than a few times a year. Carving the Thanksgiving turkey. Slicing up the Christmas ham. Other than that, it stayed put inside its charger mounted to the kitchen wall, right behind the wood block of knives.

After a couple seconds of hesitation, he snapped out of his trance and rushed over to offer his help. He picked Dylan up and whooshed him away to Dylan's bedroom. Meanwhile, Heather placed the electric knife back on the wall before entering Dylan's bedroom where Mike struggled to keep Dylan still.

"What is going on?" he asked her.

She rushed to Mike to help him restrain Dylan, who wouldn't stop screaming. "He's lost his mind. He sneaked out of our bedroom where he and I were asleep and was going to use the electric knife to cut his hand off," she replied.

"What's wrong with his wrist? I thought the ER doctor said there wasn't anything wrong with it."

"I don't think there is anything wrong with his wrist. It's in his mind."

"His mind?"

"Yes."

Fatigue was a friend in the eyes of Mike and Heather, and now Dylan started to wind down like an old clock. Not long after, he was asleep, once again, for now.

With care, she picked up Dylan like he were a newborn baby, and carried him to her bedroom where she tucked him into the bed, kissed him on his forehead, and closed the door, leaving a slight crack between the door and its frame to allow some of the light from the hallway to shine inside the room.

In the kitchen, Mike sat at the kitchen table while Heather heated him a plate of leftover spaghetti. Both were still in a state of shock over Dylan's erratic and dangerous behavior. Hell— dangerous was an understatement. His *fatal* behavior.

"Is there somewhere we can take him to be evaluated by a psychologist?" Mike asked.

"I've called a psychiatrist at St. Catherine's. His name is Dr. Thomas Ivy. I left him several messages already."

"I doubt you'll get a call this early in the morning. Has Dylan been like that all night?"

She placed the plate in front of him and shoved a fork into the pile of spaghetti. Steam rose from the heap of pasta as the fragrance of garlic and tomato sauce seeped into his nostrils. He rotated the fork and crammed a large coil of the noodles into his mouth. She stood in front of the sink and turned on the faucet.

"Yes—on and off," she said.

"Why didn't you call or text me about this?" Mike asked. "I could have somehow helped. Tried to do something."

"Because your job is dangerous and I didn't want you to worry. Also, we need the money. You know that as well as I do."

He nodded as he shoved some more pasta into his mouth, which had tomato sauce smeared all around it. His mouth resembled that of a hooker after orally servicing a truck driver in the back of his cab. Unlike the truck driver who may want seconds but would have to wait for his gonads to recharge, Mike asked for another plate of spaghetti.

"He's a danger to himself," Heather said. She slammed a scoop of spaghetti onto the plate and then another. "I think we need to bind his hands and feet as a precaution."

"That's awfully extreme, don't you think?"

"No, I don't. He's trying to harm himself. He is convinced something is wrong with his wrist. I don't want to wake up to my son dead."

Mike scoffed. "We're not going to hogtie him as if he were cattle at a rodeo. He's in our room. We'll be in there soon and ensure he doesn't harm himself."

On that note, Heather rushed out of the kitchen to check on Dylan. She thanked the cosmic rulers he was alright.

When she returned to the kitchen, he was pulling his plate out of the microwave. He nearly dropped it though. He rushed to the kitchen sink and ran cold water over his fingers. While he tended to his burned fingers, she placed his plate on the table, using a paper towel as a makeshift oven mitt.

Mike sat and without skipping a beat dove into eating his landfill-sized pile of spaghetti. Heather sat next to him with splayed fingers covering her eyes.

"I strongly feel we need to bind his hands and feet," Heather admitted. "You know I have good intuition, and something is telling me if we don't restrain him, he's going to harm or kill himself."

"Your emotions are in hyperdrive. I think it's clouding your thinking," Mike said.

"It's not clouding my thinking. Did you see me having to pin my son to the ground as he fought me to get to the electric knife?"

"We're both tired. We should get some sleep."

"I don't think I'll be able to sleep. Not after what I've dealt with tonight. My son is mentally unstable, convinced his wrist is injured when it really isn't."

But was Dylan's perception of his wrist being injured fact or fiction?

23

After the plane reservation was made, Thomas coordinated arrangements to rent a car. He figured he would stay in Georgia up until it was time for his daughters to fly up to Chesterville to stay with him. Now, though, he'd be accompanying them on the journey rather than the two of them flying on their own, which was probably a prudent move.

Within the past hour, he had received nearly a dozen calls from Nikki who provided updates on her mother, and they weren't pleasant either. Nikki relayed to her dad her mom was screaming obscenities and breaking objects in her bedroom.

He checked the time on his cellphone. It was six-twenty-two in the morning. He only had a few hours before he had to be at the airport. *Please don't let me get on a plane with a nut pilot on a suicide mission,* he thought. He leaned back in his chair, rubbing his eyes.

Thomas answered his cellphone and said: "Hey, care bear. How's your mom doing now?"

"She's freaking me out, Dad," Nikki responded. Her voice trembled.

"Tell me what she is doing."

And Nikki did. Sharon was shouting statements like: You can't do this to me; I'll kill you, you fucker; Quit being a pussy and show your face.

Pussy, Thomas thought. *Hmmmm.* "Is Dalente in the room with her?"

"No. He texted mom an hour ago and said he was held up at work."

"Pffft. Work. That fool has no job."

Nikki heavily sighed. "I don't care about Dalente right now. I care about mom."

"As do I, care bear."

And he did. Even though they were no longer married, he still loved her, just not romantically. His love for her was more of an agape love.

In the background, Thomas heard Sharon shouting: "Why is this happening? How can this be real?"

"Don't worry about your mom, care bear," Thomas said to Nikki. "She's having a hard time accepting the fact you and your sister will be spending six weeks away from her. She'll adjust." *Maybe I'll write her a script for some happy pills.*

"I didn't think she'd take me and Ashlee leaving her to visit with you this hard."

"How is Ashlee doing? Is she able to sleep through your mom's rants and raves?"

"I don't know. I'm not in the room with Ashlee right now. I'm in mom's closet."

With a stern tone, Thomas ordered Nikki to get out of her mother's room for her own safety. His fear was Sharon would find her in the closet and lash out at her, maybe even shoot her. Aside from that, Thomas and Sharon raised their daughters to be respectful of other people's privacy.

24

The first chance Nikki got, she slithered out of her mother's bedroom and tiptoed up the stairs to her bedroom, which she shared with Ashlee, who was sitting on her knees in her bed when Nikki entered it.

Ashlee, though the younger of the two daughters, was taller than Nikki. She had brunette hair that ran about an inch passed her shoulders.

"Why did you leave me?" Ashlee asked. "I'm scared."

"Dad is on the phone. He said not to be scared," Nikki responded. And to her dad: "I'm going to put you on speaker."

"I can't help it. Mom is going bat-shit crazy," Ashlee said.

Thomas said: "Hey. That's not ladylike."

"Dad, that's such a sexist thing to say," Nikki replied. "Nobody should—"

An ear-piercing scream, which was the melding of Nikki and Ashlee's individual scream, startled Thomas and caused his heart to nearly explode.

But the sound he heard before the ear-piercing scream sent a chill through his bones. A gunshot rang out.

"Shut and lock your door!" Thomas said. He picked up his office phone and dialed 911. When the operator answered, he frantically explained the situation and she connected him to the Palm Beach Police Department's 911 call center. "A gunshot rang out and it was loud. I think it came from inside my ex-wife's house."

The operator immediately dispatched a unit to the house.

25

When Mike woke up around eight-thirty in the morning, his heart repeatedly slammed against his chest when Dylan was no longer sleeping in between him and Heather. In fact, Dylan wasn't on their bed at all.

He's probably sitting at the kitchen table eating a bowl of cereal, Mike thought. And this thought put a smile on his face. He wouldn't mind if there was a lake of milk on the kitchen table dripping on the floor or if cereal was scattered all over the table. Mike would love to walk into the kitchen and see Dylan making his usual early-in-the-morning breakfast mess.

After Mike used the bathroom located in his bedroom, he wandered into the hallway, yawning like a lion as he scratched his bare chest.

"Dylan?" Mike called out. After a few seconds passed, he said: "Come out. Let's have some breakfast together before I have to go to work."

He had no fear yelling across the house. Heather was one of the soundest sleepers in the Midwest. When she slept, she was dead to the world—and it to her.

He walked down the hallway leading to Dylan's bedroom and knocked on his door, but there was no answer. He opened the door and walked inside the room. His bed was made and all of his toys were put away.

On Dylan's desk were some drawings on standard printing paper. One was a of a humanoid-shaped figure—like a shadow man—with no eyes, nose, or mouth—just a head.

Another sheet of paper displayed numbers—written in small print—in an hour:minute:second format, such as 24:00:00, which was the first number in the upper left-hand corner of the page. Underneath that was 23:59:59 followed by 23:59:58 and 23:59:57. And so on all the way down the page. When Dylan reached the bottom of the page, he moved to top again, creating a new column. And then another. And another. And another, until the entire page was filled margin to margin.

On the back of the page, the time didn't follow directly from the last entry on the front side of the paper. The last entry on the front side was 17:22:47; the first entry on the backside was 08:12:44 followed by 08:12:43, 08:12:42, 08:12:41, and so on.

Unlike the front page which was filled corner to corner, the backside wasn't. The last entry Dylan wrote using the same format was 05:17:52, but it wasn't the last entry on the page. Taking up the bottom right of the page was the numeral zero, 0— and inside of it was a face with tears dripping from both of its eyes.

But what did these times mean? Mike scratched his head searching for an answer but drew a blank. He chose not to dwell too much on it since he still didn't know where Dylan was, and that was now his top priority.

When he stepped into the hallway from Dylan's bedroom, he stopped in front of the bathroom door. Typically when the bathroom was occupied, the light was on and the crevice between the door and the floor would be illuminated.

But the light wasn't on based on the dark void between the door and the floor. To be sure, Mike knocked on the door and called Dylan's name. There wasn't any answer. Intuition was the nudge he needed to open the door and make certain nobody was inside of it.

He opened the door. Darkness turned to light, happiness to despair. His body fell forward. Before he hit the floor, his head struck the top of the toilet bowl.

26

When the alarm on his phone blared, Bruce promptly disengaged it, almost in a fit of rage, irritated he had to get up for work. He wouldn't be the same until Derrick was back home where he belonged.

He walked to the bathroom, washed his face, and pondered whether or not he should shave the five o'clock shadow on his face. A minute later he was out of the bathroom, unshaven face and all.

A clatter in the kitchen sent him into a panic. He grabbed his 9 mm and tiptoed down the hallway. When he reached the entryway to the kitchen, he peeked his head inside to see who was in it.

"Freeze!" he shouted.

"It's only me!" Gayle shrieked. Her hands were pointed skyward.

"What are doing here? How did you even get in my house?"

"You never changed your home alarm code like you said you would after we broke up. And you still have a house key outside the door stashed away. Remember?"

Gayle interpreted these things as signs Bruce was still in love with her. Their breakup was not pretty. A lot of hurtful words were exchanged from both sides. Though he believed their future was non-existent, she did. She couldn't seem to let go.

After Bruce lowered his weapon, Gayle did the same with her hands and she resumed cooking at the stove, next to which on the counter was a mixing bowl with batter dripping from its rim.

Bruce tucked his weapon in between the two mattresses on his bed and flounced to the coffee pot in the kitchen. He yanked the pot out of its catch, poured some into his cup, and slammed back into its catch.

"What's wrong?" Gayle asked. "You're going to break the coffee pot."

He slammed his coffee cup onto the counter after finishing his first sip. "Seriously? You have to ask me what's wrong? You come over unannounced, you break and enter into my house, you nearly cause me to shoot you dead. Need I go on?"

"Have some pancakes. You'll feel better."

"I don't think you're hearing me—or maybe I'm not communicating effectively." He inhaled deeply as steam gyrated upward from the pancakes. He layered each pancake with butter—as if icing a cake and drenched them with caramel sauce. "I wish you would respect my home."

"Any word on Derrick?"

It was as if she wasn't listening to a word he said. He cut into the three-high stack of pancakes and crammed a large bite of it into his mouth. After setting a plate of pancakes for herself on the table, she poured herself a cup of coffee and sat at the table.

"Yeah. I'm picking him up tomorrow from St. Catherine's," Bruce said.

"Why don't we go visit him today."

"There aren't any visiting hours on Sundays… Besides, part of me isn't happy with him right now anyway, that two-faced son of a—"

"Bruce! That's your son you're talking about, not some punk kid on the street. He's not a son of a bitch."

"Meet his mother one time and you'll think differently. On top of that his uncle is an asshole meathead—dead from the neck up—and down, too." He flashed a Machiavellian smile.

She cut her pancakes into several smaller pieces before savoring the first bite. Unlike Bruce, she preferred old-fashioned maple syrup on her pancakes, topped off with copious amounts of Hershey's chocolate syrup.

"Tell me. Why are you so upset at Derrick?" Gayle asked.

"He wants to meet his mother and begin a relationship with her. Can you believe that shit? After all these years I've taken care of him after that two-faced bitch broke my heart and stepped out of Derrick's life as if she had died?"

"Well, she is still his mother. And the two of you were awfully young when she abruptly left."

It wasn't abrupt, he thought, slightly grinning. "You're right. She did leave abruptly—much too quick. And, yes, she may be Derrick's biological mother, but she's not a mother in terms of other facets. Why should she get a second chance with him after she did what she did?"

Gayle put her hand on top of Bruce's. "I know what's wrong. You're afraid Derrick might get hurt again, aren't you?"

He skewered a pancake and folded it a few times, turning the circular-shaped pancake into wedge—like a piece of pie. He smeared the compacted pancake in some syrup and crammed it into his mouth.

After he chewed a few times—with his mouth open just as Derrick had a bad habit of doing—he said: "Yep."

Gayle smiled. "You're his protector, aren't you?" He nodded. Then she said: "It's kind of scary, isn't it?"

"What is?" Bruce asked.

"The number of suicides in the past two weeks has skyrocketed according to a news report I watched this morning before driving over here."

"People have problems. Sometimes their problems overtake them."

"Well, this sudden spike in suicides isn't just in Chesterville though. It's around the globe."

"Do the experts have any explanation?"

"Nothing concrete. Some have written it off as an anomaly."

Bruce nodded. Gayle stood, snagged his plate, and loaded it with a new helping of four fluffy pancakes. When she opened the microwave door, he stopped her, insisting the microwave would change the flavor and to not nuke his pancakes.

And she didn't. Now the two of them were back to eating their pancakes, and they were like hot and cold, sweet and sour—polar opposites. Bruce devoured his pancakes with only a bucket of syrup and tubs of butter smeared on them, chewing with his mouth open. Gayle, on the other hand, cut her pancakes into smaller bite-size pieces, which were drizzled with some syrup (no butter) and ate one piece of pancake at a time, always with her mouth closed.

"Are you going to support Derrick if he chooses to reconnect with his mother?" Gayle asked.

"I don't know. I don't want him getting to close to..." Bruce said. *Dead bitch, she is. That bitch is dead to me.*

She cut Bruce off—one of her annoying habits she initially worked so hard to curb—and did. Now it seemed she was reverting back to her old, nasty habits.

"Oh, Bruce. That's incredibly selfish. It's not so much you're worried he's going to get hurt again by his mother as it is you're threatened by her, threatened Derrick might love you less."

No nod from Bruce this time. He shook his head. "It's not that at all. I don't want the two of them to get close again only for her to break his heart again."

They continued to eat their pancakes as they discussed the weather, gripes about their jobs, and their excitement for the Pierogi Fest—always the last weekend in July.

Bruce looked up from the table and started to choke on pancakes as he pointed towards the living room. Gayle turned to see what startled him, but nothing was there.

She stood and patted him on the back, which helped alleviate his choking. He peeled out of the kitchen and into living room like a race car driver at the Indy 500.

"I saw the silhouette of a man in here," Bruce said. "That goddamn shadow guy was in here again."

"Oh, yeah? Was he cute?" Gayle asked. *He's been drinking again. Silly Bruce, silly goose.*

He stomped his foot. "Goddamn it, I'm serious!" *Dummy. I said it's a shadow, so no facial features!*

"Maybe it was the spirit of a deceased relative popping in to check on you. I see things like that all the time."

He shook his head. What he saw wasn't any family member—no way, no how. Had it have been he was certain the family member would have not masked its appearance, shrouding its face and body in darkness.

"This is something sinister, malevolent," Bruce said. "I want the hell out of my house." *Then again, it's not hurting anyone.*

"How can you be sure? Did it threaten you?" Gayle asked.

"Its mere presence made my heart tense up. It's still sore."

"Do you need to see a doctor? I'll call 911!" She yanked out her cellphone.

He gripped his hand around her phone to prevent her from dialing. "No! I don't need emergency services!" He laid on the couch and took some deep breaths. "I'll take some aspirin as a precaution."

She stepped into the kitchen and fetched him a glass of water and the bottle of aspirin. She stood over him, waiting for him to see her. His eyes were closed and his arm was covering his eyes. After a minute passed, she cleared her throat, which caused him to shudder and spring up like a jack-in-the-box.

He downed two aspirin with a deluge of water. When Gayle stepped out of his path to sit on the couch next to him, the figure he had seen from the kitchen was walking up the stairs.

With his head he gestured towards the stairwell and whispered: "Look."

And she did, but apologized for being unable to see whatever it was his eyes was seeing.

He ran to the stairwell and looked up at it. The figure stood in front of a closed bedroom door. It turned its head towards Bruce, then turned its head back before walking through the bedroom door.

"The shadow entity went into Derrick's room," he said. "Stay here." He raced up the stairs and stormed into Derrick's room. To the entity, Bruce said: "Get the hell out of this house. You don't belong here."

The shadow figure appeared out of thin air behind Bruce and whispered: "How's the old ticker, Moosey-Moose?"

Bruce backed up out of Derrick's room and closed the door.

27

Sitting in the waiting area to board the plane, Thomas struggled not to cry. He called Nikki. When she answered, she herself was crying. Thomas did what he could to console her. Hearing her cry ripped his heart from his chest.

"Why did mom do it?" Nikki asked. "Why did she have to kill herself?"

"I don't know, but all I can say is sometimes people feel like they're in a situation they can't escape."

"I'll never get the image of the wall out of my mind for as long as I live. It was painted with mom's blood, her brains and bone fragments."

Sharon had shot herself by placing the barrel of her gun, a .357 Magnum, towards the roof of her mouth and pulling the trigger. When Nikki stormed into her mother's room a waterfall of blood was flowing from her nose.

"I'm sorry you saw what you saw," Thomas said.

"Nothing you could have done," Nikki replied.

"You, too."

But he believed there was something he could have done even though he couldn't put his finger on exactly what that could have been.

Soon he would be on a plane to Georgia to make funeral and burial arrangements for his wife. Then there was the issue of her house and what to do with it. Rent it out. Sell it. So many decisions needed to be made and he did his best to keep his head level, a mighty challenge given the circumstances. He told himself he needed to be the strong one, not for his own sake, but his children's.

They talked for another few minutes. After the call, Thomas diddled on his phone before a stranger sitting across from him interrupted him. "Vacation?" the elderly woman asked.

"Not exactly," he said.

"Oh. A death in the family then. I can see it on your face."

"As a matter of fact, yes." He tore open a Twix, removed one of the two chocolate-covered cookie bars, and began nibbling the caramel off of it. "How'd you know?"

"I've been around a long time, sonny. I've worn the same face you're wearing right now several times. Who was it? A parent?"

"My ex-wife."

The elderly woman coughed a few times, hacked up some phlegm, and spat it out into a furled tissue she pulled from her handbag. Thomas asked her if she was okay, and she nodded.

"I'm sorry to hear your ex-wife passed." She coughed a few more times again, but didn't have any phlegm to spit this time. "Was it illness? Cancer?"

"It was illness, but no, it wasn't cancer."

She tried to guess what the illness was. Heart attack. Stroke. Pneumonia. Kidney disease. He shared with her the story and she offered her condolences.

"Where are my manners," she said. "My name is Joyce."

"Thomas. Nice to meet you, ma'am."

She glanced at the back of her wrist. "Time is just about up. It's been a fun ride. Ninety-two years on this planet, ninety-two glorious years." She hacked and spat again. This time the phlegm contained some blood.

Thomas offered to get her some water and a bite to eat. She smiled and accepted his offer, but when he returned with the goods, she was gone.

Permanently.

28

"I still don't know why you want me to stay with you," Usha said. She painted another fingernail.

"In another twenty-two hours and nine minutes, you will," Alejandro said, stretching his arms with his wrists facing him. He glanced at the cuckoo clock on his bedroom wall. The time was two-twenty-seven in the morning.

Though she found his response and his stretching odd, she let it slide.

They both sat on his bed doing their own thing. She continued to paint her nails. He—unbeknownst to her—was drafting his Last Will and Testament.

When the thunderclap roared, Usha screamed. She accidentally knocked over the bottle of red nail polish onto the blanket of his bed.

"I'm so sorry! It was an accident," she said.

In a calm, soft-spoken tone, he said: "It's only a blanket. It's not the end of the world."

His reaction was a complete one-eighty compared to how he typically reacted, which consisted of shouting, swearing, and rolling his eyes. Oftentimes, his face would tense up and he'd clench his jaw.

She pulled the blanket off of the bed and immediately treated the stains. Then she placed the blanket into the washing machine, located in the hallway, just outside the bedroom of his apartment.

He sat on the floor, undeterred. He needed to get his affairs in order before the inevitable happened.

CHAPTER 3

1

The release process flew by, much to both Derrick and Bruce's surprise. As the two walked out the automatic sliding door entrance to the hospital, Derrick had an ear-to-ear smile on display for everyone to see.

When they reached Bruce's car, Bruce handed Derrick the keys. Derrick didn't accept them though.

"I don't have a license, Dad," Derrick said. "I don't even have a learner's permit."

"So what?" Bruce asserted. "I'm giving you permission to drive us home."

"You know I can't get behind the wheel. I'm not ready yet."

Bruce made a scowl. "Well, hurry the hell up, damn it. I wish you'd stop being such a scared little girl and get your permit. Then you could run errands for me."

"That wouldn't work either."

"Why not?"

"Because a new law goes into effect July 1 that stipulates you must have a licensed driver of at least eighteen years of age in the vehicle with you if you possess a learner's permit."

"Well, that's a stupid-ass law," Bruce snapped. "We can pretend that doesn't exist."

"I'm sorry, Dad, but Indiana doesn't go by Bruce's Laws."

Bruce sneered at Derrick and ordered him into the car. Along the drive, they didn't say much of anything to each other. Eating Derrick alive from the inside out was his desire to meet his mother, but he couldn't find the courage to bring the topic up, especially when Bruce—who was a bit surly—was behind the wheel.

After turning the air conditioning dial to the OFF position, Bruce pushed the turn signal level down and rotated the wheel to the right, pulling into his driveway. Scott was outside watering his lawn—just as he always did before leaving for work.

"Home sweet home," Derrick said.

"It's great to have you back home," Bruce replied. *My little slave boy.*

"I'll cut the grass later today," Derrick replied. "I won't let it linger like I did last time."

Now just at the tail end of Bruce's sentence, he and Derrick observed a moving truck pull up in front of the house next to theirs. The house had been on the market for several months after the owner inside died of natural causes. The place was given a slapdash makeover and placed on the market.

A few minutes after the moving truck parked in front of the home, a minivan pulled into the driveway and like clowns at the circus, everyone piled out of it.

Five kids, two parents, one dog. One of the children who exited the van was a girl Derrick's age. Though Danielle was his one and only, he didn't see any harm in checking out the goods so long as he didn't touch them, and assumed Danielle was of the same mind (boy was he mistaken).

"Hey, get your eyes back in your head," Bruce said.

"I can't help it," Derrick said. "Did you see her glutes?"

"No." He hoped Derrick couldn't see through his lying eyes. "Why don't we be good neighbors and introduce ourselves."

They sauntered over like they were the cat's meow and introduced themselves to the family—the Saporowskis. Adam— the patriarch of the family was average height for an adult male, no more than five-foot-seven with a muscular build. His wife,

Melinda, was taller than Adam by about a foot and was pencil-thin, kind of like Olive Oyl.

Adam worked as a middle management executive at a computer software company, but now he decided to quit his job to focus on his true passion: botany. He, along with two of his best friends, also living in Chesterville, bought a small space within a strip mall located on Indian Boundary Road and was in the process of remodeling it before their grand opening.

At first, all three men's wives were reluctant to take such a leap, but after much open dialogue—and sometimes heated—all three families voted yes to the decision to support the business venture.

Now, the Saporoskis were not all born from the same mother. The five children were the combination of two from Adam's first marriage, two from Melinda's first marriage, and one from Adam and Melinda's union together. The ages of the children were nineteen, sixteen, twelve, nine, and six.

The sixteen-year-old—Coreyann—whose biological parent was Adam—had blond hair and blue eyes, just as Derrick did. They conversed for a few minutes before Derrick suggested they go for a walk so he could show her around.

As they started to walk down the sidewalk, a car abruptly stopped. Danielle stormed out of the passenger seat of the car, slamming the door, and zoomed towards Derrick. Make no mistake—she was hell on wheels, a force to be reckoned with.

"What the fuck is this shit?" she bellowed. "You get out of the mental ward and you're already trying out a new flavor of the month?"

"It's not what—" Derrick started to say before Danielle cut him off.

"Save it. You can have this skank. We're through."

Coreyann clenched a fist. "Bitch, who are you calling a skank?"

"You, skank! Slut!"

They ping-ponged insults for several seconds, often overlapping each other. When Coreyann called Danielle a flat-chested floozy, it was on, and Danielle grabbed Coreyann by the hair. Coreyann did the same and the two of them struggled to break free from the other's grip while trying to maintain their grip on the other. Derrick tried to break them up as did Andrew, who was waiting in his car until the brouhaha ensued, but it was of no use. These two girls were out to kill each other.

(I love a good cat fight. Say the words that invited me in, Sir Der-Dick-Lick. Say them again so I can finish what I started.)

But Derrick didn't acknowledge the voice this time. He was too consumed watching his girlfriend and new neighbor beat each other's asses.

Coreyann and Danielle yanked each other's hair and slapped each other's heads. And now the two of them were rolling about on the ground like pigs in mud.

Bruce and Adam arrived on the scene, each carrying a bucket of water. Both of them tossed the contents of their bucket onto the two fiery, feisty girls, and this extinguished their burning rage.

Derrick took off his shirt and started to pat dry Danielle's skin with it. He walked her back to his house where she took a shower at his insistence. While inside the shower, he left her a pair of clean shorts and a T-shirt on his bed and waited for her downstairs.

Not long after the shower water stopped—three minutes roughly—Danielle screamed. Derrick rocketed up the stairs to see what scared her. A spider, perhaps? Maybe a mouse?

"I saw a dark figure in your room," she said.

"A dark figure?"

"A ghost. It was a shadow person."

But Derrick wasn't worried. Bruce had already tipped him off there was some apparition roaming about in the house.

The fact still remained though: this was odd. Never had there been paranormal activity in his room before—let alone the house—at least none he could remember. So, who was this dark figure Danielle—and two days ago, Bruce—saw? What did this entity want?

Derrick and Danielle walked outside to the backyard and sat at the black-cherry-stained picnic table Bruce had built last summer. He was a master builder. As a decorative feature for last year's Halloween, he—along with the assistance Derrick and Gayle—built two wooden coffins, the base of which was shaped like an irregular pentagon. The idea to build coffins for Halloween was sort of a family activity Bruce suggested they do together. Oddly enough, after all of the blood, sweat, and tears shed to build the coffins, they never got placed out in the front yard, which was where Bruce had told Derrick and Gayle he wanted them to go once he was finished decorating the front yard with other Halloween regalia.

But that never happened either. Not wanting their hard work to be all for naught, Derrick and Gayle decorated the front yard and placed the coffins side by side with a skeleton resting in each—one wearing a top hat and clutching a black cane and the other wearing a blond wig with a necklace resting on its ribcage.

"I need your help," Derrick said. "Will you help me?"

"Depends on what it involves. If it's killing someone, no," Danielle said, her tone snide.

Derrick displayed a derisive look. "Nobody is going to kill anybody—"

(You're wrong, dear Der-dick. You are destined to die by your own hands. Do it! I'm losing my patience with you.)

[Go to Hell!]

(Been there, done that, got the T-shirt. Hell won't have me any longer. Just do as you're told! Kill yourself!)

Are you alright?" Danielle asked, genuinely concerned. *Bruce told me this may happen. Poor baby.*

"I'm fine… I will be fine. Anyway, I want to confront my mom about abandoning me and my dad, get her side of the story, and then depending on her answer, start a new relationship with her. Will you drive me to her?"

"Where does she live?"

"I don't know. I need to find that out, too. Maybe you could help me."

"You want me to ask Bruce for you?" She reached into her purse and pulled out a canister of Ice Breakers.

Derrick grabbed a mint out of the canister and popped it into his mouth. "Not ask him for me. I'll ask him where she lives. I doubt he will give me the complete address. I'll have to do some research to find that. Got any gum?"

Danielle rummaged through her purse. The various objects inside clattered as they struck one another. She managed to find a singular stick of gum but it wasn't inside its packaging where the other sticks would be found. Only the aluminum-like wrapping was around the stick of gum. Derrick was none the wiser, and he wouldn't have cared anyway.

"No, you don't need to ask him for me," Derrick said. He pushed the stick of peppermint-flavored gum into his mouth. "I would need you to drive me to wherever she is living."

"What if it's in California or Washington? That's awfully far. My car isn't equipped for long-distance driving."

"Shit. You're right." He chewed the gum for the world to see. Aside from the chomping sounds emanating from his mouth, he was silent. "Maybe Bruce could use your car and he could use yours while we are on our road trip."

"Will you please chew with your mouth closed?" she snapped at him, unable to handle the gum tumbling around in his mouth like sneakers in a dryer.

He firmly clamped his jaw shut and made a conscious effort to not chew with his mouth open. She popped open the canister of Ice Breakers, threw a mint into the air, and managed to position herself just right for it to land in her mouth.

Derrick mockingly clapped much like Thomas did when he finished his sit-ups. She held up three fingers on her right hand pointing to the left. That was a coded message only Derrick and she knew the meaning behind. Three fingers was Danielle's way of giving Derrick the middle finger without explicitly showing it.

"So, what do you think about me asking Bruce if we can use his car and he use yours?" Derrick asked.

"I don't like the idea. It's one thing if I wreck my own car, but someone else's is another. Also, I don't think he'd let me drive his precious car. He treats it like a newborn."

"It wouldn't hurt to ask."

"But won't he flat out say no when he finds out you're borrowing it to meet with your estranged mother?"

Derrick rolled his eyes. "No. He doesn't need to know that."

"Then what are you going to tell him you need the car for?"

"I don't know. I'll think of something. And if you have any ideas, please tell me."

She shook her head. "No, I can't be dishonest like that. It's not who I am. You can though if you want to—I mean if that's what you feel you need to do."

And that is what he felt he needed to do. There is no way Bruce would have let Derrick and Danielle use his vehicle to visit Derrick's estranged mother. That would be like aiding the enemy.

Derrick and Danielle went back inside to find Bruce and Gayle play wrestling on the living floor. They meandered their way around them and scurried upstairs to Derrick's room.

Upon entering his room, one could not help but notice the numerous White Sox posters strewn across his dark blue walls, which he had accumulated over the years. Some he bought himself through money he earned doing odd jobs around the house; others were given to him as gifts from Danielle and Gayle.

But it wasn't only White Sox posters plastered from one wall to the next. He also had posters of Albert Einstein, Niels Bohr, Edwin Schrödinger, and Madame Curie interspersed with the White Sox posters.

Immediately to the right of Derrick's bedroom door was a bed stand and to the right of the bed stand was his bed—the head of which was against the same wall of his bedroom door. Against the wall perpendicular to the wall against which his bed was located was a writer's desk on which he did his studying and reading. A microscope sat in the upper right-hand corner of the desk—a microscope he purchased about two years ago to replace the previous one he had purchased about six years before that. Bruce had no interest in paying for it. A plastic tub to the right of his desk on the floor contained used microscope slides.

A five-drawer dresser was positioned near his bedroom door in such a way the maximum angle the door could open was ninety-degrees.

"I don't see any shadow person," Derrick said. "Coast is clear. It's safe to come in."

She took a breath, standing outside the threshold of his bedroom. "I've got a bad feeling about your room," she replied, standing outside the threshold of it. "I'm reluctant to come inside of it."

He pulled his eyeballs out of the eyepiece, grabbed her by the hand, and led her into his bedroom. She sat on the bed while he resumed his analysis of cell specimens he collected a few days before he was discovered by the Chesterville police officer. He jotted down some notes about his observations into an official science laboratory notebook consisting of white and yellow pages—the white pages of which were no carbon required.

Bored to tears, Danielle fell back onto Derrick's bed and sighed. She closed her eyes and drifted off to sleep while Derrick continued to review his microscope slides.

(Look at the two-timing slut laying on your bed. Slice her like a Christmas ham, slit your throat!)

[Talk all you want. You're not going to get me to bite.]

(You underestimate my power. Do I need to prove just how dangerous I can be?)

[Do what you got to do. I'm so scared.] Derrick snickered at his own retort.

(Get ready for it! Here it comes!)

It's all in your mind, Derrick thought. *Just ignore it and it will go away.*

A few minutes passed, during which time Derrick peeked into his microscope, then eyed his notebook to jot down observations, only to return to the microscope a few seconds later. As he did this he fantasized about one day being the scientist who discovered a cure for cancer or MS—a mighty feat for which he would be awarded the Nobel prize.

The sound of someone choking startled Derrick. He turned around and gasped. He rushed to Danielle who was grasping at her neck. Derrick picked Danielle off of the bed and whisked her out of the bedroom.

He placed her on the floor of the hallway outside his bedroom. She sat up and pressed her back against the wall.

"What happened?" Derrick asked.

"Something was choking me! It wanted to kill me!" Danielle said. "I felt cold fingers on my neck. Its death grip nearly sent me on a one-way trip to the cemetery."

"I can understand why you might think that, but that's not what happened," he assured her. "What happened was you were choking on your saliva. I heard you trying to swallow in between snores."

"What about the hands I felt?"

"They were your own. I should know. I saw it with my own eyes."

2

Bruce downed a shot of Wild Turkey. "I spent your college fund money."

"You what?" Derrick shrieked.

"It's true. An account was created for you by your mom and—well me." He cleared his throat, downed another shot, and continued. "I spent it."

"You fucking bastard!" Derrick shouted. "How could you do that knowing I had dreams of going to college one day?"

Derrick stormed out of the kitchen and Bruce ran after him. When Bruce caught up to Derrick, he grabbed his shoulder. Derrick pulled back, freeing himself.

"Fuck off, Dad!" Derrick screamed. "You're a selfish piece of dog shit!"

"Look, I understand you're upset, but I needed the money to keep us afloat."

"How much was in the account?"

"Not a lot. Maybe twenty-five thousand. Your dad—I mean mom—was highly intelligent and she won a lot of money on a show called *Who Wants to be a Millionaire?* Some of the money she placed in a savings account for your college fund."

"That wasn't your money, you slovenly, surly motherfucker!" He rushed towards the stairs. As he stomped the first three, he said: "I want to kill myself."

A dark mass appeared in front of Derrick on the fifth stair and looked down on him. Derrick tried to speak and move, but he couldn't. Some force compelled him to stay put and stay silent. His ears were like Dumbo's, keenly listening to what this dark mass shaped liked a human had to say.

The dark mass said: "And in twenty-four hours, you shall and you must. That's exactly how much time you have to kill yourself. Congratulations, Derrick—you're one of the chosen ones—one among millions. At the end of the twenty-four hours, if you haven't killed yourself, I will kill you myself. If you do kill yourself, your spirit will live eternally in unbridled ecstasy. If you don't, however, I will own your soul and torture it until the end of time. And, speaking of time, a countdown watch located on the back of your wrist will show you how much time remains for you to kill yourself. Only you can see the countdown timer. Go ahead. Take a look."

And he did just that. He couldn't believe his eyes.

"Once I finish my little spiel, the countdown timer will begin. It won't do any good to tell anyone about the countdown watch—which only you can see—and if you do I may kill you on the spot. I'm everywhere and anywhere all at the same time. Do the right thing and kill yourself. Get creative with your suicide. Grandstand. The more gore, the higher score, as I like to say. Make your choice: die or be killed." The dark mass faded to invisibility.

Derrick shot up out of bed in a cold sweat, hyperventilating.

"It was just a nasty dream," Derrick muttered. "Thank god."

3

Tomorrow was Sharon's funeral. Thomas laid out a black suit on his hotel room bed and inserted a hanger inside of the jacket, then slipped the matching black slacks through the metal rod at the bottom of the hanger.

Nikki and Ashlee sat on the other bed in the hotel room watching TV and perusing the cellphones Thomas had purchased for them the day before.

After Thomas hung his suit up in the closet near the hotel room door, he sat on the bed behind his two daughters and kissed both of them on the top of their heads. He told them he loved them and they said the same back.

Thomas checked his phone for updates from the acting administrator of the BAU, Dr. Lauren Winters. He called her and they had a brief conversation. She reported to him everything was fine except for a patient whose behavior was erratic. Her name was Anisa Egarton, a seventeen-year-old.

"How do you girls feel about moving up to Chesterville?" Thomas asked.

"Yeah, Daddy! I want to move there! I like it there!" Ashlee said, her tone gleeful.

Nikki said: "Not me, Dad. All my friends are here. Can't you move here?"

He kicked himself for asking instead of telling. Now he would have to either insist they move or persuade her.

He placed a hand on Nikki's shoulder. "It would be too difficult for me to move here, Princess. I'd have to find a new job, a new house."

"But, Dad, we already have a house," Nikki said. "We could stay at mom's house."

While true, Thomas didn't want to live in the house where his ex-wife and the mother of his children committed suicide, but he also didn't want to state that outright.

"You'd be able to stay in contact with your friends through Facebook, SnapChat, and text messaging," Thomas said. "And even though we'd have a house, I would still have to find another job, and that's too much of a gamble to take."

"You've got time, Dad. It's June. We could spend some time in Chesterville for the next six weeks like planned. During that time I'm sure you could find another job." Nikki said.

"It's not that simple. I'm happy where I'm at right now."

"As am I."

"So I'm supposed to give up my whole life and start over? Chesterville sucks. I want to stay in Macon. Please, Daddy. Move here."

And then there was the issue of their mother's grave. Sharon was going to be buried in a cemetery in Macon. Both Nikki and Ashlee wanted to have opportunities to visit their mother's grave to lay flowers and pay their respects. If they moved to Chesterville with their dad, it would be much more difficult to do this.

The debate raged on for another forty-five minutes with no consensus reached.

4

Around three in the afternoon, Derrick stumbled out of bed from a brief nap. He nearly took a tumble down the stairs when his ankle gave out. He wanted to get himself a glass of water and nibble at some leftover spaghetti with meatballs, which he had made for him and his dad's lunch and dinner.

When he turned the corner of the stairwell, the kitchen fan was already spooling and Bruce was sitting at the kitchen table enjoying some shots of Jim Beam.

"Want some?" Bruce asked.

"No, thanks," Derrick said. "I tried that stuff once and it nearly knocked me flat on my ass."

Bruce slammed the shot down his throat and then the glass onto the table. "When did you try Jim Beam?"

"At one of Aaron's family functions. I don't remember which one it was exactly though. His Uncle David let me try some—and Aaron, too."

Derrick pulled out a bottle of water from the refrigerator, uncapped it, and consumed it in one gulp. The slurping sound Derrick made as he drank the water grated on Bruce's ears like a high-pitched scream. Before sitting at the table with his dad, Derrick pulled out the pot of spaghetti and meatballs.

"Want some?" Derrick asked.

"Horse testicles and noodles? No thanks," Bruce responded.

Derrick snickered. "Horse testicles. They're meatballs, Dad."

"Imitation meat. Next time I want you to make the meatballs from scratch. None of the pre-packaged shit."

(Isn't he Father of the Year?)

Derrick massaged the sides of his head. "Okay. I will." He twirled his fork in the pot and ate the helping of spaghetti on it. "I don't mean to open this wound, but can we talk a little about mom?"

Bruce slammed an open hand on the table. The look of hatred in his eyes made Derrick's skin crawl. *He looks as though he wants to steal my soul.*

(Wrong, Derrick! That's me!)

"Easy, Dad. Let me explain," Derrick said. "I think if we talk about mom a little maybe then I won't be so eager to seek her out. I'm interested in learning what things were like when you two were together."

"Does that voice in your head thrive on seeing me suffer? I don't want to talk about her. Every time I talk about her my mind fixates on her leaving us and I relive the hurt she inflicted on me when she left me—and you."

"Have you ever thought of seeing a counselor to resolve these feelings?" He twisted some more spaghetti on his fork.

"I dealt with it in my own way and it helps me get by."

"What way?"

"Like I said: in *my* way. That's *all* you need to know."

Derrick chewed with his mouth open and Bruce reprimanded him for it. Then Bruce stuck his grubby stubby fingers into the pot of pasta and bit into a meatball, chewing with his mouth wide open.

As Derrick relished in the taste of the spaghetti, he tried to muster up the courage to ask Bruce another question about his mother. He wanted to involve his dad and not keep secrets from him, but if Bruce didn't want to participate in helping Derrick find his mom, then Derrick decided he would stop being open about his intentions.

"Where is my mom now?" Derrick asked.

"Galveston, I think," Bruce responded, after releasing an exasperated sigh. He didn't slam his palm on the table this time though.

"Galveston, huh? Maybe—"

"No, wait. That's not it. Richmond—that's where she— no, that doesn't sound right either. Albany. That's it. Actually, no—that's where my now-deceased cousin lived… I remember now. Victorville—no. Evanston."

Derrick sighed. "Are you sure?"

"Yeah."

"Man, you were all over the map. Galveston, Richmond, Albany, Victorville, Evanston."

After Derrick placed the pot of spaghetti back into the refrigerator, he placed his hand on his Dad's shoulder and wished him a good night's rest.

Derrick ascended three stairs before he doubled back and stepped into the kitchen again where his dad was firing more shots into his liver.

"What was mom's name again?" Derrick asked.

"Bethany," Bruce said, pouring himself another shot. "Who gives a shit let alone two?"

Derrick snickered. "First it was Heidi, then Tabitha, then Catrina, then Ingrid. Now it's Bethany. I bet if I ask again in three minutes, you'll give me a different name, won't you?"

The Jim Beam went from bottle directly to belly. No pouring it into a shot glass this time. Bruce downed it like a thirsty camel.

"I thought you were going to bed," Bruce shot back.

"I am. Good night."

This time Derrick ascended all of the steps, climbed into bed, and shortly after was dreaming again.

5

After Derrick prepared some banana flapjacks for his dad—who took them to go, he stepped into his dad's room and slid open the chrome-trimmed mirror door leading to the closet. *It's got to be in here somewhere,* Derrick thought, contemplating where to start his search.

(That's it! Find that gun and have some suicidal fun!)

Without acknowledging the voice speaking to him from within his head, Derrick stormed out of his dad's room and into the kitchen where he whipped out the first bottle he touched, and that was a rectangular bottle labeled Disaronno. He unscrewed the cap and sent several milliliters of it down his hatch, but not before tossing a few of his dad's Risperidone into his mouth.

Confident the booze silenced the smack-talking voice, Derrick began removing boxes from his dad's closet. *Shit! I should have taken a picture first so I know exactly how he left the closet,* he thought. He yanked out his camera and snapped a quick picture of the boxes that remained inside the closet.

Once all of the boxes—some big, some small, others tall—were removed from the closet, Derrick started to rummage through each one, delicately sifting through the contents.

Danielle called from the living room: "Derrick? Where are you?"

"In my dad's room," he responded back to her.

"What are you doing?" she asked as she stepped into the room. "Why are you going through your dad's personal things?"

"I'm looking for my birth certificate. I need you to help me find it."

She took a step back and shook her head, declining to have any part of what he was doing, not wanting to invade Bruce's privacy. He explained she didn't need to gawk at documents. If something wasn't a birth certificate, skip over it.

But she asserted herself, unwilling to risk violating Bruce's trust. By all outward appearances, their relationship was already essentially non-existent and she didn't want to put herself in a position where Bruce could use her misdeed as ammunition to drive a wedge between her and Derrick.

"He's not going to know, damn it," Derrick snapped. "I need your help. Please. I'm in such a state of disorientation, I may have even skipped over it. Check the boxes I've already gone through."

Danielle folded her arms and sighed. "Why is this so important to you?"

The inhuman voice crept it, but this time not as brash sounding. The voice was muffled, sort of in the way a voice would be if one was trying to hear someone through thick glass.

(You're wasting your time. Kill her, Bruce, then yourself. Or just yourself. Either way, you must die! And you will!)

He rushed out of the bedroom, popped another Risperidone, and gulped down some Disaronno to wash it down.

The inhuman voice cackled, though like the words he spoke no more than fifteen seconds ago, it was muffled, too.

(The drugs and booze can only keep me away for so long. Down the whole bottle—both bottles. Please! Let's play the game I like to call Kill Thyself. I'll be back, you bas—)

"What the hell are you doing?" Danielle said in a motherly tone, standing akimbo at the entrance to the kitchen. "You can't mix booze and meds. You could die. Maybe you are suicidal after all."

"It's not that at all. Don't worry about that. Just help me find my birth certificate, please." He walked past her and continued down the hall to his dad's room.

"Why don't you leave it alone? Obviously your dad has reasons he doesn't want you have contact with your mother."

I should have accepted Coreyann's offer to help me find my birth certificate. "It's kind of like forbidden fruit. The more he tells me don't pick at it, the more I want to pick at it. What reasons could he possibly have to deny me a relationship with my own flesh and blood?"

Danielle picked up where she left off, looking through a box Derrick already did, cross-checking his work. A part of her felt naughty, and she liked it.

"I don't know. Maybe she's a felon. Maybe she's a drug addict. Maybe she's a sex predator," Danielle said.

"I would think if she's really a vile person, my dad would want to tell me those things, not conceal them from me. Those things you mentioned all would sway me away from wanting to find her. But he won't tell me anything, and what he does tell me I think is complete bullshit."

"What do you mean?"

He pushed another box he finished going through towards her across the bed. She stopped it just before it fell off the bed, which would have almost certainly resulted in the papers and other objects in it to scatter across the floor. She chided him, insisting he be more careful.

Derrick squinted his eyes and rubbed his forehead. "Like this morning. This morning, I asked him once again what my mom's name was. Keep in mind he told me the names Heidi, Catrina, Tabitha, Ingrid, and Bethany before this morning. Now my mom's name is Donna. I don't get why he's playing games. That's why I need to find my birth certificate. Her name—her *real* name—will be on it. From there, I can take the next steps to find her."

"Not trying to stick up for your dad, but maybe he doesn't want to give you up," she replied.

"You sound like Gayle. She said the same thing to me recently."

"It's not too hard to fathom, is it? After all these years it has been only you and your dad. Now you're talking about bringing someone into your life who left you when you needed her the most. I can see Bruce's frustration and anger."

She finished going through another box and without skipping a beat began inspecting the next and then the next and so on. After about ten minutes passed, she had finished going through all of the boxes Derrick had already checked and began to inspect boxes he hadn't gone through as of yet.

As if selecting clothes off of a rack in Macy's, she eyed the different boxes—which were stacked in an unequal row-column fashion—left to check. One in particular stood out to her: a shoe box with duct tape wrapped around it in such a way the box had the appearance of a gift left nestled under the tree on Christmas morn.

On top of the box was a five by eight pink index card which bore the inscription: BLISSFUL MEMORIES.

She handed the box to Derrick. As he rubbed his left eye, he asked: "Why would someone seal up happy memories like this? It doesn't make sense."

"I don't know either."

"Open it and find out."

"Won't the removal of the tape ruin the box?"

She had a point. After some contemplation, Derrick suggested they cut the tape on three of the sides, leaving the last side's piece of tape to function like a hinge. After they searched the contents of the box, they would re-tape the box and place it back into the closet so the undisturbed side faced outward. The other three sides would be surrounded by boxes and the closet wall.

"I don't know about doing this," she said. "I don't feel it's right for us to look at what is inside of this."

"Why not? If anything that's probably where my birth certificate is. That's why it says blissful memories on the box. In fact, I bet you that box has all my important documents in it."

"Fine. Then you open it."

"I would be privileged and honored if you opened the box. Please."

Danielle sighed and snatched the box from him. After the tape was cut—Derrick did those honor in such a way one would have thought it was a ribbon-cutting ceremony—she opened the box. Inside were several newspaper sections. Danielle pulled out the folded newspaper section that was on top of the pile of others in the box. The newspaper was a rusty color; the paper had faded over the years. The section was the first section—labeled A—of a Milton Messenger newspaper, and the top headline snagged her attention. Rather than focus on helping Derrick find his birth certificate she started to read the article.

The headline: 2 FOUND DEAD IN HOUSE FIRE. The victims discovered in the fire were both middled-aged people and were each other's spouses. Their names were Harold and Gertrude Rice—ages 43 and 44, respectively.

"Why would your dad save this article?" Danielle asked. He handed Derrick the newspaper. "That's kind of creepy."

Derrick glanced over the article before thumbing through the other pages of the paper. With slightly slurred speech, he said: "Here's why he saved the newspaper, and it wasn't because of that ghastly article." He pointed to a news article that was circled on page A6.

She glanced over the article with the red-inked circle around it, and it wasn't at all as shocking and intriguing as the main article on the front page. The article focused on fiscal discrepancies uncovered after an audit of the city's books had been conducted.

"Put that back and stay on task, please," Derrick said. "This is bullshit. In all the boxes I've checked I've found no important documents related to me. No social security card, none of my old report cards, nothing."

Danielle's eyes and facial features shifted in such a way to convey she liked the way Derrick had just asserted himself, which was so unlike him. She was mildly turned on by it, but knew Derrick wouldn't smash with her.

After a few seconds of Danielle regrouping, she said: "Maybe he has your birth certificate and social security card stored in a safety deposit box at a bank," she suggested, as she glanced over another newspaper from the shoe box. It was another raggedy, discolored A section of a Milton Messenger newspaper. Though she wanted to read the top article—a story about a couple killed in a car crash—she didn't. She folded the newspaper.

The article detailed a tragic fatal accident of two people who were traveling westbound on The Borman Expressway when the driver lost control of the vehicle, which tumbled several times along the four-lane highway before being struck by a semi-truck.

"Is that where your parents keep your important papers?" He looked up from the box he was searching. "Come on. Put that back and seal the box. There's no birth certificate in there."

She slammed the paper in the box and then the lid, which caused the box to slightly deform. "Well, no, but my dad has a safe in his home-office."

The search continued for about another twenty minutes, at which point all of the boxes had been checked. No birth certificate.

(Oh, Deeeeer-riiiiiick. How are you, buddy? Are you ready to swim in my Lake of Fire? Are you ready for your soul to be eternally tortured and tormented?)

As if his head was on fire, Derrick sprinted out of the bedroom, popped another Risperidone, then placed his mouth in the stream of water from the kitchen faucet and washed it down.

(I'm through playing games with you. I've tried to reason with you, I've tried to encourage you to do what needs to be done. Now things are about to get ugly.)

[Fuck off.]

Derrick stumbled back to his dad's room where Danielle had already started putting the boxes back into the closet, not at all in the proper order or arrangement. At this point, Derrick didn't care. He took over. He put the boxes away as she handed them to him.

After the last box was placed back into the closet, Derrick closed the sliding door. He stood for a few seconds, staring at himself. Danielle screamed when an unseen force struck the mirror, leaving a dime-sized-and-shaped indentation, which rested on the forehead of Derrick's reflection—almost as if he had been shot.

The indentation had several irregularly-shaped rectangle-like pieces within it. Derrick ran his finger over the circular impact zone, lightly massaging it in a circular motion. He turned around and scanned the room, trying to ascertain where the object originated. He also checked the carpet—as did Danielle—both trying to find the projectile that struck the mirror.

Derrick concluded his telekinetic ability got away from him and caused something to strike the mirror. He searched the carpeting, but never found a projectile.

"What are you going to tell your dad?" Danielle asked.

"I'll play dumb. Pretend I have no knowledge of the damage. When he shows me, I'll look surprised and shaken."

Danielle folder her arms and gave her a look of disappointment similar to a way a mother would her mischievous child.

"What?" he asked, confused.

"It's not right to be dishonest. Just tell the truth," she advised him, her tone assertive.

"What am I going to tell him? I was in your room rummaging through your boxes in your closet when a ghost broke your mirror?"

She mockingly laughed.

"Who knows. He drinks so much, maybe I can pin the blame on him. Hell—he may even think he did it himself. I may not have to say anything at all. Or if he does blame himself, I can play off of that."

"Listen to yourself. If you're lying to your dad, how can I be sure you're not lying to me."

"What do you mean?"

She rolled her eyes and folded her arms. "Like when you tell me you haven't been spending any time with Coreyann. How did I know you and her aren't hooking up and smashing?"

"Because I wouldn't do that to you. I want to be with you—and only you."

She smiled. "Talk is cheap. How do I know you're not lying to me? And especially now after you're conspiring to lie to Bruce about an accident."

It was rare Danielle could make his blood boil. Her goody-two-shoes-higher-than-thou attitude every once in a while awoke a beast within him. He'd never physically assault her, but sometimes he wanted to give her a piece of his mind, he wanted to scream at her.

He took a breath and promised her he would be forthright with his dad and tell him about the damage to his mirror. She hugged him and told him the old adage about honesty being the best policy.

He looked at the indentation and said: "It's minor anyway. I don't think he'll get mad."

Now, at the tail end of sentence, a multitude of cracks radiated from the indentation, and each crack had several cracks branch off of it, and then more off of those. The entire right-hand sliding door had the appearance of a car windshield after an accident: still intact but smashed to shit.

The pieces were still within the frame. Derrick and Danielle stood stunned at the sight. They were both baffled and impressed.

Danielle ran out of the room. Derrick stood staring at himself in the smashed mirror. In the reflection, a pair of shoelaces was wrapped around his neck from behind. His reflection's face seized up, and a fraction of a second later, the pieces of the smashed mirror rained onto the floor.

(Try explaining this mess to your so-called dad.) The inhuman voice let out an equally inhuman laugh for several seconds. *(I warned you to kill yourself. Your soul belongs to me, and I'll stop at nothing to get it. I won't be at peace until I have your soul.)*

No more than three seconds later, Derrick's cellphone chirped. It was a text message from his dad.

Why would you send something like that to me? his dad asked in the text message.

Derrick pressed his thumb over the home button and a few seconds later he was in his list of text conversations. He clicked on the one between him and his dad.

"What the fuck," Derrick muttered.

I swear I didn't send you that, Derrick texted back.

His dad responded back with the okay emoji.

I don't know what's happening, Derrick texted him.

Bruce responded in a text: *I understand you're pissed I won't help you find your mother, but that doesn't give you the right to send FUCK YOU DAD!!!! to me.*

Though Derrick made a valiant effort to convince his dad he wasn't the one responsible for the text message, he ultimately ended up taking responsibility for it, convinced he telekinetically texted and sent the message. There was no way of proving he didn't send the text message and all roads let to him anyway.

"Why'd you leave the room?" Derrick asked Danielle, whom he found sitting in her car.

"A voice whispered in my ear: leave or die," she responded. She was visibly shaken. He hands still trembled.

"Are you sure?"

She shot him a look of irritation. "I know what I heard. I even felt the arctic chill of the spirit's breath on my ear lobe and neck." She shuddered. "I don't know if I'll be able to come over here anymore. That house is too scary."

(Strangle the bitch! Use the seatbelt! Then drive the car off of the Rickety-Rackety Bridge! It's the perfect ending to your doomed relationship!)

[Why do you taunt me? What do you want?]

(Your soul, mon frère. Clean the peanut butter out of your ears. You're destined to be an angel—one of my angels. You must kill yourself though. It's the only way it will be.)

While listening to the voice in his head speak, to Danielle he said: "Don't do that. There's nothing in the house to be afraid of. If it makes you feel better, I'll—"

"No, Derrick," she said in a firm tone. "That voice that whispered in my ear means business."

"There's nothing—"

As her eyes widened, Danielle released a blood-curdling scream. She started her car and peeled backwards out of the driveway and down the street before turning into an intersection, at which point she threw the shifter into drive and peeled out once again, but this time traveling forward.

Derrick tried to run after her as she backed out of the driveway, but she accelerated once in the street. He immediately called her on his cellphone but she didn't answer.

6

"Why did you buy this with money you stole from me?" Scott asked.

"I thought it would be nice," Aaron said.

In the garage they stood in front of a Craftsman ten-inch table saw, which Aaron had purchased. He wanted to make amends to his dad for selling the table saw his dad originally had.

The money he received for the table saw was used to purchase narcotics.

Scott shook his head, struggling to find the words to express himself. On one hand, the gesture was nice; on the other, it made no sense and wasn't a gift at all. Aaron snapped a selfie next to the table saw and posted it to his Facebook page.

"I can appreciate the thought, but it's a little asinine, don't you think?" Scott said.

"What do you mean?" Aaron asked.

"First you steal my table saw and pawn it for money. Then you use the money to buy who knows what because you refuse to tell me, but I bet it was drugs. Now you stole money from me to buy me a table saw, which I already had in the first place until you sold it." He lit a cigarette and enjoyed a drag of it.

Aaron sighed. "I know. I'm sorry, Dad, but I'm trying to do better."

"You are? How? You sleep all day, you're gone all night. You don't respect the rules of the house. You smoke dope. You pop pills. You steal. You lie. You leave messes all over the place. You don't help out around here, but you're doing better. Yeah, okay."

His sarcastic tone could cut through one's heart like a surgical blade, and it did Aaron's.

"I know, Dad! I'm nothing but a worthless piece of shit, aren't I?"

"No, now I didn't say that. All I'm saying is—"

"I swear! I should kill myself! Then everyone in the house would be happier, wouldn't they? Everyone's lives would be easier. I want to kill myself sometimes!"

"Hey! Quit talking like that."

"But it's the truth. If I weren't around, things would be better. You wouldn't have to worry about your money being stolen or your tools being sold. The house would be cleaner. I should hang myself from one of the rafters of the garage."

Scott dropped his cigarette onto the concrete floor and snuffed it out, then lit another cigarette. As Aaron was storming through the garage to get to the door, Scott blocked his path. Aaron tried to bypass him, but didn't fight tooth and nail to overpower his dad.

"If you're going to talk like that, making threats to kill yourself, I'm going to have to take you somewhere to talk to someone, just like Derrick had to do," Scott said.

"I don't care. I'm not talking to anyone."

"Look—don't be saying things like you're going to kill yourself. It's okay to be angry, but it's not okay to say things like that unless you're serious."

"I'm sorry. Now will you get off my nuts?" He slithered passed Scott, closing the hinged door behind him.

Scoot shook his head. *That kid is going to be the death of me, that is if I don't end up killing him first.*

7

After the pastor finished his oration at Dylan's gravesite, the casket was lowered into the ground. Now the sobs and cries intensified. The sun broke through the dark clouds, which Mike interpreted as Dylan saying to his family members and friends to not be sad and to move on with their lives. Mike told this to nobody though, strongly believing everyone must deal with grief in their own way.

As Mike stood at Dylan's open grave with Heather by his side—his arm around her waist—family members each walked by and dropped a rose onto Dylan's casket, then headed for their vehicles. Some of the roses slid off of it as the pile's height increased.

The last person remaining with Mike and Heather was Natalia—Mike's mother. All three stood together, looking down at Dylan's white satin-finished casket. All three simultaneously reminisced in their minds different experiences they had with Dylan. Birthday parties. Christmases. Other experiences that didn't revolve around a holiday.

Natalia sniffled, then blew her nose. "Bye, sweet boy," she said. Her voice consisted of a thick Ukrainian accent. "We will see each other not so long from now."

"Yes—we will," Heather whispered.

"He was good boy with big heart," Natalia said. "My heart crumbles each time I think about the way he left this world." She kissed Mike on his cheek. Then Heather. "I'll be by car. You two take your time." She blew a kiss towards Dylan's casket after dropping a rose onto his casket.

When Natalia was out of earshot and sight, Heather pulled away from Mike. He didn't try to pull her back. Their marriage had flatlined; it was dead on the operating table. She said a silent prayer for Dylan before dropping a rose onto his casket. Then she walked the car where Natalia was waiting.

Now Mike was all alone. He pulled out a Kleenex and wiped the lenses of his glasses. He normally wore contact lenses, but ever since he found his son dead in the bathtub, he didn't give two shits about them.

"Dad? Let me out. Please," Dylan said.

He looked down at his son's casket. "Dylan? Is that you?" He rubbed his eyes.

"Come down here and open this casket. Then we'll play together."

He questioned his reality for several seconds, wondering if he was in a dream or somehow stepped into an alternative dimension.

"What's taking so long? It's hot and dark in here," Dylan complained. "I'm weak, dad. I can't open the lid."

And to Mike's amazement and bewilderment, the casket lid slightly lifted a centimeter—if that—and fell again. Then two more times.

Convinced his son was alive but morbidly weak, he jumped onto Dylan's casket—the lower half, crushing many of the roses as his hind end pressed upon them. He was seated on Dylan's casket as if on a saddle, a leg on each side. He opened the upper lid and Dylan sprang up at the waist like a jack-in-the-box and grabbed his dad's throat. "You killed me!" Dylan sneered, then rapidly fell backwards and when the back of his head hit the pillow, the casket lid slammed closed.

Scott didn't dare try to open it again.

8

After Derrick completed another workout routine, he finished a bottle of water and headed upstairs to read some more chapters from a book on mechanics he had checked out from the Chesterville Public Library.

After he finished reading two chapters along with drinking six bottles of water, he left his room, heading for the bathroom. Along the way, he checked his text messages and social media accounts. Somehow word got out he had been in the BAU at St. Catherine's, and for the past few days people commented on this fact on his Facebook, Instagram, and Twitter pages. Most people were supportive and considerate, but there were a few who poked fun or even ridiculed him. Water off a duck's back though.

After he took care of his call from Mother Nature, he walked downstairs to get something to drink. Bruce was sitting at the kitchen table working on another Sudoku puzzle. Derrick passed Bruce in the kitchen and patted him lightly on the shoulder.

Pointing to the box located in the fourth column, third row, Derrick said: "Three should go there."

"Good eye." He wrote the three inside the box.

Derrick poured himself a glass of cranberry juice and downed it in one gulp. Then he poured himself another glass. This one he didn't down though. He sat at the kitchen table and took a swig of it, exhaling heavily after.

Bruce snickered.

"What?" Derrick asked.

"Nothing." He chuckled again.

Derrick had another swig, then exhaled sharply. Bruce snickered once more. Confused, Derrick asked Bruce to tell him what was so amusing to him.

"It's nothing, really," Bruce said. "You just remind me of this guy at work who exhales every time takes a drink of something. He's relatively new to the medical equipment repair team."

"Oh, sorry. I didn't realize I was even doing it."

"It's okay. He's been under some stress lately. He caught his wife cheating on him—the bitch. He's in a dark place right now."

"It's not all that difficult to see why." He took another swig of his juice. No exhale this time.

Bruce poured a shot of Jim Beam and took it down like a champ, then exhaled—and more obnoxiously than Derrick ever did. "That's another reason I don't want you speaking to your mom. She not only left you and me, breaking up the family, but chose to run off with another man—the de-" He cleared his throat. "The bitch."

"I'm sorry she did that to you, but I still would like to—"

"I didn't bring your mother up as a way for you to start trying to persuade me to give you my blessing to reestablish contact with her."

"Did she marry that guy? Does she have other kids?"

"Don't know, don't care."

"But, Dad, if she had kids, they would be my half-siblings. I'd like to meet them, and I'm sure they'd like to meet me. Will you tell me where my mom lives? Will you take me to visit her?"

"I'll think about it."

"Thanks, Dad."

And with that Derrick didn't want to push his luck any further. He was elated his dad was giving greater consideration to his feelings.

Bruce carried on with his puzzle, frantically searching for clues in order to place digits within his Sudoku puzzle. Derrick finished his cranberry juice. Bruce asked Derrick to run through how he managed to bust his mirror again, and Derrick gladly told him the story. When Derrick finished, Bruce rubbed his stubbly chin for a few seconds.

"So I was demonstrating my golf swing for you when I lost control of the club and it struck my mirror?" Bruce asked, confused.

"I can't say it was completely your fault, Dad. I asked you to do it after you were pretty hammered. After the club smashed your mirror, your response was hilarious," Derrick said.

Something was gnawing on Bruce's mind, but he wasn't sure if he should ask Derrick about it or not. He didn't want to risk Derrick remembering events related to or leading up to his alleged attempted suicide.

Derrick asked Bruce: "How's Gayle?"

"She's doing fine. She told me she texted you a few times, but you haven't responded."

"I will. I haven't had time to yet."

"If you've had time to read her texts, then you certainly could have had something back to her. She's been blowing up my phone asking about you every hour on the hour, kind of like WMAQ's traffic and weather on the eights."

Derrick snickered. "Doesn't she annoy you?"

"No. Not really… Okay, well, maybe sometimes, but most of the time she has the best of intentions. Also, I don't think she realizes some of the things she does. She's not fully self-aware."

He finished the rest of the cranberry juice in his glass and exhaled sharply. He set the glass in the sink, but when Bruce unnecessarily cleared his throat, Derrick knew what that meant and he walked back to the sink and washed his glass.

As Derrick walked out of the kitchen and entered the living room, Bruce asked: "Hey, I'm curious. Have any memories surfaced about the night you and I had our little fracas?"

This was the first time Bruce asked this question in the house. He asked it before—once at the hospital and then on the car ride home. Bruce could see Derrick standing still in the living room. He walked to him and saw Derrick had his eyes closed.

"I remember us yelling and swearing at each other, sort of the way Aaron and Scott do when they fight." He opened his eyes. "I don't remember what we were fighting about, so will you tell me?"

"That's not important. But I want to ask you something about that night."

"What's that?" *Why won't he tell me what we fought about? What's he hiding?*

"You ran out of the living room and started to stomp up the stairs, but on about the fourth step, you stopped and looked up towards the top of the stairs. Do you remember?"

Once again, Derrick closed his eyes and thought intently about the night he and Bruce had their argument. His mind drew a blank for several seconds, but then he had an epiphany.

"I remember the spirit of one of my family members talking to me," Derrick said. "I can see myself on the stairs and I can hear someone talking to me, but their voice isn't their natural voice."

"What did he or she say to you?" Bruce asked, genuinely interested.

"I don't know. In my mind, all I hear right now is garbled chatter from the spirit. It's as if the spirit was talking to me through a pane of glass."

Was there any significance to the occurrence Derrick had with the spirit on the stairs the night he and Bruce had their verbal tiff?

9

When Usha woke up around seven in the morning, Alejandro wasn't in bed next to her. She slipped out of bed—only wearing a T-shirt and put on a robe from his closet.

Still half asleep, she galumphed out of the bedroom and down the hall the living room of Alejandro's apartment. The sound of a pan hit the stove. With squinted eyes, she walked into the kitchen where Alejandro was preparing some breakfast for them.

"Did you even sleep?" Usha asked.

"Nope. Not a wink, and it was wonderful." He walked over to her and kissed her. Not a simple peck. A long kiss on the lips. "How did you sleep?"

"Great."

He poured her a cup of coffee, but he didn't hand it to her. He asked her to sit down first, then set it in front of her. After he set it down, he glanced at the back of his arm.

He whisked some eggs in a bowl and added some green pepper and ham to it. He opened the sliding door to the balcony when smoke built up in the kitchen immediately after he added the eggs to the overheated pan.

"Why do you keep doing that? Is there something wrong with your arm?"

"Yes, but nothing for anyone but me to worry about. Are you hungry?"

"Yeah, I could eat."

Once the eggs finished cooking, he placed the omelet on a plate and set it in front of her. He instructed her to start without him, but she refused, insisting they split the omelet he made for her so they could eat together.

Midway through their breakfast, Alejandro skewered a piece of the omelet with his fork and held it in front of Usha's mouth. She did the same, and they fed each other bites of omelet.

After they finished eating breakfast, Alejandro rinsed off the dishes and loaded the dishwasher. He dried his hands and wrapped his arms around her from behind. He thanked her once again for dropping her plans and spending time with him. He wasn't sure if what he was told would happen to him if he didn't follow through with what he was told he should do.

"Is your arm okay?" she asked him when he looked at the back of it again.

"It's fine. Nothing to worry about." He glanced at the back of his arm again. *Another nine hours left.* "Why don't we go for a walk? Get out of the apartment for some time."

10

While both boys readied themselves, their burger containers opened and both of their hands armed on their burger, Derrick announced the countdown.

Andrew stared into Derrick's eyes as if trying to pull the soul out of his body.

"Three…two…one…" Derrick said. "Go!"

And now the battle started. Both of them ravenously ate their Double Whoppers, but Andrew won the competition this time.

"Great job," Derrick said, chewing with his mouth open.

Andrew dropped his jaw and then pushed it back up with his finger. This was their agreed-upon signal to remind Derrick when he was chewing with his mouth open, a habit he honestly wanted to break.

"Thanks," Andrew replied. "So, tell me, how have you been feeling?"

"I told you earlier when you picked up," Derrick responded. "Remember?"

"I know, but something tells me you're not being completely upfront with me. I'm your best friend, so come on, out with it."

Derrick shook his head. "I don't know about this. I mean I don't want you to get the wrong idea about me."

"Whatever it is, I'll always be your friend."

"Okay, this is getting weird," Derrick admitted, smiling. "But, you're right, there is something that has been bothering me."

"Tell me," Andrew said, cramming a wad of mustard-ladened French fries into his mouth.

Andrew had an interesting and unique food palate. He liked ketchup on scrambled eggs, but not on French fries—only mustard—and gobs of it, too.

"I've been hearing this voice in my head quite regularly," Derrick said, sheepishly. "I don't know what to make of it."

"Voice?"

(Your destiny is inescapable. You will be dead, and then your soul will be mine forever and a day!)

Derrick shook his head. "It just spoke to me again."

"It?"

"The voice."

"What does it say to you?"

"It tells me to kill myself."

Andrew turned his head, not wanting Derrick to see his eyes widen, but it didn't do any good. Derrick dipped one of his French fries into a small pool of ketchup and bite into it.

"Have you talked to anyone about this?" Andrew asked, genuinely concerned.

"No, only you," Derrick said. "And I'd be appreciative if you keep it to yourself."

"I will." He paused briefly to chew another wad of French fries. "What do you think is causing this voice to talk to you?"

Derrick shrugged his shoulders. "Not sure, really. My best guess is it is a manifestation brought on from my attempted suicide. Or murder. Not sure which."

"Murder?" Andrew shrieked.

Nearly all eyes shifted to Andrew and Derrick. Andrew nervously chuckled and crammed another wad of French fries into his mouth.

A few moments passed and it was as if nothing even happened. The other patrons resumed their conversations while eating their food.

"Yes, it's hard to explain, but I saw the shoelaces I was going to use to kill myself lift up on their own and pull me backwards from neck against the fence. Then the ligature tightened until I passed out. The next thing I remember is waking up to this Barney Fife dude standing over me."

"Does the field have any security cameras? I mean maybe if someone did try to murder you, it was captured on camera."

"I'm not sure. Could we swing by there after we leave from here?"

"Sure," Andrew said. "And, tell you what, why don't we hit an empty parking lot and you can practice driving."

"I'm not ready. I still have an innate fear of driving. It was difficult enough for me to get used to riding in cars as a passenger for the longest time."

A couple months back, Derrick and Bruce were riding in Bruce's car with Derrick at the driver's seat—illegally—since he didn't even have his learner's permit yet. While on a desolate, empty road, Derrick lost control of the vehicle and it tumbled several times down a hill.

Miraculously, neither were seriously injured, but the car was totaled. Bruce lied to the police and took the heat for Derrick.

"Well, let me ask you this," Andrew said. "Let's go back this voice."

"Yeah," Derrick said. "What about it?"

"At the BAU, you had a psychiatrist, right?"

"Yeah, I had a very, *very* weird psychiatrist. Why do you ask?"

"Why didn't you tell your psychiatrist about the voice or voices you are hearing in your head?"

Derrick finished chewing—this time with his mouth closed—which was a mighty feat only achieved because he consciously forced himself to do so. Andrew excused himself to refill his soda cup and offered to refill Derrick's, too.

About a minute or two elapsed before Andrew returned with the refills.

Derrick said: "I wanted to tell my psychiatrist, but I was deterred when I found out it could prolong my stay."

"I don't follow."

"I asked Dr. Ivy—my looney tunes shrink—if someone admitted to the BAU was hearing voices if it could prolong their stay, and he said yes, it could possibly result in the person having to stay longer. At that point, I put the brakes on telling him anything that I believed could result in me having to stay there longer."

"But what if there's something seriously wrong up there in your mind?" Andrew asked, deeply concerned. "Wouldn't you want to find out what it is so it can get fixed?"

Derrick pushed his glasses back up. "I guess, but I didn't want to be confined a second longer. I was going to go nuts there."

"Maybe you should call your psychiatrist and tell him."

"Fuck that. No way, no how."

"So, then what? You're just going to live with the voices in your head."

"One voice—well one unfamiliar voice—not multiple. I think what I will do is call a neurologist and see if they will perform some tests on my brain."

"Good idea."

The two finished their burgers, fries, and beverages before driving to the baseball field where they discovered there wasn't any security cameras.

What was this inhuman voice speaking to Derrick from within his mind? Was the voice real? Imagined?

11

A mother and her young child—a four-year-old girl—were in the cereal aisle of a Kroger supermarket. Hit pop songs from the 90s and beyond played over the store's speakers. NSYNC, Celine Dion, Fastball, and the New Radicals were a few of the different artists whose songs that played while they were in the store.

The mother—who looked like a kid herself (she was only nineteen)—picked up a box of Cheerios off the shelf and set them in the cart. She asked her daughter which cereal she wanted. The little girl with a rose flower hair band wrapped around her head of blond hair pointed to the box of Cinnamon Toast Crunch.

"Okay, sweetie pie, you can have it. Get it off the shelf," her mother said. The daughter complied. "I'll take it."

"No, Mommy, I put it in the cart for us," the little girl said.

The mother lightly chuckled at how adorable her daughter sounded. The little girl—Melanie—climbed into the lower level of the car clutching the box of cereal under her other arm. She dropped it into the cart.

"Good job, sweetie pie," the mother, Roberta, said. "We need to get a few more items and then we can leave."

They turned into the next aisle over to get some pastas and sauces. As Melanie's mom placed several packages of generic spaghetti and macaroni noodles in the cart, Melanie hopped off the cart and walked up the aisle.

"Stay by me, sweetie pie. Don't wander off. There are all sorts of weirdos and creepos who might try to hurt you."

"I'm sorry, Mommy."

"It's okay. I just don't want you to get hurt."

A man wearing a business suit with a full-length trench coat and dress shoes turned into the aisle. His shoes made a click-clack sound as he walked up the aisle towards them.

"Can we get McDonald's?" Melanie asked.

"Not today. Maybe when I get paid in two weeks."

"But I want McDonald's!" Melanie screamed. "You promised me!"

And Melanie wasn't making that up. Her mother did promise her McDonald's about a week ago, but due to unforeseen circumstances with her car (it needed a new muffler and some other exhaust repair work), she had to get her vehicle fixed, which drained what savings she had, and cut into her paycheck she received earlier that morning. The only money she had left was to pay for food and other bills. She didn't have any mad money to spend until her next payday.

"I can't do it today," Roberta said. She tried to rub Melanie's back to console her, but Melanie pulled away from her.

Melanie stomped up and down and screamed: "I'm gonna kill myself if I don't get McDonald's!" She did this several times over, attracting stares from customers as they passed by the aisle. "I want to kill myself!"

At this moment, the man in the suit was passing their cart, but now he stopped, took two paces back, and approached Melanie. He knelt down and placed a hand on each of her shoulders. "You need to be very careful with what you say, because you never know when *it* will make its move. I'm hunting it to protect you and everyone else from it. But, remember: be careful what you say. You got lucky this time."

He stood, walked down the aisle past Roberta, and stopped when he reached the end of it. He turned around and tipped his fedora at Melanie's mom, who stared back at him with bewilderment. She slightly nodded her head back to him. Then he turned left and a second later he was out of sight.

12

The doorbell chimed three times and Derrick answered it. Standing on the front porch was Coreyann; she was wearing a floral-patterned blue bikini and flip flops.

He didn't want to be rude, but at the same time he wanted to maintain his distance with her. He knew if Danielle saw the two of them together, it could be the end of their relationship.

He asked her if there was something he could do for her and she requested he fulfill his offer of showing her around the city of Chesterville. He asked her if he minded if Danielle tagged along, which she didn't.

He invited Coreyann inside and offered her something to drink. She chose a bottle of water, which was all she drank since cutting out soda altogether two years ago. She sat on the couch while Derrick excused himself to use the bathroom.

He commanded Siri to call Danielle and about ten seconds later, she answered. After some preliminary gushy talk, Derrick asked: "Could we skip going to the beach and show Coreyann around Chesterville instead?"

"Um, no," she said, almost instantly.

"Why not?"

"I don't like her, and I don't like the idea of you hanging out with her either."

He was relieved he didn't mention Coreyann was in the house as they spoke. The two of them argued for a few minutes before she finally relented and agreed. They ended the call with their usual tennis match of I love yous.

To add authenticity to his ruse, he flushed the toilet and pretended to wash his hands.

When he exited the bathroom, Coreyann was drying her eyes with some tissues. The TV was on, and Derrick figured she had seen a sad part of a movie or a dramatic segment of a soap opera. He asked: "Something I can do to help?"

"No. I'm sorry."

"Do you want to tell me what you saw on TV that got you upset?"

"My brother."

"Your brother was on TV? What happened?"

She lightly chuckled. "No, there was a news segment a few minutes ago about a school bus driver in Knoxville, Tennessee who veered in front of a semi-truck and was killed on impact. It reminded me of my brother's death."

This was news to Derrick. He didn't know she had a brother who died. She explained the reason she nor anyone in her family brought it up is because it wasn't something they felt comfortable telling people, especially new neighbors. Also, they were still grieving. Finally, they didn't want to receive pity support.

"Can I be nosy and ask what happened?" he asked.

"Basically, he stole my stepdad's car in the middle of the night and sped off. He got on the expressway. Once on the expressway, he accelerated to over one-hundred-miles per hour, then jerked the wheel to the left, traveling into the path of a semi-truck." She started to sob again, but a few seconds later compelled herself to stop.

This was eerily similar to the accident Derrick was in as a baby—unbeknownst to Derrick. For a moment, he had a flashback of his body crashing through the windshield and landing on the side of the shoulder in some tall brush, but wasn't sure why he recollected it.

Derrick offered his condolences, then asked: "How old was he?"

"Twelve."

"I don't mean to pry, but why did he do it?"

She shrugged her shoulders. After she blew her nose, she said: "It was out of nowhere. He was such a happy kid." After a brief pause, she continued. "The night before he stole my stepdad's car, he and mom had a fight over him wanting to go over to a friend's house. She said no. They argued. He said some nasty things to her and threatened to kill himself. Later that night, Shawn made good on his threat."

Derrick's eyebrows raised and his heart sunk to the bowels of his stomach. Coreyann dried her eyes with a tissue he handed her.

A voice in Derrick's head told him the story didn't pass the sniff test. The notion an otherwise happy and content kid who over an argument—a seemingly trivial argument—with his mom ended his life was atypical.

After some additional contemplation, the possibility Shawn was masking his true internal state seemed more likely—perhaps depressed about something else—but Derrick didn't want to pry into the nitty-gritty. He figured it wasn't any of his business anyway. If she volunteered anything, however, he'd be receptive.

"There was something odd about his behavior after their argument," she said. "I passed his room a few times. His door was open. He kept rocking back and forth, clutching his arm, just below the wrist. It was the strangest thing. I've never seen him behave that way before."

"Did you talk to him at all about why he was acting in such a bizarre manner?"

"I did, but he said he couldn't tell me. He said if he did he'd be in trouble."

"With who?"

With whom, not with who. Don't correct him though. She shrugged her shoulders.

Before Derrick could comment, Danielle stepped through the front door. After she used the facilities, the three of them piled into her car—which had been out of commission due to a damaged transmission until earlier that day—and Derrick and Danielle showed Coreyann around Chesterville.

And after dropping Coreyann off at home, Derrick and Danielle headed to the beach. Along the way, she chided Derrick for having anything to do with Coreyann. She warned him if he ever spoke to her again and she found out about it, she would end their relationship swiftly, like the coup de grâce to a terminally-ill animal.

13

"He's dead," Lauren told Thomas over the phone.

"What the hell happened?" he snapped.

"Someone dropped a pen in his room. The patient used the ballpoint to stab himself repeatedly in the neck."

Lauren explained the patient—Carl Faulkner—exhibited hallucinations and delusions. He also declared if he shared any information about his state of mind, the bad entity would torture him to death. Finally, during the twenty-four-hour period he was in the BAU, he constantly announced resolutely he wanted to live and didn't want to die.

Though Thomas was upset at the loss of a patient in the BAU, he was more concerned about the potential lawsuit the hospital could now face. He asked for more details about the suicide.

"Michelle was inside his room, monitoring him."

"Right. Suicide watch. Makes sense."

"While he lay on his bed, she sat in the chair, slightly facing away from him. He slipped out of bed to stretch. He knelt down on the side of the bed opposite Michelle, picked up the pen, and repeatedly stabbed himself in the neck."

"No warning?"

"No, but as he stabbed himself, according to Michelle's statement, he shouted things as if someone else other than Michelle was in the room with him, as if someone else was stabbing him in the neck."

This made no sense to Thomas and he asked for clarification. The sound of papers being shuffled traveled into Thomas' ear. Soon after, she clarified. She hypothesized Carl was suffering from dissociative identity disorder, and it was one of his multiple personalities who killed Carl, not Carl's personality.

Carl had no prior history of mental illness. He was a happily married man of two children who recently was fired from his job due to the company going bankrupt. For two months, he tirelessly submitted applications, but nobody called him back for an interview even though he was qualified. His savings depleted and his house now heading into foreclosure, he slipped into a dark place.

The nail in the coffin was when he arrived home after traveling from one place to another seeking work to an empty house. No wife. No kids. No dog. A note was left on the kitchen table. It read: FUCK YOU, YOU LOSER OF ALL LOSERS. Underneath that endearing heartfelt message was an outline of a middle finger—Brandi's middle finger which she herself traced.

Because their cellphones were shut off, Carl galumphed to his neighbor's house with his head slumped in his chest. And like a good neighbor, she let Carl use one of their cellphones to call his in-laws, thinking that's where his wife and children would be.

But his in-laws had already changed their cell numbers—all part of the master plan his wife had hatched weeks ago to leave with the children with the aid of her parents—two people who detested Carl since the first moment Brandi introduced him to them. They condemned her for marrying him and disowned her for nearly a year after they married. It wasn't until Carl and Brandi's first child was born they started to mend broken fences.

"Did you place Michelle on administrative leave?" Thomas asked.

"Yes. Immediately."

"We will need to terminate her."

"Why? No, that's not right. She didn't do anything wrong."

"It's a sacrificial firing, if nothing else," he said, "and rest assured if we don't fire her, it won't look good in court. Our asses will be crucified."

They argued for ten minutes about the potential firing of Michelle who appeared to be a victim of circumstances. Lauren believed Michelle did nothing improper and didn't deserve to be fired. Thomas was adamant about firing Michelle, arguing she had a duty to ensure the room was free of any weapons at all times.

"Well, if you want her fired so badly, you can do it yourself when you get back. Until then, she'll be on administrative leave," Lauren said. "I'm not doing your dirty work for you, and as I've already made clear to you, I think she's free of any wrongdoing. She didn't leave the pen in there."

Maybe you need to be fired, too, then. "Alright. Fine. I won't make any final decision until after I read all the documentation."

"That makes me happy. And take into consideration she witnessed Carl stab himself several times in the neck. She tried to stop him, but he fended her off."

"It sounds like an absolutely ghastly way to die."

"It is, and the scene itself was ghastly. There was a tremendous amount of blood. It was on the walls, the ceiling. Chunks of flesh flung into Michelle's hair."

The conversation switched from the suicide at the BAU to how he and his children were coping with the death of his wife. He was vague in his responses. He thanked her for her concern and ended the call.

14

A storm front was moving in. Lightning flashed and thunder rumbled, but several seconds apart. Alejandro checked the back of his arm when he stumbled to the ground after his shoe dipped into a hole he didn't see while walking along the beach. Usha asked if he was okay and he answered he was fine.

The two of them spent the last four hours walking around Chesterville. They stopped at a small cafe that served quiche— one of his favorite dishes. Then they walked to the beach where they sat next together, listening to the waves crash against the shore. After that, they walked in the woods before returning to the beach once more with quiche.

Usha tried a number of times to convince Alejandro to have his arm examined by a doctor, but he refused, insisting spending time with her doing romantic things was more important than the issue with his arm. Besides, he was adamant no doctor could help anyway.

Wanting to avoid the dangers of the storm passing through, they parked themselves under a roofed area containing picnic tables at the softball field.

"Do you ever think about death or dying?" he asked.

"Sometimes, but I try not to because there's no point. It's going to happen one day. It can't be stopped, only slowed." He nodded. Then she asked: "Do you think about death?"

"More so now than I ever did before."

Her eyes widened. "You're starting to scare me now. What do you mean by that?"

"Nothing for you to worry about."

Now her radar was pinging. She feared he was treating her right and showing her a nice time only to kill her and then take his own life. This wasn't too far-fetched either. During their two-year relationship, a few times he openly expressed he wouldn't let her or himself live if she didn't stay with him. But he always played it off as a joke, so she never put too much emphasis on it.

She took out her cellphone and sent a quick text to her mother, then quickly tucked her phone back in her pocket.

"Sorry. I know we agreed no cellphones, but I had to check my email for messages from my boss," she said.

"You don't owe me any apology."

She smiled, not knowing what else to do.

He placed his hand on hers. "I want you to know you were the best girlfriend I ever had."

And she was. His other girlfriends didn't stick around long after they discovered his volatile temper. The slightest, mildest thing could set him into a frenzy of fury. And the faces he made when he was angry oftentimes caused his girlfriends to shudder.

One girlfriend—the one before Usha—proclaimed he was possessed by an evil spirit, a demon, which he denounced.

But what if he was wrong? What if he was possessed by some sort of evil entity? What if his denouncement of being possessed was the evil spirit allegedly within him the one speaking on Alejandro's behalf?

Usha's cellphone rang and she reached into her pocket while looking at Alejandro's eyes. He nodded, which signaled to her she could answer the call if she wanted.

"It's my mom. Excuse me," she said. She walked to the nearby restrooms, which were adjacent to the sheltered area where Alejandro remained.

He checked the back of his arm again. "Time stands still for nobody," he muttered. He walked to the edge of the concrete floor and stated at the angry sky. "You may as well go ahead and do it now… Because I won't." After a brief pause—two seconds or so—he added: "But then again maybe I will once the hours switch to minutes and then dwindle to seconds."

"Do what?" Usha asked.

He didn't hear her approach. He was too engrossed within his own mind, his own world, his own reality—which seemed unreal to him, even though it was *real*.

He jumped from being startled, then chuckled. "You caught me. I was practicing some acting. I've always wanted to be one."

She bought it.

15

Sitting on the couch, Derrick flipped through the channels, searching for something educationally stimulating to watch. Eventually he stopped at MSNBC, not interested in any of what CNN had to say, which was fake news—in the words of Donald

Trump. Derrick's mindset was if the President of the United States said it was bad, then it was bad. Yes—Derrick was a sheeple.

The time was five-fifty-seven in the evening, and a preview of the next news program was being broadcasted, which was a special report on the recent spike across the world in suicides.

While commercials aired, Derrick took some time to grab himself a bite to eat and something to drink. He sauntered into the kitchen and pulled out a new loaf of bread from the cupboard along with a jar of organic peanut butter and a bottle of honey.

(Want a jolt to perk you up? Take that fucking butter knife and stab it into toaster!). Maniacal laughter from the voice followed.

Unlike before, Derrick didn't pop another Risperidone though. He decided it was better to do his best to ignore the voice.

He spread some peanut butter on each slice of bread. As the butter knife slid across the second slice, the sensation eyes were watching Derrick caused him to stop what he was doing. Part of him didn't want to turn around to see who—or what—was behind him.

But he did ever so slowly, and to his amazement and horror, a young woman about five-foot-five wearing a pair of jeans and a Christina Aguilera T-shirt. She had golden hair and a Oompa-Loompa-looking-tan complexion—as if she liked to frequent the tanning beds.

"This isn't happening," he muttered.

She nodded her head.

"Who are you?"

She reached out her hand as if she wanted him to place his in hers.

"No! I will not come to Hell with you!" Derrick shouted. "Now you go back to Hell and stay there!"

The apparition faded away after two seconds. He released a sigh of relief and finished spreading the peanut butter on the bread.

"Who are you yelling at?" Bruce asked. "You woke me up, goddamn you."

"Sorry. Are you hungry? I can make you a sandwich while I've got the stuff out."

Bruce walked over to Derrick. "What the hell are you making?"

Derrick picked up the bottle of honey and squirted a deluge of it on top of the peanut buttered slices. Bruce's eyes widened at the puddle of honey on each slice.

"Goddamn, Derrick," Bruce said. "You apply honey the same way Burger King applies mayo to its Whoppers. Jesus."

"At least honey is healthy."

"It's actually not. Maybe you need to pull your nose out of those biochemistry books and read about the dangerous allure of honey. You should use honey in moderation."

Yeah? And you should drink in moderation. "I'll look into that. Thank you."

"Make me three of those sandwiches, will you? I'll be in my room."

And Derrick did, though he didn't add quite as much honey. With a stoic expression on his face, Derrick brought his dad the plate of sandwiches. Bruce was laying on his bed with his back against the headboard. The flat screen TV aired one of Bruce's favorite shows—Grip It and Rip It—hosted by Jon Daly.

(Your dad is a killer, and he's gonna kill you. Kill him before he does you! Then yourself!)

[I don't give a shit what you say. You can't convince me to kill myself. Or my dad. I love him, even if he can be a complete prick sometimes.]

The fact this voice—this ungodly, inhuman voice—would not stop talking to Derrick reached a breaking point. Because it had not subsided on its own, Derrick made the decision to find a neurologist in the morning and get his brain scanned.

"Are the sandwiches okay?" Derrick asked.

"They're fine," Bruce said.

"Dad? I want to know if you've had a chance to find my birth certificate."

Bruce slammed the sandwich he was nibbling at onto the plate. Derrick took a step back as his heart raced. As Bruce glared at Derrick with hatred-filled eyes, Derrick's body trembled, which was ironic because Derrick was a muscular guy who dwarfed his dad. If one were to hedge their bets as to who would win in a fight based upon sheer brawn, they would choose Derrick.

(Who does he think he is keeping you from your mother? You want to see your mommy? Blow your brains out! Then you can haunt—I mean visit—her whenever you want!)

[Why do you torment me this way?]

(Because your soul is mine. Give it to me now!]

[Who are you?]

(I'm not a who. I'm what Satan himself fears. I'll be seeing you soon.)

Bruce's eyes were no longer fixated on Derrick. He was munching away on the sandwiches and trying to solve his latest Sudoku challenge. It was always fun to watch Bruce try to solve a Sudoku puzzle when he was hammered. He would duplicate digits, add digits beyond 9, and sometimes even include letters.

"I don't think I have it here," Bruce said.

"Where is it?"

"To be honest, I think I have it in my locker at work. I'll check tomorrow and let you know."

"Dad, if it is easier, I could go to the courthouse and request a new copy."

"Just let me check my locker at work first. I think I have an envelope with your SSN card and birth certificate in there."

"Actually, I'm wrong. There is an easier way. Just tell me who my mom is, where she lives, and how I can reach her."

Bruce slowly turned his head in Derrick's direction and glared at him with those piercing menacing black eyes of his.

"I'm going to be honest with you. Your mom—Allison—has a—"

"Allison?" Derrick said, confused. "You told me last time her name was Donna. Now it's Allison?" *What the fuck! Heidi, Catrina, Tabitha, Ingrid, Bethany, Donna, Allison.*

"Damn it, boy! Now you are pissing me off! It doesn't matter what her fucking name is, okay! She's dead to me! You hear me! Dead! Dead bitch she is—that's all she is to me!"

Bruce's face was red and sweat dripped from his forehead. Drool covered his chin. Derrick apologized for getting his dad riled up—a side he wasn't used to seeing all too often. Sure, there were times would get mad—resulting in him swearing—but never was his temper this volatile.

"I apologize for losing my cool," Bruce said. "It's just she is rotted—I mean rotten—to the core. She's evil inside and out. I don't want you getting mixed up with her."

Derrick lowered his head. "Dad, please don't take this the wrong way, but are you saying these things about her because you're angry and spiteful or because you know pertinent facts about her and you're trying to protect me?"

"She's dead on her feet, often spaced out. Mind, body, and soul in the clouds. I haven't personally kept in contact with her all that much, but I know friends of mine who know friends of hers and based on what I've been told, she's not someone you need to be around."

"Tell me some things you've heard."

Bruce's facial muscles clenched and his forehead crinkled. Derrick asked him why he was getting so mad about a simple question about his biological mother. He even told Bruce if he heard the specifics of his mom's deviant ways, he likely wouldn't want to meet her after all.

But this brought no comfort to Bruce. He wanted Derrick to lay the topic of his mother to eternal rest and never resurrect it for as long as one or the other lived.

Bruce felt betrayed by his own son. He was enraged that Derrick would want to forge a relationship with the one person who should have always been by his side no matter what.

And part of Bruce explained to Derrick he didn't want his mom to simply be able to reenter his life and pretend like nothing happen, act like the slate is clean, like nothing ever happened. And who could blame him? After all, though Bruce certainly wasn't ever going to win Father of the Year, he was the one who provided Derrick with food, clothing, and shelter. Bruce was the one who for all these years raised Derrick. He did all the heavy lifting, not her.

The inhuman voice spoke within Derrick's psyche again.

(Hey, if you want, I can introduce you to your mom. She's mighty fine. I'd love to smash her sometime.)

[You're a figment of my imagination, a by-product of my attempted suicide. I'm going to get rid of you.]

The damage to Bruce's mind, heart, and soul were evident, and it hurt Bruce exponentially more Derrick didn't seem to recognize this pain and suffering.

But Derrick couldn't help how he felt either. Ever since the top was brought up in the sessions with Thomas, he couldn't stop wondering about who his mother was, how she now felt about leaving, if she ever wondered how he was doing and what he was up to, and if they could potentially begin to knit a relationship together.

"Tell me about her, Dad," Derrick said.

"I'm sick of talking about her," Bruce said. "I'm so pissed off I need to take one of my heart pills. Look at this." He lifted his arm. "You got me goddamn shaking." He wanted to scream his thoughts as they entered his mind: *That woman is one dead bitch to me. Dead bitch she is! And that is all she will ever be to me.*

But he didn't.

Derrick sat on Bruce's bed and said: "Maybe if you talk about mom you'll—"

The plate crashed into the undamaged side of Bruce's closet mirror door. A mixture of shattered glass from the plate and mirror littered Bruce's bedroom floor.

"At least both sides match now," Derrick said as he walked out of his dad's room.

16

Alejandro laid on the couch while Usha fixed dinner. She figured since he made her breakfast, she could make him dinner. He didn't have much in his fridge or cabinets. He hadn't gone shopping since their last break-up, which occurred six days ago.

As Usha seared two steaks in a cast iron skillet, she turned her head towards the living room. Though the back of the couch was to her and she couldn't see Alejandro's body, what she did see was all she needed to see.

"I think we should get your arm examined," she said. "You keep staring at it." She sprinkled copious amounts of meat seasoning onto the sizzling meat.

"Nothing to worry about." His arm was no longer sticking upward. He had abruptly yanked it down after she started to talk, hoping she didn't catch him staring at it.

"Then why do you keep fixating about it?"

"Only time will tell, as the hours dwindle to minutes, then to seconds." He looked at the back of his arm again,

She curled her lip, though he didn't see it. She gave up trying to figure out the meaning behind his last remark, along with all the other random quotes about time he said throughout the day, the majority of which were from books he read. Some statements he said included: The past is never dead. It's not even past. Time takes it all, whether you want it to or not. As if you could kill time without injuring eternity.

In another pan with melted butter, Usha tossed in some onion rings and started to sauté them. They both would be eating good tonight. Steak was a luxury for Alejandro, who worked as a custodian at a Pinnacle—a casino in a different city. Usha worked as a part-time waitress during the day and attended classes at night.

"Why don't we watch some TV?" Usha asked.

"Every second counts, and I'd much rather not waste it away on the TV… Do you hear that?"

"What?"

"Listen carefully."

"The raindrops hitting the window. It's a beautiful sound, peaceful."

Usha popped the steaks into the oven to finish them off. She stepped into the living room and walked to the couch. Alejandro was wiping his eyes with his shirt.

"Why are you crying?" she asked.

He snickered. "I'm not."

But he was. The end was approaching.

17

The sounds of intense sobbing snapped Mike out of his trance as he sat on Dylan's bed. Two days had passed Dylan was laid to rest, and ever since Dylan's death, Mike slept in Dylan's bed.

Mike stumbled out of the bedroom wearing only a pair of ratty boxers, his face unkempt with facial hair. He had not shaved since Dylan's death.

"It's good to see you're out of bed," Mike said, his voice faint. "You haven't been out of our bedroom since we got back from the cemetery."

She lifted her head off of the table. "All I want to do is die now that my son is dead." She lifted another tissue out of the box and wiped her eyes and blew her nose, then crumpled the tissue and tossed it in front of her where a landfill of other used crumpled up tissues littered the kitchen table. "I can't go on."

"Don't say stuff like that."

"It's true. I'm telling you how I feel. A big part of me wants to kill myself so I can be reunited with my son. Besides, I don't deserve to live anyway. I *should* kill myself."

Mike started to sob, but fought the urge. "I've already lost one of the two most important people in my life. I don't know if I could handle losing the other."

The sentiment was nice, but it was as if Heather didn't even hear what he said. She yanked out another tissue. Wipe. Blow. Crumple. Toss. She laid her head back onto the table, silent.

Now Mike was inside the kitchen. He pulled out a chair and sat. He placed his hand on hers, but she retracted it, as if he had transferred an electric shock to her.

For about four minutes, no conversation took place. The only noises during this four minutes included sniffles and snorts from Heather as she cried.

"We'll have another baby," Mike said. "When the time is right."

She lifted her head slowly. Strands of her hair covered her eyes, though not completely. He was able to see them in between the strands. She asked him to repeat himself and he did.

"I don't want another baby! I want my fucking son back!" And now she swiftly rose. "And I'll tell you something else, you fucker! I blame you our son is dead!" She ran out of the kitchen to their bedroom and slammed and locked the door.

He walked down the hall towards his bedroom, but stopped at the bathroom. The door was shut and two strips of yellow crime scene tape ran across the door from corner to corner, one strip from upper left corner to lower right corner and the other from upper right corner to lower left corner, forming a big X.

"Dad?" Dylan said.

Mike turned his head towards Dylan's bedroom and flipped on the hallway light. "Dylan? Is that really you?" The apparition of Dylan stood with its right shoulder pointed at Dylan's bedroom door.

"It's me, Daddy."

Tears fell from Mike's face onto the floor. "I miss you."

"I miss you, too, Daddy. And Mommy." Dylan looked towards the floor as he fiddled with his fingers. He released a heavy sigh. "The bad shadow man made me kill myself, Daddy. I didn't want to do it, but I had no choice. Die or be killed."

"What bad man? Tell me who. Where can I find him?"

But before Dylan could respond, he faded away. Mike stood in the hallway, unsure what to make of the experience he just had. Before he could reach a conclusion, Dylan's bedroom light turned on. Mike snickered once and wandered down the hallway to Dylan's bedroom, assuming Dylan's spirit was playing in his bedroom.

But his assumption was dead in the water when he turned the corner and stepped into the bedroom. Mike kept his wits about himself and bravely confronted the entity. "Are you who killed my boy?"

The apparition cocked his head slightly to the right and then returned it back to a normal position. When Mike confronted the apparition a second time, it vanished, and when it did, Dylan's bedroom light turned off and his door slammed closed.

Though his heart raced, he was undeterred. He laid down in Dylan's bed and soon after fell asleep.

18

The morning was filled with birds chirping. A calm breeze passed by Derrick's face as he stood outside waiting for Andrew to pick him up.

The front door swung open.

"Hey!" Bruce yelled. "Where the hell is my breakfast?"

"I can't make it this morning, Dad," Derrick replied. "I have to go to Chicago today."

"Chicago? For what?"

Derrick sighed. "I told you this a week ago. I mentioned again on the way home from the store. And then once more last night."

Bruce picked out a few hairs of his chevron mustache and rubbed them in between his fingers, letting them fall to the ground. Derrick removed his glasses and held them up above his head. The lenses were scratched up pretty severely.

After snuffing out the flaming itch in his crack (four-finger scratch), Bruce said: "Well, what am I going to do for breakfast now? Make me some eggs really fast."

"Dad, I can't," Derrick replied. "Andrew will be here any second now to pick me up."

"What are you going to Chicago for anyway?"

"To check out the University of Chicago. It's one college I'm thinking of attending after I graduate in two years."

"Let's think priority here. I need my breakfast now, but you've got two years to visit the University of Chicago." Bruce scratched his head. "Hmmmm. Which should you choose to do first?"

Annoying slave driver! "Fine. I'll make you some eggs, but they won't be my usual five-star quality."

And with that, Derrick stormed into the house, cracked some eggs in a bowl, and whisked them. Meanwhile, Bruce sat at the kitchen table, drinking his cares away.

A noxious scent filled the kitchen when Bruce belched for about thirty seconds straight. Derrick immediately sprayed the area with Lysol.

"Hey!" Bruce yelled. "Don't microwave my eggs! I want them cooked in the pan."

"This is faster, Dad."

Standing with a slacked jaw and eyes wide, Derrick listened to the inhuman voice from within his mind talk to him again.

(Don't let him treat you like this anymore, Der-der. Gas yourself to death! So says the song, it's as simple as one-two-three. One: Open oven. Two: Turn on oven. Three: Stick head in oven. The rest will work itself out for the dead—I mean best. Kill yourself!)

"What is wrong with you?" Bruce asked. "You look as though you've seen a ghost. Is that it? You saw that black mass apparition again?"

Derrick shook his head. He was fed up with this voice that would not stop speaking to him; he was even more fed up with the things the voice was instructing him to do.

After the microwave dinged, Derrick removed the steamy eggs from it and placed them in front of Bruce.

"I can't eat these," Bruce said. "These are not cooked eggs."

"Yes, they are," Derrick replied. "And if you don't like them, then you can make yourself some eggs in the pan. I need to go back outside and wait for Andrew."

That was Andrew for you. Always late. If he ever was on time, it was on accident.

The time was now eight-fifty-three, and Derrick's patience wore thin. He called and texted Andrew but received no reply.

While sitting in a chair on the front yard, Coreyann sauntered over wearing a tank top sans bra and a pair of speedo shorts.

"How are you doing today?" Coreyann asked.

"Fine. How are you?" Derrick answered.

"Good. Just babysitting. This is Madison."

Indeed, this was the same Madison who threw a fit over McDonald's. Derrick politely introduced himself to Madison and lightly shook her hand. Had he have been any more of a gentleman, he would have kissed it, but he squashed that idea for fear of being labeled a child predator. Can't be too careful these days.

The three of them talked for a few more minutes—up until Andrew finally pulled up in front of the house. He exited his vehicle and approached the group.

"Sorry I'm late," Andrew said. "Traffic."

"Traffic? You live three streets over from me," Derrick replied.

"I know. I'm sorry. I got caught up…doing something." He raised and lowered his eyebrows.

Coreyann snickered. She was right on target with pinpointing what Andrew eluded, but she didn't embarrass him for it. Everyone has to be their own mate, even if only once in a while, but for Andrew, it was constant. He was a horndog.

Derrick and Andrew said their goodbyes to Coreyann and Madison.

Once in the car, Andrew asked: "Have you still been hearing that voice?"

"All too often, but I searched for some neurologists, and I think I'm going to make an appointment. I don't understand why my mind has created this personality persuading me to kill myself."

Andrew slammed on the brakes. A car weaved around him, honking. The female driver said: "Dumbass! Burn in Hell!"

A split second later, Andrew extended his middle finger out of his window and honked his horn a few times. Yeah—that'll teach her not to mess with him.

She slammed on her brakes and extended her middle finger out her window. At the same time, a car had to swerve around her this time, but this driver didn't honk or use obscene gestures. He simply sped past and continued on his journey.

"Dude, quit engaging people," Derrick said. "I don't want to end up dead today."

(But that's how I want you. Your soul is mine.)

"I don't remember you telling me this voice was enticing you to kill yourself," Andrew said. "This is more serious than I thought."

"Don't worry," Derrick said. "I'm not going to kill myself."

(You will if you say the words again that invited me into your life to destroy it. For now, you're safe, but once you utter those words—which I'm desperately trying to get you to do—your soul will become mine, and that will be a rejoiceful, glorious day!)

"It's talking to you right now, isn't it?" Andrew asked. "I can see it in your face."

"It was talking to me, but I've blocked it out."

And, now, like a ditsy high school cheerleader whose boobs were bigger than her brain, this voice started to chant a cheer, loud and proud: *(Kill your-self! Kill your-self! Kill your-self!)*

Andrew let off of the brake and punched the accelerator. On the way to Chicago, he encouraged Derrick to get professional help—and fast.

But this wasn't the only plea Andrew voiced to Derrick.

"So, how are things going with you and Danielle?" Andrew asked.

"Great," Derrick replied. "I can't wait for us to walk down the aisle together and start a family."

"You know, Derrick, you might want to pump the brakes a little. I mean you're talking about becoming a biochemist, and that takes years of school. Danielle seems to be more of a carefree spirit. Aren't you worried after you two graduate, she'll leave you coughing in the dust?"

With no hesitation, Derrick snapped back. "No, not at all. She wouldn't do that to me. What we have is special."

"All she wants is sex, Derrick."

"She's been less persistent for a while now."

And Andrew had a suspicion why, but he simply didn't have the testicular fortitude to tell Derrick. And, to be fair, he had no ironclad evidence Danielle was cheating on Derrick, and so he double-knotted his tongue.

As the traveled on I-94 to Chicago, they jammed to some tunes on the radio, chatting in between songs. The pair were so adorable together, especially when one or the other would sing the wrong lyrics, which induced a hearty laugh from both.

Traffic was light when the pair first merged onto I-94, but not longer after—maybe after three or four miles—a bottleneck ensued. That was Indiana for you: The Men-At-Work Roads of America.

"We were doing a steady seventy-five miles per hour," Andrew said. "Now we're at a standstill."

"It'll be alright," Derrick said, reassuringly. "We can always get off at the next exit and take the scenic route. It will probably be faster."

"I don't think that's a good idea. I don't want to risk getting lost."

"We won't. I can get us turn-by-turn directions using the Maps app."

(Let me give you turn-by-turn directions, you walking-talking corpse. In the glove box is a switchblade. Take that switchblade, open it, and cram the blade into your heart, dead center.)

This time Derrick's inner voice replied back to the ungodly-inhuman voice.

[Why don't you go die? I'm not going to do anything you say. I'm not going to kill myself or anyone else.]

(I'll never die. I've been born, lived, died. Now I'm the undead.)

[Why did my brain create you?]

The inhuman voice cackled—and it wasn't a friendly one either. It was demonic sounding.

(Is that what you think? Your mind created me? Okay— have it your way. You can think that.)

[Am I wrong?]

But the voice seemingly slipped into a black hole, not answering Derrick's question.

19

The seven o'clock news aired on TV as Usha had her head in Alejandro's lap. She was asleep, tired from the events of the day.

"Nearly four hours left before it's go time," he muttered.

"What?" Usha muttered back.

"Nothing, beautiful," he said. "Go on back to sleep." He rubbed the side of her head, as if it were a fluffy kitty cat.

She smiled. "You're too good to me," she said faintly.

"No, no. You've got it all wrong. You're too good to me." *I hope I've impregnated her. We've had sex three times in the last sixteen hours.*

On the news there was a segment about another suicide whereby a sixteen-year-old girl, Aleisha, one who no more than a month ago survived an attack with a crazed loner who brought a machete to school—the last day of school—and hacked people in his algebra class with it, including her, had impaled herself on a metal spike she had planted into the ground in her backyard. She impaled herself by swan diving off of the roof of her garage, skewering her center mass.

The mother of Aleisha confessed for the last day her daughter had been acting out of the ordinary, her mood deflated and her attitude despondent. Aleisha's mother went further to share with the viewers that Aleisha refused to tell her what was wrong.

Usha opened her eyes and asked: "Why do you think she would kill herself, and in such a spectacular fashion?" Though partially asleep, she had been listening to the news.

"Survivor's guilt, I suppose. I know the killer who murdered his classmates with the machete was able to kill about ninety-five percent of the class, including the teacher. I think only two people survived that attack, Aleisha being one of them."

"But I asked why would she kill herself in such a grandiose way? It's as if she were putting on a performance. Who pierces the ground with a metal spike, climbs onto a garage roof, and dives onto the stake? Why didn't she slit her wrists or take a bullet to the brain or down a fistful of prescription pills?"

"I don't know, love." He glanced at the back of his arm again. His heart pummeled against the inside of his chest. The hours were dwindling, soon only minutes would remain, followed by seconds. "Have you ever experienced something that was real but seemed unreal?"

She took a deep breath, then yawned. She sat up and rested her head against his left arm. "There was this one time I encountered a mean spirit living in my house when I was growing up. It was the spirit of an old man who previously owned the house before he died. When I first encountered him it was an experience that seemed unreal—almost unbelievable—but it was real. Why do you ask?"

At first, she thought he didn't hear her because he didn't respond. Right before she was going to ask him again, he indicated he was only making small talk. She kissed him on the cheek.

Now he stood and took her by the hands, playfully pulling her off the couch. He led her into his bedroom, and along the way, she made it clear she was too tired for another ride on his love wand, but he wasn't interested in that right now anyway. Time ticked away, and he needed to make certain she knew some things in the event that what he had been told the day before happened.

He opened his closet door and pulled down from the shelf near the ceiling an accordion-style file organizer. He didn't open it though. He only provided information about what she was to do with it if anything happened to him before the night was over.

She took two steps back. "You're scaring me now. What's in there?"

"Don't be afraid. There's nothing to worry about."

"Really? You sound like you're going to do something to yourself. I'm about to call the authorities and have you taken to be given a psychiatric evaluation."

"I don't need one. All I need is you."

"That's sweet, but I can't ignore the signs. On and off today you've wavered between lucid sanity and clouded irrationality. What's going on?"

He placed his hands on her shoulders. "Just promise me if something happens to me before the night ends, you'll take this file folder to Esteban Ledesma. He's my attorney. Inside of it you will find all the answers."

"Okay. I promise." He hugged her, and when that was over, she asked: "But will you please tell me what's going on? Maybe I can help. Is it money issues?"

"No."

"Are you sick? Do you have some sort of terminal disease?"

He looked down at his feet, then back at her again. "Something like that, maybe. We'll see. We just need to let the sand continue to fall from the hourglass." He walked out of the bedroom.

She stood in his bedroom, aghast. In her mind, all the pieces snapped into place. She believed he had finally seen the doctor for his memory lapses and violent mood swings, and news he was given was grim. Brain cancer maybe—or some other terminal degenerative disease.

But she was wrong, at least to an extent. What afflicted him wasn't degenerative nor was it a disease. It was something far more sinister.

CHAPTER 4

1

As Derrick lay on his weight bench to start lifting weights, Bruce walked in and confronted him about the front lawn not being cut yet. Derrick was supposed to cut the lawn two days ago, but kept saying he would do it the next day. Derrick offered the same response again, but this time Bruce warned Derrick if he didn't have the grass cut by the time he returned from work, he would be grounded for two weeks and he would no longer have access to the weight room. Initially, Derrick argued with Bruce, insisting his tyrannical tactics were not fair, but then he stopped and promised to have the grass cut before Bruce returned home from work.

When Bruce stormed out of the weight room, he muttered: "Ungrateful bastard." Derrick heard it, but didn't verbalize himself, instead choosing to exercise his middle finger, which Bruce obviously didn't see.

A part of Bruce was tired of being a surrogate parent. He was never cut out for parenthood, and regretted not being the first one to jump ship from raising Derrick. Perhaps that was another reason he resented his wife so much: she beat him to the punch to back out of raising Derrick.

Now the bits and pieces of the fight Bruce and Derrick had started to assemble themselves together and come back to Derrick. He sensed it was about not cutting the grass when he was asked, though a part of him had a suspicion the fight was over something more serious than that.

A voice within Derrick's mind spoke, but he didn't recognize whose voice it was.

(Have you figured out what I am yet? Do you remember me?)

"Yeah, you're the result of damage sustained to my brain when I attempted suicide?" Derrick asked aloud, though softly. "Am I right?"

After a four-second period of silence, as if someone had struck the catch of his bench press table with a dinner fork, a ping sound caught Derrick's ear.

Derrick lunged off of the bench and stared it, perplexed. He asked the entity to show itself, but it didn't.

"What do you want?" Derrick asked.

(I've told you that before. Your soul, and I'll get it one way or another.)

Whereas most people would run out of the room screaming, Derrick remained in the room, laughing at the supposed entity's threat, undeterred.

To be quite candid, Derrick didn't even believe this was an entity at all. The object that struck the catch was a quarter that was originally on a small TV dinner table. *My telekinetic power is revving up again,* Derrick thought.

(I almost had your soul once, and I'm determined to get it. You won't get a second chance to save yourself. So, you may as well off yourself before I do.)

"Oh, really? And how do you suppose I do that?" Derrick asked, genuinely interested in the response.

(Get creative. Make your death memorable. Grandstand. The more gore, the higher the score, as I like to say.)

"I suppose you'd like me to rig the lawn mower in such a way the blade can spin without me holding the safety release down. This way, I can propel my face into the rotating blade."

(Do it however you like, mon frère, but do it soon.)

He sat on his weight bench and an image flashed into his brain—a horrific image of his head splattered from the weights. "You're crazy, you know that," Derrick said, "and I'm not going to kill myself. You're using the fact I was recently released for an attempted suicide to taunt me."

(If you don't take care of the loose ends, you'll leave me no choice but to handle this matter myself. I don't like doing that—interfering with one's free will—but I will if I need to. You shouldn't be alive right now.)

"What's your name? Who are you?"

(Does it matter?)

"Why don't you leave before I banish you from here?"

The entity's laugh was deep and growly. That's right—it found Derrick's threat humorous. Derrick was serious though. He read about ways to cleanse a house of unwanted spirits after Danielle saw the entity in his bedroom after her shower.

The entity advised Derrick not to underestimate its power, which made Derrick laugh, who commanded the entity to move something within the room or turn on the ceiling light to prove it was real.

(I don't dance for anyone. If you know what's good for you, you'll take your own life, you psychotic suicidal nut job. Go on. You know you wanna do it. GO DO IT! NOW!)

"Maybe I am a nut job," Derrick said. *Am I losing my mind?*

(Yes, you are, and my mission is to taunt you until you utter the words I need to hear to invoke my command over you. And when I do, you'll surely be dead this time.)

"What's your name?"

(If it makes you feel better, you can call me T-U. Bye, now.)

After unsuccessful attempts to get a response from the entity, Derrick strongly considered the possibility something was wrong with his mind. Maybe the attempted suicide damaged his brain. He searched high and low in Bruce's room for Thomas' card, hoping to give him a jingle and gain some insight from him.

But he couldn't find it, so he called the BAU at St. Catherine's and left a message for him after he found out Thomas was still in Florida, tying up some loose ends of his own.

2

"What did the spooky man in the store mean when he said I should be careful with what I say?" Madison asked her mother.

"Think before you speak. Say what you mean," Roberta said.

They were both seated on the couch. One of Madison's favorite movies was playing on the TV: *The Incredibles 2*. In between them was a large mixing bowl of popcorn, heavily buttered and salted—just the way both of them liked it.

Madison reached into the bowl and like a two-jawed crane, grabbed a handful of popcorn and crammed it into her mouth. Butter dripped down her chin. She washed the crunchy snack down with some grape juice.

"Mommy? What did the man mean when he said *it* may hear you?" Madison asked.

A fair question, but one she wasn't expecting Madison to ask. Roberta grabbed a few popcorn pieces and ate them one by one, buying herself some time to think of an answer, and it was a struggle to come up with one. While Roberta contemplated, Madison patiently waited, watching her movie.

"Maybe the Devil, honey," Roberta finally said.

"Oh."

"I mean when I was a kid I was told if I say things like I'm going to kill myself or I'm going to kill someone, the Devil gravitates to toxic talk like that."

With eyes squinted, Madison placed a finger to her chin, then scratched her head. "What's gravitate mean?"

"It means to be attracted to something, kind of like how you are when we are at Wal-Mart. You gravitate to the toy aisle."

They both shifted their focus back to the movie. After about ten minutes passed, the movie switched off to what appeared to be a news conference, but by the looks of the image quality, either the camera used was old or the footage was recorded decades go.

A heavyset balding man wearing a black suit and a red-and-pink-striped tie—which alternated between the two—was speaking to roomful of people. But what was said wasn't heard because the audio within the footage wasn't audible. The camera was facing the man's right side as he spoke.

"What happened to *The Incredibles,* Mommy?" Madison asked. She stuffed another handful of popcorn in her mouth.

"I don't know, but I'm curious."

He handed an envelope to each of two men, one at a time. After handing the envelope to first man, he said a few words to him, then called the next gentleman up, handed him an envelope, and said a few words to him.

With those formalities out of the way, the man produced a manila envelope and pulled out a revolver from it—a bluing Smith & Wesson .357 Magnum. Some onlookers screamed while others pleaded with him not to go through with whatever it was he was going to do. Though there wasn't any audio, Roberta read the man's lips. He said to the crowd: "Please leave the room if this will affect you." Moments later, he warned: "Don't, don't, don't, don't…this will fuck someone up quick."

As the events unfolded, Roberta predicted the inevitable, and she frantically tried to turn the TV off to prevent Madison from seeing it. The remote didn't work though. Roberta rushed to the TV to turn it off, but this didn't work either. In an act of desperation, she yanked the cord from the wall from behind the entertainment stand. The TV shut off.

But only for a second. And then it happened. The man placed the gun in an upright position into his mouth and fired a single shot. That's all that was needed. A piece of his scalp shot upwards as the bullet traveled through his skull. He slumped to the floor and a waterfall of blood flowed from his nostrils and mouth. Blood also pooled from out of the exit wound, dripping towards the left front of the top of his head, dripping down his face.

Roberta tried to warn Madison to close her eyes before the man shot himself. Madison tried to close them, but couldn't. Roberta scurried to her, whose eyes were widened and face and body like the dead.

"Madison..." Roberta said. Then a little louder: "Madison!"

Whatever trance Madison was in she snapped out of it and immediately started to cry. Roberta hugged her and rubbed the side of her head.

Now the TV was off, which made sense since Roberta had unplugged it, but it turned back on, displaying a white screen with the translucent silhouette of a man. Though he was nothing more than a black mass, Roberta felt as though he was looking at her, looking *through* her. A few times, the silhouette of the man slightly cocked his head, then back to an upright position again.

"I'm scared, Mommy," Madison said. Roberta covered Madison's eyes, unaware she was watching the TV screen. "What is it?"

"I think the TV is broken. I'll take it in to get it fixed."

The TV—a birthday gift to Roberta—from her best friend, Erika, was relatively new. The likelihood there was some internal malfunction was slim. Besides, the TV *was* unplugged, so there wasn't any way the TV could have been displaying any sort of picture anyway, and Roberta knew this. She did find some solace in her lie to Madison.

Now the TV turned off once again, and when it did, the screen cracked as if someone had punched it.

Both of them screamed and Roberta carried Madison into the bathroom. Roberta drew Madison a bath while she called Erika, hoping she could come over and keep them company.

Ever since Roberta and Madison moved into the apartment—which was a few days ago—weird things happened soon after. Lights would turn on by themselves. Drawers Roberta knew she shut would be opened. Sometimes objects would turn up missing only to be found where they should have been a few minutes later.

Roberta believed a playful spirit was the jokester, probably the spirit of a child. But the silhouette of the man she *felt* staring back at her consumed every corpuscle of her body with angst and dread.

And what about the TV being smashed by some unseen force. What did that mean?

Madison slipped into the tub while Roberta chewed the fat with Erika, sharing with her the disturbing events that unfolded just moments ago.

When Roberta was finished flapping her gums with Erika—and boy could they talk for hours about nothing significant, though this conversation was considerably brief compared to their usual conversation—Madison asked: "Mommy? Why did that man blow the top of his head off?"

Roberta rolled her eyes, wishing Madison hadn't brought it up. She wanted to forget it and it seemed it was out of her mind until Madison asked her question.

"I don't know, but I don't think that was real. I think it was staged, like in the movies or on a TV show."

"But why do people kill themselves?"

She hesitated to answer; she didn't want to answer at all. But sweeping it under the rug might do more harm than good. As Roberta squirted some shampoo and distributed it throughout Madison's hair. "Some people do it because they have something wrong with their mind. Others do it because they are extremely sad. And some do it to prove a point."

"I wonder what it would be like to commit suicide."

"Sugar, please don't think about things like that. I want you to think about life and living, not death and dying."

"All that blood from the man's nose. Gross."

After Madison's bath, Roberta read her a bedtime story, which helped her fall asleep. Then she slipped into the bath herself—a bubble bath—where she reflected on her previous suicide attempts.

3

After Derrick finished cutting the front lawn, he took a seat on the porch swing, located on the front lawn near the walkway to the front door. Aaron was in his driveway, bouncing a basketball and shooting hoops.

His cellphone pinged. It was a text from Danielle. She sent to him: *Miss you.*

He replied back: *Miss you, too. Just finished cutting the grass in the front. Backyard next.*

She was in Hannibal, Missouri, visiting relatives—her aunt and cousins—along with her mom, dad, and two younger sisters.

Coreyann walked over and asked if she could sit on the swing with him. When she sat, he stood, claiming he didn't like to sit for too long. Fact of the matter was he didn't like the idea of sitting next to another woman while his girlfriend was out of state.

"Thank you again for showing me around Chesterville," she said.

"No problem. I'm still a little embarrassed at those assholes making fun of my suicide attempt in front of you though."

"Why? We all think about ending our lives now and again."

"You have?"

"At least once a day." Before Derrick could respond, she put a finger up. "What I mean is I think about death every day, not killing myself."

"Doesn't that make living less enjoyable?"

"I guess, but I can't help thinking about death and dying."

Derrick nodded. "I don't think about death every single day, but ever since I got out of the BAU I feel as though I'm living on borrowed time, like I *should* be dead."

(Exactly. So, how do we fix this problem, egghead?)

The basketball Aaron was bouncing and tossing rolled into Derrick's yard after Aaron shot the ball towards the basket and it hit the rim, ricocheting off of it. Coreyann picked the ball up as Aaron gallivanted into Derrick's yard.

"That's mine," Aaron said, his voice lethargic.

Coreyann smiled. "Oh, is it?" she asked. "Come and get it."

"I'm not in the mood." And to Derrick: "Get your bitch in line, laces."

"Who are you calling a bitch?" Coreyann asked.

"Laces?" Derrick said, confused.

"That's my new nickname for you, suicide boy," Aaron said. "Next time I see Bruce I'm going to tell him to keep only Velcro shoes in the house."

"Man, that's not funny," Derrick said. "Don't call me that."

Aaron apologized with his middle finger extended as he walked towards Coreyann to retrieve his ball from her.

What happened, Aaron? Derrick thought. *We used to be best friends. Drugs—that's it.*

Coreyann rolled Aaron's ball into the street. A car swerved to avoid hitting it and ended up veering onto a resident's front lawn. The driver's reverse lights illuminated, and then the driver—an elderly man—abruptly backed up and parked in front of Derrick's house. He exited his vehicle and Coreyann stood behind Derrick.

"What the fuck's your problem?" the man said as he waddled up the front lawn with his distended belly partially hanging out of his ripped blue T-shirt. "You stupid asses have nothing better to do but to endanger people's lives on the road for your amusement."

"It was an accident," Coreyann said.

"Bullshit! I saw you roll that motherfucker into the street!" the man said, shaking his finger at her. "This ain't no fuckin' bowling alley!"

"We're sorry," Derrick said.

"Man, fuck y'all!" the agitated man bellowed as he scratched his belly. He did an about-face and waddled to his car while announcing: "You pull that shit again, Missy, and your ass is gonna be hurtin'!"

Being the smartass she could be, Coreyann rolled the ball in the man's direction. It struck the back of leg, causing him to trip over it and nearly fall. He whipped out a pocketknife, released the blade, and stabbed the ball. Then he picked the deflated ball up and tossed it into his car. Then he drove off, traveling down the street to the end of the block. He pulled into a driveway and turned around. As he approached Derrick's house, the old man tossed the ball onto his lawn, honking twice afterwards.

Aaron livestreamed the old man's actions using his smartphone. Many of his viewers commented the man was crazy but funny.

"I'm sorry about your ball," Derrick said to Aaron.

"It's cool, Laces. I've got a few more in the garage," Aaron replied. "Besides, that was funny as fuck."

"I'm sorry, too," Coreyann said.

"Would you stop calling me Laces?" Derrick asked.

As Aaron walked back to his own yard, he extended his middle finger again to Derrick. He turned around and mouth the word: laces.

"It's not right the way he makes fun of your suicide attempt," Coreyann said. "Maybe you need to be a little more assertive with him."

"Naw, it's alright. He doesn't mean any harm. He's taking his anger out on life on me. He doesn't mean anything harsh by it."

The torment all began when Derrick was in the first grade and Aaron was in the second. Aaron liked to sneak up behind Derrick and smack his ears. He also gave Derrick the nicknames Der-dick and Der-dickless. Then there were the times Aaron would see Derrick leave the classroom, presumably to use the bathroom. When Aaron would see Derrick pass by his classroom, he'd ask to use the bathroom, also. Once in the bathroom, he would discreetly enter one of the stalls and unroll several sheets of toilet paper. Then he would wet it and toss it into Derrick's stall.

Derrick picked up the basketball and tossed it into one of the two garbage cans inside the garage before entering the house to get a quick drink. Meanwhile, Coreyann sat on the swing and rocked back and forth.

"You're still here?" Derrick said when he walked out the front door.

"No, not at all," she said. "I'm not sitting on the swing."

"Like a ghost?"

"Yeah, that's it. I'm a ghost." She started to laugh.

"Speaking of ghosts, I think I have one in my house. There's something lurking in there."

"Have you seen it?"

"Yes."

"Why don't you confront it then?"

Derrick shrugged his shoulders. "I don't want to trouble him. Besides, I don't know what its intentions are. What if it isn't a friendly ghost?"

"Good point."

Derrick was operating by the mottos: *if it isn't broke, don't fix it* and *let sleeping dogs lie.*

"I heard you and your dad arguing last night about your mom," Coreyann said, pulling up the top of her bikini, much to Derrick's viewing pleasure. "What's that all about?"

"My dad doesn't want me to have any contact with mom, even after all these years," Derrick said. "But, you know what?"

"What?"

"I'm about done relying on him to help me find her. I can do it all by myself. And, yes, I may never find her, but at least I'd die peacefully knowing I tried."

(Dying peacefully is out of the question, you worthless shit smear!) Demonic cackling ensued.

"What are you going to do?" Coreyann asked, sincerely intrigued.

"Well, I think I'm going to visit my school and see if I can view my cumulative file. My birth certificate should be in there," Derrick said.

"Most likely, yeah."

Derrick nodded. "My mom's name will be on there along with the hospital I was born in. That should give me two solid clues to start tracking the whereabouts of my mom."

"Good plan," Coreyann said, standing. "If you need me to help, I'm happy to do it." She glanced at her iWatch—similar to the one Bruce had. "I've got to be going now. I'm on my way to babysit Madison."

"How's she doing?"

"She's doing fine, though the last time I babysat there, she said she saw this little boy ghost in her bedroom in the middle of the night when she woke up, feeling as though all of the breath had been sucked from her lungs."

"That sounds like a lot more sinister spirit then this shadow figure I see every now and again in my house."

"Yeah, well, I hope it stays away while I'm there. I fear ghosts. Talk to you later."

After Coreyann left, he pushed the lawn mower to the backyard and started to cut it. As he went up one way—away from the house—and down the other—towards the house, his mind wandered from one thing to another. His weight-lifting goals for the week. What to make for lunch. Where he may want to take Danielle for the anniversary. Now his mind started to think about suicide. He pictured himself sticking his face into the spinning blade of the lawn mower. The blood. The brain matter.

To combat the horrific thoughts of him committing suicide, he forced his mind to imagine Danielle in a bikini on the beach of the Indiana Dunes, standing in the waters of Lake Michigan as the waves crashed onto her tanned skin. He could hear her laughing as he chased after her in the water, grabbing at her legs as she fought desperately to swim away from him.

His vivid and ecstatic memories of Danielle went up in smoke when the lawn mower produced the most terrible grating sound and the motor cut off.

Derrick turned the lawn mower on its side and inspected the blade. He reached his hand into the mower to untangle the shoelaces wrapped around the shaft connected to the blade. It took twenty minutes to get the laces removed. Derrick tossed them onto the back porch and resumed cutting the grass.

Once the grass was cut, he placed the lawn mower in the garage and went inside to fix himself a snack: four raw eggs.

4

Scott scurried down the stairs in a panic. He normally left for work at least twenty minutes earlier when he worked midnights. When he was about to turn into the kitchen, something in the living room caught his eye.

"Are you okay in there?" Scott called from the hallway. After a brief pause, he asked again, speaking louder. Then he shouted: "Hey! Wake up! Are you alright?" as he walked into the living room.

"What?" Aaron answered, his voice faint and lethargic. He rubbed his eyes and turned towards the backrest of the couch. When he did, Scott picked up a prescription pill bottle, which Aaron had been lying on until he repositioned himself. "I'm trying to sleep."

"I don't care. Explain to me what this is."

But Aaron didn't respond. He didn't turn his head to see what Scott wanted information about nor did he ask his dad to be more specific.

The bottle had the patient's name scratched out, but the medication inside the bottle was still visible, and that was OxyContin, or as Aaron's supplier liked to call it, hillbilly heroin.

Scott twisted the cap off the bottle and inspected the pills. He tapped the bottle against the palm of his hand a few times until one of the pills spat from the bottle into the palm of his hand. One side of the circular white pill had OC engraved on it while the opposite had 10.

"It's not enough you do dope and steal money, now you're popping prescription pills?" Scott asked, his voice tense.

Now Brandon walked into the living room. He was wearing a pair of Toy Story pajamas. He put on his glasses and watched as Scott continued to berate Aaron.

"Is Aaron okay?" Brandon asked.

Scott rubbed the top of Brandon's head. "No, he's not okay. He's taken himself some pain pills that weren't his. He'll be out of it for a while."

Concerned, Brandon nudged Aaron a few times, hoping he'd wake up, but Aaron continued to snore, undisturbed.

"I'm so sick of this kid," Scott muttered as he walked into the kitchen. "Stupid son of—!" he shouted.

Scott fed the contents of the OxyContin bottle into the mouth of the garbage disposal and tossed the bottle into the garbage can. He opened the refrigerator and ransacked it looking for his lunch. Karen stepped into the kitchen and asked him to calm down before he woke up the baby.

"Where's my lunch?" Scott asked.

"I'm sorry. I got caught up taking care of the baby. I didn't get a chance to make it yet. I'll do it right now."

He slammed the refrigerator door. Many of the magnets on the face of it fell to the floor. He kicked them as if his leg were a hockey stick and the magnets were pucks, all the while shouting expletives and caustic remarks. Karen stood with her arms folded, unaffected by his explosive behavior.

Brandon ran out of the kitchen, crying. He didn't like seeing this side of his dad, the Mr. Hyde side of his personality.

When Scott stopped the kicking of the magnets, Karen asked: "Are you done?"

He nodded.

"Do you feel better knowing you scared Brandon again? And that you've woken up the baby?" She stormed out of the room.

"Thanks for making my lunch," he shouted from the kitchen.

5

The head custodian of the high school—Mr. Elmore—was perched on his tractor like a king on his throne, rapidly traveling up one direction of the landscape and down the other.

"How may I help you?" the lady's voice emanating from the speaker asked.

"Hi. My name is Derrick Johns. I'm a student here. May I come in, please?"

"Do you have an appointment with someone?"

Derrick swallowed some of his Red Bull before answering. "No, I don't, but I wanted to speak to the guidance secretary, if possible."

After a six-second period of silence, the door clicked and Derrick pulled it open. He entered the building and ascended the stairs to get to the second floor of the building, which is where the main office and guidance department were located.

Once on the second floor, Derrick made a left, passed two doors, then made a right into an office. A pixy-stix-thin woman with grayish hair and a few wrinkles on her cheeks was seated at the front desk. The collagen in her cheeks was starting to deteriorate. Getting old—ain't it a bitch—as she would like to say. Her name was Mrs. Fraser, and she was a new face to Derrick, replacing the previous guidance secretary from last year, whose husband hanged himself in their basement just weeks before the school year ended.

She sat slouched in the chair with her arms folded. Derrick stood at the desk waiting for her to offer assistance. A few times he glanced at her and nodded.

But she never offered assistance, so Derrick took the initiative, but in a roundabout way.

"If now is a bad time, I can come back," he said to her.

"Now is fine. I was waiting for you to state your business, that's all," she fired back.

"I'd like access to my file. I need to view what's in there."

She shook her head. "I'm sorry, I can't let you do that."

"Why not?"

"Because FERPA doesn't allow it."

Derrick had no idea what FERPA was, so he asked for a primer on it. Mrs. Fraser explained FERPA was a federal law pertaining to privacy of a student's records.

"But they're *my* records, so why can't *I* view them?" Derrick asked, rubbing the lenses of his glasses clean with his shirt.

Mrs. Fraser took a drink of her coffee, then folded her arms again. "FERPA only allows for your parent or guardian along with other personnel who have a legitimate reason to do so to view the records."

"I don't understand. The records I want to see are my records, not another student's. Are you sure you're understanding the law the correct way? It doesn't seem right."

"Listen, four-eyes. I've been in numerous schools serving as a guidance secretary for many moons. I know what I'm talking about. Now, you and everyone else of your useless generation have these phones that can give you answers to questions in an instant. If you don't believe what I'm telling you, why don't you take out your phone, look it up, and read it for yourself?"

Derrick didn't appreciate the comment about his new glasses, which he never needed until a recent eye exam—which he had before his suicide attempt—indicated otherwise. He scheduled his own appointment for the eye exam, got himself there, and paid for the co-pay—and just yesterday—the glasses himself through money earned from tutoring summer school students. Bruce certainly wasn't going to play papa to Derrick and ensure he had his routine checkups.

He did, however, pull his phone out of a new case he had clipped to his shorts and read about FERPA like Mrs. Fraser suggested.

"So, did you learn something?" she asked.

"Yeah, I can't view my own records until I'm eighteen," he replied.

She nodded her head. "That's right. It's not me being a total queen B to you. I'm just following the law."

He slumped in a chair and folded his arms, mirroring the quick-draw-pistol-witted Mrs. Fraser. He sat for several seconds, tapping his foot, sulking.

Mrs. Fraser stood, and when she did, her heels clacked against the floor, startling Derrick. She walked around the front desk and sat next to him.

"Listen—why don't you have your dad write a note and sign it giving you authorization to view your file? Then there won't be any issue," she said.

Derrick sighed and slumped a bit further into the chair. She started to walk back to her desk.

"I guess it's not meant to be," Derrick said.

"What's not meant to be?" she asked.

"Me meeting my mom."

"I'm not following you."

"My mom left me and my dad before I can remember. I never really questioned why she left or wanted to meet her for many years. It was just me and my dad. But recently I've had a change of heart. It was her who gave me life, and even though I'm angry she broke my dad's heart running off with another man and abandoning us, she's still my mother, and I'd like to meet her, even if only once."

As Derrick shared his story, Mrs. Fraser filed her nails. When he finished speaking and she didn't say anything after a few seconds, he started walk towards the exit of the guidance office.

"Hey, specs. Come here," she said.

"Yeah?" he asked, walking towards the front desk.

"Why can't you ask your dad for your birth certificate? I'm sure he has a copy of it."

"He doesn't want me to reestablish contact with my mom. He is doing everything he can to prevent me from finding her."

"Why?"

Derrick opened up like an encyclopedia and shared the multitude of reasons his dad didn't want him reaching out to his mom. Mrs. Fraser understood his dad's position, but ultimately believed it was wrong for Bruce to deny Derrick any contact with her.

"Were your parents married or were they just dating?" Mrs. Fraser asked.

"I don't know."

"What did your dad do? Destroy all the evidence reminding him of her—well except you of course."

For some reason unknown to Derrick, a fragment of a memory flashed into Derrick's mind. He remembered one time Bruce tried to strangle him. Derrick saw himself sitting on his bed. The sheets and blanket had different dinosaurs on them. Tyrannosaurus Rexes. Pterodactyls. Velociraptors. Bruce walked in with a menacing glare in his eye and wrapped his hands around Derrick's throat for several seconds, but the rest of the memory didn't play.

"No, but the evidence was destroyed. A fire, I think my dad said."

"Bullshit." She immediately covered her mouth. "Oops. Sorry about that," she announced to the counselors in their offices. They snickered. And to Derrick: "He's lying. He just doesn't want to tell you he burned the pictures and documents reminding him of her. There wasn't any house fire. Your dad destroyed the records in a rage."

"Who knows. He lies to me constantly about my mom, so it wouldn't surprise me if he did burn the stuff himself and now he's projecting the blame elsewhere. Classic Bruce."

"I hope you find your mom. I really do, but there's nothing I can do to help you."

(Now's your chance, Der-dick-sucker! Take that calligraphy pen and stab her in the neck! The blood squirting out will be a divine sight—one to behold! Then you can stab yourself in the neck!)

"Are you alright?" she asked when he didn't respond to her. "What's the matter with you?"

(You know you want to do it, so what's stopping you?)

Derrick swallowed hard. "I'm fine." He took a breath. "Maybe there is a way you can help me."

"How's that?"

"You have access to the files, right?"

She nodded. "Yes, they're right behind me within these eight large file cabinets. Why?"

Derrick took one step to the left and leaned forward to find the drawer containing the Js. The drawer labeled I-K caught his eye. He so much wanted to leap over the counter and steal the file.

"Can you view my file and tell me the name of my mother on my birth certificate?" he asked.

"No, I can't do that. I don't have a legitimate reason to pull your file and be rootin' through it, and that would be unethical."

"I give you permission though."

She chuckled. "Well, thanks, but you don't have the authority to give me permission. Only your dad does."

"Please. All I need is her name."

"It's not going to happen. I can't help you in that way. Get permission from your dad. Bring me a signed letter from him and you can look at anything and everything in your file."

She had about enough of his nagging, but she remained cordial and politely reiterated what he needed to do in order to see his records. Even still, he didn't want to leave until he had what he wanted.

He asked if he could speak to his guidance counselor, Mr. Micklo, and she said she would see if he was available. His office was tucked away at the end of the guidance office hallway on the left. As she walked away from her desk to get to Mr. Micklo's office, there wasn't any click-clack sound from her heels; she had taken them off, a practice she had done for years at her other positions.

Derrick pinched his nose at the acrid aroma striking his nostrils like a hammer to an anvil. He grabbed the bottle of Purell hand sanitizer and squirted copious amounts of it in his hands. He rubbed his hands together, flattening the blob of the green goop to a thin layer. He swiped his finger across his nose a few times and breathed deeply, which masked the scent of Mrs. Fraser's rotten foot odor.

And to be honest, her foot odor was on par with the aroma one might encounter when a bloated, decomposing body is opened up for the first time. A pungent knock-you-on-your-ass scent.

"I'm sorry, Derrick," Mrs. Fraser, "but Mr. Micklo isn't available right now. He's with a parent conducting an entrance interview. If it's important, you're welcome to sit and wait."

"No, that's okay," he said. The inhuman voice continued to insist he murder Mrs. Fraser and then kill himself. Derrick pulled out his Ice Breakers container and removed two pills. He averted disaster by stopping himself from swallowing them when they almost went down the wrong tube. Sometimes his epiglottis had a mind of its own. Once the pills were in his stomach, he said: "I did want to ask you something though."

"And what's that?"

"If I were to give—"

The interim principal of the school—Dustin Verta—scuttled into the guidance office with a terrified expression on his face. Whenever he walked, he swung his arms back and forth at his sides—as if the motion of his arms was what propelled him forward—in opposite directions at a proportional rate to his speed of travel. Also, the faster he walked, the longer the distance his arms traveled. Low speed, short distance; high speed, long distance.

"With me, you come," he said to Mrs. Fraser, using his head to motion towards a room since his arms were too busy to do that for him. "Information for you, I have."

This dude talks like Yoda, Derrick thought, lightly snickering. *I can't wait to see how the student population reacts to this guy.*

The previous principal—Rick Wilson—resigned abruptly after it was discovered he was engaging in sexual relations with the previous guidance secretary, who wasn't fired or asked to resign, but was bounced to another school. None of the current assistant principals had an interest in moving up, so the superintendent of the school district brought in Dustin—who served as an art teacher at a middle school for a few years before becoming assistant principal and eventually principal there—to fill the role of interim principal with the prospect of being board approved as principal.

Mrs. Fraser and Dustin stepped into a conference room in the hallway where the counselor's offices were located. Dustin scurried with his arms flailing back and forth out of the conference room and stepped into one of the counselor's offices, indicated he needed to speak to her, and then led the way into the conference room. Seconds later, he vamoosed out of it and entered another counselor's office, then escorted him into the conference room. Dustin did this four more times. Now all six counselors along with the guidance secretary were inside the conference room. Derrick could see some of them since Dustin didn't shut the door when he entered it.

Although they were in separate rooms, Derrick was still able to hear the announcement Dustin had for the counselors and Mrs. Fraser.

"One of our students committed suicide earlier this morning," Dustin said. Gasps erupted from the crowd. "I just got off the phone with the parents a few minutes ago."

"Who was it?" one of the counselors asked.

"Jessica Jensen," Dustin replied.

"Why?" Mr. Micklo asked.

"Her parents don't know. The past day or so Jessica had been in a strange mood. She didn't want to go anywhere, do anything. She confined herself to her room and rarely came out of it. She didn't eat much either."

(Why don't you join dear Jessica? Remember her? You sat next to her in English class last year? It was beautiful the way she offed herself! I wish you could have seen it! It was orgasmic to the nth degree!)

While it was true Derrick sat next to Jessica in Honors English last year, they didn't talk much, primarily because Derrick didn't want to upset Danielle by talking to another woman of the same mental caliber as he. He wouldn't dare make that mistake again, especially after the argument he and Danielle had after she caught Derrick talking to and laughing with another girl from his World Civilization class in the hallway. She cut into Derrick like an axe into a watermelon.

At first, he didn't understand why she was so upset. It wasn't until after a four-day hiatus from each other—during which neither said anything to the other, including via text message—she explained to him why she didn't like him talking to other girls, especially those who were in his advanced classes. She feared he would leave her for another girl, someone smarter than her.

Dustin went on to tell the guidance staff Jessica drew a circle around the back of her wrist in permanent red marker. When Derrick heard this piece of information, he looked at the back of his wrist as a vaguely familiar feeling came over him.

Mrs. Fraser walked out. "Is there anything else I can help you with before I leave for lunch?"

"Yes. If I were to ask you to add something to my file, could you do that?" he asked.

Dustin ambled out of the conference room. His arms hardly swayed back and forth at his side.

"Depends on what it is."

"A letter of commendation from one of my teachers."

"No, that is not something I can add to your cumulative file."

He asked her for items he could potentially give to her so she would have a reason to peek into his file. She mentioned the typical things that go into a file. Proof of residency, immunization records, birth certificate, assessment data, parent handbook signature, report cards, among other items—depending on the student and their individual circumstances.

"What if I asked you to check if there was an item in there?" Derrick asked. "While you're looking for that item you could just happen to stumble upon my birth certificate and glance at my mother's name. Would that work?"

"I can't do that either. I'm sorry." She folded her arms, effectively placing a stone wall between him and her. "Enjoy the rest of your summer."

He nodded. "Well…thanks anyway."

He turned around and left the office.

Empty-handed.

6

Detectives were eager to get Usha's side of the story. They watched her through a one-way mirror as she sat in an interrogation room.

The lead detective of the case, Benito Monteleone, stood next to his partner, Desiree Bingham. Both were attracted to each other, even they both were married—unhappily, yet they never openly expressed those feelings to each other.

"What do you think?" Benito asked his partner. *The vanilla scent of her lotion... I can't get enough of it.*

"It's a suicide," she said. "All the evidence points in that direction."

They walked into the interrogation room and placed a plastic cup in front of Usha, who grabbed the cup, but then instantly let go of it, as if she had wrapped her hand around a steam pipe. Using a few tissues, she wrapped them around the cup and took a few sips of coffee.

The two detectives didn't sit at the table together. Desiree sat in a chair, which was tucked into a corner of the room near the door. Benito—who preferred to be addressed as Ben—sat at the table with Usha.

After the two detectives introduced themselves to Usha, Ben started the interrogation. He sat with his arms on the table, fingers interlocked. Slouched in the chair, Desiree had a padfolio in her lap, opened and ready for business. Her job was to remain silent and take detailed notes, and that's what she did.

"Walk us through the events leading up to the discovery of Alejandro's body, please," Ben said.

"How far back do you want me to go," Usha asked.

"As far back as you feel you need to, but I will say the more information we have, the better."

Usha took another sip of coffee. "Alejandro woke me up a little over twenty-four hours ago. He wanted—"

"Sorry to interrupt," Ben said. "Can you give us an approximate time he called you?"

"Twelve-forty-five-ish, I think."

Desiree, who was seated behind Usha, scribbled down the time.

"What did he want?" Ben asked.

"He asked me to come over right away. His voice was frantic, like someone in his family had just died or something," Usha said. "I told him I would come over later, after I got off work, but he pleaded with me to come over now and call off from work."

Ben nodded, but it wasn't him agreeing, it was him prompting, it was a nod that suggested she should continue her statement since he had no questions at the moment.

And she did continue. She said: "I asked him to clarify over the phone, but he wouldn't. He insisted I come over where he would explain further."

"And did you agree to come over then or did you wait until you got off work?"

"I gave it some quick thought. Alejandro wouldn't play games with my mind. I figured whatever was eating away at him was authentic, so I decided to go and visit him."

Usha shared with detectives when she arrived at Alejandro's apartment, he was lying on his couch, staring pensively at the back of his arm, as if there was something on it. She told them she called his name a few times, but he didn't seem to hear her. He was too obsessed with his arm, running his fingers over his wrist—the back of it, then caressing it with his thumb while his other fingers were wrapped around the front of his wrist.

The sound of Desiree's pen dancing in a frenzy across the page momentarily distracted Usha, but then she continued, sharing with detectives Alejandro insisted she stay with him until time was up.

"Those were his words?" Ben asked. "He said until time is up?"

"He did. I didn't know what that meant, but I think I do now."

"And what's that?"

"He had set in his mind a plan to kill himself and have me find his body. That's why he was so persistent about not pissing time away."

"But don't you think that's a little outlandish? You told me at the scene he wasn't suicidal, so why would he have this elaborate plan to off himself?"

Usha folded her arms. "I don't know what the fuck to think right now. I'm in a dark room hunting for the light switch. I wish I could understand what possessed him to kill himself, but I don't know." *Should I mention the possibility he had a terminal illness?*

Ben took off his glasses and wiped them with his tie. He placed them back onto his nose and leaned back in his chair. Desiree continued to write, finishing up notes based up what was said up to the conversation ceasing.

"I think you bring up an interesting point there. Now, I know you didn't come outright and suggest it, but is it possible Alejandro was possessed?"

"Seriously?" Usha asked. "You think Alejandro was literally possessed by a demon and that's why he killed himself."

"If you're a religious person, it's not too far-fetched."

"You want me to believe Alejandro was possessed by a demon who convinced him to kill himself rather than he willingly killed himself?"

"The logical side of my brain wants to believe Alejandro willingly ended his life, that it was something he truly believed he needed to do. The religious side of my brain thinks other forces were at play."

Unconvinced of the detective's assertions regarding the possibility of something beyond the physical world having a hand in the matter, Usha continued her account of the day's events. The time they spent together on the beach, in the park. Then she moved to her making dinner, them eating together. Ben took a sip of his coffee as she spoke, listening.

"Around ten-forty-five, he excused himself to the bathroom. He also said he wanted to change into some more comfortable clothes. I knew what that meant. Fresh boxers and a T-shirt. When he didn't return after about fifteen minutes, I went into his bedroom to check on him."

"So the time you went to check on him was approximately eleven, right?" Ben asked.

"Yes, that's right. I walked into his bedroom, didn't see him, so I figured he was likely in the bathroom—the one in his bedroom."

"But we both know he wasn't. How did you end up finding him?"

"Sixth sense, I guess. Then again, maybe it was just that—a guess. Something compelled me to open his bedroom's closet door, but I didn't think I'd find Alejandro hanging from the rod with his belt wrapped around his neck. I figured he would have popped out and startled me. You know—like a prank."

"So you found Alejandro deceased in the closet around eleven. But the 911 call was placed at eleven-thirty-two, according to records. Why?"

"I fainted. When I saw Alejandro's body, his face a purplish-blue, his tongue partially sticking out of his mouth," she said, "all the strength in my knees gave out." Now she bawled for several minutes and Bill and Desiree gave her all the time she needed. "I'm sorry."

"No need to apologize," Desiree said.

After Usha signed her statement, she was released from the interrogation room. Ben offered to drive her home himself, but she declined his offer, preferring to take an Uber.

He waited outside with her until the Uber arrived. Before she got into the car, he handed her his business card with his cell number written on the back of it. He told her if she thought of anything or just needed to talk to someone, he was her man.

She accepted the card, thanked him for his candor, and then drove off in the Uber. Upon the car driving away, she considered crumpling up the card, believing she would never speak to Ben again, but she placed it into her pink Coach wallet. Then she closed her eyes and dreamed about Alejandro—the good times they had together.

7

"Buckle up nice and tight," Thomas said. He fastened his seatbelt. And to Nikki: "Please help your sister."

And Nikki did. Meanwhile, Thomas lowered the tray and placed his laptop on it. He pressed the power-up button and waited for the home screen to appear.

The first thing he did once logged into his laptop was type an email to the BAU staff thanking them for their condolences and expressing his enthusiasm to return to work.

"Listen, girls," Thomas said. "I know you may not be happy about moving to Chesterville on a more permanent basis, but I think you'll adjust just fine."

"It's okay, Dad. It's going to be nice to see the old city again," Ashlee said.

"That's the right attitude to have, princess," Thomas said. And to Nikki: "How about you? How do you feel now that we are on the plane and getting ready to take off?"

Nikki folded her arms. "I'm super excited about it."

For the past three days, Thomas and Nikki fought relentlessly about her and her sister moving to Chesterville. Nikki's biggest hang-up was the fact her mother's remains would be in Florida while they would be in Indiana. A compromise was reached when Thomas suggested they bury their mother's urn in a grave in Calvary Cemetery—a cemetery within walking distance from Thomas' house.

The girls agreed, but for some reason Nikki still wasn't content. Thomas tried to get to the root of the issue with her but she was one tough nut to crack.

"Daddy? Where's mommy at right now?" Ashlee asked.

"She's in the belly of the plane with our other luggage," Thomas said. He hammered away on his laptop keyboard, adding narrative to a report due to the state in a few days. "Why do you ask?"

Ashlee put a finger to her chin and tilted her head slightly. "No, that's not what I mean, Daddy. I mean is Mommy in Hell because she killed herself?"

This was a question Thomas hadn't given so much as a thimbleful of thought to, and he was taken aback by the question. His mind struggled for several seconds to come to an answer. On one hand, if he did believe his ex-wife was in Hell, he wasn't sure if he should share that with Ashlee. On the other hand, he himself was unsure what he believed.

Both Nikki and Ashlee looked at their dad with eager anticipation for his response.

Thomas took a drink of his water, then spoke: "No, princess. I don't believe if a person commits suicide they go to Hell. Now, you should know some people do believe that, but don't listen to them. You believe what you think is the truth, and don't let anyone change that. So, tell me, princess, where do you think your mom is?" When she didn't offer a response, Thomas added: "Don't be afraid to tell me what you think."

Ashlee smiled. "I don't think, Daddy. I *know*."

"And what is it you know?" he asked, sincerely eager to know.

"I know Mommy is in Heaven," Ashlee said. She smiled as she spoke, and from that alone it was obvious Ashlee believed what she said. "I know Mommy is an angel, and she's going to protect us from the spirit of darkness."

"The Devil?" Thomas asked.

"No, but The Devil, too," Ashlee said.

The safety announcements started and Thomas insisted his girls pay close attention to the flight attendant's instructions, because it could mean the difference between life and death.

Nikki gave Thomas shit about the instructions, but ultimately obeyed. Ever since he suggested she and Ashlee move to Chesterville with him, she'd been mouthy and defiant. Then again, he hadn't been around her since Sharon moved to Florida after the divorce was finalized, so he wasn't sure if this was a manifestation of terrible teens or if her Jekyll-Hyde personality was because of the abrupt move.

Once the divorce was finalized and Sharon was granted full custody of their two daughters, Sharon decided to sell the house (both Thomas and Sharon were on the deed) and move to Florida, which created another battle between Thomas and Sharon. He refused to sign the agreement with a real estate agent to sell the house. He didn't want his girls to move to a different state.

Ultimately Thomas decided to swallow his pride and support Sharon's decision. Otherwise, she was going to let the mortgage default and move to Florida anyway.

All Thomas wanted to do now was to help his daughters heal from the emotional battle wounds they endured over the past few years. The divorce, the suicide, and now the move.

"So, Dad, I will get my own room, right? You didn't just say that to butter me up?" Nikki asked.

"Yes, Angel. That was the agreement. You will get your own room," Thomas replied.

"You're leaving me?" Ashlee asked.

"Nothing personal, Sis," Nikki replied, smiling. "Besides, you'll have your own room now, too."

Thomas could read the hurt in Ashlee's eyes. It was like a divorce. Since Ashlee was old enough to have a big-girl bed, she shared a room with Nikki, and now that was ending. She didn't want her older sister—her protector—to have her own room. A big part of her prayed something would happen to prevent Nikki from getting her own room, but only momentarily. That was her selfishness kicking in and she didn't like that side of her. She took back her wish.

He shut down his laptop, packed it away in his black leather satchel, and excused himself to use the latrine. Once inside of it, he texted Nikki a message containing a request, knowing he'd catch hell for it, but it was worth a shot.

He waited a few minutes for her to reply back, and when she didn't, he sent her a question mark. He was fairly confident she saw the message since she was typically on her phone any given minute. A cellphone-rush junkie, she was.

After waiting another ten minutes and sending a barrage of question marks, she texted him: *Fine! I'll sleep in Ashlee's room for a few weeks and gradually phase myself out! Happy?*

Just as Thomas was about to reply to Nikki's text, his cellphone vibrated as a call came through. It was Lauren. His heart sank, fearing it was another call about a suicide.

"What bad news do you have for me now?" he asked. No hello. No how are you. He went right between the eyes.

"No bad news, all things considered, but I wanted to let you know in the last twenty-four hours, the BAU has had five people admitted with suicidal ideation."

"I want two orderlies assigned to each patient with the slightest hint of suicidal ideation. We've got to recover from the shitstorm Carl created for us."

"That's a rather cynical thing to say about someone who suffered a devastating blow and is now deceased. I think you need to… I'm sorry. I know you've endured, too."

"I have, but you make a good point."

"So two orderlies per suicidal patient. We'll have to call in reinforcement."

"Why? How many total patients do we have with suicidal ideation?"

The sound of papers being rummaged about bled into the Thomas' ear. He quickly sent Nikki a text telling her he was taking care of some business to which she replied she pitied the fool who uses the bathroom after he gets done in there. He snickered and took it as a sign she was getting back to her old self.

"Twenty-six," Lauren said.

"Out of forty rooms, twenty-six have patients exhibiting suicidal ideation? What the hell is going on? It's like a pandemic. Very, *very* disturbing."

But Lauren didn't understand why this shocked Thomas. For the past few weeks, news channels worldwide had aired segments about the recent sharp spike in suicides without any warranted explanations. Then again, she took into consideration Thomas was grieving, and perhaps wasn't thinking clearly.

"That's not too far off base," Lauren said. "I've conferred with friends and colleagues who work at other hospitals, both in our state and outside. Their psych wards have experienced a spike in patients with suicidal ideation. Even outside the USA suicides are spiking."

A pandemic, yes. But what was causing the outbreak of suicide and suicidal ideation like it was typhoid fever? What drove people to contemplate and carry out suicide without any advanced, prolonged warning signs? Could the pandemic be contained or was the human race on the brink of total destruction?

8

After enjoying a breakfast consisting of French toast and eggs—which Derrick prepared—for Bruce and Gayle—who lately had been spending more and more time with Bruce after work and on his off days, Derrick retired to the weight room to begin his exercise regimen.

Since his encounter with the spirit (only its voice), Derrick hadn't heard from it nor had he seen it. Sporadically, he would notice a palpable change in the atmosphere. Thick, electrically-charged air. The sensation of someone watching him, much in the same way he was watched while at the BAU, but with a greater intensity, as if the unseen eyes never blinked, remaining fixated on Derrick's every move, occurred more often than the change in the ambient air.

Whenever Derrick experienced these sensations—most often occurring either in his room or the weight room—but sometimes other rooms of the house also, he paid no mind to them, preferring to focus on his energies on his exercises, his strength training, and soon after shifting his focus, the sensations faded away.

Now, the feeling of eyes on him and the drastic changes in atmosphere didn't bother him nearly as much as some of the dreams he recently had—and visions he had while fully awake. Take, for instance, last night while Derrick was soaking in the bathtub after his shower (he showered first because he didn't want to soak in dirty bath water). While soaking in the tub with a damp, warm rag over his eyes, he dozed off and dreamed about committing suicide—multiple times in a variety of ways. Slashing his wrists. Blowing his brains out. Hanging himself from a tree in the local park. Pills. Carbon monoxide poisoning. It wasn't until he dreamed himself at the baseball field he snapped out of his sleep, mainly because the events he dreamed at the little field felt real, like his mind and body had been transported out of the tub to play his part in his dream.

Gayle sauntered into the weight room and stood on the treadmill. "I hope you don't mind me getting a little exercise in while I'm here," she said.

"Be my guest," he responded. He continued to lift the barbell up—stopping for two or three seconds—before lowering it down and waiting two or three seconds, and then back up again. "Are you and my dad dating again?"

"I don't think so. I'd like us to, but I've decided to take it slow this time. Not push him into a relationship. I think that was the mistake we made in the first place."

As Derrick lifted the barbell up, he grunted as if trying to relieve constipation. After another two reps of five, he sat up on the bench and wiped sweat from his brow using an Everlast towel he received as a Christmas gift from Danielle last year. It was the only towel he ever used in the weight room. He washed it every day, which was a source of frustration to Bruce, who found it ridiculous to wash one item, even though Derrick set the washing machine dial to LIGHT LOAD.

He stood and walked over to the pull-up bar which hung from the top of the entrance to the room. He started to do pull-ups, grunting as he pulled upward. When his chin surpassed the bar, he counted out—in a grunting voice—the number of pull-ups he had done up to that point.

"Did you think about killing yourself when my dad kicked you to the curb?" Derrick asked.

Wow. Thanks for the kick in the teeth, Gayle thought. "No, it wasn't that serious, but it was emotionally painful—and draining," she answered.

"Have you ever thought about killing yourself?"

She answered without any hesitation, like she was expecting the question before it was even asked. "Sure. Who hasn't?" But her response was actually a knee-jerk reaction; she was taken by surprise by the question.

"When?"

She increased her pedaling on the bike. Clearly the conversation was making her uncomfortable. Derrick didn't want to pry, but at the same time he was curious about the times she thought about suicide, interested to know what was the furthest she went with attempting suicide.

He grunted a little louder now as he cranked out his pull-ups. The lactic acid in his muscles was causing his arm to start to cramp a little, but he pushed himself and managed to crank out six more pull-ups, bringing his total to seventeen, a new record for him.

"If you don't want to tell me, you don't have to," Derrick said. "I'd understand if you didn't reveal that part of yourself to me."

Gayle wavered between sharing that side of her she kept concealed in a vaulted safe in her brain or shutting the conversation down like cops at a frat party.

Now, she and Derrick weren't enemies per se, but their relationship wasn't the strongest either. She considered using this situation as an opportunity to become closer to Derrick.

"I'll give some insight into my experience with suicide," she said, "but you have to promise me you'll not blab it to other people, not even Danielle. Do you promise me?" She smiled, but not enough to show any of her off-white teeth. She was always self-conscious of her smile, and she look forward to the day she could get dental implants—or at the least removable dentures. After Derrick agreed to keep it to himself, she said: "Let me get a bottle of water first. I'm thirsty."

"I'll get it." Moments later, he returned with an uncapped bottle of Dasani water and handed it to her. "Sorry we don't have any more flavor packs to add to the water."

"That's okay. Thank you," she said. She slurped the entire bottle of water down like an alcohol-starved lush would a bottle of beer. She capped the bottle and set it on the floor, and when Derrick tossed it in the garbage, she retrieved it. A save-the-planet junkie, she was.

"Will you tell me now?" Derrick asked with a hint of impatience in his voice. He laid on the floor and started to do sit-ups.

"Would you like to know the first time I thought about suicide or the first time I *attempted* suicide?" she asked.

He abruptly stopped his sit-ups and remained in a forward crouched position, contemplating which he would prefer. He considered asking her to share the details about her first attempted suicide but thought it may a ploy for him to open up about his alleged attempted suicide. Aside from what, he wondered what she would think of him for wanting to know such details.

"How about you tell me both?" he said. He resumed his sit-ups.

"Alright." She took a deep breath and exhaled. "The first time I contemplated suicide was when I was in first grade," she revealed. "I was made fun of constantly because I had big ears that stuck out like Dumbo. Kids also made fun of me for being Mexican."

"But you're not Mexican."

"Exactly! That's why I was always like *what the fuck* when I'd be called different Mexican racial slurs. At first, the crude remarks about my ears and erroneous race occurred every so often, but gradually it picked up steam. I hit rock bottom when the principal himself made fun of my ears in front of the whole class, saying if I learned how to flap them, I could fly away."

"Wow. What a dick."

"I kept a brave face for the rest of the day, but I wanted to kill myself right then and there. I saw the pair of scissors—the sharp scissors—on my teacher's desk in an old mayonnaise jar. I wanted to take those scissors, kill the principal, and then kill myself."

Derrick saw her eyes filling like a clogged sink. He told her she didn't have to continue to share the story if it was too painful.

But she didn't stop. She said: "When I got home, I told both of my parents what had happened. Neither gave two shits. They told me to get over it. They told me that day I learned the most important lesson in life."

"What was that?"

"Life is painful. Learn to deal with it."

In the closet in the weight room were a few boxes of tissues. He opened one of them and handed it to Gayle. She thanked him and wiped her eyes and blew her nose.

"Would you help me with something?" Derrick asked.

"Depends on what it is," she answered.

"Do you think you can extract some information from my dad? He won't tell me, but maybe he'll tell you."

"Tell me what?"

"What my mother's name is. Where she lives. Maybe a phone number."

"You mean he still hasn't told you?"

"He's given me names, but I don't think a single one of them is correct." *Heidi, Catrina, Tabitha, Ingrid, Bethany, Donna, Abigail.* "Even if I didn't want a relationship with my mom at this point, I'm determined to at least find out what her name is—her *real* name. Not one my dad tells me."

He shared with her the seven different names Bruce had supplied to him. She told him she would try to get what information she could, but not for him to get his hopes up.

She glanced at her cellphone when it vibrated. It was her boss from the law firm she was employed at. She excused herself to take the call, and about five minutes later, she returned to the weight room and regretfully announced she had to leave because her boss needed her to help with a last-minute deposition.

Before she left the weight room, he hugged her, wishing the experience she had with the adults she likely trusted the most who shattered her heart never happened.

9

For the last two weeks—since Dylan's burial—Heather confined herself to the bedroom, only leaving it to use the bathroom, though sometimes she went in the bed. Not because she didn't give a shit, but because she was consumed with depression and couldn't conjure up the strength to get out of the bed.

Mike did his best to stay strong for her sake. He also tried to sustain a living at the house, but with him being the only one working, they were back to struggling financially again. He didn't burden her with this information though. He simply spoke to their creditors and made arrangements to pay what he could. Most were sympathetic; others were complete douchebags.

The reality was they would no longer be able to stay in the house if Heather wasn't going to return to work—and soon.

They would have to move back in with his mother—once again—until they got back on their feet.

Now, the day Heather and Mike returned from Dylan's burial, she immediately packed her bags and attempted to leave, but Mike blocked her at the front door and convinced her to stay.

Or so he thought he did. The truth was she didn't stay because of his sweet-talking soliloquy he orated. She stayed for her own reasons. She wanted to be close to the spot where Dylan died, where he took his own life, and for the first week, she spent all of her minutes in the bathroom inside of the bathtub. She ate in it; she slept in it. The white plastic of the inside of the bathtub was tarnished with Dylan's blood, the blood that pooled from the gashes in his wrists and neck, the gashes Dylan inflicted using razors from an unopened package of disposable razors that sat underneath the bathroom basin for who knows how long.

Mike knocked on the bedroom door and opened it. Heather was balled up with her knees to her chest, laying on her side. He didn't dare sit on the bed next to her nor touch her. He wouldn't make that mistake again. And she did provide him with notice. She made it clear she did not want his murderous hands touching her ever again when they returned from Dylan's burial.

"I fixed you a plate of food," he whispered.

But she didn't budge. He didn't repeat himself or try to wake her up. He set the plate of piping hot food onto her dresser, which was situated directly across from their bed. He hoped the scent of the slow-cooker-prepared pot roast with potatoes and carrots would function like a smelling salt and snap her out of her slumber.

He waited a few minutes for her to wake up, but she didn't. She was resting almost as peacefully as Dylan was. Only her light snores every once in a while confirmed she was still alive.

He returned to the kitchen and dished himself a plate of the pot roast and vegetables, then sat at the table and started to eat.

He buttered a few slices of bread and placed some of the meat and potatoes and carrots on them, folding each slide in half, which made what he called a fancy American taco.

He finished one of the three taco-like pieces of bread. He placed his face in his hands and rubbed his eyes with his fingertips.

"Dad?" Dylan asked.

Mike didn't remove his hands from his face nor did he open his eyes. He was emotionally drained and didn't want to deal with Dylan's ghost again.

"I already know what you're going to say," Mike muttered. "I'm your killer."

"Why'd you do it, Daddy?"

"I didn't, son. Honestly, I didn't. I never wanted you dead. I never wanted to hurt you."

"Then why did you?"

"I didn't!" he screamed as he pounded his fist on the table.

The laugh of an innocent child ensued. Mike looked around the kitchen, but Dylan wasn't around anymore. Looking down at his plate, Mike picked up one of the two pieces of folded-up bread, one of which had a small bite taken out of it, as if a child had bitten it.

Mike whispered: "I'm sorry, son. I didn't mean to yell at you."

At about that time, Heather galumphed into the kitchen with her head slumped down, carrying the plate of food he had brought into the room no more than ten minutes prior. She pulled out a chair from the kitchen table—Dylan's chair—and placed the plate of food in front of her. Her hair covered her eyes and she kept her head beveled towards the plate.

"Please eat," Mike said, his voice straining.

"Is this supposed be a fucking joke?" she asked.

"What?"

"It's bad enough you killed our son, but now you're bragging about it."

"I've said a thousand times. I didn't kill Dylan."

She scoffed. "Liar. If you would have bound his hands and feet like I wanted, Dylan would be here today."

"I'm not culpable for Dylan's death." About three seconds later, he asked: "What did you mean by I'm bragging?"

"Maybe bragging wasn't the right word, but you're plunging the knife which stuck out of my heart into my back by making Dylan's favorite dinner."

She continued to stare down at the plate of food with her hair covering her eyes.

"I thought it would be a nice gesture. I thought it would be a way for us to remember and celebrate Dylan."

"Celebrate? I bet you are celebrating now that bastard of a burden is no longer here to tie you down. Am I right?"

He almost lunged up and slapped, just as he did one other time long before they got married when she mouthed off at him. She pressed charges initially, but then dropped them.

"I never wanted Dylan dead," Mike insisted. Then after a two-second pause. "Please eat a little something. If not for me, for Dylan."

She hadn't eaten much of anything over the past two weeks. She'd nibble on a bagel or swipe a piece of cheese out of the mini-fridge in their bedroom, but nothing other than that.

She stood, picked up the plate of food, and slammed it vertically onto the linoleum floor before falling to the floor and rolling in the food and broken glass like a pig in mud. "This is me celebrating Dylan! This is me celebrating our fucking son is dead! He's fucking dead! And I will be soon, too!" She grabbed a handful of food with both hands and smeared over her face and into her hair as she cackled like an evil witch. She picked up a remnant of broken glass and placed it to her wrist whilst continuing to roll side to side in the mess. "Mommy's coming to see you, Dylan! Get ready for the Mommas!"

Before she could inflict injury onto her wrist, Mike intervened by lunging towards her and pushing the hand grasping the sharp shard of glass away from the wrist over her head. She was pinned to the ground but mercilessly fought to break free. Fearing she was a threat to herself and to him, he kept her pinned down with his body weight and prevented her two arms—which were also pinned to the ground with one of his arms—from moving while using his other arm to phone 911.

No more than three minutes later, paramedics and police arrived on the scene. Heather was placed on a gurney, tied down, and loaded into the back of an ambulance.

Mike left the mess on the kitchen floor. He needed to help ensure his wife would be okay. He initially was going to ride in the back of the ambulance with her, but decided it would be best if he drove himself.

When the ambulance drove away, he turned towards the house, the inside of which was illuminated. Standing in the house behind the glass front door was Dylan. He placed his wrists and face onto the glass door. A deluge of blood fell from his neck and both wrists.

Mike covered his mouth in horror and closed his eyes for two—three seconds—tops. When he opened them back up, reality was restored. He walked inside the house and packed a few belongings for Heather—some clothes, toiletries, and her cellphone and charger. When he picked the tote bag off the bed and turned around to walk out the bedroom door, Dylan stood in the doorway looking into his parents' bedroom.

"Please help me help your mom," Mike said.

"Why'd you kill me, Daddy?" Dylan asked as blood started to exude from the slits in his neck.

"I didn't, son. I swear, I didn't."

"Why did you let the bad shadow person do this to me?"

Mike shook his head, confused. "What shadow person? What are you talking about, Dylan? Tell me."

But Dylan faded away.

Mike walked out of the bedroom into the living room with his head down since he was checking messages on his cellphone. Once in the living room, he lifted his head up, then dropped the tote bag and gasped. A single word was repeatedly painted in a reddish-hued substance in capital letters and in different sizes across the walls, ceiling, and furniture. The word: KILLER. He stared at the floor, which initially didn't have the word written on it, but then it started to appear—a letter at a time—as if someone was writing it.

The sound of Dylan chuckling startled Mike. Then Dylan said: "That's you, Daddy. You're the killer—an accomplice to murder. And when you die, you're going to straight to Hell to become Satan's whore."

Mike grabbed the tote bag and rushed out of the house without closing the front door.

10

The four of them—Derrick, Danielle, Codi, and Andrew—were lying on their towels on the beach, soaking in some sun and listening to the waves crash onto the shore of Lake Michigan. The gentle breeze was a warm welcome, offering a brief reprieve from the excessive heat and humidity.

Codi and Andrew both had their ear buds crammed in and wouldn't hear an atomic explosion if one occurred.

Wiping sweat from his brow using his White Sox towel, Derrick placed his hand on top of Danielle's, but said nothing. She gently caressed his palm with her long, painted nails.

"Do you think I tried to kill myself?" Derrick asked.

Danielle turned to him, lying on her side, propping her head up with her arm. "Honestly?"

"Of course."

"I don't know what to think. You left my house pretty angry that night. I'm actually relieved you don't remember what happened that night." She covered her mouth. "I've said too much already."

"What do you mean?"

She hesitated to answer him and lay back down, but this time on her stomach. She attempted to deflect attention by asking Derrick to put some suntan lotion on her back, which he did, but still pressed her for answer.

It didn't make sense to him why she was keeping information from him. Though it angered him, he managed to keep his emotions under wraps.

"I promised your dad I wouldn't say anything," she said. "He doesn't want me stirring the pot, he doesn't want you to remember."

"Remember what?"

"That night, the argument, the attempted suicide."

But this made Derrick want to remember the events even more so now than ever. Still, though, no pervasive memory sprang forth.

He stood and walked into the water, trying to make sense of why his dad didn't want him to remember that night. Now, his suspicions peaked. Was it possible the argument between the two of them was so heated, his dad tried to strangle him—like that one time before—and plant his body and stage the scene at the baseball field to make it appear it was a suicide?

Now the waves were crashing against Danielle's legs just as they were against Derrick's. She placed a hand on his shoulder and he started to sob, but then tried to stifle.

But Danielle encouraged him to cry and to not be afraid to shed his suit of armor and show his softer side.

"Why wouldn't he want me to remember?" he asked.

"To protect you," she said.

"From what?"

"Yourself."

11

A six-foot-two slender man wearing mechanics overalls and boots sped near the tree in the woods and hopped off his motorcycle. From inside one of the saddlebags, he pulled out a metal wire having roughly the same thickness as a cellphone charger cable and the length of a standard jump rope—which is exactly what he intended to use the wire as. A rope.

He wrapped the metal wire around the tree and threaded one end of the metal wire through the noose at the other end. He slipped his neck through the noose, then checked his wrist to see what time it was and how much time was left. He removed his wedding ring and iWatch—he didn't need these things anymore, especially for where he was going.

He swung his leg over the seat of his Honda CBR1000 and started it up. He revved the engine a few times before releasing the brake and speeding off into the night. An instant later, what he saw changed at a breakneck pace. He saw concrete followed by night sky followed by concrete followed by weeds, gradually fading to darkness—and then nothing but.

His motorcycle ghost rode into some thick brush, where it crashed to a stop.

12

Sitting at her vanity in her room, Melanie morphed her hand into a pistol—the barrel of which she inserted into her mouth—the same way the man on the TV did. Then she pulled the trigger by pushing her thumb forward and back again. No sound effects though. She did hear the sound of the gun firing in her mind though, and then she imagined what her head would look like after the bullet exited it.

But once wasn't enough. She did it several times, all while compelling herself to understand what it must have felt like when the bullet ripped through the man's brains and skull.

The image of the blood gushing from the man's nose and exit wound hadn't escaped her, and it was as prevalent in her mind as it was when she first bore witness to it.

She also asked herself questions. Why did the man do it? Why was he so sad or mad? Was there an alternative to him killing himself? What's it like to die? What's it like after we die?

In the reflection of her mirror, she saw the little boy around her age standing behind her again. His eyes were closed and his head was angled towards the ground.

"Who are you?" she asked.

And this wasn't the first time she confronted him either. But he didn't answer. About four seconds after she asked her question, he opened his eyes, which were black. She screamed and her mom rushed into her room, and this was something she had never seen before.

"What happened, honey?" Roberta asked.

"There was a boy in my room. He was scary. His eyes were dark as your hair."

"Are you sure that's what you saw?"

"Yes, mommy. Why don't you believe me?"

Roberta rubbed Melanie's head and assured her it wasn't that she didn't believe her but that she wanted to make absolutely sure what she thought she saw was actually a boy, and not a shadow or something like that, since Roberta herself had passed by Madison's room a few times. There were also shadows of tree branches on her walls—and her mirror—from outside the window that occasionally swayed to and fro due to a gust of wind.

Melanie emphatically insisted there was a little boy in her room. Roberta shuffle Melanie out of the bedroom and they walked to the nearby park.

13

After Derrick dropped a heaping pile of homemade mashed potatoes onto Bruce's plate, he took his seat at the dinner table and cut into his meatloaf.

Bruce poured himself another shot of whiskey and slammed it down in a New York second.

"Dad, I have a question for you?" Derrick said.

"If it's about that dead bitch mother of yours, don't ask," Bruce bellowed, then belched.

"It's not about her. I have a question about something else."

"Yeah? What?"

Derrick smeared some mashed potatoes onto a bite-sized piece of meatloaf, then placed a carrot coin on top of it before placing it into his mouth. Bruce struggled with hand-eye coordination, inebriated out of his mind, unable to get the fork into his mouth without stabbing his lip or cheek.

The oven timer dinged and Derrick sprang out of his seat as if he had sat on a spike. He pulled the crescent rolls out of the oven and dropped two onto Bruce's plate.

"The night I attempted suicide at the baseball field," Derrick said. "I wanted to ask you something about it."

"Well, go on, ask then," Bruce snapped. *What lie should I tell him now? I don't want him to remember.*

"Were you there that night? Did you intervene somehow?"

Bruce twiddled some of the hairs in chevron mustache, a few fell out and garnished his meatloaf. Derrick snickered, but played dumb, not sharing what he saw.

"Dad? Will you tell me?" Derrick asked.

"No, I wasn't there," Bruce replied. "I was here drunk off my ass. I drank until I passed out. The ring of my cellphone woke me up."

"You're telling me the truth?"

As if someone pulled a lever, Bruce's demeanor flipped. "Yes! That's all I tell! I'm not going to lie! You understand me? You ask me a question, I'll give you an honest fucking answer! If you ask me do I want to fuck Donald Trump I'm going to be like: Ewww! Fuck that shit! Now leave me the hell alone about that night!"

Unsure whether to laugh or be afraid, Derrick shot between the middle and played it safe, not showing any emotion at all. Bruce resumed eating his meatloaf—chevron hairs and all.

Why did that voice say my dad intervened and ruined my death?

(Because your dad DID intervene.)

14

"I don't know," Mike said. "She just snapped," referring to Heather. He was observing her through a one-way mirror.

"It's probably a good thing you had her brought here," Lauren said. "She'll be in good hands."

Heather sat on the floor in an empty padded room with her knees to her chest. She rocked slightly back and forth. Occasionally she glanced at the back of her wrist. Sometimes she would even run her finger across it a few times—a behavior Mike saw her do on occasion at home.

"How often did she do that?" Lauren asked.

"Do what?"

"Inspect the back of her wrist?"

"A few times. Why?"

Lauren shrugged her shoulders and wrote a note on her notepad. Mike looked on at Heather, reminiscing about happier times with his now mentally-distraught wife. Their courting years when Mike was the king of romance, their wedding when it seemed they would never have any problems and life would be nothing but roses and sunshine and laughter and love.

"But you can't say for sure, right?" Lauren asked.

"No, I had to work, but Stacey might be able to tell me."

"Who's she?"

"Our babysitter and my wife's best friend."

Though Mike didn't have a fancy doctoral degree like Lauren did, he was smart enough to pick up on the fact there was significance to Heather looking at her wrist, believing it extended beyond her concern for him and his wife.

He sent Stacey a quick text asking for her best guess as to how often in a twenty-four hour period Heather glanced or touched her wrist. He also asked her if she ever said anything about her wrist.

"Are there any meds she can be given so she can rest at home?" Mike asked.

"I'm sorry, but she will not be going home for at least twenty-four hours, maybe longer depending on the results of the assessments."

"Why?"

"We have a legal obligation to society to ensure she isn't a threat to others or herself. We're already in a shitstorm without an umbrella because of the suicide we had happen on our watch. I'm sure you heard about it?"

He shook his head. "No, I didn't. I've been too busy burying my son and dealing with his accusatory ghost to follow the news. Is my wife safe here?"

"A lot safer than she would be at home where I'm sure there are at least a hundred different ways she could inflict harm on herself there."

Rocking back and forth in the padded room, Heather glanced at her wrist again. Then she caressed it. Lauren made another tally mark on her pad. That was Lauren's seventh time in a ten-minute period, according to her observational notes.

Mike asked if he would be able to stay in the observation room a while longer. He was too afraid to go back home, especially after the accusatory message Dylan left for him in the living room.

15

Though the coffee was cold and tasted like something siphoned from a septic tank, it still managed to hit the spot, at least in Thomas' view. Sitting in front of him on the kitchen table was the urn containing the ashes of his ex-wife.

The dimly lit kitchen coupled with the rumbling of thunder gave Thomas the sensation something was lurking in the shadows—and perhaps there was.

Tonight was the first night Nikki and Ashlee were in their new permanent home. At the time Thomas was sitting in the kitchen having a heart-to-heart with his wife's remains, his two children were upstairs in their room.

Nikki—wearing a teal nightgown—shuffled into the kitchen and poured herself a glass of tea. At the circular table, she sat next to her dad.

Thomas unwrapped a Twix bar, but he didn't nibble at it right away like he usually did.

After Nikki placed her hand on the side of her mother's urn, she said: "I hope you're resting peacefully in Heaven."

"I'm sure she is," he said to her.

"I looked at the other room. I think I could have it cleared out in a few days."

The room was chock-full of boxes stacked to the ceiling. When Thomas moved into his new house—which he didn't own but rented—many of the boxes he didn't unpack, choosing to leave his belongings in their boxes. He had his reasons.

But then his perceptions shifted. Still, though, he never got around to going through the contents of the boxes and putting the things where they belonged. It made no difference though. As far as Thomas was concerned, it was better this way.

"I think it would be best if we go through the boxes together," Thomas said. "I need to know where things are." He started to nibble the top layer of his Twix like a rabbit to a carrot.

"I didn't plan on rummaging and organizing your possessions," she said. "I was going to move the boxes from the room to the garage."

"Oh, angel, we can't put all of those boxes in the garage. I won't be able to park my car in there if we do that."

"Dad, you promised me I would have my own room here if I moved in with you."

A rage ignited within him. He wanted to backhand his daughter—much the same way his dad and mom did to him for so much as looking at them cross-eyed—but he didn't. He was appalled at her lack of appreciation for what he was trying to do for them as well as her selfish attitude.

"You will have your own room," he said as he chewed up the cookie layer of the Twix. "I am a man of my word. I need you to be a little more patient though, okay?"

She placed her cup in the sink and went back upstairs to go to bed. In between those two events she managed to plunge a knife in his chest by kissing her mother's urn goodnight but not him. He let it slide.

A few moments after she left the room, his cellphone jingled. The news wasn't good. Another suicide.

16

When Derrick stormed into his dad's room, the blankets and sheets on Bruce's bed were rapidly rising and falling, as if they were the lungs of the bed, in which case the bed was hyperventilating.

But actually it was Bruce and someone else—Derrick presumed Gayle—who were the ones hyperventilating.

"You're hiding stuff from me and I'm going to find out what it is!" Derrick announced before making his grand exit by stomping out of Bruce's room, slamming the bedroom door behind him.

Chris Rellim

THE UMBRA

CHAPTER 5

1

Walking hand in hand with Danielle along the sidewalk of Olivia Court, Derrick reminded himself how lucky he was to have a girl like her. He never understood what she saw in him, but he didn't care. Nor did he question it.

They were on their way to Chesterville League Park—where the ballpark Derrick attempted suicide was located. They both hoped that by being in the exact location of where Derrick's attempted suicide took place, he may remember something.

Two kids on tricycles chased each other on the sidewalk on the opposite side of the street, laughing along the way. *Enjoy your childhood while it lasts,* Derrick thought.

Though Derrick's childhood wasn't all peaches and cream, it wasn't nearly as bad as those of other children in the nation. Indeed, Bruce exploited Derrick and was essentially an absentee parent, but in spite of this Derrick had a relatively decent home life.

Danielle asked Derrick about how things were between him and Bruce since the night Derrick stormed into Bruce's bedroom and accused him of withholding information from him.

"Things are better. We talked the following morning about it," Derrick said. "After I stormed into his bedroom and confronted him, he leapt out of bed and chased after me."

"What was he doing?"

"Sliding his stick in Gayle." *I think it was Gayle.*

Danielle gasped. "Eww. Gross. You walked in on your dad doing the nasty with Gayle again?"

"I didn't see anything this time. The room was dark. Both he and Gayle—I think it was Gayle—were under the sheets and covers."

"So, you really don't know who he was with then, right?"

"Not with absolute certainty, no."

She smiled. "I'm relieved to hear that."

Now they stood on the sidewalk in front of the Chesterville League Park near one of the two outfields the field had. Later the field would be filled with players and parents, sports enthusiasts and spectators.

As they stood in front of the field, a car pulled up next to them and honked. The passenger window descended. "Need some laces?" the passenger, Jason Robbins, said, cackling at his own remark.

After chuckling at Jason's remark, the driver Brian said: "Follow through this time! Don't choke this time!"

Derrick lowered his head. Danielle ran towards the car, but before she could strike Jason with her fist, the driver punched the gas and hauled ass away.

"Ignore them, Derrick," Danielle said, rubbing the back of his neck.

"I hate those guys. I hope they crash and burn." He removed his glasses and wiped the lenses clean.

"I agree they're assholes, but don't wish them dead unless you mean it."

"Why the fuck not?" Derrick snapped. "They just wished me to be dead. They just encouraged me to kill myself."

"It's beneath you."

Walking hand in hand again, they crossed the threshold from the spectator area to the baseball field. Derrick asked Danielle to wait near third base—which is where he hoped to get with her later that day in his room—while he walked to the area he was found by Officer Chubbs.

While heavy-footing it to the spot where his near-dead body was discovered, he thought he saw an opaque figure—a *shadow* figure—of a person bolt across the outfield as it was rapidly—almost instantaneously—fading away.

He turned to Danielle, but her head was down perusing her cellphone, chuckling. He didn't asked her if she saw it; the answer was obvious.

All at once the sky went from brightness to deathly darkness. A storm front was moving in unexpectedly.

But this didn't stop Derrick from trying to retrace his steps from that near-fatal night when his shoelaces snaked around his neck and strangled him—almost to death.

After a blinding flash of lighting came and went, he closed his eyes and let go of the harnesses of his mind. Flashes of the events that occurred that night played in his mind. In between the bright flashes of recollection were nothing but darkness—much like the sky above his head.

A hand touched Derrick on his shoulder and he shuddered.

"Did you remember anything?" Danielle asked.

"Bits and pieces," he said. He paused for two seconds. "I know I didn't try to kill myself though."

2

With a swift kick from Scott's worker's boot, Aaron's door flung open and struck the wall. Aaron sprang out of bed and onto the floor like a piece of bread from an overzealous toaster. Emily started to cry from her crib.

Scott swept his hand across Derrick's writer's desk, pushing everyone atop of it to the floor. Then he flipped the desk over as if it were a fellow wrestler in a ring.

"What the hell did you need four-hundred dollars for that you had to forge another one of my checks?" Scott demanded to know. He kicked the swivel chair out of his way. "I'm not working for you to steal my money, Aaron!"

But Aaron offered no response. His eyelids were heavy and he was zonked out on the floor. That didn't stop Scott from continuing his tirade though.

"Now guess what I've got to do? I've got to take out a payday loan just to make sure we don't fall behind on our mortgage!" he shouted. "Do you like the living on the street? Do you? Because that's where we're going to end up if you keep stealing my money from the family."

Brandon stepped into Aaron's room with his lower jaw looking like a necktie. And about a few seconds later—four tops— Karen entered holding the baby.

"I can't believe you would do this, Scott," Karen said. "Look at the damage you've done to the room, to the door, to the stuff on the floor."

"It's not going to matter none," Scott said. "This kid right here stole more money from my checking account."

"Oh, no. Aaron, that was a bad thing you did," Brandon told his older brother. "Right, dad?"

"Yeah, it's a despicable thing to do," Scott said, shaking his head like one of those bobble head people. "And as far as the damage goes, who cares? We're going to be living in a dumpster behind the Dollar General on 169th thanks to this piece of shit bastard."

Karen stomped her foot. "He's not a bastard. He's your son, Scott."

"Why are you always sticking up for him? Do you even care about the damage he's done to us as a family? The trouble and turmoil he's caused all of us?"

"What he did was wrong. I'm not disputing that, but you shouldn't be calling your own flesh and blood bad names. That's just how I feel. That's my opinion," Karen said. "You love your kids no matter what."

This remark sent Scott into a rage. He was fed up with being the only one in the household working while Karen did next to nothing except occasionally made a meal or two and made sure the baby was taken care of—well, most of the time.

During Scott's rant, Brandon ran out of the room with his fingers in his ears. He took refuge in his room, slamming the door and locking it. Scott shouted from Aaron's room: "You better watch it! You want a whoopin'? Don't be slamming the fucking doors in the house! Only I can slam and kick the doors."

And then he did. He punctured Aaron's door several times with his fist.

Karen replied after he was done yelling. She said: "Sometimes I wish I were dead." Then she walked out of the room.

"What did you say?" Scott asked, irritated.

"I said I sometimes wish I were dead. Then things would be easier for you."

"You should be careful with what you say. It might come true."

"Is that a threat, Scott? Are you threatening me now?"

"Fuck off. Shut up."

Lightly nudging Aaron with his foot, Scott asked for Aaron to explain his actions. Moaning and groaning like a sick animal, Aaron pulled the blanket over his head.

"I'm about fed up with you," Scott said to Aaron. "You better just watch yourself around here."

Scott walked from Aaron's room to Brandon's door. He knocked it two times with the second knuckle of his pointer finger. Brandon opened the door and looked up at his dad.

Before Scott said anything, he knelt down and hugged Brandon. Then he said: "I'm sorry for losing my temper."

Brandon looked at the inside of his palm and with a finger traced some of the lines in it. He sighed. "But, dad, that's what you always say. You get super mad, go insane, and then apologize."

"I know. I need to work on my anger issues. I'll try and find someone who can help me get a grip on my anger. Does that make you feel better?"

After a brief pause, Brandon lightly nodded. Scott stood, rustled up Brandon's hair, and walked away, going downstairs.

3

"It was a shadow man," Ashlee said. "He was standing by Mommy's urn in the family room."

Thomas sat up in his bed, flipped on a light switch, and lit a smoke. "Are you sure that's what you saw, sugar bear?" he asked, struggling to believe her.

Ashlee nodded her head. In her hand was a teddy bear Thomas gave to her a few years ago as a no-special-occasion gift. She slept with it every night since then.

"By Mommy's urn?" he asked.

As a family, it was decided to move the cremated remains of Sharon in the china cabinet in the family room along with some other of Sharon's items she treasured during her time on Earth.

Thomas picked Ashlee up and caressed her back. She coughed and choked from the stench of his cigarette smoke. He snuffed out the cigarette in the Chicago Cubs ash tray and walked downstairs to the family room.

The room was a ghost town. Nobody there.

4

"You can't be serious," Ben said. He rolled his dress shirt sleeves up to his elbows. He sat on edge of the table in the interview room looking down at the person he was questioning. "You say it looked like he *didn't* want to kill himself even though he tightened the extension cord that was already around his neck by pulling on it in opposing directions?"

The woman to whom Ben asked that question folded her arms. The name tag on her blouse read KELLY, and above that was the company name, which was called RICORDANZA. The woman folded her arms and locked eyes with Ben's.

"I saw it with my own eyes," she said.

5

"Come on, darling. It's time to go," Roberta said to Melanie, who was skirting across the monkey bars at the local playground. "We've got to get home."

"Can I go down the slide one more time before we leave?" Melanie asked, her eyes wide. She had a pair of big brown eyes that you didn't want to say no to when she asked for something.

"Okay, darling, but let's hurry, okay?"

"Okay, Mommy!"

Melanie jogged in an uncoordinated manner to the ladder and ascended it. When she reached the top, she walked towards the slide, but stopped about halfway along the platform and turned around—as if someone had called her name.

Only being able to see Melanie's backside, Roberta moved to a different spot to get a closer look at her. A few seconds after Roberta got into position, Melanie turned to her mother, then two seconds later back again.

"Come on, Melanie. It's time to go," Roberta said.

Melanie put up a finger.

"No, not in a minute. Now, please."

"I'm talking right now! Wait!" Melanie screamed, stomping her foot on the platform.

Under normal circumstances, Roberta would have reprimanded Melanie swiftly, but she was intrigued with Melanie talking to nobody and decided to let Melanie finish up her conversation.

Melanie extended her hand out and moved it up and down, as if shaking hands with someone in spite of nobody being in front of her. She slid down the slide. When she reached the bottom, Roberta was there to greet her.

"Who were you talking to?" Roberta asked.

"A boy. He's really nice," Melanie responded. "He's the boy who was in my room that one day. Remember?"

"What's his name again." *How long has she been interacting with this boy spirit? What does he want with her?*

Melanie put a finger to her chin. "I can't tell you. He told me not to tell you. He told me not to tell anyone."

"Why can't you tell me? What does he have to hide?"

There wasn't a word spoken. Melanie shrugged her shoulders.

Not overly concerned about Melanie interacting with a spirit—which she did as a child herself—Roberta made the decision to not make a fuss about it.

Roberta did, however, make a mental note to reach out to other single moms and get Melanie involved in a play group, get her to make some friends—*real* friends, friends made up of flesh and bone.

Once Melanie was buckled into the back seat, Roberta stabbed a straw into a juice box and handed it to her. When Roberta opened the driver's side door of her 2003 Ford Taurus, it generated an ear-grating shriek. The hinges needed some WD-40 badly, but it was the furthest thing from Roberta's mind most of the time.

As they drove back home, Melanie said: "The boy I talked to is dead."

Roberta abruptly pulled over and turned to Melanie. "Say that again for Mommy, please." Every atom in her body trembled.

After a light chuckle, Melanie complied with her mom's request. "The boy. My new friend. He's a ghost, Mommy."

"I know. Can you tell me how he died?"

Melanie scratched her head. "Hmmm… I don't know." She turned to her left. "How did you die? My mommy wants to know." she asked nobody visible to Roberta. Melanie nodded as if someone was responding to her. A few seconds later, she said: "Sorry, Mommy, but he said for you to mind your own fucking business."

Roberta gasped. "Excuse me, young lady? You don't talk to me like that. Understand?"

"But, Mommy, he told me to tell you that. I was only repeating what he told me to say."

Being a good sport, Roberta turned to the empty seat next to Melanie. "Little boy ghost. This is Melanie's mother speaking. Listen to me. If you want to be friends with my daughter, you can't use profanity around her. Do you understand me?" Two seconds later, she added: "Good."

But then Melanie relayed a message to her mother from the boy ghost. She said: "He said for you to go slip your neck in a noose," Melanie said. "He said he can't wait to see your swinging corpse. He wants to try and bust it open like the piñata he had at his last birthday party."

Roberta tried to mask her feelings of fright. Her body juddered. What shocked her even more is how Melanie repeated the awful things the boy ghost was telling her to say as if she didn't understand the meaning behind them.

Pissed beyond belief on the outside but terrified on the inside, Roberta let the pissed part of her handle the situation. She flung open her car door, exited the vehicle, and opened the driver's side back door.

"Mommy? What are you doing?" Melanie asked.

To the boy ghost, Roberta said: "Listen—little boy ghost. You need to find a different ride. You're no longer welcome in my car. Stay away from my daughter, stay out of my car, and stay out of my house."

Melanie covered her mouth and giggled.

"No, Melanie, this isn't funny," Roberta snapped. And to the boy ghost: "Come on! Get out!"

Now Melanie pointed towards Roberta, who turned around to see what Melanie was pointing at, and when she did, she screamed after bumping into a man.

"I'm sorry. I didn't know you were behind me," Roberta said.

In a thick Bronx accent, the man said: "Hey, not a problem. I couldn't help but notice you was talking to nobody there. Is everything alright with you? How youse doing today?"

Roberta chuckled at the thought of how she must have looked to the man. He smiled in turn, masking his true concern for her sanity, especially since there was a child under her care.

"Fine. Just fine," Roberta said, nodding her head. "Thank you for asking."

"Hey, forget about it, no problemo. It's just the kinda guy I am, ya know what I mean?" he said, looking up at Roberta, who was a skyscraper compared to him.

Roberta closed the back door and extended her hand and introduced herself. The man shook her hand and did the same.

His name was Jimmy Palmaneti, a recent college graduate. He had a head of thick black hair with barrels of gel incorporated into it. His face was clean-shaven and he reeked of cheap impostor cologne. He was a short fellow, standing only five-foot-one—four inches shorter than Roberta.

"Tell you what," Jimmy said. "Why don't the four of us get a bite to eat together on me, huh? What do youse say?"

"Four?" Roberta asked, bewildered.

"Yeah, you, me, the sweet angel eyes back there along with your ghost."

She smiled. "I guess we could do that, but let me make sure Melanie would be okay with it." *Ghost. Please don't let it be true.*

After getting Melanie's blessing, Jimmy then asked for Roberta and Melanie to decide to go. Soon after, Jimmy was following Roberta and Melanie in his 2018 Cadillac CT6.

6

As Derrick scrambled some eggs in a mixing bowl, Bruce ripped off the rubber band and read the main headline of the A section of The Times—the region's lead newspaper agency. Bruce's mom, Robin, once worked as a newspaper carrier for The Times and treated the job with the same care as a surgeon does their patient. After eight months, she was promoted to an assistant manager.

"Anything good?" Derrick asked.

"The main story is another boring article about the recent spike in suicides," Bruce said. "Hey, maybe they can interview you, huh?" He started to laugh.

"In Chesterville?" Derrick asked, raising a knife behind Bruce's back.

"Yeah… Hey, your psychiatrist Thomas is quoted in here. He has zero explanation for the spike in suicides. All those fancy years of schooling and he's nothing more than a man with no answers."

I wish he would have called me back, Derrick thought. He called Thomas' office number once more and this time received a response. Thomas apologized for not getting back to Derrick sooner, admitting he hadn't even had a chance to listen to all of the voicemails on his phone since he was too busy dealing with suicides within the BAU. Thomas informed Derrick they didn't perform any heavy-duty neurological tests, but that he shouldn't be concerned.

When Derrick stepped into the kitchen after the call, Bruce held up his coffee cup and obnoxiously cleared his throat. Derrick stopped chopping up the green pepper for the omelet and played a quick game of step-and-fetch with Bruce. After Derrick refilled Bruce's cup with coffee, he set down three French Vanilla creamers in front of Bruce.

Once the vegetables were chopped, Derrick added them to the whipped eggs, did a rough stir, and poured the mixture into the skillet.

"Once more, I'm sorry for barging in on you that one night," Derrick said.

"It's alright. You were upset. Please understand if I keep things from you, it's for your own good."

"Can I be nosy and ask who you were making thunder under the covers with that night I barged into your room?"

"Who do you think?"

"Gayle?"

Bruce sipped his coffee without acknowledging Derrick's question. Derrick furiously scraped the eggs in the skillet, destroying the omelet Bruce requested for breakfast. To boot, he sprinkled in a little pick-me-up seasoning into the now-scrambled eggs.

One of Bruce's passive-aggressive tactics he used was ignoring. Derrick wouldn't have cared if Bruce told him to fuck off or it's none of your business—at least that would have been something other than blatantly ignoring his question.

"We've got to register me for school," Derrick said. "I'd also like to visit some college campuses next summer."

"Oh, really? What campuses?" Bruce asked.

We've talked about this before, Derrick thought. "Yale. Harvard. Stanford."

Bruce whistled. "Whoa, wow. And how do you expect to pay for tuition? Do you know how much it costs for a single year—*not* including summers—to attend any one of those schools? And do you even have the grades to attend a school like that?"

Another one of Bruce's flaws was his lack of involvement in Derrick's education. He never once asked to see a report card. Never once took time to access Derrick's grades during the school year to keep up on his progress. If it wasn't broke, don't fix it—or put another way, if the school didn't sound any alarms, don't worry.

"My grades are good," Derrick said. He scraped some eggs onto a plate for Bruce.

"Are they good *enough*?"

"Yes. They are good enough. I need to focus on the SAT. I was thinking about taking an SAT prep class."

Derrick was being modest, and not all that direct either. He was a straight-A student, and had been since seventh grade. Bruce never attended any of the awards ceremonies.

"How good is good?" Bruce asked.

"Straight As, Dad," Derrick replied.

"Oh."

"But I need to start preparing these college admissions tests. SATs. ACTs. I need to find some classes to help me better prepare."

Bruce scoffed. "Why don't you just get a job, save, and pay that asshole we've been hearing about in the news who doctors up SAT scores or pays off coaches and college administrators to get students admitted."

"No way. I'm going to get admitted because I'm one of the chosen ones. Because I earned it."

"I'm just the opposite. I takes what Is can gets."

Derrick dropped the plate of eggs in front of Bruce. The plate crashed onto the table. Some of the eggs bounced off the plate and landed in Bruce's lap.

"What's wrong with you?" Bruce asked.

"It was an accident," Derrick said.

"Just like you."

"What's your problem all of a sudden?"

"Nothing. Forget it. Anyway, if you really want to go to a school like Harvard or Yale you better start working and making some money. You can't assume you'll get a full-ride scholarship to one of those schools. Besides, there are still other expenses even if you did."

"Aren't you going to help me pay for college expenses?"

"Sure—I'll help…some. But I don't have a quarter of a million dollars to pay for four years of school for you."

"But you do have money in an account set aside for my college expenses?"

"Not exactly, but I'll contribute something. You'll still want to get yourself some employment and start saving yourself though." *Maybe I can charge him a little rent.*

Bruce crammed a forkful of the eggs in his mouth and three seconds later spat them out. He rushed to the kitchen sink and did several rinse-spits. Derrick tried his best not to laugh, but it wasn't easy.

Curious as to how bad the eggs tasted, Derrick picked up a little piece out of the skillet and placed it one his tongue. Two seconds later, he spat it out and ran to the bathroom to douse the flames burning his tongue.

Derrick returned to the kitchen and put his hand on Bruce's back and apologized for putting cayenne pepper in the eggs. Bruce demanded Derrick whip up a new batch of scrambled eggs—sans cayenne this time.

"By the way, I want to say thank you for telling me that story about my mom last night while we watched the news together," Derrick said.

"Ah, don't mention it," Bruce replied. "I don't even remember what I said." He poured himself a shot of vodka.

"So her name was Ericka, huh?"

"Yeah. Ericka." *Dead bitch she is to me, and that's all she'll ever be—as she will be to you, too, Derrick, if you ever manage to find where she's rest—I mean—residing.*

"What is her last name?"

Bruce slammed the shot glass onto the table. "I don't remember what her last name was—is. I wish you'd let this go." He grinned like the Grinch—ear to ear. "And, actually, you may have to postpone finding your estranged mother."

"Why is that?"

"Because I don't have two-hundred-and-fifty-thousand dollars sitting in a vault or in a Swiss bank account just waiting to be spent on you when you start college. I don't have much money, actually. We may even have to move somewhere else."

(He deserves to die! That fucker doesn't have any money for your college expenses. Bust that bottle of Svedka over that useless booze-soaked brain of his! Then use the jagged glass to slit his throat! Then your own throat!)

"Goddamn it!" Derrick said as he pounded a fist on the table. *[Stop!]*

"What the hell is your problem? How can you be a straight A student but not know with my income and expenses I wouldn't have money to send you off to some nose-in-the-air school?"

The question Derrick now asked himself was whether or not he should tell Bruce about the voice in his head he had been hearing since the night he was admitted to the BAU. He feared Bruce would take him back to the BAU, and if admitted, he would be there for a long time.

Derrick released a sigh. "I guess I'll start working more hours then. Cutting grass. Washing cars. Tutoring in math and science. Other odd jobs."

"Why don't you apply at the local Burger King you and those other goober friends of yours like to eat at?"

"I don't like the idea of working in fast food. Besides, I don't want to be committed to a schedule. I'd rather make my own hours." He cracked some eggs into a mixing bowl.

Bruce raised his coffee cup up and cleared his throat again even more obnoxiously than the first time. After Derrick finished whisking the eggs, he refilled Bruce's coffee and dropped some creamers on the table.

No thank you? Derrick thought. *What an asshole.*

With a meat cleaver, Derrick bisected the green pepper. When the cleaver struck the cutting board, it produced a loud thwack. Then he bisected each of the two halves. *Thwack! Thwack.* As Derrick hacked away at the fresh green pepper, he started to envision the flier he would type up after he finished making and eating breakfast. He thought about what the flier would look like, what it would have on it, what services he would offer along with their respective rates.

"Hey! Why are you butchering the bell?" Bruce asked, referring to the green pepper.

"I'm not," Derrick responded, knowing he really was. He was pissed at Bruce for not saving money for his college expenses. He had years to set aside something, anything.

"Bullshit. Knock it off. I want the pepper pieces to be roughly the same size, damn it."

Derrick raised the meat cleaver above Bruce's head and instantly imagined the meat cleaver's blade puncturing Bruce's head and nothing but hot air whooshing out of his skull, which shrunk and shriveled like a balloon. Derrick lightly snickered at the sight before redirecting his complete attention to finishing breakfast.

After the eggs were finished cooking, Derrick plated them and placed them in front of Bruce. He admonished Derrick for making him scrambled eggs instead of an omelet, but ate it anyway.

7

After Derrick pushed the lawn mower out of the garage, he fired it up and started cutting the grass. While pushing the mower, he had a vision of himself sticking his face into the path of the rotating blade. The sight of blood and tissue and bone flying out of the mower induced Derrick cover his mouth with one hand and clutch his stomach with the other.

(Not a bad way to go, so give it go. Go on! Your destiny is death! I'll talk to you 24-7 until you say the words to let me back in.)

Rather than acknowledge the voice that crept into Derrick's head, he ignored it—just as he had done the last two weeks.

(I'll make you looney! I'll make you beg for death!)

After twenty minutes passed, Derrick was finished with the front yard and pushed the lawn mower to the back. He couldn't help but glance at Coreyann next door who has standing on the deck leading to the above-ground pool her dad had recently installed. She was wearing a solid black bikini, the top piece of which had frills across it.

She waved at him with a slight smile before pinching her button nose and jumping into the water. She screamed from the water's icy chill.

"Why don't you take a break and come over?" she asked.

"That's okay. I don't think I should."

"Why not?"

"I don't know. I wouldn't feel right about it. I'd feel like I'd be cheating on my girlfriend."

Coreyann rolled her eyes. "That's all in your mind. We're just friends. Nothing more, nothing less. It would be two friends swimming together."

"I appreciate the offer, but maybe another time. I've got too much work to do around here. Cut the grass. Type up and distribute fliers. Study."

"Study? Why? It's still summer vacation."

"I know, but I want to be a biochemist, so I need to up my game if I'm going to make it to the big leagues—and when I say big leagues, I mean Ivy Leagues."

"Suit yourself," Coreyann said. She pushed herself backwards using the sidewall of the pool and performed the breaststroke.

Derrick couldn't help but notice her well-endowed Northern states. He shamed himself for looking at another woman and feeling a physical attraction to her, but he reconciled his feelings by remembering Danielle once told him she found Bruce attractive—you know, for an older guy. Derrick shuddered at the thought of his dad and her slapping skins, and worse, the image of the two of their two naked bodies melding together in bed. Hoping to take his mind off of things, he fired up the lawn mower and began cutting the grass.

(Go ahead. Give that rotating blade a kiss—just like you wanted to do to Coreyann's nether-regions. Can you imagine how wonderful a sight it would be for your dad to see? Give it some tongue action like you did Andrew that one time.)

Unwilling to acknowledge the voice, Derrick resumed cutting the grass, but he didn't realize the spirit speaking within his mind could hear his *subconscious* thoughts.

(Try and ignore me, Derrick! It doesn't matter if I get your spirit or not! I just want you dead! I want the satisfaction of seeing you kill yourself!)

Amazing. This inner voice within Derrick's mind finally called him by his actual name for the first time.

8

Sitting on her bed with the lock box Alejandro had told her to take to his attorney, Usha debated whether or not she should open the box and see what's in it or wait for the attorney to do the honors. She also wrestled with bringing the lock box to Ben—one of the two detectives who took her statement the night of Alejandro's suicide.

Next to the lock box was a picture of Alejandro. She picked it up and embraced it, as if it was his physical body. A comforting warmth washed over her from head to toe.

"I know you're here," Usha said. "I can feel you." A few seconds later, she said: "Can I see you? Will you show yourself to me if you're here?"

But he didn't, and Usha chided herself for uttering such nonsense. She set the picture on the bed stand on the left of her bed and picked up the lock box and walked into kitchen, setting the lock box on the counter next to the stove. She pulled out her phone and looked up Esteban Ledesma's law office. She poked her phone a few times and minutes later a lady with a smoker's lung and a baritone voice answered.

"Ledesma and Ledesma Law Office. Alex speaking."

"Yes, sir. I need—"

"Excuse me, miss thing." She coughed several times into the phone—deep, throaty coughs. Hacking coughs. "I'm a female. Thank you."

"I apologize. I need to schedule an appointment with Mr. Ledesma."

"Well, which one? We have three Ledesmas attorneys here at the law firm."

"Esteban."

"Good choice, honey." More coughing and hacking. Usha heard Alex swallow some liquid—it was Fanta. "He's the youngest among the three and he has a nice pair of buns you just want to bite. How soon can you—" She started to cough again. Another swig. Exhale. Now Alex's frog-like voice was back in Usha' ear. "Can you come in Thursday at one?"

"That works for me. I'm Usha, by the way."

"Nice to meet you, Usha. And may I ask what this is in reference to or do you prefer to keep that to yourself until you meet with him?"

Usha paused for a few seconds—three or four—and decided it was best to keep hush-hush. Besides, she had no idea what was inside the lock box, though she hungered to know, and her appetite was growing each passing minute.

"Are you sure you don't want to give some information upfront?" Alex asked. "It might speed up your initial consultation."

"According to Alejandro, Esteban should already know what it is about."

"Who's that?"

"My dead ex-boyfriend." She chided herself for blurting out such an in-your-face response, one of morbidity, too. "Sorry. I didn't mean for me to respond that way. I'm still shaken up by his suicide."

"I'm sorry for your loss, ma'am. I, too, lost a son to suicide many years ago under the strangest of circumstances. Anyhow, I've got you down for one o'clock next Thursday. It was nice to—" An eruption of coughing and throat clearing exploded through the phone. This last for about thirty seconds upon which time the sound of Alex gulping replaced the coughing and throat clearing. "Sorry about that. I'll see you next Thursday at one," she said, her voice horribly strained, sounding as if a ligature was coiled around her neck, much like the extension cord that ultimately killed Timothy Owens two nights ago—a waiter at a local upscale restaurant, Ricordanza.

"See you—"

The sound the call had been terminated stopped Usha from finishing her sentence. She snapped her cellphone back into the case that was clipped to her shorts.

"Why'd you do it, Alejandro?" she whispered. "Why'd you kill yourself with me there?"

The same warmth she felt when hugging his picture embraced her again. She wept.

9

With a stack of fliers printed on neon yellow card stock in his hand and a White Sox cap on his head, Derrick started on Heritage Road—located three streets over from his street Fremont Circle, placing a flier in the mailboxes of the Chesterville residents homes. He never cut across the residents' lawn, but instead would use the driveways, walkways, and sidewalks to get from one house to the other, something his mother encouraged him to do when he helped her deliver newspapers.

As he walked along the walkway to a mailbox, the owner stepped outside. His name was Adam Gray, who recently moved from Texas to Indiana. He was wearing sunglasses and a Cubs baseball cap.

Derrick introduced himself and Adam did the same in kind. When Adam asked Derrick what he needed, Derrick handed him a flier and explained his services and rates and specials. At the bottom of the flier were several coupons for discounts on bundle services. Adam shook Derrick's hand, but respectfully declined the use of any of the services he had to offer. Derrick thanked him for his time and turned around to venture on to other prospective customers' homes.

"Derrick?" Adam said.

"Yes, sir?" Derrick responded as he twirled around.

"Take this." Adam handed Derrick a twenty-dollar bill. "Although I won't need your services, I still would like to contribute to your educational fund raising. Education is important."

"Thank you, kindly."

10

"Dad, I thought you were going to smoke outside," Nikki whined.

Thomas blew smoke from his mouth towards the ceiling. He said, "I'm sorry, angel. I promise I won't smoke in the house anymore." He walked to the back door, opened it, and stepped outside onto the back porch.

Not more than thirty seconds from the time he stepped onto the back porch did his cellphone squawk. He yanked it out of the breast pocket of his shirt and glared at the screen.

"What's up, Doc?" Thomas said.

"Bad news. Another suicide. You better get here."

"Goddamn it. What the hell happened?"

"One of the patients bashed her skull in using the floor." She whimpered for a moment before speaking again. "The scene is gruesome. I'll have nightmares about it until I take my dying breath."

Thomas did what he could to console Lauren as he rushed into the house to tell Nikki she would need to watch Ashlee while he went into work even though it was his vacation time.

"But, dad! We are supposed to start moving the boxes out of the bedroom so I can move my things in there," Nikki said.

"I don't have time to argue right now, angel. Take care of your sister. Answer your phone when I call you. Understand?" When Nikki failed to respond after a few seconds, he spoke with a stern tone. "Do you understand me?"

"Yes! I understand! God! I should just kill myself!"

"Hey! Don't be talking like that! That's enough of the attitude. I'm counting on you to take care of your sister."

"And I counted on you to help me move into my own bedroom that you promised me. Looks like that's never going to happen. I hate it here! Why did I even come here with you!" She stampeded rapidly up the stairs and slammed the bathroom door.

Ashlee—who was sitting on the couch playing a game on Thomas' iPad—shook her head. "She's cruisin' for a bruisin', isn't she, Dad?"

Thomas lightly snickered. "She's just upset right now. She'll calm down soon. I love you."

"I love you, too, Daddy."

He closed the door behind him, started his engine, and fled to the scene.

11

Stumbling and fumbling around in the garage, Aaron could hardly keep his balance, still under the influence of his last OxyContin fix. Drool dribbled off of his chin.

He tripped over a tool chest, but managed to regain his balance before hitting the pavement of the garage floor, latching onto the table saw he had bought for his dad with money he stole from his dad.

The blade of the saw caught his eye. He turned the power saw on and gazed at the stainless-steel blade as it spun around numerous revolutions per second. The teeth of the blade were nothing more than a blur as it spun, and Aaron was thunderstruck at how innocuous the blade appeared—its whirring sound soothing—looking like nothing more than a Frisbee or dinner plate rotating. *The blade looks more dangerous when the saw is off than on,* Derrick thought.

As the table saw whirred, Aaron pulled out a blunt from his shorts pocket, lit it, and inhaled. A cardboard barrel containing an assortment of tools—rakes, hoes, shovels, and edgers—in the corner of the garage had a Kool Kids doll's feet sticking out of it.

Aaron pulled the doll out of the barrel by its leg. Its freckled face had dirt and oil smeared all it; its lips had lipstick on it. The sight of the lipstick induced a chuckle out of Aaron, remembering the situation in which the lipstick eventually ended up on the doll's lips. Aaron and his cousin Autumn had been shooting the shit in the garage while smoking a cigarette followed by another recreational substance. While smoking and chatting, they also drank some wine coolers. Autumn—tripped out of her mind—grabbed the Good Guys doll from Brandon when he walked into the garage with it and started giving it a makeover.

The doll's clothing consisted of a rainbow-patterned shirt and overalls. Out of the box, the Kool Kids doll would be wearing a hat, but Brandon lost to one his doll.

When Aaron squeezed the doll, it said: "What's up? I'm Ricky. What's your name?"

"Fuck off, bitch," Aaron said, chuckling at his own response. "That's my name." He squeezed the doll again.

"I've got a headache from too much laughter. I need to lie down."

The saw blade continued to spin and the motor rotating it continued to whir.

"A headache? Awww. You poor baby. Let me fix that splitting headache for you," Aaron said. He slammed the Kool Kids doll onto the table saw. "Oops." With his face a hair's width away from the Kool Kids chest, he started to push the Kool Kids doll towards the saw blade, a centimeter at a time.

"Aaron?" Brandon shouted.

"Ahh!" Aaron responded in turn. As a knee jerk reaction, he pushed the Kool Kids doll forward. The saw blade bisected its head. He turned to Brandon, who was standing in the doorway of the garage. He turned off the table saw and the motor died. "You realize you nearly killed me just now, right?"

"How?"

"My face nearly hit the blade. Can you imagine Mom or Dad or you walking into the garage and seeing my face spliced in two with blood doused all over the pavement of the garage?"

"I'm sorry. I don't want you to get hurt or die."

Aaron pulled out a cigarette and lit it. He was a Marlboro man and had been since age seven when his other cousin—Shane—let him have a puff of his cigarette—a Marlboro.

"What are you doing now?" Brandon asked as Aaron climbed the steps of a portable ladder.

"Gotta get something. What do you care anyway?"

"Quit being a dick, dick."

"Quit being a fag, fag."

"Why don't you go suck on Lucifer's cock?" Brandon said, giggling. He hardly could get his words out he was giggling so much.

"I can't. You're in the way."

Brandon extended his middle finger.

Now they both were laughing. This was something Aaron and Brandon used to do before Aaron started his deadly dance with drugs. They would hurl insults and nasty directives back and forth, but always in jest.

On top of the rafters in the garage was a plank of plywood. On top of the plywood were several boxes—one of which was labeled AARON'S BABY CLOTHES. The box was about the size of a cooler, the type you'd see carry onto the beach or to a picnic.

"You want to try some?" Aaron asked Brandon as he climbed down the ladder.

"What is it?"

"Disaronno. Can't you read?"

"Fuck yourself."

"Sorry, but I'm not anatomically built to do that."

Brandon had no idea what Aaron meant and he didn't ask for clarification either. Aaron took a drink from the bottle and then another. Disaronno was his favorite alcoholic beverage, introduced to him by his Uncle David a few years ago at a wedding reception. His Uncle David was outside smoking a cigarette—not Marlboro though like Aaron preferred—his brand was Capri, and he didn't smoke from the cigarette directly, but used a French cigarette holder—a black one.

His Uncle David spoke his mind and lacked a social filter. He was quite the diva.

But Disaronno wasn't the first alcoholic beverage Uncle David offered to Derrick while outside Dynasty Banquets—the banquet hall where the wedding reception was held. The first beverage Uncle David offered Aaron was a little Jim Beam. When

Derrick swallowed the shot of Jim Beam, it cleared his sinuses out and caused his eyes to water.

"Want to try some?" Aaron asked Brandon. He lit a fresh cigarette.

"No, thanks. I better not," Brandon replied, sheepishly.

"Quit being a pussy. Try some of this, you'll like it."

"No thanks."

Aaron took another drink from the glass bottle. Brandon walked over to him and pulled the cigarette from in between his fingers. He looked at the cigarette, then back up at Aaron. He closed his eyes for a brief second. When he opened them he dropped the cigarette to the pavement and stomped on the cigarette.

"What the fuck did you do that for, shit stain?" Aaron asked.

"Because I love you and I want you to live a long time."

Brandon walked out of the garage.

12

An ear-piercing scream from another room awoke Penny from her sleep. She sprang out of bed and scurried to the bedroom from where the scream originated, the room of six-year-old Jillian, Penny's daughter.

Penny switched on the hallway light, flung open the Jillian's bedroom door, and stood with her arms folded, sporting a cold, hard stare.

"The shadow man wants me to do bad things," Jillian said, sheepishly. "He wants me to…"

"Wants you to what?" Penny asked, her tone caustic.

Jillian lowered her head and fixed her eyes onto the back of her left wrist. Penny demanded an answer to her question, but Jillian didn't offer one.

Penny flipped on Jillian's bedroom light, causing Jillian to squint her eyes for a few seconds.

"The time left is two-thirteen-forty-two," Jillian said.

"What? It's one-sixteen in the morning," Penny said. "And now it's lights out."

Penny turned off the bedroom light and closed Jillian's bedroom door.

"But, Mommy!" Jillian pleaded. "He wants me to kill—"

"Lights out!"

And indeed—later that night—it was lights out for little Jillian.

Permanently.

13

"All you have to do is kill yourself," Dylan said to Madison. "Then you'll be in Paradise in the Sky with me. Won't that be fun?"

Madison stopped playing with her Legos and looked up at the boy. He smiled at her, but it wasn't a friendly smile. It was a diabolical one.

"But I don't want to die," Madison said. "I love my mommy. She would miss me too much."

"I know you love your mommy. But she doesn't love you. She wants you to die, she wants you out of her life. You cost her too much money."

"She does so love me. Stop lying."

"Don't be afraid to die, Madison. If you want, I could help you."

"No! I won't do it!" she shouted.

With a swift kick, he struck the Lego skyscraper she was building. Several Legos traveled across the room, some of which struck the wall across from her bedroom door.

Roberta stormed into her bedroom and swiftly reprimanded Madison for treating her toys in a poor manner and for making a mess. When Madison blamed the mess on the boy ghost, Roberta demanded she stop making things up and take responsibility for her actions.

14

Sitting in Thomas' office across from his desk, Lauren pulled out a bottle of prescription pills—Valium—and swallowed two of them without the aid of any liquid to help wash them down.

Thomas wrapped his dried lips around a cigarette, swiped a match across the striker, lit his smoke, and shook the match, effectively killing the flame.

They sat silently for several minutes. Thomas was skeptical about Lauren's observations. It seemed illogical.

He dropped his cigarette in an ash tray and tore open a Twix. "What do you think the significance of people obsessed with their wrist is? What does it mean?" he asked.

"I don't know, but it means something. It has to. It's more than a coincidence."

"I disagree. I read the monitoring reports of the orderlies who observed Carl while he was on suicide watch. The orderlies assigned during his suicide watch didn't mention anything about him being preoccupied with his wrist."

"That doesn't mean it didn't happen," she snapped. She grabbed his pack of cigarettes. "All it means is they didn't report it. Maybe they didn't think it was worth reporting. It's a seemingly insignificant thing."

The scent of her body lotion was arousing him, and now wasn't the time for it. He stood and opened his minifridge, pretending to look for something to drink. In reality he was trying to reign his horses back in before he lost control of his urges.

She approached him from behind and reached over his shoulder, grabbing one of the Pepsi cans in his fridge. The scent of the body lotion was even stronger than it was before. He wanted to take her over the desk right then and there. But truth be told, his attraction to her wasn't only the scent of the lotion; it was Lauren herself.

But he knew they would never be an item. She was ten years younger than he was, had a slender frame, and had indicated in passing she would never date men again. Her divorce was too painful—as was the loss of her child—and she refused to risk her heart being broken once again.

"How's this for more than a coincidence?" Lauren asked. The soda can hissed as she pulled the tab to open it. "We have a patient here named Heather. Her son recently committed suicide and he had a preoccupation with his wrist. Now she's a patient of ours and every forty-five seconds or so she glances at her wrist, sometimes caresses it. Now doesn't that tell you something? That maybe there is something we need to watch for when a patient is obsessed with their wrist?"

"No, it doesn't. I think you're overanalyzing."

She swallowed a gulp of Pepsi. "Is that so? So, then what do you conclude about Heather?"

"How did her son commit suicide again?"

"He slit his wrists and neck in the bathtub."

"And there you have it. Her behavior is a manifestation of her son's suicide. Are any other patients overly concerned about their wrists?"

"Some, yes, but I haven't had much time to thoroughly investigate." Thomas asked for her to elaborate since she affirmed she had seen patients other than Heather exhibit a preoccupation with their wrist. "I have to clarify. Though I have seen some patients touch their wrists or glance at their wrists, it doesn't mean they may have an obsession with it. They could have touched their wrist to scratch an itch."

Thomas gave Lauren kudos for pointing out a logical explanation for people touching or glancing at their wrists, but she pressed that it didn't negate the possibility those people she observed scratch or look at their wrist were obsessed with it either. She suggested her and Thomas instruct the orderlies watching the suicidal patients to document when a patient interacts with his or her wrist.

But Thomas disagreed with her, convinced she was turning something out of nothing. He suggested the two of them spend more time with patients and less time in the office on administrative tasks.

"I think that's a good idea," she said.

"Of course it is. I thought of it."

15

As the sun beat down on Derrick's face and sweat dripped off his forehead, he carried on his mission of distributing fliers throughout the Chesterville area.

Throughout the past hour he started distributing the fliers, he had received a few calls already. One caller requested him to walk their dog twice a week. Another caller asked if he would tutor their son in biology when the school year started, the parent hoping to make a preemptive strike at their daughter acing the course.

As he walked down the sidewalk to get to the driveway of the next house, a yard in the distance caught Derrick's eye. Its grass was knee-high. *Maybe the property owner works long hours,* Derrick thought. He hoped the owner of the property would be another source of potential business.

Now he was walking in front of the house with the jungle-like front yard. The resident's mailbox was overflowing with letters and adverts. The morbid—yet realistic thought—of the resident—or worse residents—being deceased in the house lit up in his brain like a bright digital billboard, like the one located in 80-94, the interstate near where Chesterville's city limits started.

The inside front door was partially ajar, and through the crack Derrick could see a body slumped on the couch. Strewn on the floor near the couch and atop the coffee table in front of the couch were bottles of alcohol—some empty, others partially full. Derrick opened the outside front door and pushed the inside front door open.

"Sir!" Derrick yelled. "Sir! Wake up! Are you alive?"

The man awoke and sat up. He rubbed his eyes, then grabbed one of the bottles on the floor—ABSOLUT VODKA—and guzzled. Derrick laid his cellphone to rest in his shorts pocket, now that he no longer needed to call the police or an ambulance.

"I'm fine," the man said, his speech lethargic. "What do you need? You selling Girl Scout Cookies or something?"

This would have been a perfect opportunity for Derrick to be sarcastic, but he didn't want to risk losing any potential customers. He explained his business and asked if he could come in to hand the man a flier. The man obliged and even offered Derrick a drink—Smirnoff. This situation reminded him of the story Aaron told him about the experience he had with his Uncle David. Though he and Aaron weren't the best of friends, they still chatted every once in a while, though most times Aaron was a complete dick to Derrick, jealous of his mind and muscles.

"I can't help but ask," Derrick said. "Are you sad about something?"

For a few seconds, the man wrestled with whether or not he should tell Derrick about his strife. "I'll be alright."

The scent of carpet cleaner, bleach, and ammonia started to disorient Derrick. *Did this man murder some people here and try to cover his tracks?* Derrick wondered. *Maybe I should call the police.*

The man informed Derrick he would be back shortly. He needed to use the bathroom and freshen up. Once the man was out of the room, Derrick walked over to the couch, on top of which were some bottles, but also some pictures in frames. One in particular pulled at Derrick's heartstrings. It was a photo of three people: the man Derrick was speaking to, a woman—whom Derrick presumed was his wife, and a young child—a boy. The picture was taken by a professional studio. In the picture there were nothing but smiles—a happy family—or so at least the picture conveyed.

But that wasn't the only picture where all three of the family members were smiling. Several of the pictures littered on the couch, floor, and coffee table were candid photos taken at different events. Parties. Barbecues. Birthdays. Some even appeared to have been taken during no special occasion at all.

All of a sudden Derrick's intuition sounded an alarm. He turned around and there he was—the man standing in the hallway, staring at Derrick.

"I didn't mean to be nosy. I'm sorry," Derrick said.

"It's okay. I'm proud of those pictures, and of my family. What's the point of taking pictures if you aren't going to share the memories with other people?"

"You have a lovely family."

"Had."

Derrick swallowed hard and placed his hand in his pocket—the same pocket his cellphone was entombed—you know, just in case he needed to hit the panic button.

"What do you mean *had?*" *This son of a bitch did it. He actually killed his family. That explains the strong chemical scents of bleach and ammonia.*

"My son, Dylan, committed suicide. My wife is in the mental ward of St. Catherine's."

"I'm sorry for your loss. I've experienced loss myself. Both my parents."

The man offered his condolences and introduced himself as Mike. He spent the next ten minutes talking about how much he missed Dylan, sharing stories about his deceased son. Derrick listened and enjoyed the stories, but at the same time he also needed to be going. He had other houses to distribute his fliers and he wanted to get some study time in before he had to make dinner for him and Bruce.

"Would you like to see Dylan's room?" Mike asked.

"Sure."

"Great."

Mike led the way to Dylan's room, walking down the hallway and turning into the last bedroom on the left. He said: "I haven't touched his room since that fateful morning my wife discovered Dylan in the bathtub."

On the walls were posters of Dylan's favorite cartoon characters. Tom and Jerry, Bugs Bunny, Daffy Duck, to name a few. Scattered on the floor of Dylan's bed were magazines a young age his age likely wouldn't have any interest in reading. People, Cosmopolitan, Good Housekeeping, among others.

"Do you mind if I thumb through some of these magazines?" Derrick asked.

"No, I just ask you put them back exactly where you found them."

"I will," Derrick said. He picked up an issue of People and thumbed through it. He gasped.

"What is it? What's wrong?"

"In every picture where a person's wrist is exposed, someone has dragged something sharp across it."

This was new information to Mike. He, after all, had never once flipped through the magazines on the floor in Dylan's room. He had no reason to since Dylan had a hobby of cutting pictures out of the magazines and making mosaics—some of which were displayed on Dylan's wall.

Mike picked up one of the magazines on the floor and thumbed through it. As he did, a bent-out-of-shape paper cup fell out of it.

"He must have been contemplating suicide for a long time," Mike muttered. "You should see of some of the pictures he drew before he committed suicide."

Derrick looked at his watch—a gift Danielle purchased for him for their two-year anniversary—and apologized for being unable to stay longer. Mike understood and asked Derrick to come over tomorrow to cut his lawn. He handed Derrick a ten-dollar bill. When Mike admitted that's all he could pay instead of the full twenty-five dollars Derrick quoted him, Derrick told him not to worry about it. He would do the front and back for ten dollars, telling Mike to consider the difference of fifteen dollars a contribution from him to his family in memoriam of Dylan.

16

"Why can't you tell me about the shadowy apparition you saw?" Tao asked his eight-year-old adopted son Julian. "And what it wants you to do?"

"Because he'll kill me if I do," Julian answered.

He was a scrawny dimple-cheeked kid with stick figure arms and head of thick brown hair. In a lot of ways, he resembled the Kool Kids doll Aaron had accidentally destroyed, slicing its face with the circular saw.

Tao adopted him from the USA and then brought him to China to care and raise for him.

"Nobody is going to touch you," Tao assured. "I will protect you. Why don't you come sleep in my room tonight?"

Julian shook his head. "I don't think you can protect me from this, Dad." He paused for a few brief seconds. "This shadow figure is more powerful than God. I'm not safe anywhere."

Tao pushed the side of Julian's face onto his chest, using every ounce of energy not to start crying. Moments later, Julian and Tao fell asleep.

Around seven-thirty-two the next morning, Tao woke up and zombie-walked to the kitchen to prepare Julian and him some breakfast. He whipped open the refrigerator door, pulled out the Eggland's Best egg carton—Grade A Large—and from the crisper drawer a package of bacon.

He placed two skillets on the stove and lit a fire underneath each.

As he cracked eggs into an old sour cream container, Julian walked into the kitchen, eyes half open, and poured himself a glass of orange juice.

"Morning," Tao said. "You slept well? Yes?"

"Not really," Julian answered. He gulped down some of the juice. "The shadow person wants me to do something terrible."

"Tell me."

"I can't. He'll kill me."

(Bingo, baby!)

Tao turned the heat down a smidge for the skillet containing the eggs and tossed some bacon into the other skillet.

Julian traced the back of his left wrist with his finger.

"He can't hurt you, Julian," Tao assured. "He's a ghost, a spirit."

"Dad, I tried to text you what this shadow figure wants me to do. As I did, an unseen force gripped my hands and squeezed them. I heard the bones crack. If I do anything to tip you off, I'm as good as dead… Actually, I'm as good as dead regardless."

(So what are you waiting for? Let's get it in gear!)

"I'll do whatever I can to protect you, but I think this is all in your mind," Tao said. "I think you're overreacting."

"I'm not. This spirit isn't any ordinary spirit. It's the embodiment of evil."

"The embodiment of evil. That sounds awfully scary. Maybe I need to get a spiritualist in here to rid the house of the shadow figure."

"It won't do any good. This entity is too powerful."

Tao scraped some eggs out of the skillet onto a plate. Julian poured himself another glass of orange juice.

With the two of them seated at the table, they began to eat their breakfast. Tao read some news article on his cellphone while Julian played with his food using his fork.

"Come on," Tao said. "Eat. You need your energy."

"I just had a epiphany, Dad," Julian said, slightly grinning. As he spoke, his voice became higher pitched and louder. "If this shadow entity thing wants me to do what it says and I don't it's going to kill me anyway. So, what the hell, I say! I'm going to reveal all to you!"

"You're freaking me out. Please calm down a few pegs."

Julian pointed to his wrist. "Do you see the numbers there?"

"No, I don't. What numbers?"

"06:12:13, 06:12:12, 06:12:11. See it counting down? That's how much time I have left to kill myself before the shadow figure does it for me."

"Cut out this talk," Tao demanded. "It's not funny. It sounds like something straight out of a horror movie."

"But this isn't a movie," Julian said, walking towards the silverware drawer. He pulled out a steak knife and returned to the table. "This is my reality."

"What's the knife for?"

"I don't know. I don't know why I brought that to the table. Weird."

They both resumed eating their meals. Out of the blue, Julian grasped the steak knife and stabbed himself deep in his right eyeball. The knife pierced his brain, killing him.

17

Walking home after distributing another set of fliers, Derrick received a text message from Bruce—and not a nice one either. Rather than waste time arguing through text messaging Derrick called him.

"I thought you were going to cut the grass today," Bruce said, irritated. "The grass is longer than it was when I left. What have you been doing all day? Jerkin' your gherkin?"

"I did cut the grass," Derrick said. "I did it before I left to disperse fliers."

"Bullshit. I'm looking at the yard right now. The grass is not cut. And the Code Enforcement for the city placed a notice on the front door we are in violation. We've got two days—forty-eight hours—to get the grass cut, the weeds removed, and the loose trash scattered against our fence in the alley cleaned up. Otherwise we get fined seventy-five dollars."

"I'm being straight—"

"And next time we don't even get a warning before we are fined. You want to pay seventy-five dollars to the city? If I pay it, it's coming out of your college fund—what little is in there."

By this point, Derrick was hyperventilating from running. He turned onto his street and increased his speed. Though he was built like a Mack truck, he wasn't much of a long-distance runner.

Bruce terminated the call when he saw Derrick running up the sidewalk. Danielle pulled up in front of the house and exited her vehicle.

Derrick tried to kiss her, but she denied him, claiming he smelled like shit from a dead man's ass. He wasn't expecting her over today, but still was pleased to see her.

"Cut the grass, Derrick," Bruce ordered. "You can romance your bitch later."

"Hey! Don't call her that!" Derrick snapped. He walked onto the grass. "I know I cut the grass today. Coreyann even saw me earlier doing it. She talked me for a few minutes before I started to cut the backyard."

Bruce contested Derrick cut the grass. The evidence spoke for itself. The grass was not cut. Bruce tried to give Derrick the benefit of the doubt, but he couldn't. He initially considered the possibility Derrick cut the grass using a raised-blade setting, but this didn't make sense. There were no wheel trails left on the lawn and the grass was *longer* than it was when Bruce left earlier in the day for work.

Determined to be vindicated, Derrick sprinted next door and rang the doorbell. Coreyann answered it.

"What do you want?" she said, her tone sharp.

Derrick's eyes widened. "I'm sorry. Is now a bad time?"

"No. What do you want?"

"You and I talked earlier, right?"

"Yeah. So?" *Reject me. Nobody rejects me! Nobody!*

"And you saw me cutting the grass, right?"

"No. We talked, but you *never* cut the grass."

He started to second guess his own recollections now. He wondered if it was possible he *thought* he cut the grass, but actually didn't. But he was sure he cut the grass, which he did.

But if it was true he did cut the grass, how could it grow back—and even longer than before it was cut—in a short time span? And why would Coreyann claimed he didn't cut the grass?

"Are you pranking me right now?" he asked her.

"No—I'm not." She closed the door.

Derrick walked back home and after poking at the keypad on the garage, the door opened and he pushed the lawn mower out and checked the fluids—just as he had done earlier when he cut the grass.

As Derrick was about to fire up the lawn mower, Danielle approached him.

"Are you okay?" she asked.

"Kind of. I don't know what's happening." *I need an MRI or CT scan.*

Convinced he suffered brain damage from his attempted suicide, he believed his memory was fooling him into believing he had done something when in fact he hadn't

"I'll wait inside for you," she said. She kissed him on his cheek, not on the lips—which she used to do up until about a week ago.

Just as she was about to open the outside front door, Bruce stormed out of it and got up close and personal with Derrick.

"What the fuck is wrong with you leaving a mess like that in the kitchen?" Bruce shouted. "It looks like a rabid animal ransacked it."

"I didn't do that. I don't know what you're talking about. Maybe Gayle came by and made the mess. I know I didn't." *At least I don't think I did... Or did I?*

"You better shape up or I'm going to toss you out of here," Bruce warned. He walked away from Derrick, hearing him speak, but not listening to the words actually said. "And quit being a little bitch and get your learner's permit!"

Derrick fired up the lawn mower and began cutting the grass. Up one way and down the other. A voice in Derrick's head suggested he film himself cutting the grass. At least this way there would be ironclad, irrefutable proof he cut the grass.

But he didn't do this, figuring Bruce and Danielle both could—and likely would—look out the window and see him doing it.

When Derrick was nearly three-quarters finished with the front yard, Mr. Brink—who lived across the street—straggled over to the yard.

"Hey there, Derrick. What do you say?" Mr. Brink asked. He extended his hand after coughing on it.

Derrick extended his other hand, hoping Mr. Brink would shake it with his untainted (presumably) left hand, but Mr. Brink didn't.

"Something I can do for you?" Derrick asked.

"Yes, there is," Mr. Brink said. He pulled out of his pants pocket a neon yellow flier—Derrick's flier. "I understand you don't have what I am about to request of you as a service, but I thought I'd run it by you anyway."

"I'm all ears."

Mr. Brink glanced at the back of his arm, caressing the brown patches on it. "I need you to enter my back door tomorrow at seven in the morning and let Meowser out. Can you do that?"

Meowser was the name of Mr. Brink's Himalayan cat—a stray he found inside a dumpster about three years ago when he was out for one of his nightly walks. For past three months, Mr. Brink discontinued his walks for reasons unknown to Derrick. He only saw Mr. Brink every once in a while, usually when Mr. Brink would step outside to retrieve his mail.

Mr. Brink was Derrick's fifth-grade teacher when he attended North Haven Elementary School—recently renamed Donald G. Brink Elementary School. Mr. Brink taught at North Haven for forty-two years before retiring, though he retired out of practicality. He and several other teachers were offered a buyout deal along with continuation of the district's health insurance for another two years.

But he didn't want to retire. He loved teaching and his students, even when that supercilious shithead Tony Bennett along with the clueless out-of-touch-with-the-reality-of-teaching assholes in the Indiana General Assembly dismantled public education in the state.

"Sure. I can do that for you," Derrick said.

"Thank you," Mr. Brink said as he extended his hand—his left hand this time—for Derrick to shake it. But before Derrick could grab his hand, he coughed on it. Rather than shake Derrick's hand, he patted him on the back. "You're a good kid. You're going to go far in life."

Mr. Brink strayed back to his house. Derrick resumed cutting the lawn down to size. Once he was finished with the front yard, he walked inside to fetch himself a drink of water only to find Bruce and Danielle play wrestling on the living room floor—as they did from time to time.

Though Derrick found the behavior odd since it was his first time witnessing it, he didn't think much of it. And, actually, he was somewhat happy to see the two of them getting along better than they had in the past. Bruce labeled Danielle a slut who would open her legs for just about anything with a proboscis.

When he finished his drink, he stepped into the living room.

"Who are you?" he asked the apparition on the stairs. "What do you want?"

18

"Karen! Karen!" Scott screamed from Emily's bedroom. "Hurry! Something is wrong with the baby!"

Karen stormed into the room. "What's wrong?" She looked into Emily's crib. Emily's face was cyanic in color—just like it was that one other time. "I'm calling 911!"

This was the second time in three months something catastrophic was wrong with their daughter.

"What happened?" Karen asked, her voice frantic as she delivered compressions to Emily's chest with two fingers.

"I came in to give her a bottle and she wasn't responsive," he said. "Is she dead?"

"No. She has a pulse—but it's faint."

Karen continued to administer chest compressions to Emily. When paramedics arrived, Scott leaned against the wall and observed them work their medical magic on his near-non-responsive daughter.

19

"Andrew! Get down here this instant!"

And he did, stampeding thunderously down the stairs. When he reached the living room, his mother handed him a notice from the Chesterville Police Department. It was a red-light ticket.

"Mom, there's a mistake," he insisted.

"Mistake nothing. Open the notice up," she said. "They included a picture." She tightened the sash of her robe wrapped around her turgid abdomen and unfurled the towel around her head. "I'm not going to let you drive my vehicles if you're going to break the law and cost me money."

"I'll try to be more careful. It was an accident."

"If you get another red-light ticket, parking ticket, speeding ticket, any kind of ticket, you will be taking the bus to school. Are we understanding each other?"

Andrew nodded and strolled into the kitchen to retrieve the silverware he needed to set the table. While in the kitchen, he received a call from Derrick. Once the bullshit pleasantries were out of the day, Derrick cut to the chase.

"Do you believe in spirits?" Derrick asked.

"Not really," Andrew replied. "Why?"

"I think there's a ghost haunting my house, and especially my bedroom."

"That's weird. Have you tried communicating with it?"

"I've tried ignoring it."

Andrew expressed an expletive when he dropped the fork he was placing on his napkin. As a quick fix, he exchanged what would have been his fork for his mother's—which was already safely and securely resting on her napkin.

"What's it look like? A dead relative?" Andrew asked.

"It's nobody. It has no face. No skin as you and I have. It looks like nothing more than a translucent shadow."

"The fuck? That sounds kind of creepy, bro. Has it done anything to hurt you?"

"No, not that I can think of."

"You better tell your dad about it."

"I don't know. He's pissed at me."

Derrick proceeded to explain the scenario in which the front yard, which he had cut earlier in the day a few days ago, miraculously grew back. Andrew experienced difficulty swallowing what Derrick was feeding him, but he didn't argue with Derrick. Instead, Andrew shifted the focus of the conversation back to the apparition Derrick saw.

"What do you think it wants?" Andrew asked.

"I don't know, but it seems to have some sick fetish with wanting to see me kill myself—or get killed."

"What? Run that by me one more time."

And Andrew didn't need to tell Derrick twice, whose mouth spewed different situations in which the apparition tried to persuade Derrick to end his life. Rather than going back to the first encounter Derrick had, he focused on some of the most recent situations. As an example, last night while Derrick was buttering a bagel for his dad he had just toasted, the voice of the apparition told Derrick to stick the knife into the toaster. Later that evening, as Derrick was getting into bed, the voice of the apparition suggested to Derrick he defenestrate himself, encouraging him to run from the hallway into his bedroom and dive through his bedroom window. The third—though far from the last encounter—Derrick shared with Andrew the voice of the apparition supplied the idea of hanging himself from the oak tree he often climbed up and played on when he was younger.

"But you say the voice of the apparition, right?" Andrew asked. He pulled the casserole dish out of the oven and placed it on the metal cooling rack.

"That's right."

Andrew scratched his head. "So, then how do you know it's the apparition speaking to you?"

"I'm putting two and two together, that's all."

"But the apparition and the voice you're hearing could be unrelated. One may have nothing to do with the other."

"I don't know about that. I mean it seems logical one relates to the other." Derrick paused for about three seconds. "Then again maybe the real apparition—the owner of the voice—wants me to think the apparition I've been seeing is the voice I've been hearing… But why?"

"I'm still trying to understand this. You'll be sitting in a room and out of nowhere you hear a voice speak to you?"

"Not exactly. The voice speaks to me from within my head."

Concerned Derrick might either be losing his mind or in danger, Andrew implored him to talk to his dad about the apparition and the voices he was hearing within his mind. Andrew's thinking was if it can get inside your head and speak to you, it may be able to manipulate your actions, too.

The two spoke for a few more minutes before Andrew had to end the call so he and his mom could eat dinner.

20

An angelic voice announced over the intercom for Thomas and Lauren to report to the BAU's nurse's station at once. Thomas arrived first and standing at the station were two African-American individuals who introduced themselves as Carl's parents, Everett and Margaret. Thomas welcomed them to the BAU and suggested they speak privately in his office given the sensitive nature of the situation.

Thomas escorted Everett and Margaret to his office. He unlocked his door, swung it open, and extended his hand as if to say enter please.

Before Everett entered Thomas' office, to Thomas he said: "I hope you won't feel the need to admit us to the BAU after you here what we have to say, but my wife and I feel it's important you know this information. It may save lives."

Thomas looked up at the towering near-seven-foot gentleman and grinned. "I look forward to any information you have." *And I'm relieved you're not here to discuss the possibility of a lawsuit.*

"Would either of you like something to drink? Or some junk food?" Thomas said, waddling to his minifridge. "Water? Pop? Candy?"

They both declined insisting they were on a strict diet—a keto diet—and refused to poison their body with harmful indulgences such as Twix candy bars and Pepsi products.

"Smart," Thomas replied as he yanked out two Twix bars and a can of Pepsi. "I should probably jump on that bandwagon myself one day."

"Why not today?" Everett asked.

Margaret smacked Everett's arm and Everett lightheartedly chuckled. He apologized to Thomas and assured him he spoke in jest. Thomas was a good sport and didn't take the remark personally. Besides, Thomas believed Everett had a point.

After Thomas offered his condolences, he asked: "So, what can I do for you folks?" He reached into his desk drawer and whipped out an opened pack of cigarettes.

"Well, I'll take one of those, if you don't mind," Everett said. And, overlapping Everett, Margaret said: "Give me one of those smokes before I flip my shit."

Thomas chuckled on the inside, laughing at their hypocrisy—and Margaret's off-the-wall remark. He fulfilled their demands, giving each one of his cigarettes.

Not long after all three were huffing and puffing, the room was nothing more than a haze of smoke—every cubic inch filled.

"You wanted to talk to me about Carl, right?" Thomas asked.

"That's right. I don't think he killed himself," Everett said.

Suicide was no laughing matter, but Thomas had to force himself not to chuckle at Everett's illogical claim.

"I can see it in your face, doc. But my husband and I both think Carl was murdered," Margaret said.

Now Thomas went from chuckling on the inside to choking on the outside. He wondered if his ears deceived him. He asked for Margaret to repeat herself, which she did.

Thomas didn't bother finishing his cigarette. He murdered its flame and dropped it in the ash tray. He swallowed hard.

"I understand you may think we're out of our right minds, but hear us out," Everett said.

"I'm not sure I can continue this conversation," Thomas admitted.

"Why not?" Margaret asked, her voice firm and motherly.

"Because you're implying one of my staff members murdered your son. If you honestly—"

"We don't think that. We *know* one of your staffers didn't murder our son," Everett said.

If Thomas wasn't confused before, he was now. With each additional exchange of words between him and Carl's parents, the less he understood.

Thomas downed some Pepsi before he spoke. "Alright. If not one of my staff members, then you must think one of the other patients did it, right? Is that it?"

"No. Not one of your staff members, not one of the patients," Margaret said, reaching for Thomas' pack of cigarettes. "Do you mind if I have another?"

Thomas signaled for Margaret to help himself to another cigarette, which Margaret did. Then Thomas lit one and puffed on it a few times, all while trying to make sense of what Everett and Margaret were driving at, though no answers surfaced.

But this was understandable. The medical examiner, after all, ruled Carl's death a suicide. Then there was Michelle who witnessed Carl puncture his neck with a pen. There was no question in Thomas' mind Carl took his own life.

"Is it possible for you two to give it to me straight?" Thomas asked. He ripped into the Twix wrapper. "Who do you think murdered your son?"

"Not a *who*, doctor, but a *what*," Everett said.

"A what? Like a spirit?"

"Exactly. A spirit—and a deadly one, too."

Thomas asked for evidence, but Everett said one of his relatives from the hereafter spoke to him a day ago and divulged to him a malevolent entity presented Carl with an ultimatum. When Carl didn't fulfill his part of the proposition, the entity killed him.

Everett's fists clenched when he observed Thomas stifling his snickers. Margaret lightly tapped Everett's foot and he relaxed.

"How would I even begin to investigate this?" Thomas asked. "Or the police? How can we show an entity is responsible for your son's death?"

"We can't. But I think you should know there is an entity ever-present throughout the world either convincing people to kill themselves—or if they don't—it does it for them."

Everett stood, then Margaret, and they both left on that note.

21

Today was the forty-fourth annual Pierogi Fest—held in Whiting—and Derrick had no plans to miss it. For the past eight years—ever since his mom up and left—he and his dad attended, and for the past two years, Derrick and Danielle spent time together at the Pierogi Fest.

But this time around was different. Danielle was unable to get time off from work and Bruce was called into work at the last minute—ironically because someone had called off to attend the Pierogi Fest.

After Derrick paid the Uber driver at the BP on the corner of Indianapolis Boulevard and New York, he crossed the street and walked towards 119th Street—the street on which the majority of the Pierogi Fest was held.

As Derrick passed by the streets intersecting New York, he thought to himself the same thing he always did when he saw the houses on the streets, and that was how he would detest living in a city where the houses were so close together. And they were close together, so close in fact you wouldn't need to leave your house to borrow a cup of sugar from your neighbor. You could simply reach out your window and knock on theirs.

Once he was bored with bitching about the proximal distances between one home to the next, he pulled out his cellphone and poked at the Facebook icon on his home screen. With tremendous thumb technique, he whipped out a new Facebook status and posted it, letting the world—well at least his Facebook friends—know where he was and what he was doing. Over the past year, he limited his Facebook posts to bigger events—a drastic flip from his old habit of posting every event in his life. Eating a taco. Walking in the store. Taking a super mondo duke.

After posting his status update, he scrolled through his Facebook wall and was alarmed to see one of his friends posted a sobering message. It read: MY COUSIN TAHANA HAS PASSED. SHE DOUSED HERSELF IN KEROSENE AND BURNED HERSELF ALIVE. RIP CUZ.

Pablo Ortiz was Derrick's friend's name and he knew Pablo's cousin. Without thinking twice, Derrick double tapped the home button and then smacked the Contacts app. He swiped upward several times, choosing not to take the path to least resistance to get to the contacts with last names starting with O. He could have simply clicked on O along the alphabet vertically listed along the right side of his screen.

"I'm sorry to read about Tahana," Derrick said. "Why did she do it?"

"I don't know," Pablo admitted. "Two days ago when he hung out, she was fine. Smiling. Laughing. Joking around. Then yesterday she calls me in a panic."

"What was she panicking about?"

"She started talking all *loco*. She said she had a limited amount of time to transcend to the next dimension. She said she would always remember me."

Derrick turned onto 119th Street, but then double-backed since there was too much noise. He sprinted down the sidewalk and turned into an alleyway. Pablo sniffled a few times in the phone.

"When she said those things, what was going through your mind?" Derrick asked.

"I feared she was going to kill herself. Never did she talk like that, not once that I can remember at least."

"Did you tell anyone?"

"Not exactly. I decided to rush over to her house. When I got there she wasn't there though."

"Where was she?"

"In Riley Park where her body was found, I think. The canister of kerosene and box of matches my uncle kept in his garage. I think after she got off the phone with me, she went into the garage, packed the kerosene and matches in her backpack, and pedaled her way to Riley Park."

"I think I know how this ends. You don't have to give me any additional details."

But Pablo disclosed the rest of the details and then some. He shared with Derrick information not even the police were aware of, and that was the fact Tahana had Facetimed with Pablo prior to ending her life.

The two of them talked for another ten minutes. Derrick invited Pablo to meet up with him at the Pierogi Fest, but he declined.

With Pablo no longer in his ear, Derrick walked back to 119th Street, located his favorite pierogi vendor—Lynnethe's, and took his meal to a bench along one of the side streets intersecting 119th.

As Derrick dipped one of his pierogis into some sour cream, a man stuck his arm in Derrick's face.

"Do you see it?" the man asked.

"Do I see what?"

"Look at my wrist, kiddo. Do you see the numbers?"

(Remember when you had your numbers on the back of your left wrist, buddy? Your dad fucked things up for me! I'm hunting him just as he is hunting me! I'm gonna kill him. I'm gonna slay his spirit! He'll be reduce to nothing more than particles in the Universe!)

Derrick stood and walked away without answering the man or the voice. The people he came across at the Pierogi Fest seemed to get stranger and stranger each passing year.

"Look for my name in the obituary page tomorrow! I'll be dead in—" He checked his wrist. "Four hours, eleven minutes, and now six seconds." When Derrick didn't turn around to respond, the man shouted: "You hear me! Look for the name Alan Gallmeier! Death is my date today, kiddo!"

"Crazy old man," Derrick muttered.

Wanting to get away from the noise and chaos—two things Derrick didn't care for, he walked to the Lakefront—one of the recent additions to the city.

When he crossed the entrance, he immediately locked eyes on an empty swing near the lake. Fortunately he was able to claim it as his before the family of three sprinting towards it did. He felt bad, and almost offered it to them.

He finished his pierogis while listening to the waves roll in and out, all the while thinking about Danielle and wishing she was there with him by his side, just as she was the past two years.

Refusing to be a litterbug, Derrick walked to a trash can about a hundred feet away from his swing—and behind it also—and dropped his garbage into it. Once he turned around to wander back to the swing be was sitting on, someone had already beat him to the punch. Fortunately, there was another swing with nobody on it, and he started to walk towards it.

When Derrick passed the man who snagged the swing from Derrick, the man tipped his fedora to him. "Lovely day, isn't it, Derrick?" the man said.

Had the man not said Derrick's name, he would have kept on walking while responding. But the man somehow knew Derrick's name, and this concerned him, who stopped, turned around, and walked towards the man.

"How do you know my name?" Derrick asked. *Why is he wearing a full-body trench coat in this ninety degree weather?*

"There's a lot of things I know about you," the man responded. "You're lucky to be alive. I don't think you'll ever know just how close to death you came."

"What are you talking about?" *How does he not sweat even though he is in a three-piece suit and it's hotter than Hades out here?*

"That night at the baseball field. It's probably best you don't remember." He stood and tipped his hat once more before walking away along the concrete walking path.

Derrick walked a few steps in the opposite direction of the man before turning around. Derrick wanted to confront the man, thinking he was somehow involved in his near-death experience.

But the man was nowhere to be seen. This raised red flags in Derrick's mind, convinced the man to whom he had spoken was no longer of the physical world—but of the spiritual. The only way the man could have escaped out of sight so quickly was if the man had jumped over the railings into Lake Michigan, but Derrick discounted this because he never heard a splash—only the same crashing sound of the waves hitting the pier and receding from it.

Bit by the hungry bug again—probably due to the combinations of food aromas permeating the air—Derrick ventured back to 119th Street to get some more food. Along the way, he responded to a text from Danielle, who expressed her frustration she couldn't be with him at the Pierogi Fest.

After fighting his way through the sea of people in between the two sides of the street where the vendors were set up, Derrick opted for a Philly cheesesteak, and once he had that in his hand, he stood in line to get a freshly-squeezed lemonade.

A bench along one of the side streets of 119th Street was available. He enjoyed his meal while listening to some *Second Chance* by Shinedown—his now-favorite band—to drown out the ambient cacophonous noise of people chattering as they either stood in one of numerous lines or traveled through the densely-packed area between both sides of 119th Street.

"You're in danger," someone from behind Derrick said.

Derrick turned around as he swallowed a mouthful of Philly cheesesteak. "You again?" Derrick said—his tone irritated—to the fedora-sporting man he encountered in the Lakeshore.

"Me again," the man said,

"Who are you and what do you want?"

"The shadow of death wants your soul. You escaped it once, but it will stop at nothing until you're dead. I'm your protector. I saved you from The Umbra once before. Now, I'm hunting it to destroy it."

"What the hell are you talking about?"

"You didn't try to commit suicide. Thank goodness I intervened before it was too late. Still, though, you're in danger—mortal danger."

As if someone pushed a button, the suit-dressed man with the fedora vanished into thin air in an instant, much like a light being turned off.

Onlookers glared at Derrick with an expression of bewilderment and concern, and he asked why they were staring at him.

"You were talking to nobody," the pleasantly-plump-and-puny woman said.

"Yeah—are you off your meds or something?" her husband asked. He was needle thin. A male Olive Oyl. "You're *loco en le cabeza*, aren't you?"

"Harold, don't disparage the young man. Mental illness isn't something to be making wisecracks about. It's a serious crisis in our country."

"Oh, get a grip, Beth. Besides, I was only funnin' with the boy." And to Derrick: "Now, seriously, do you need us to call someone for you? Or was what you just did an act?"

Derrick wasn't sure how to respond. It seemed either way he would look bad. If he said yes, it meant he was having conversations with people from the spirit world, which other people likely couldn't see. On the other hand, if he said it was act, he'd look bad since in a sense he was mimicking people with delusions and hallucinations.

"I'm fine," Derrick said. "Just sleep-deprived from working and studying. I think I'll go home and take a nap."

"I hope you feel better," Beth replied. "See a doctor for your insomnia before things proliferate."

"I will. Thanks," Derrick said. He threaded his fingers through his hair. "I'll call my psychiatrist right now." He walked back onto 119th Street, but this was the street where the majority of people attending the Pierogi Fest congregated and traveled.

After walking several feet along the sidewalk, Derrick cut in between two vendors and crossed 119th Street to get to the other side. When he stepped onto the sidewalk and turned right, he was surprised to see his dad and Danielle talking and giggling as they walked down the sidewalk towards Derrick. Neither Danielle nor Bruce saw Derrick because they were too consumed with each other. Derrick followed behind a group of people in front of him, trying to blend in with them. Right before Danielle and Bruce passed Derrick and the group in front of him, he jumped out in front of them, causing both of them to scream.

"What are you two doing here?" Derrick asked, his tone exuberant. "I thought you couldn't make it."

Both of them stammered for a few seconds before Danielle said: "We wanted to surprise you. Are you surprised?" She put her arms around Derrick.

"Yeah. I'm surprised," Derrick said. He smiled widely.

Damage control. Check.

Bruce said: "We love you and we decided to convince our bosses to let us out of work."

(You're a fucking moron. They both hate you. Why don't you impale your skull with one of those metal skewers Mr. Pierogi is standing by. Get his fucking costume all bloodied up. Go out with a showstopper suicide!)

Derrick smacked his forehead a few times. Danielle asked him if he was alright and he told her it was a migraine brewing. She reached into her purse and handed him a bottle of Midol and instructed him to take two of those.

"Thanks, but I had my period last week. Remember?" Derrick said.

"I can vouch for that," Bruce quipped. "He was a moody son of a bitch last week."

Danielle laughed at both of their remarks. And to Derrick: "Just take two of them. They will help your headache."

(You want to cure your headache? Kill yourself. The clock is ticking and my patience is dwindling.)

Now another voice crept into Derrick's head. It said with authority: "Leave my son alone!"

(Make me! His soul—)

Danielle snapped her fingers in front of Derrick's face a few times and he snapped out of his trance. He apologized to her. At this point, Bruce was long gone—waiting in one of the boa-constrictor-like lines for some brats and a beer.

Walking side by side with his hand in hers, they talked as they walked to the Lakeshore, and not longer after arriving there found a swing on which to sit.

She kissed him on the cheek and placed her head on his shoulders. They listened to the waves rush in and out, the sound soothing their over-stimulated minds. She rubbed his chest and told him she loved him.

(That bitch hates your guts! She's cheating on you! Take many Midols and swan dive into the water! Drown your sorrow—and yourself!)

"Do you ever think about finding your mother and starting a relationship with her?" Danielle asked.

"Sometimes."

"Why don't you then?"

"Because I fear rejection. She already left me and my dad once. Why should I risk getting hurt all over again? Besides, I don't have much respect for people who cheat on their significant others or spouses."

Danielle nodded and without blinking an eye said: "I can understand why you'd feel that way."

(Here's an idea, lover boy. Why don't you kill her, then yourself? You love that promiscuous bitch, right? Poison her to death, then blow your brains out. Then you two can fornicate for all eternity after you enter the pearly gates of Heaven.)

Once again, Derrick smacked his forehead a few times. His inner voice told the voice of the spirit in his head to stop bugging him. Danielle yanked out the Midol package out of Derrick's pocket, removed two from the tray, and forced him to swallow both. He took the bait just to get her off of his back.

22

The office smelled stale and gross. Usha spritzed some perfume on her before approaching the lady—Alex—at the desk.

After Usha signed the check-in sheet, in her gruff frog-like voice Alex said: "Have a seat. Esteban will be with you shortly." After a few seconds elapsed, she said: "I love that dress you're wearing. Royal blue is a good color on you."

"Thank you. It was a gift Alejandro got for me last Christmas," Usha said. She took a seat in one of the four padded chairs against the wall in the lobby. "And allow me to say that tie on you looks nice."

Alex was a wearing a white dress shirt with a dark red tie and a pair of men's black slacks. She wasn't wearing any makeup and had a bit of five o'clock shadow on her cheeks and chin.

In Usha's lap was the lock box Alejandro had asked her to take to his attorney Esteban Ledesma. Usha had her original appointment weeks ago, but she had to cancel to appointment when the lock box turned up missing. After weeks of searching high and low, she finally found it buried under bags of clothes she received from her sister as hand-me-down gifts.

"You're in for a real treat," Alex said. "Esteban has a pair of buns that will give you goosebumps."

"Great. I can't wait," Usha said, unconvincingly.

"If I remember correctly from the last time we spoke you said your boyfriend passed away, right?"

Usha nodded. "I still haven't come to terms with his death. I don't get why he did it, why he hung himself using his belt in his closet."

"I know exactly how you feel. My son ended his life a few months ago, but you know what's frightening? He didn't display any warning signs. He seemed to be a happy kid. He was doing decent in school. He was captain of the football team. He had a host of friends. He had plans to join the service after graduating this school year."

"I'm sorry for your loss. I'm not a parent, so I can't even begin to imagine what you're going through. How did he—I'm sorry. I shouldn't ask that."

Alex started to respond but choked on her own saliva, inducing her to cough and choke. She downed some of her Dunkin' Donuts iced coffee. "Sorry about that. My son—Bradley was his name—ended his life by carbon monoxide poisoning. He woke up one morning, went to the garage, placed one end of a hose in the exhaust and the other end inside the car, started the car, and let the CO do the deed."

Usha couldn't help but ask if Alex knew why her son ended his own life, especially since he seemed to be a happy child. Alex expressed about a day before his suicide, Bradley's mood had been deflated, spending the majority of his time in his room.

But Alex didn't think too much about it. Everyone has their peaks and valleys and she figured Bradley was experiencing a case of the blues—as he had done every once in a while over the years.

"I wish there was a way we could go back in time and fix things," Usha said. She pulled out a Kleenex from her purse and blew her nose.

"Me, too, but we both know that's not the reality we live in. All we can do is cherish the memories we have of the ones we've lost."

The phone on Alex's desk chirped like a bird. It was one of the strangest ringtones Usha had ever heard. Alex smacked the bottom of the receiver as if disciplining a naughty child, causing it to fly upward, and she caught it. The telephone pyrotechnics Alex displayed reminded Usha of Tom Cruise in Cocktail when he would show off by tossing a bottle upward and catching it behind his back. Sure—Alex's trick wasn't as impressive, but it still put a smile on Usha's face.

Based on the things Alex said, Usha presumed she was speaking to Esteban, most likely informing her he was running a little behind schedule with the client he was currently seeing and he wanted to let Alex know to tell Usha. But then Usha's assumption changed when Alex gasped into the phone.

"I'll let her know," Alex said. "Okay, cinna-buns. Ta-ta for now." She blew a kiss into the phone.

After Alex placed the receiver on its base—which she did in a most peculiar way by slowly inching the receiver to the base and once the receiver was about a centimeter or two above the base, she slammed it down—she informed Usha that Esteban was running late from the tennis club.

Usha looked at her cellphone and sighed. "I'm not going to lie. I'm a little irritated it's already about fifteen minutes past my appointment time and Esteban isn't even here."

"I'm sorry. He's stuck in traffic on the expressway due to an accident. Some wacko intentionally bicycled in front of a semi."

Alex offered Usha something to drink, and Usha chose coffee with cream but no sugar. When Alex returned with a cup of steamy coffee in hand, she divulged to Usha there was an interesting—yet sobering—article in the paper about suicide.

After enjoying a small sip of the java, Usha picked up the paper on the square glass coffee table to the left of the chair in which she was sitting. The article focused on the increase in suicide among children, attributing the increase to greater demands placed on children to achieve and cyberbullying.

Just as Usha was finishing the article—which continued to the sixth page of Section A of the paper—Esteban walked in wearing skin-tight white shorts and a pink polo.

"You must be Usha," Esteban said, smiling. "Sorry I'm late, but some loon riding his BMX on the shoulder of the expressway turned into the path of a semi-truck."

"My goodness. That's unbelievable."

"Yeah. He took a look at the back of his wrist and seconds later veered into traffic. His body exploded as if a bomb detonated."

When the semi-truck collided with the biker's body, the remains splattered onto the side of Esteban's car—who was driving slightly ahead of the semi-truck to the left of it. After giving his statement to police and rinsing his car off the best he could using water from a bottle of purified water, he hightailed it back to the office.

Usha was surprised he was even in a proper state of mind to drive. She didn't think she would have been able to function, especially after already dealing with one recent suicide.

"Well, let's get to it," Esteban said. He walked ahead of her to lead the way.

Alex turned her head towards Esteban as he passed, not wanting to miss any of Esteban's ass action.

"Didn't I tell you?" Alex asked, smiling.

Usha gave a thumbs-up and continued to follow Esteban, trying her best not to stare at his well-toned tushy, but it was a mighty feat for her. A part of her felt guilty for looking at another man, believing not enough time had elapsed for her to start playing the field again.

She followed him down a hallway and they turned into the second office on the right. Inside the office was a large L-shaped executive-style desk along with bookshelves upon bookshelves of law books. A twelve-seat conference table—

which matched the executive-style desk—is where Esteban stood, pulled out a chair for Usha, and invited her to sit at the head of the table, which she did.

He offered something to drink and she accepted, requesting a bottle of water, if he had it, which he did. He sat to her right with a legal pad in front of him. After making some preliminary notes—the date and time and her name—the session began.

"What brings you here?" Esteban asked, with his wide blue eyes twinkling.

"My boyfriend—well ex-boyfriend—well now deceased ex-boyfriend—asked me to bring this to you," Usha said. "He said you would know what to do with it."

"Refresh your memory. Who is—excuse me—was your boyfriend?"

"Alejandro Reyes."

"I don't believe I know who that is."

Usha pulled up a picture of Alejandro off of her cellphone and handed him her phone. He studied the picture closely while fiddling with his ear lobe—twisting it, fondling it, flicking it.

After about four minutes, Esteban said: "Oh, okay. Now I remember. He came in here about a month ago asking me about estate planning. I never serviced him as a client though."

"I don't understand. He wouldn't have sent me here without a purpose. He said you would know what do with this lock box. When you two met did he give you anything?"

His eyes lit up. "Now that you mention it, I think I remember he dropped a key as he was walking out of my office. In the words of Celine Dion, it's all coming back to me now."

He rustled through a few of his desk drawers before he stepped out of his office. Usha could hear faint chatter and the voice of Alex bleed from the lobby area of the law office into Esteban's office.

23

When Thomas walked through the front door, Nikki didn't offer so much as a hello before she tore him a new one. As he walked from the living room to the kitchen to the bathroom, she was right behind him speaking her mind about how he had done nothing but strung her along over the past few weeks.

"It's been weeks now, Dad, and I'm ready to have my own room now," Nikki said.

As Thomas walked back into the living room, he said: "Princess, please. I'm in deep trouble. We had another unexplainable suicide at the BAU this morning. I've been dealing with the authorities and the patient's family members and the media all day."

"Then let me start moving the boxes out of the room."

"Some of those boxes are quite heavy, Princess. I don't like the idea of you trying to move heavy boxes from the upstairs to the downstairs. My fear is you'd trip going down the stairs and hurt or kill yourself."

Nikki sighed. "You broke your promise to me, Daddy. And it's breaking my heart."

His heart ripped into two, kind of like the exam of a student who was caught cheating. He poured himself a cup of coffee and lit a cigarette. Nikki walked to the back door, opened it, and pointed to the patio, and without skipping a beat, he followed her non-verbal directives, stepping onto the porch to enjoy his smoke and Joe.

As he stood on the porch, he thought to himself about Nikki's desire to have her own room. He wanted to tell her she couldn't have her own room after all. She was only nine and could hold off for a few more years before getting her own room. Besides, he wasn't certain he was going to employed much longer at St. Catherine's BAU. Too many suicides on his watch took place, and though he wasn't at fault, he himself was about to become a sacrificial firing, much in the same way he wanted make Michelle one.

After he finished another smoke and drained his cup, he stepped back inside and sat at the kitchen table where Nikki was, sitting with her arms folded and a scowl on her face. In front of her was a neon green flier.

"What's that?" Thomas asked of the flier.

"There's this person named Derrick Johns who does odd jobs for money," she replied.

"Yeah. And?" *That name sounds familiar.*

"Well, I was thinking he could help move the boxes into the shed in the back yard. This way, when you are ready, you can go through them yourself."

He placed another cigarette in his mouth and reached for the flier. He glanced over it and set it back on the table before walking back outside to the patio.

While outside he strained to reach an answer as to why the last three suicides occurring on his watch all involved the person having an obsession with looking at their wrist, including Carl, based upon interviews with orderlies who were assigned to Carl during his brief stay. They didn't think much of him glancing at his wrist or scratching at it, which is why they made no mention of it in their observational reports. They also told Thomas that Carl's interest in his wrist seemed innocuous enough.

But then there was the outlandish claim an evil entity murdered Carl that gnawed at Thomas' brain. Why would they assert such a thing? All it did was negate their chances of winning in a lawsuit because it absolved everyone within the BAU of responsibility.

As he stood leaning over the porch railing, a gentleman from next door called out to Thomas while simultaneously waving at him. In turn, Thomas waved back, not knowing who the man was or what he wanted. Thomas spent so many hours at the BAU he didn't even met his neighbors let alone knew what they looked like.

"How are Nikki and Ashlee?" the man asked.

This sent a chill down Thomas' spine. Now he worried for the safety of his daughters while he was at work more so than he ever did before. His blood boiled, also, because Nikki never mentioned any interaction between herself and the neighbor.

Thomas walked over to the fence dividing the two properties and introduced himself to break the ice. The man shook Thomas' hand and introduced himself as Dan Jagadich.

"So, you've met my daughters?" Thomas asked.

"Only once," Dan said. After two—three seconds top—he added: "Don't worry. I never did anything improper with your daughters," his voice insistent and assuring.

"How did you know I—"

"I'm a father myself. I know that look you gave me. I'd give someone the same look myself. No offense taken."

After Thomas apologized to Dan, he asked him about his children.

"Kids all grown up now. They flew the nest a few years ago. Then last year I lost my wife to ovarian cancer." After Thomas offered his condolences, Dan continued. He said: "Thank you. Yeah, it was a rough time seeing her deteriorate day after day. She's at peace now though. Anyhow, after she passed, I sold my house and moved here. This used to be my brother's house—well still is—but he had to leave for business, so I'm housesitting for a time until he gets back from his stint in Abu Dhabi. Anyway, enough about me. Tell me about you. What's your story?"

After Thomas offered Dan a cigarette, he lit one for himself and puffed it a few times. Before Dan lit the cigarette

Thomas offered him, he pulled the filter out using his teeth and spat it onto his lawn.

"I'm a nervous wreck," Thomas admitted. Dan had to force himself not to laugh at how funny the cigarette flopping up and down looked as Thomas spoke. "I'm the chief psychiatrist and administrator of the BAU at St. Catherine's."

"Oh, my. I must say you've definitely got blood on your hands in a sense. What's happening there? How are your patients managing to kill themselves in a ward of the hospital that's supposed to prevent that very thing?"

"It looks bad. Goddamn does it look bad. I have no idea. You're going to hear about this sooner than later, so I'll tell you know. We had another suicide in the BAU today. A twenty-year old female."

"Good lord. What happened?"

"She stood out of the chair across from the orderly assigned to her suicide watch at the time, walked over to her hospital room doors, and closed it. She walked back to her chair on the opposite of the door and rammed her head as fast as she could into the door."

Dan flicked his cigarette across his backyard. "Around the world there has been a spike in suicides across all ages, races, genders, and socioeconomic statuses. There's definitely something unexplainable by the rational laws that govern our reality we're accustomed to that make us feel warm and toasty side at work."

"What are you suggesting to me? A ghost is behind the suicides?" *This guy must be friends with Everett and Margaret.*

"If I said yes would you believe me?"

"What would you think of me if I said I believed you?"

"Touché, my good fellow."

About five minutes later, the two shook hands and parted ways. As Thomas walked towards the back porch, he couldn't help but wonder what the implications would be if an evil entity was responsible for all of the suicides at the BAU—and other places, too.

The BAU hadn't had a suicide in several years. This was due in large part to the orderlies who were assigned to patients in a one-to-one correspondence. The BAU also prided itself on ensuring patients didn't spend every waking moment in their rooms. They had structured activities each day, such as group and individual therapy sessions, but also had time to talk with other patients and walked the length of one of the BAU's sidewalks with orderlies supervising them to ensure the safety of the patients.

When Thomas stepped into the kitchen, Nikki was still sitting at the kitchen table, tinkering on her phone while stuffing her face with ice cream laden with buckets of hot fudge. Twilight was turning into night. He turned the kitchen light on and then poured himself another cup of coffee—the last of the pot. After starting a fresh pot of coffee, he sat at the table with Nikki. He added some creamer and stirred his coffee before taking a big sip of it.

"Why didn't you tell me about Dan?" Thomas asked.

"I didn't think it was a big deal. Ashlee and I were playing outside in the backyard and he started talking to us," she said. "Afterwards we went inside and stayed inside until you got home."

"I wish you would have told me. That's all."

"I'm sorry."

"It's okay."

She rinsed her bowl out in the sink and placed it in the drain. Then she made another bowl of ice cream with not nearly as much hot fudge this time. She told her dad she would be right back. The ice cream was for Ashlee who was in her bedroom playing with some action figures, such as Batman, He-Man, Iron Man, among others.

While Nikki was out of the room, Thomas looked over the neon flier. The name Derrick Johns—prominently displayed near the top of the flier—resonated with Thomas. As he read over the services Derrick offered, he tried to remember where he heard that name before, but an answer never came to him.

The sound of something crashing to the floor shifted broke Thomas' concentration. The sound seemed to originate from the living room, and when he turned to enter it, his heart skipped a beat. He stood just before the ingress of the living room, his bones and muscle like concrete.

On the floor was the shattered urn containing the remains of his late ex-wife Sharon. Standing next to the scattered ashes and shattered glass was a shadow-like apparition with a translucent appearance. Thomas swallowed hard and considered retreating, not at all interested in sticking around to see the magician's next trick.

"You don't belong here," Thomas said, his voice straining. "Leave and don't come back."

But the apparition moved no more than Thomas did. Though the apparition—which was nothing more than a quasi-translucent shadow—had no eyes—at least none visible to Thomas' naked eye—Thomas felt the apparition had a hundred pairs of eyes, all of which were staring at him and *through* him.

"What do you want?" Thomas asked the apparition.

The apparition raised its right hand as if being sworn in to testify on the stand in a courtroom, but he didn't stop raising it. Up and up it went, and as it did, its shadowy hand closed except for one finger, which was pointing towards the second floor of the house.

"You stay away from my daughters," Thomas said. And now louder: "You hear me? You stay the fuck away from daughters!"

The sound of footsteps pounded the stairs. Seconds later, Nikki and Ashlee stood in the hallway. Thomas put his hand up like a crossing guard, ordering his daughters to stay put.

"What's wrong, Daddy?" Ashlee asked.

"Nothing for you to worry yourself about," Thomas said, his eyes fixed on the apparition as if in a stare-down contest. "Everything is going to be okay."

But Nikki wasn't a fool nor was Ashlee. It was obvious to them something was wrong, and neither appreciated being patronized.

Nikki started to walk down the hall towards her dad, but he once again put his hand out and verbally ordered her to stop.

The apparition moved its hands as if bringing two objects on a table closer together. The scattered ashes formed into a volcano-shaped pile.

The apparition gestured as if unzipping its pants and reached into them. A second later—two tops—a stream of liquid shot out from the apparition's crotch area and followed a parabolic trajectory onto the ashes. When the liquid hit the pile of ashes, a sizzling sound coupled with smoke filled the air. The pile of ashes started to dissolve down its middle, forming a hole. The apparition continued to spew its stream of miasmic mystery juice onto the pile of cremation remains for another ten seconds, at which pointed it zipped up and stood with its arms folded.

Beads of sweat skimmed down Thomas' face. His clothes stuck to his body.

The volcanic pile of cremation remains continued to sizzle and smoke. The sizzling sound intensified. The scent of acid eating away at rotten flesh pervaded the entire house. Even Nikki and Ashlee had their hands over their noses, at times coughing and gagging—as did Thomas.

The apparition raised its hand displaying three fingers. Then he counted down. 3…2…1. When his final finger folded, he disappeared and the volcanic pile of cremation remains erupted and exploded radially in all directions.

"Dad! Oh my god! What happened?" Nikkie asked.

But Thomas didn't answer. He removed a handkerchief from his left pocket and wiped the cremation remains off of his face, but the burning sensation was unrelenting as was the pain. Remember his days as a chemistry student in college, he rushed to the shower, flipped it on, and started to remove his clothing.

"Go outside! Now!" Thomas ordered his daughters. "I'll be out there in a second. Go wait by the car."

And they did. Thomas treated his chemical burns, threw on some clean clothes, and burned rubber as he peeled out of the driveway. As he stopped the car after backing up to thrust the shifter into drive, Ashlee screamed.

Thomas jerked his head to look at her. She was sitting in the backseat on the driver's side. "What's the matter?"

"Daddy, look!" Ashlee said, pointing to her bedroom window.

And he did. Standing in front of the window of both girls' well-lit bedroom was the shadowy apparition. All at once, every light on inside the house shut off. Thomas slammed his foot onto the gas and sped away into the night.

24

As Derrick finished cutting the front yard, Coreyann strolled over wearing a tight-fitting American Eagle tank top and an even tighter pair of Adidas shorts. As she strolled over her fun bags flopped fro and to.

She stood with her arms folded in the center of the lawn, watching him finish cutting the grass. When he looked in her direction, she would casually bend down as if she were picking something she had dropped, candidly revealing her massive mammaries.

The engine of the lawn mower sputtered off when Derrick released the safety bar. He wiped his forehead with his shirt and approached Coreyann.

"Did you need something?" he asked.

"I wanted to come over and see if you wanted to go get some ice cream," she responded, retying her hair, which caused her ample bosom to protrude outward.

"As I've said before, I don't think it's a good idea for us to be hanging out—at least not without my girlfriend. Aside from that, I'm on my way to someone else's house to cut their grass."

Coreyann rolled her eyes. "You know, about your girlfriend, Danielle, she's not what you think she is."

"Okay. Thanks for the tip. I've got to go."

He walked towards the lawn mower. After setting the gas can on top of it, he began pushing it along the sidewalk. Though many of his customers had their own lawn mower, he refused to use them, not wanting to be liable if it broke.

As he passed Aaron's house, he and Scott were outside working on one of the vehicles. Aaron waved to Derrick as he passed; in turn, Derrick waved back. It was a breath of fresh air to see the two of them—father and son—doing something productive together, sharing each other's company.

After Aaron waved at Derrick, he glanced at the back of his wrist and cupped his hand around it.

(Remember when you had to go through that?)

[Piss off. I'm gonna snuff you out of me.]

(Please do, Derrick. How are you going to kill yourself? Shotgun blast to the face? Dive headfirst into a spooling jet engine? Climb Chesterville's water tower and somersault off of it?)

[I'm going to see a doctor and get put on some meds to drown you out.]

(That's laughable. No meds can drown me out. I'll be in your ear year after year unless you silence yourself—permanently. You belong to me. Gotta go. But we'll be in touch.)

The birds chirping a happy tune lifted Derrick's spirits. Over the past few recent days, he and his dad were at odds with each other. Bruce purchased a new TV a few days ago and the next morning a pickaxe was planted through it, and he blamed Derrick. The day after that Bruce came home only to find he and Danielle making out on the couch. He firmly condemned their behavior, sent Derrick to his room, and afterwards retired to his own room to release some tension with the help of another. Most recently, this morning, Bruce woke up to find a butcher's knife plunged into the backrest of the couch with ketchup smeared around it to pass of as blood.

But Derrick denied responsibility for all of these incidents, and this created a heap of contention between him and his dad.

What happened that night I attempted—allegedly attempted—suicide? Did someone try to murder me? Did I actually try to kill myself? Why can't I remember?

Ten minutes passed from the time Derrick left his yard to the time he arrived at Mike's house. He knocked on Mike's front door and Mike answered a few seconds later.

"Come on in," Mike said. "Today is a glorious day."

"It's nice to see you're in a better mood," Derrick responded. "What's happening?"

"My wife is returning home. I pick her up later today."

"That is good news. I'm glad to hear that."

"I hope she has come to terms with our son's death." Mike his Adam's apple. He cleared his throat. "I need your opinion. Do you think it would be a bad idea to create a shrine for Dylan? I thought about creating it as a surprise for my wife—you know, for when she comes home today."

"I'm not so sure it's the best thing to do right now. Didn't you tell me it was the death of your son that drove her to St. Catherine's in the first place?"

Derrick checked his watch—a gift from Danielle—and Mike lashed out. "Just go outside and get started. I don't want to keep you."

"You're not keeping me. I can't help looking at this watch though. My girlfriend gave it to me earlier this week as an anniversary present."

Mike apologized for his outburst. Against Derrick's advice, he decided to create the shrine for Dylan as a surprise for Heather. He politely told Derrick to go to Dylan's room and gather all of the drawings on his desk and take down all of the mosaics on the walls.

And he did. Fifteen minutes later, Derrick brought the items out to the living room and set them on the couch. Mike was searching for a spot in the living room to create the shrine in Dylan's memory.

"I think the best spot for it is where the eyes land when one first walks into the living room from the front door," Mike said. He stepped out of the living room and walked back in it. "That wall next to the entrance leading into the kitchen. Perfect."

There was a large black-cherry-colored China cabinet in front of the wall he chose to construct Dylan's shrine. He and Derrick started to unload it.

"I hope your wife likes this, but aren't at all worried it might push her in the wrong direction?" Derrick asked.

"She was one hell of a mother to Dylan. She needs something to memorialize. Wouldn't you do the same thing for your mother or girlfriend if you were in the same situation?"

"I don't know who my mother is. She left me and my dad before I can remember."

"Why don't you find her and start a relationship with her?"

"She didn't want anything to do with me back then, so I don't see why she would want anything to do with me now. Besides, it's a two-way street. She could seek me out, too, but hasn't."

"She has more to risk than you," Mike said. "Let's move the top part of the cabinet to the bedroom. We can set it on top of Heather's dresser."

"Even if I wanted to seek her out I wouldn't know where to begin. I don't even know her name."

"I don't understand how that can be, but if you're being serious, start with your birth certificate. Her name has to be on there."

As they carried the top part of the China cabinet to Mike's bedroom, Derrick couldn't help but wonder what a relationship with his mother might be like, how his dad would react if he admitted to him his intentions to seek her out, and how the relationship between him and his dad might change.

They set the china cabinet on the dresser and walked into the living room to begin piecing together Dylan's shrine.

"How can you not know what your mother's name is?" Mike asked.

"My dad gave me a couple names over the years. I think he gave fake names to be honest."

"Why would he do that?"

"I don't know. He always seemed to get angry when I would ask about her, so I stopped altogether. I gather my mom broke his heart when she left and never returned. He loved her to death."

"What about your other family members? Do you have any contact with them?"

"No. My dad said his parents died when I was a baby and he was an only child. He also told me my mom's family broke off contact with him shortly after my mom left us, apparently my mom told everyone he abused her, so her side of the family disowned him—and as a result, me. It's basically been me and my dad, through thick and thin."

Mike and Derrick started to place adhesive on the back of each of Dylan's drawings and place them on the wall. Some of the pictures resonated with Derrick, but he didn't understand why. One picture was of a digital clock with the numbers 24:00:00 displayed on it. Next to the numbers was a downward-facing arrow. Another picture was of a hand with thin lines running across the wrist. In each of the four corners and in the center was a letter. From upper left going clockwise and ending at the center: A, R, B, M, U.

"There's something you're forgetting," Mike said. "And I think it's important you keep this in mind."

"And what's that?" Derrick asked, genuinely interested.

"It was your mother—not your father—who gave birth to you."

Derrick nodded.

25

Roberta pulled the neon green flier from her purse and dialed the number on it. Part of her had reservations about having a teenage boy watch her daughter, but the rates were much lower than what Madison's current babysitter, Delilah, charged—after Coreyann bailed on her, not wanting to spend all of her summer babysitting. Additionally, Madison's babysitter recently informed Roberta she would be raising her rates, and that was the nail in the coffin.

As the phone rang and Roberta waited for someone to answer, the sound of glass shattering caused her heart rate to skyrocket. The object sent glass shrapnel flying at Roberta's head when it crashed against the wall near where she was sitting in the kitchen.

"I want McDonald's!" Madison hollered as she stomped up and down.

"Young lady! Are you crazy throwing a glass vase at me?"

"But I want McDonald's! You promised me! And my friend wants McDonald's, too!"

"I told you. I've got bills to pay first. I'll—"

"Hello?" Derrick said. *Damn that kid's screaming is annoying.*

Roberta said: "Yes, hello. Hang on. Let me go into a different room… Are you still there?"

Derrick confirmed he was still on the line. She asked him if he would be able to babysit Madison for three hours a day during the school week, help her with her homework, and prepare dinner for both her and Madison.

Considering Derrick needed the money, he accepted the offer.

"Are you able to come over today and visit with Madison and me so she and I can get to know you better?" Roberta asked.

"I can't today, but tomorrow I can," Derrick said. "Does that work for you?"

"Well, actually, I was hoping you could come over today and babysit so I can get some things done. I'd pay you, of course."

Now a decision needed to be made. Cancel his plans with Danielle and make some more money to put towards his college expenses or decline and lose not only the money he could have earned from babysitting, but also the money he would be spending on the date.

But, then again, Danielle had cancelled their plans to meet up together on a number of occasions and he was always understanding. He agreed to meet Madison and Roberta, even though Danielle would likely be upset.

26

The sound of objects crashing caused Derrick to think twice about whether or not he should ring the doorbell. Someone inside was angry, throwing objects and screaming at the top of their lungs.

As Derrick retreated down the walkway, Roberta opened the front door and called him back. He covered up his cowardice by claiming he thought he was at the wrong address, claiming his dyslexia tripped him up.

She bought it, and Derrick relished in the feeling of pulling the wool over her eyes.

"Come in. Just watch your back," Roberta said. "Madison is way off her hinges this afternoon."

The sound of objects striking the walls and floor sent chills through Derrick's body. He envisioned someone like The Hulk being inside the bedroom, tearing it up like some rabid animal.

"So I hear. What's with Madison?" he asked.

"She's upset because I was called into work and can't take her to McDonald's to eat and play like we were supposed to do."

"Called in?"

"Yeah. Shortly after I hung up with you, my boss called me and asked if I'd like to come in for a few hours."

"I can take her if you want. She and I could walk there together."

Roberta smiled slightly. "That's nice of you, but she needs to be kept inside at all times. She can't even be outside in the backyard."

Naturally, Derrick asked why, presuming Madison had been ornery and was grounded for some time, but that wasn't the reason at all—far from it in fact. The reason Roberta didn't want Madison outside was for a more compelling than a result of bad behavior.

Roberta reached for a tissue and wiped her eyes. Derrick uncapped his bottle of water and took a few swigs, patiently waiting for a response from Roberta.

"She's been acting bizarre for some time now," Roberta said. She took a seat on the sofa after placing a bottle of water in front of Derrick. "Ever since she's been interacting with his boy spirit, he's been enticing her to do bad things… Dangerous things."

"Like what—I mean if you don't mind me asking."

"Yesterday, I let my emotions control my judgment. When she asked me if she could play outside in the backyard, I said yes. I was tired of her screaming and breaking things, and quite honestly, I needed a break myself. I shouldn't have done that though. Anyway, as Madison played in the backyard on her swing set, I stood at the kitchen sink washing dishes, every now and again peeking up to check on her through the window. The first several times I checked on her, she seemed fine. Idly swinging back and forth, her lips moving as if she were talking to someone."

"Her imaginary friend?"

"Right. I let my guard down again. After checking on her several times in a row and seeing she wasn't doing anything too crazy, I lost track of time as I listened to some music on my phone. Ten minutes passed by before I looked up again. Madison was securing a noose to her swing set."

Derrick swallowed hard. "That's scary. What did you do?"

The sounds of items striking the walls, ceiling, and floor continued as Madison screamed and shouted. Her vocalizations ranged from deep and growly to high-pitched and piercing.

"I ran outside and demanded to know what she was doing," Roberta said. She unwrapped a York peppermint patty and bit into it, then chewed and swallowed. "And she told me she wanted to hang her doll from the swing set."

"Oh. It's still a little scary, but at least she wasn't trying to kill herself."

"But I don't believe her. Her doll wasn't even outside with her." Another bite. Chew. Swallow. She stood and walked away from Derrick. "I'll go get her right now so you two can meet and I can be on my way to work."

Roberta knocked on Madison's door and walked inside her room. She nearly was struck in the head by the same doll Madison told her mom she wanted to hang from her swing set. Roberta lunged at Madison and restrained her from throwing anything else—just another day like the past several.

She and Madison stepped out into the living room. Madison climbed onto the couch and sat next to Derrick. She introduced herself with a smile that could melt anyone's heart.

Roberta handed Derrick a twenty and a ten. The twenty was payment for his four hours or so he would be babysitting Madison while the ten dollars was for them both to get something from McDonald's. The only stipulation Roberta had was for Derrick to give her any change back from breaking the ten-dollar bill.

"Yay! Let's go, buddy!" Madison exclaimed, rushing towards the door.

"Wait, Madison," Derrick said. "Please." And to Roberta: "I thought you didn't want her outside."

"It's okay. I trust you'll keep a close eye on her," Roberta said. "Maybe I'm being overprotective."

Madison began stomping up and down on the floor. "Let's go! Let's go! Let's go!"

"Ouch!" Derrick said. "Something stung me!"

Madison started laughing. Roberta asked him if he was okay. Derrick inspected the back of his arm. Along the length of his forearm was a three-inch deep scratch, which drew blood. Derrick felt around the armrest of the couch and came across something sharp not visible to the eye but evident to the touch. Roberta apologized and said she would have Jimmy—her new friend she met when Madison divulged she had a boy ghost friend to her—fix it the next time he was over.

But the sharp object from the couch had a singular point, not three.

Roberta left for work. Derrick and Madison began walking down the sidewalk to get to McDonald's. Derrick used his shirt to wipe sweat from his brow. The summer heat was milder than usual but still nonetheless hot and humid. An occasional gentle breeze offered some reprieve from Mother Nature's scorching fury.

"My friend said he thinks you should play a game with us," Madison said.

"What's your friend's name?" Derrick asked.

"He calls it Lie in the Street and Die."

Derrick stopped and knelt down to be at eye level with Madison. "Are you serious?"

Madison nodded with an ear-to-ear grin. Derrick's head spun.

"Why would he want to play a game like that?"

Madison shrugged her shoulders. She fiddled with her fingers for a few seconds before speaking. "I think it's because he wants me to go to Heaven with him. That way we can play all day and not have to listen to that bitch of a mother of mine."

"You shouldn't talk like that about your mother," Derrick asserted. *I really need to make time to find my mom.* "But I thought you both played together all the time already. Am I wrong?"

"Sometimes my friend gets pulled away by other spirits. But he told me he's getting stronger."

"What's that mean?"

"I don't know."

They continued walking down the sidewalk and when they reached the busy intersection of Cozza Boulevard, Derrick asked Madison if she wanted to push the button to trip the signal, which she did.

As traffic whizzed by at fifty plus miles per hour, Derrick remembered the story online he read about a boy who crossed the four-lane street and was struck by an eighteen-wheeler. The boy didn't cross at a crosswalk and the trucker was traveling fifteen miles over the speed limit while receiving some oral stimulation from his first cousin Willadeene.

Though the direct lesson from the tragic event was to cross at a crosswalk and to look both ways before crossing, Derrick extracted a broader lesson, and that was to make smarter choices and think before acting.

As the two waited for the traffic signal to change and the pedestrian signal to give them the go-ahead to mosey across the street, Madison began chuckling lightly and in spurts. Then she was hysterical.

"What's so funny?" Derrick asked, genuinely concerned.

"My friend said we should all play Lie in the Street and Die right now," Madison replied. "Let me show you how to play it." She started to run towards the street.

Derrick grabbed her before she could take her third step into the street. Madison tried to break away but Derrick was too strong for her.

"Madison, don't ever do that again, okay," Derrick said. "A car or truck could have plowed right into you."

"But nobody would hit us. They would stop, just like they did on my street when me and my friend played Lie in the Street and Die a few days ago."

Derrick's jaw dropped, and Madison chuckled. "You've played this before?" he asked.

She nodded. "It's a lot of fun. Especially when the cars slam on their brakes and honk their horns. Sometimes the people say bad words though. One man said—"

Derrick put a finger to his lips and Madison killed her voice. He took her by the hand and they played a game Derrick wanted to play, and the objective was to briskly reached the other side of the street before the static white walking person symbol switched to the blinking orange hand, warning pedestrians their time to cross the street was about to end.

As they crossed, Madison giggled as she scurried across the painted black-white crosswalk, keeping her eye on the pedestrian signal, eagerly pushing herself to get across the street, determined not to lose the game.

Derrick and Madison, 1; pedestrian signal, 0.

"Nice job!" Derrick said. "You did it!"

"Yeah!" Madison smiling, her tone exuberant, which a second or two later vanished. When Derrick asked her what was the matter, she said: "My friend said the game is stupid. He said it isn't dangerous enough."

"He can think that. Why is he so negative?"

"He died young. He killed himself."

A cloud of fear engulfed every molecule of Derrick's body, concerned about Madison's safety, fully aware this alleged ghost friend of Madison's could be one of Satan's angels. Derrick was shocked and amazed at how candidly Madison spoke about her ghostly friend, but it wasn't too hard to grasp why. She was too young to fully comprehend death, dying, and the spiritual world.

Derrick's cellphone crowed like a rooster—a new ringtone he switched to in order to alert him to numbers not saved in his contacts, because it was these unrecognizable numbers that might be people reaching out to him to retain his services.

Not long after Derrick answered the phone, the caller—Thomas from the BAU—stated his business. He said: "I know this might be awkward with you being a former patient of mine, but would you be willing to help me move out of my house? I've got so much work to do at the BAU that I can't possibly be in two places at one time."

"When and how much stuff are we talking about?" Derrick asked.

"I'm a pack rat, so there is quite a bit to move. You may want to bring some additional manpower with you."

"I'd need to come by and assess the job so I can give you a quote."

"I don't need a quote. I can cover your hourly rate of twenty dollars an hour for quote-unquote big jobs."

"I'd have to give my friends helping me a cut though, and I'd like to not have it come out of my earnings. Could we negotiate a price?"

"Look—I'm going off of what you have on your flier. There isn't a disclaimer about prices being subject to change based on the job."

(Listen to this fat fucker trying to stiff you! Take the job, kill him and his two bitch daughters, then kill yourself! That pudgy fucker touched you in your no-no spots while you slept in your room at the BAU!)

Another intersection, another game. Madison pushed the pedestrian button to trip the signal, eagerly waiting for the white pedestrian signal to flash so she could try and beat the clock. Derrick continued his conversation with Thomas, trying to convince him that the compensation needs to match the job.

But Thomas was adamant about paying extra since he was going by the language contained on the flier. He clarified it wasn't his intention to be difficult. And truth be told he wanted to pay Derrick a little more, but money would be tighter now than it ever was before since Thomas still had four months left on his lease at his former residence and was now paying additional rent at Lauren's house, where he and his two daughters were staying until his current lease ended and he could find himself a new house.

This situation was a dilemma for Derrick, and he was torn. On one hand, the job would still yield some profits and he needed all the money he could get. On the other hand, the profits earned didn't seem equitable with the amount of work required, even if he did all the work by himself.

"Could you do thirty dollars an hour instead of twenty?" Derrick asked.

"I'm sorry. I can't. Do you want the job or not? If not, I'm going to find someone else."

"Fine. I'll take the job."

"Thank you. I should warn you though. There may be an evil entity lurking about in the house. Just ignore its presence. Hell—it may even be an asset."

"How is that?"

"It will motivate you and your cronies to hightail it. I'm sure you'll have the moving truck loaded in no time. I'll see you early next week with your two buddies. What are their names again?"

"Andrew and Codi." *I hope they'll agree. If not, I'm screwed.*

(Bravo, you fucking eunuch! Five homicides and a suicide. It's going to be beautiful! Lure them into the moving truck and set it ablaze! We'll oven-roast that turgid Twix-eating motherfucker and his ugly kids! And your so-called friends, too!)

As the inhuman voice spoke, Derrick focused less on it and more on what Thomas was saying, and that was about the mute spirit that Thomas had encountered.

(I can't wait to meet that spirit! I like making new friends!)

"The spirit is dangerous. He destroyed my wife's urn and pissed on her ashes," Thomas said. "The ashes and urine mixed, causing a chemical reaction. The ashes exploded in the living room, some of which hit me. I've got chemical burns on my face and neck."

(I feel a kinship with this spirit! It's like I know him already!)

"That sounds scary," Derrick said. "I almost think I should be paid more simply because the job sounds dangerous."

"Don't start. We've already danced to that tune."

(Go ahead. Tell him about me—the voice inside your head that keeps begging you to kill others and yourself. I dare you, Derdickless. The meds you're taking will only keep me away for a short time.)

Derrick struggled with the decision between sharing with Thomas the auditory hallucinations he had been experiencing, and the possible notion his mind was destroying things around the house. But he suspected if he shared this information Thomas wouldn't retain his services, and Derrick needed and wanted the money. Instead, he popped two Risperidone and not long after the voice faded away.

Madison and Derrick entered McDonald's and ordered. Madison rocketed to the play area while Derrick took a seat and continued his conversation.

Thomas choked on a bite of Twix he was eating. Once he stopped, he said: "Maybe there is a way you and your friends can make some extra money. I planned to have a clean-up crew collect what ashes they could of my wife for me, but there's nothing all that sophisticated about it. How would you like to make five-hundred dollars?"

"Half a grand just to sweep up ashes? I'll do it."

"It won't be that simple. You'll need to do some scraping, but it won't be too bad."

"Scraping?"

"You'll understand it better once you see the living room where the eruption of remains happened. Do you accept the offer?"

After a brief pause, Derrick said: "I'll do it for six hundred. Do *you* accept the offer?"

Thomas muttered unintelligibly for a few seconds. "Fine. Six-hundred dollars. That's it—not a cent more."

And with that the deal was sealed. They said their goodbyes and ended the call. About a minute later, Derrick and Madison's food order was up, and Derrick smiled at the worker as he took the tray away from her.

"Oh my god!" the worker shrieked. "Look at that little girl!"

Derrick whipped around and dropped the tray. He scudded towards the door to the play area and caught Madison in his arms just as she plummeted from the top of the Play Place. Had he arrived a second or two later, Madison surely would have been severely injured—if not dead.

What was most shocking to Derrick was there were several people in the play area, parents sitting in the booths eating and children in the Play Place jumping, running, and sliding, yet nobody saw Madison scale the Play Place, stand on top of it, and jump off.

Looking into her eyes, he asked: "Are you crazy? Who do you think you are? Rogue? Molly Hayes?"

"I was playing a game with my friend! Now let me go!" Madison screamed, flailing in Derrick's arms. "Let go of me!" Her shoe struck his groin, and he was now down and out for the count, laying on the floor clutching his crotch. Madison pointed and laughed at him. "My friend thinks you're funny. He's laughing at you right now."

With strained speech, Derrick said: "Your friend is bad. He's not your friend at all. You need to stay away from. He's going to get you hurt or worse, killed."

"But he said if I jumped off the top someone would catch me, and you did. He doesn't want to hurt me, but he does want to hurt you. He's the one who scratched you at the house; it wasn't the couch."

"He's bad, Madison. You need to tell him to stay away from you."

"No! Don't!" Madison screamed.

"Don't what? What did I do?"

"Not you. I was talking to my friend. He was going to scratch your face."

"I'm not afraid." And to her friend: "Go ahead. Scratch me."

And her friend did, which left one four-inch scratch along Derrick's right cheek.

27

"You're a fucking waste of space," Scott said. "Why don't you do everyone in this family a favor and leave?"

Aaron closed his eyes. "Maybe I will."

"Good. I hope you do."

"Or maybe I'll kill myself. I want to die anyway. I'm tired of this cruel world."

Scoot scoffed as he tapped his cigarette against the coffee table. Aaron—who was lying in the middle of the living room floor—opened his eyes and stood. He looked at his dad who was puffing away on his cigarette, then snailed out of the room to the garage. On the way there, he waved at Derrick, who then stopped him.

"What's wrong?" Derrick asked. He was uncoiling an extension cord next to the weed whacker.

"My dad is being a total dick as usual," he responded.

"I'm sorry, man. Why?"

"I'll always be his punching bag. He likes to take his anger out on me. Just a few days ago, my sister was rushed to the hospital again. She was having breathing issues. My dad is the one who saved her from dying, and while it is a good thing, he's pissed about the medical bills that have accumulated from these trips."

Derrick swayed the weed whacker back and forth along the fence line as he said: "Isn't this the fifth time Emily has had to be rushed to the hospital?"

"Sixth."

"What have doctors said is wrong with her?"

"None of the doctors have answers. My mom is taking Emily to a specialist in a few days, which also has my dad mad." Derrick asked why and Aaron answered. "The potential cost. The specialist will likely want to run a host of tests. All my dad cares about is money."

For the past two weeks, Aaron had cleaned up his act. He was no longer popping pills (unlike Derrick), stealing money, or smoking dope. He helped out more around the house, cooking and cleaning. He also spent more time being a big brother to Emily and Brandon.

In spite of these changes, Scott still belittled Aaron. Scott constantly brought up Aaron's past transgressions and touted it would only be a matter of time before Aaron reverted back to his old ways.

"I'm sorry your dad is being such a douche canoe to you," Derrick said. "It's good you've made changes for the better."

"Thanks. I'll be the first to admit I've been a piece of shit, but I don't want to be that person anymore. I want to be someone my brother and sister look up to," Aaron said. "Something else my dad has done is accuse me of molesting my little sister all because I've started to spend more time with her."

"Wow. That's harsh."

They spoke for another two minutes before parting ways. Aaron stepped into the garage and leaned on the table saw he had purchased for his dad with the money he stole from his dad and cried for a few minutes.

Crying wasn't something he was ashamed of, and he didn't think men cried often enough. To Aaron, crying was a way of releasing emotional toxins from the body. Every few days he made time to cry similar to the way people make time to meditate or take a nap.

He caressed one of the teeth on the blade of the saw and tapped the point of the tooth a few times. He pictured the doll's face being maimed by the blade and shuddered at the thought of a human's face enduring the wrath of the saw blade.

As Aaron thought about the emotional trauma endured from his dad, he whispered: "I want to die…I just want to die. At least that way the emotional pain will be over."

About ten minutes passed by before Aaron's heart rocketed into his throat when the sound of the saw blade whirred. Scott had turned it on as a cruel way to wake Aaron up. Aaron apologized for falling asleep and left the garage feeling proud of himself for not cussing at his dad for acting like an ass clown—a reckless and dangerous ass clown.

28

Marcy Simmons stood in front of her bathroom mirror with her housecoat wrapped around her body, crying. It was end of the line for her. Last April, she was in a horrific work-related accident due to somebody else's negligence, which left her permanently disfigured. On top of that, her husband left her for another man shortly after her accident. As if these two events weren't bad enough, her dad was murdered a few weeks ago when a group of hoodlums broke into his house and bludgeoned him to death, and it was Marcy who stumbled upon the grisly sight.

A female Job, she referred to herself as when talking to family members and those friends who didn't break off contact with her.

I want to die, she thought. *This is a cruel world. I've had enough of it... But how should I do it?*

A voice external to her answered. "Jump out your living room window."

There's an idea, she replied.

"Good. Do it."

She walked out of the bathroom and stepped into her living room. She glanced out the window of her fifty-seventh-floor apartment and began to imagine herself plummeting to the ground, the exhilaration it would to travel through the air like a wounded bird before splatting onto the sidewalk, which would unequivocally provide an instantaneous death.

Downside is if I jump out of the window and then have a change of heart, I can't save myself. It would be too late, she thought.

"Quite right," the external voice said to her. "What about this? Take a bunch of sleeping pills with barrels of wine. Then lay flat in the tub. Once the sleeping pills start to make you feel woozy, turn on the bath water. You'll drown yourself."

Again, no safety net though, she thought.

"So? You're determined to kill yourself, right?"

"Yes," she answered aloud, her voice a whisper. "I want to die." She sprawled on the couch. "Besides, if I don't do it, you will."

"Exactly. Then it doesn't matter if there is a back door to escape or not, now does it?"

What about eating a bullet? I could do that. At least this way there is a back door. I can back out.

"No, you can't. Once you pull the trigger, that's it. Lights out."

"You misunderstood me."

Her stomached growled. She walked into the kitchen and slammed a frying pan onto the stove. She cracked some eggs into the non-stick pan and delicately stirred them with a fork.

She contemplated sticking her head in the oven and gassing herself to death, but discounted that almost immediately. She didn't want to risk killing other people in the apartment building if an explosion resulted—unlike the airline pilot who purposefully crashed a plane that took out over three-hundred people.

"Why don't you force the police to kill you?" her inner voice asked her. "Blue suicide."

No. Absolutely not. I don't want to put anyone in the position to choose whether I should live or die. I'm putting the burden on them that way, and it's not right.

"Are you *sure* you want to kill yourself?"

Yes.

"It sure doesn't sound like it. Wimp… Coward… Loser. Maybe we should let time run its course and then I'll take care of it for you."

Why don't you shut up before I blow your brains out?

She sampled the eggs and grimaced. To spice them up a little, she added a dash of salt and a scoop of cream cheese. As she stirred the eggs, she muttered to herself, mocking her inner voice claiming her hunger to commit suicide was nothing more than empty rhetoric—all talk, no show.

Before sitting down at the dining room table to savor the eggs, she peeked through the spyhole of her door, not wanting anyone to be around when she opened it. She believed herself to be too hideous and did a public service by keeping herself confined to her apartment like a rat in a cage. Had anyone been near her apartment door, she wouldn't have opened it to retrieve the morning newspaper.

At this point the amount of steam rising off of the eggs was minimal. She positioned herself in front of her plate and started to eat while glancing over the headlines of the main section of the newspaper. Nothing snagged her interest.

With her stomach full and her mind cleared, she wandered into the kitchen, placed her plate in the sink, and poured herself a glass of wine. Her favorite: Cabernet Sauvignon.

"Look at how pathetic you've become. Face disfigured. Hardly any friends. Mommy and Daddy are dead. Your husband left you. You're a tormented soul. You know you don't belong on this planet anymore, in the physical realm. It's like you're a round peg and the physical world is a square hole. It's like you're a left shoe and the physical realm is a right foot, and you're not the right fit. Release yourself."

A minute or so passed. Marcy failed to respond as she wiped tears from her cheeks as she stepped into her bedroom.

"You don't wanna die, do you?"

She picked up a vase with white roses inside of it and hurled it across the room. It struck the wall and shattered. "I do! I wanna die! I hate my—"

In an instant, she silenced herself and listened to *another* voice talking to her—and not one inside of her head this time. Her eyes widened to their maximum and her mouth was partially ajar. The voice supplied her with some instructions. She glanced at the back of her left wrist. Her heart rate spiked and beads of sweat started to form on her forehead.

"I guess there's no escape now," her inner voice said.

29

In his battle-wounded pick-up truck, Mike pulled into Derrick's driveway and beeped twice. Several dogs within earshot started to bark. Derrick walked out of the house and waved. He hoped into the passenger seat and thanked Mike for his help.

Mike made a valiant effort to convince Derrick to drive, but Derrick refused, claiming he wasn't quite ready yet, but was gradually building up the courage to get over his fear of driving. Mike respected this and laid the issue to rest, just as he did his son, Dylan.

The two of them were headed to Indiana University Northwest in Gary for Derrick to tour the campus and meet with an admissions counselor. Derrick was prepared to let go of his dream to attend Harvard or Yale and go to a four-year commuter college and pay for college himself by working. He had an epiphany recently, and he was determined to find his mother and start a relationship with her.

And as far as he knew, she could be some rich mogul of some type who could help pay for his college expenses—no matter what school he chose to attend. Given all the years she had missed of his life, all those years not helping raise him, helping him pay for college would be one way for her to make restitution.

"I'm being nosy," Derrick said, "but I can't help it. Any news on Heather? She coming home soon?"

"In a week or so. Thanks for asking."

"I'm glad she is doing better."

"Me, too, though she still has an obsession with her wrist, but Thomas thinks it has to do with the manner Dylan killed himself."

Heather was to be released several days ago, but told Lauren she didn't feel ready and requested she be permitted to stay a while longer and receive additional therapy. One concern Lauren had was Heather staying for too long—longer than necessary—and then not being able to adjust to life outside of the BAU.

And there was also the issue of how Heather viewed her husband. The death of a couple's son or daughter drastically changed both person's lives as individuals, but also the relationship between them. Heather blamed Mike for Dylan's death—as did Dylan's ghost—up until recently, thanks to Lauren and other mental heath care personnel who helped her see Mike didn't cause Dylan's death, and gradually she accepted this.

Mike belched after taking a length drink of his A & W root beer. "So, what's happening with you? How's the quest to reunite with your mother coming along?"

"Not good, and my dad has gone from keeping information about her from me to toying with me," Derrick replied.

"How's that?" Another drink, another seismic burp, as he turned onto the busy four-lane highway of Calumet Avenue after having to wait several minutes for traffic to clear since there wasn't a traffic signal at the intersection, only a stop sign, and cross traffic had the right of way.

Derrick said, "Today I asked him to relinquish my birth certificate. After about fifteen minutes of arguing, he relented. He told me to search through the boxes in his closet. I went through all the boxes, I painstakingly inspected each item in each box. My birth certificate wasn't in any of those boxes. After I told him it wasn't in any of the boxes, he started to laugh. His response was oops."

Mike rolled his eyes. "So he knew your birth certificate wasn't in any of those boxes."

Derrick nodded, saying nothing.

"Why doesn't your dad want you to meet your mom? She is the one who gave birth to you. If you want to meet her and try to weave a relationship with her, your dad should be supportive."

Even though the inhuman voice speaking from within Derrick's mind made a snide remark—claiming Bruce wasn't Derrick's dad—Derrick ignored it and responded to Mike. He said: "I think he's threatened by her. It's just been me and him since I was a baby. She also ripped his heart from his chest when he found out she was cheating on him, even during her pregnancy with me."

"That's rough, but that was years ago. He needs to put on his big girl britches and get over it. I'm sure your mom isn't the same person she was fifteen years ago."

"I would hope not. I don't think she is."

The traffic signal Mike approached switched to yellow and he punched the gas, but then a second later he slammed the brake pedal, propelling Derrick's upper body forward. Mike extended his arm in front of Derrick.

Mike took another swig of his root beer. He tried to burp, but couldn't. Derrick thanked the heavens above, grateful he didn't have to smell the stench of the belch.

The light changed and Mike punched the gas and switched from the left lane to the right to pass a slowpoke. He then abruptly shifted from the right lane to the left and displayed his middle finger, pressing it against the back window of the truck cabin.

"He keeps giving me different names, too," Derrick said. He counted on his fingers, then said: "Nine different names he's given me. "

"What are they?"

"The most recent one is Deborah. The first name he gave me was Heidi. So, Heidi, Tabitha, Ingrid, Bethany, Donna, Adelaide, Ericka, and Deborah."

"That's quite a list."

"Is there anything else your dad has told you about your mom?" Mike asked.

"Nothing new. She's a drug addict and prostitute, but I think he says those things out of anger."

Derrick told Mike about his attempt to view his school records in his cumulative file, but was turned down because Derrick was still a minor in the eyes of the state of Indiana. Much like Derrick, Mike didn't think that made much sense.

"It's your file," Mike said. "You should be able to view it whenever you want."

"I think so, too, but if it's the law, there isn't much the guidance secretary could do."

Mike glanced at the radio clock, swiftly turned the wheel to the right, cutting across the right lane and pulling into a vacant parking lot.

"What's going on? Everything okay?" Derrick said, trying to catch his breath.

Mike picked his cellphone out of the middle console that also functioned as a divider between the driver and passenger sides of the truck. Derrick looked at him, waiting for an answer.

After Mike tapped his greasy phone screen a few times, which made a prominent sound when his talon-like fingernail struck the tempered glass. He wiped the grease off of the phone screen with his shirt and placed the phone to his ear. He stepped out of the truck and walked a few paces down the sidewalk along Calumet Avenue.

Derrick glanced at him but shifted his eyes away when Mike looked in his direction.

(He left the keys in the ignition. Start the truck up and crash head-on with oncoming traffic.)

Without hesitation, Derrick swallowed two Risperidone. Mike opened the driver's side door, dropped his phone in the middle console, and fired up the truck.

"Everything alright?" Derrick asked.

"Perfect. I need to make one more detour. Do you mind?"

Derrick checked his watch. "I kind of need to get back home as soon as possible. I'm babysitting Madison today."

"Oh, yeah, you told me about her and her imaginary friend. It sounds like her friend is one evil asshole." Mike smacked the back of his neck. A warm liquid transferred to his fingers. "Something scratched me."

"I don't see anything sticking out of the seat. That's strange." Derrick peeked at Mike's neck. "You have a scratch on your neck."

"It's probably my dead son. He resents me."

"He still accuses you of his death?"

Mike nodded. "About this stop I need to make, it will be quick. I promise."

Not too many words were spoken after that. Derrick read a textbook on his Kindle app while Mike flipped between burping his soda and pushing buttons on his radio, searching for a song he liked.

About ten minutes later, Mike turned into the Chesterville High School parking lot and found a space close to the main entrance of the building. He didn't care the space was reserved for PRINCIPAL. Besides, he figured he would be in and out, and even if he wasn't, it made no difference to him.

"What are we doing here?" Derrick asked, perplexed.

"I'm going to speak to someone about substitute teaching. My wife quit her job after our son died. When she is released, I think it would be good for her to get a job to keep her mind occupied. I'd rather her be out of the house doing something productive than her sitting the house all day depressed. I'm going to inquire about substitute teaching."

"I don't think substitute teaching is the job for someone who is already mentally fragile, no offense. I mean high school kids are assholes—all of them, including me. Whenever there is a sub in the room, it's party time. It's a thankless job. Even the faculty is treated like garbage by the students, administration, parents, and society as a whole."

Mike took a swig of his soda—which was now tepid and lost its fizz—and burped in Derrick's direction. "Did you want to come inside or were you going to stay here?" he asked.

"I'll wait here."

"Suit yourself." *You've got a surprise coming to you.*

Derrick wanted to rest in the truck while Mike handled whatever business it was he needed to handle. There was no reason for him to accompany Mike inside.

Part of Mike felt snubbed by Derrick's rebuff and was close to backing out on his plan. He grabbed his cellphone and his near-empty bottle of A & W. As he walked towards the main doors and the sun beat down on his face, the sound of taps striking the pavement prompted Mike to turn his head and look behind him. Midway in the parking lot was a man wearing a trench coat and fedora caught—who was walking across the parking lot—caught his attention. The man was approaching school—just as Mike was. Derrick's eyes were closed with a White Sox baseball cap covering them.

Before pressing the button to alert someone inside he wished to be granted access to the building, he finished the remainder of his soda and pitched the bottle. Once inside he stepped into the main office and asked to be directed to the guidance office. The main office secretary—Mrs. Ladd—led the way.

Mrs. Fraser wasn't at her desk at the moment. Mrs. Ladd offered Mike something to drink and he accepted. Meanwhile, he sat in a chair near the front desk. To pass the time, he texted his mother and called the BAU to check on his wife.

Five minutes passed and by this time he had finished the bottle of water. He pulled out a folded-up piece of paper, opened it, and gazed at it with a pensiveness expression. It was a sketch Dylan had drawn, and in the sketch was a picture of an arm with an open-palmed hand. An arrow pointed to the wrist. Next to the arm was a shadowy figure shaped like a human. The shadow had no eyes, nose, or lips. It was simply a humanoid-shaped black mass.

The discordant sound of shoes striking the tiled hallway pierced Mike's ears. The volume increased with each step, but then all at once stopped. The door to the guidance office crept open and the man sporting the fedora and trench coat walked inside. Though the door crept open, squeaking intermittently, the man violently pulled it towards him, stopping it just before it slammed, then gently shut it.

The man lightly pulled down the brim of his fedora and nodded. Mike didn't nod back, but instead pointed a finger pistol at the man and smiled.

"Is this seat taken?" the fedora-sporting man asked. His voice was deep and resonant.

"Nope."

"That's an interesting picture you're holding there. What's it mean?"

"I don't know what it means. My son drew it."

"He's pointing out to you who his killer is."

"Excuse me?"

"I'm hunting it. It tried to murder my son. I nearly killed it, but it got away from me."

"It?"

The man nodded. "It—yes."

Mike sputtered a snicker, but then his laughter switched to anger. He didn't appreciate this man disparaging Dylan's death.

"I know what you're thinking," the man said. "You think I'm making a mockery of your son Dylan's death, but I'm not. I'm here to tell you your son didn't kill himself, but he was killed."

"Who are you? How do you know my son's name? Did you kill my son?" *I'm calling the police.*

"Don't call the police. There isn't a thing in this godforsaken world they can do to help. Not even an atomic bomb can stop it."

"You're crazy, you know that. My son slit his wrists in the bathtub. He committed suicide, you son of a bitch!"

"I wish that were true, but I'm afraid it's not."

Mike looked into the man's eyes and read nothing but truthfulness in them. His heart skipped several beats as he thought about the implications of the man's claim someone murdered Dylan.

"Sir?" one of the counselors said, which in turn caused Mike to turn in the direction of the person's voice. "Are you alright?"

"I'm fine. Thank you." Mike turned his head towards the fedora-wearing man but only emptiness was in the chair.

As if he had sat on a cactus, he sprang out of the chair, opened the guidance office door, and checked left and then right and then left once more.

"Sorry I'm late," Mrs. Fraser said after she turned the corner and saw Mike standing in front of the guidance office. "Traffic was a mess on Kennedy. Some driver leapt out of their car while it was in motion and was run over by a city bus. As a witness I had to stay and give my statement to police."

"I'd like to inspect and photograph the contents of my son's file, please," Mike said. "My son's name is Derrick Johns."

"You finally caved, huh? Well, good. I think you should let the mother of your son have another chance." She opened a file drawer and thumbed through them. Her fingers mimicked a runner jumping over hurdles. "Alright. Inspecting shouldn't be a problem, but I'm not sure about photographing."

Mike placed his cellphone into his pocket. "I'll just inspect his records then. That will suffice."

It shocked him the guidance secretary didn't request any form of identification to prove—or in this case to disprove—Mike was Derrick's father and had a legal right to view the records in Derrick's file.

He opened the file and attached on the inside cover of it was a pink paper with two bulleted lists on it. The first list indicated all of the required items that should be inside the folder. Two proofs of residency, birth certificate, and immunization records, and there was a checkmark by each of these bullet points.

The second list included required documents on a case-by-case basis. Divorce decree, health and dental records, adoption paperwork, social security card (copy),…

Mike shuffled through the folder, searching for Derrick's birth certificate. As he thumbed through the documents, he cracked a slight smile, recollecting his times in high school. Derrick's grades were impressive—certainly better than the grades Mike often received when he was in high school.

But soon his smile flipped. He never would get to see Dylan cross the stage and this tore his heart clean from his chest.

"Are you about done?" Mrs. Fraser snarled. "I feel like you're looking down my blouse." *I'd love to ride him on the conference table.*

Mike grimaced. "Hell no, I'm not. If I'm bothering you so much, why don't you go somewhere else?"

"I can't. I need to supervise you."

Mike finished his business and exited the guidance office without so much as saying anything else. He had what he needed and that's all that mattered.

As he walked back to his truck, his cellphone rang. It was the BAU. He took the call and learned that Heather had a nervous breakdown and would need to spend a few more days at the BAU.

After the call, he sighed, feeling deflated and alone. He walked back to the truck. Along the way, his mind began to question what name he had read on the birth certificate. It was between two names.

30

"Morning, boys," Thomas said, exiting the moving van parked in his driveway. "Thanks for coming. Where are your other two friends you said would be coming?"

"They're running late," Derrick said, apologetically, his tone deflated. "But Aaron and I can get started in the meantime."

Thomas nodded as he extended his hand to Aaron. "Alright. That's fine. But remember: a deal's a deal. No overtime pay." He handed Derrick the key to the front door. "It's nice to meet you, Aaron. What's your story?"

Aaron snickered. "Story? I don't know what you mean, sir."

After Thomas clarified and Aaron gave a brief introduction about himself—going so far as to share with Thomas his struggle with drugs and crime and his recent about face—Thomas gestured for the pair to follow him. He flipped the latch to the back door of the moving truck and threw open the door. He handed Derrick a five-gallon bucket, and inside of it were putty knives, smaller containers, and a glass urn—a replica of Sharon's.

"Aren't you coming inside?" Derrick asked.

"No," Thomas said. "After seeing that shadow ghost do what he did to my wife's—excuse me ex-wife's—remains, I can't. I'm too terrified."

"I can appreciate that."

"I want you two to work expeditiously and efficiently. The sooner you can get my wife's remains to me, the sooner my children will feel better. I've been lying to them for days now about their mother's urn."

Derrick and Aaron walked to the front door, unlocked it, and stepped inside. The two couches were turned over, the glass coffee table was shattered to bits, and flat-screen TV that was once mounted to the wall was on the floor with a large indentation in the middle of it—as if someone had punched it in a fit of rage.

"This is freaking me out," Derrick admitted.

"Don't be scared. There's nothing to worry about. Must be an angry spirit," Aaron responded.

"It looks like a demon or something was in this room and went ape-shit. Look at the couch. It's been ripped to shreds."

"Time is money, man. Let's get the remains of his ex-wife collected so we can get paid and be on our way."

They ambled down the hallway leading to the sitting room. With each step, the aroma of rotten flesh increased in intensity. They both plugged their noses and carried on down the hallway.

Once inside the sitting room, Derrick removed his shirt and coiled it around his nose, tying the shirt into a knot at the back of his head. Aaron did the same. It did little to mask the scent, but for some reason or another it made it at least tolerable.

"This is disgusting," Aaron said. "Look at these blobs and flecks of ashes all over the wall and ceiling. How did this happen?"

Derrick cleared his throat. "A ghost pissed on the ashes and they erupted like Mount Saint Helens."

Aaron started to laugh, but then Derrick shot him a look that conveyed honesty and sincerity. Aaron swallowed hard.

Reaching into the bucket, Derrick pulled out two putty knives and two containers and handed one of each to Aaron.

"Why don't you start on the ceiling and I'll start on the walls," Derrick suggested.

(Why don't you slit your throat with the putty knife and let him watch in delight? Make that tree trunk neck of yours smile.)

[I've had it with you. I'm going to get my brain evaluated.]

(Go ahead, Der-Dickweed. Tell the doctors you're hearing voices. I can't wait to see the expression on the doctors' faces. They'll commit you to an institution for sure. Then you'll never see your mom.)

Aaron scanned the ceiling. There were several clumps of Sharon's remains scattered along the area of the ceiling. Derrick started to scrape her remains from the wall.

"You're the boss," Aaron said. He positioned the ladder near Derrick, ascended its steps, and began scraping the ceiling.

Derrick spatted a few times. "Hey, man, watch what you're doing up there."

Some of Sharon's ashes landed in Derrick's mouth when he looked up to see where Aaron was scraping. Derrick ran out of the sitting room and into the hallway bathroom to rinse his mouth out, which at this point was starting to burn.

(That's the only woman you'll ever have in your mouth, Der-dick-licker! Kill yourself and I'll give you all the women you want!)

Without responding to the voice in his head, Derrick swished some water in his mouth several times before discharging it into the sink. Then he popped three Risperidone.

(You're a fool. All this time you've thought I'm a voice within your mind, and in a way, I am. But I am much more than that. I am not a product of your imagination. I am not a result of brain damage due to your so-called attempted suicide. I am an entity who is after your soul, which I should already have, but someone interrupted me during. He's hunting me and I'm hunting him. I will not stop until I have your soul. You said the words that let me in, and now it's time to pay the price.)

[Yeah, okay. Whatever you say. You're an entity. I believe you.]

(You will.)

Before Derrick returned to the sitting room to pick up where he left off, he readjusted the shirt around his nose. Now the shirt covered his nose and mouth, sort of like a mask a bandit getting ready to rob a bank would wear.

(Do you like my handiwork?)

[What the fuck are you talking about? God, I am sick of you.]

(Look at the walls, the floor, the ceiling. I did this.)

[No, I didn't.]

(I said I did it, not you, Der-dick-tickler. You still think I'm a manifestation of your brain, huh?)

(If you're not, then do something to me. Scratch me. Slap me. Better yet, kill me.)

[I can't.]

Out of nowhere, a new voice spoke from within Derrick's mind.

<Quit interacting with The Umbra, son! But let me tell you a little secret. The Umbra can't hurt you unless you say the words you said that night you had the argument with Bruce. Do you remember the words? Don't say them again. If you do, you negate your protection, and The Umbra can invoke his proposition the same way he did the night you and Bruce argued about him spending your college fund money.>

College fund money? Derrick thought. *Yeah. Okay.* He chose to ignore the inner voice and focus on his job: salvaging cremation remains. There was no doubt in his mind now. He wanted to get his head examined, confident something wasn't quite right with it. He hoped that given the time that had passed since his attempted suicide, more damage to his brain hadn't occurred.

After apologizing to Derrick about the cremation remains falling into his mouth, Aaron asked: "Are you ready to tell me the big news you have?"

"You know how I've been arguing with my dad about gaining access to my birth certificate?" he asked.

"Yeah. Did he finally cave?"

"Of course not, but I found out my mom's name."

"That's great news," Aaron said. He pushed the ladder to a new location in the sitting room as Derrick continued to scrape the wall. "What is it?"

"Wendi Price."

"Have you found out where she is?"

Derrick turned to Aaron, but Aaron was preoccupied scraping cremation remains off of the wall. "It's a fairly common name, but I'm starting with three Wendi Prices I found doing a simple Facebook search who reside in Chesterville."

"It's too bad your dad won't be more helpful. Everyone deserves second chances. His refusal to help you is like a blade to the face. Did you message those Wendis through Messenger?"

"No, not yet."

"Why not?"

"Fear."

Aaron asked for some elaboration on what Derrick meant. Both scraped away.

Before Derrick could get an answer out, the doorbell rang. Derrick said he would answer it, but Aaron insisted he would do it, wanting to take a brief break. Derrick had no qualms with this at all, and suspected Andrew and Codi were the ones who rang the doorbell.

But Derrick was wrong. It was Thomas asking for a status report on their progress, which Aaron provided. Meanwhile, when Derrick realized Andrew and Codi were not the ones at the door, he checked the messages on his phone to see if they had sent him a line about why they had not yet arrived.

When Aaron entered the room, Derrick said: "Andrew and Codi said they should be here by ten."

"Assholes. First it was 9:15. Then 9:30. Now it's 10, but whatevs." He handed Aaron a piece of paper with a list on it. "Those are the specific items Thomas said we needed to ensure we load into the moving truck. Those items are priorities."

Derrick nodded and they both resumed scraping the walls and ceiling.

"So, tell me," Aaron said. "What fear is stopping you from reaching out to the Wendi Prices you came across on Facebook?"

"Rejection. There's the rejection of her flat out not wanting anything to do with me. Then there's the rejection of her accepting me and we start building a relationship only to have her cut me out of her life again. I'm also afraid to discuss with her the attempted suicide."

"Why?"

"She may think I'm mentally unstable and kick me to the curb."

"Well, look—if she does, then you're better off without her. All I can tell you is without risk there's likely little gain."

(If you really want to see Mommy, kill yourself. Then you can spend all the time you want with her.)

Derrick pounded his head against the wall a few times, startling Aaron who nearly lost his balance on the ladder.

31

The doorbell rang and Marcy fled from the couch to answer it. When she opened the door, she embraced the person standing before her—Karla—who was her best friend since high school. They were Class of 2000 and graduates of Chesterville High School.

Marcy was still wearing her housecoat from the previous morning. Her hair was a rat's nest. Her skin was ashen.

In contrast, Maxine was dressed in a purple blouse with a matching scarf and black slacks. Her Elvira-hued hair dangled about a half inch past her shoulders. Her face was dolled up quite nice with just the right amount of makeup to accentuate her facial features without looking like a clown from Barnum and Bailey Circus. In her left hand she was clutching a bag from Panda Express.

"You're shaking," Karla said, embracing Marcy in her arms. "What's wrong?"

But Marcy didn't say a word. She tightened her embrace around Karla and started to sob.

"What is it? Tell me what's going on," Karla whispered. After a several more seconds passed, Karla said: "Let's at least go inside."

And they did. Karla led the way to the couch with Marcy's arms still wrapped around Karla. A few seconds after they sat, Marcy pulled away from Karla.

"I'm glad you came," Marcy said. "Something terrible has happened."

"What? Tell me," Karla said. With sincerity, she said: "Maybe I can help."

"It told me I can't tell, but I'm going to anyway."

"*It*?"

"Yes. This isn't a person I'm talking about, but something otherworldly, something as powerful as God—if not more so."

"What are you—"

Marcy's eyes widened. She whipped her head to the right.

"I'm not afraid of you! Do what you got to do. Kill me." A few seconds passed. Then she screamed: "Fuck you! I know I've got eleven minutes and thirty-some-odd seconds left!"

Karla shook her head in disbelief. For the first time in a long time, she found herself in a situation where she didn't know how to respond. She was flummoxed. Marcy stared pensively at the back of her wrist and began to make tick-tock noises by clicking her tongue.

After Karla cleared her throat, she said: "Please tell me what is happening."

"In about ten minutes, I'm going to die. I need you to witness my death."

"What?" Karla shrieked, lunging off of the couch.

She snickered. "I'm sorry."

"Jesus Christ, Marcy, please don't toy with me like that." She sat again.

Marcy held out both of her arms with the back of the wrists pointing towards the ceiling. "See anything?"

"A slight rash, maybe, on your left wrist. You want me to get you some lotion? Or some Cortisone."

"No. It won't help any." Marcy sniffled. "You really don't see anything else other than some redness."

Karla inspected Marcy's wrist a bit closer. "No. What should I be looking for? What is it you want me to see?"

"I'll tell you what I see. What I see—" Her decibel level went crashed through the roof. "I don't give a fuck what you told me! If I want to tell someone, I will!"

Weighing heavy on Karla's mind was the notion Marcy was cracking up, losing her screws. Marcy had spent the past several weeks cooped up in her apartment, ostracizing herself from the outside world.

"Who are you talking to?" Karla asked.

"It. The evil bastard that did this to me." She flashed the back of her wrist to Karla.

"A ghost gave your wrist an Indian burn?"

"No, no. Can't you see the numbers on my wrist?"

Karla looked again even though she didn't feel it necessary. She shook her head. "All I see is redness from irritation. Have you been scratching at your wrist?"

"Yes."

As Karla wiped the sweat from her palms and silently did some breathing exercises, she questioned whether or not she should ask Marcy about going to talk to someone. For the past few weeks, Karla urged Marcy to see a therapist and even gave her a business card to the therapist she saw when she was struggling with depression and anxiety.

But Marcy wanted no part of seeing a therapist, who would likely judge her just the same as everyone else did. She vowed to live like a recluse until the lights in her eyes flickered out.

"Four minutes, sixteen seconds," Marcy said, her voice almost inaudible. "See?" She presented the back of her wrist to Karla again.

"You're scaring me," Karla replied. "Do you want to go see a doctor?"

"Only doctor I'll be seeing is a forensic pathologist."

"Is there anything I can do to make you feel better?"

Marcy glanced at the back of her wrist once more, then back at Karla. Marcy took a deep breath. "Could I see that scarf you're wearing? It's beautiful. I'd like to die holding something beautiful in my hands."

Karla glanced down at the scarf and removed it. She handed it to Marcy and told her she could have it if she wanted it. Karla just wanted to see her best friend happy again.

Marcy caressed the scarf in her hands, relishing in the texture of the fabric, silky smooth and soft to the touch. She wrapped it around her neck once and looped both ends up and over the neck loop.

"You look pretty in it," Karla said.

"I don't feel pretty. Look at my face. Look at how mangled it is."

"I don't see any of that."

Marcy placed a hand on each end of the scarf and lightly tugged on them. About ten seconds later, the scarf tightened around her neck and she gasped for air.

"Stop!" Karla shouted. "Why are you doing this?"

The color in Marcy's face went from pale to purple. Karla tried to loosen the scarf, but the force being applied to the ends of the scarf was too great for her to overcome.

Karla rushed to the kitchen to get a pair of kitchen shears. She opened the shears and tried to slide the blade under the scarf, but she couldn't.

Marcy's gasps died, as did she.

Karla immediately called 911. Paramedics and police were dispatched and arrived within five minutes.

CHAPTER 6

1

Summer was over. School was starting.

Another year of school, Derrick thought as he sat up and stretched his arms. *I'm so ready to go back. Gotta be valedictorian, gotta rise above the pack. Dead tired though.*

He silenced the alarm on his cellphone and rose out of bed like the soul from a corpse. Deep down he was excited to start the school year, determined to rise to the top of his graduating class, eager to attend an Ivy League school in the future.

After grabbing a towel from the hallway closet, Derrick hopped into the shower and started to lather himself up with some Old Spice body wash Danielle grew to love over time, although she initially detested it. Interestingly, though, it wasn't on Derrick she first came across the scent. It was someone else. Eventually, though, she bought Derrick a bottle and asked him to use it.

(Look how pathetic you are, you limp-dicked loser. Your dad hates you. Danielle hates you. You're worthless and stupid.)

[A few more days and I'll have my neurology appointment. They'll give me something to silence you!]

The inhuman voice laughed with a demonic, guttural timbre as Derrick re-lathered his body using his pink loofah.

(You think there is a medicine than can block me out of your mind?)

[Yup. Now leave me alone.]

(You're mistaken. I'm not a voice at all, but something much more. I'm a supreme being.]

[Okay, Mr. Supreme Being. Go away now.]

(Not before I tell you this. Your little love Danielle is fucking another man right under your nose.)

The thought incensed Derrick. With the bottom of his palms, he smacked his forehead several times, almost as if he was trying to punish his own mind for thinking such a thing.

After his shower, he towel-dried his body, layered his armpits with some Old Spice deodorant, and dress himself in a Harvard T-shirt and a pair of khakis. Although he hated the scent of the Old Spice body spray—which his dad always wore—that Danielle also liked, he sprayed some onto his shirt, khakis, and neck. He also mimicked the way his dad wore cologne and body sprays: a little dab on the wrist, then rub it onto the other wrist.

He raced down the stairs.

"I didn't hear you come in," Derrick said when he stepped into the kitchen. He kissed Danielle on the cheek. "Hungry? I was going to whip up some oatmeal."

She grimaced. "No, thanks. How did you sleep?"

"Not good, actually."

"Why?"

He glanced at her, then turned away to prepare a bowl of oatmeal. She pressed him once more, even though truth be told she didn't care.

"I've been hearing voices," he said. "But one in particular taunts me, threatens me. It tries to get me to…kill myself."

"You need to tell your dad right now."

"He doesn't need to know. Besides, I've already made an appointment with a neurologist, Dr. Pritchard. Hopefully she can help."

"*She?* Excuse me?" she asked, displaying a derisive look.

"What? Women are doctors, too."

"No, you're not seeing a female neurologist. You need to find a different doctor—a male doctor."

Derrick sighed. "There's nothing to worry about. I'm not going to cheat on you with my neurologist. She's in her fifties." He pushed a few buttons on his phone and showed Danielle a picture of Dr. Pritchard, and next to her picture was her biography. "She's married. She has kids and grandkids."

"I don't care. Find a different doctor."

Derrick sighed. "Fine. I'll find a new doctor."

"Good," she said, smiling. "That's my baby. Now call her office and leave a message telling her you're cancelling your appointment."

(Fuck that bitch, Der-Small-Dick! Her love tunnel has been toured more than once. She's banging another dude, and I know who, too! Kill her! Then kill yourself! Beautiful.)

[Not hearing you.]

(Yes, you are, dumb shit. Otherwise, you wouldn't have responded.)

Derrick pulled the bowl of oatmeal out of the microwave and sat at the table next to Danielle. She applied some more lipstick.

"I'll call on the drive to school," he said.

"No. Do it now. I want it done now."

She grabbed his phone and clicked on the phone number, and when the voicemail beeped for the message to be left, she handed the phone back to Derrick. He said what needed to be said and placed his phone in his pocket.

With the oatmeal now cool, he stabbed his spoon into it and crammed it into his mouth.

"Happy?" he said, chewing with his mouth open.

"Yes. Thank you. Any luck finding your mom?"

He shook his head. "All of the Wendi Prices I've reached out to have said they have no clue who I am."

"What if the name Mike gave you is wrong? What if it isn't Wendi Price?"

Derrick rolled his eyes and she snapped her fingers. He apologized for his rude gesture. She warned him not to roll his eyes at her again, which he promised not to do.

She stuck her finger into his bowl of oatmeal and licked it off in a seductive manner. He almost rolled his eyes, but cracked a slight smile, even though her actions repulsed him, especially since moments ago that was the same finger she rotated in her ear.

He scraped the rest of the oatmeal out of the bowl into the garbage and placed the dirty it along with the spoon into the sink.

"What do you mean though? Why would Mike give me the wrong name?"

She rolled her eyes. "That's not what I'm saying. What I mean is what if your dad had a fake birth certificate planted in your file as a preventive measure from you finding out what your mom's real name is?"

"No offense to my dad, but he's not that cunning."

"I'm trying to throw you a bone here. Why don't you request a copy of your birth certificate from the courthouse?"

Derrick rolled his eyes, but she didn't see him. "My mom's name is Wendi Price. I need to get some other information about her though, where she lived or is currently living. I think we need to go through those boxes in my dad's room again and sift out any information that might be relevant to my mom."

She shook her head. "You're on your own. I helped once, but I can't do it again. I can't violate your dad's privacy like that, and you shouldn't either."

"Fuck my dad. He should be doing everything he can to help me find her, which on that note I think he knows where she is." He rolled his eyes. "Fuck that guy."

She wasn't about to get into it with him about how she believed he needed to leave it alone. She stood and walked to the living room. He followed her.

As they walked towards the front door, the TV turned on, yet neither Derrick nor Danielle commanded it to do so. The channel was airing a news broadcast about a man who was piloting his private plane over Little Rock, Arkansas with his wife and two kids inside of it. Upon reaching their cruising altitude, he leapt out of it, leaving his wife and children to fend for themselves. His body crashed through the roof of a house, landing on top of a couple who were still asleep in their bed, killing the both of them instantly.

(You like my handiwork, Der-dick? You should have seen the expression on his family's faces when I opened his door and tossed him out of his seat. Get ready! You'll soon join him!)

"What's wrong?" Danielle asked.

"Nothing. I'm fine. That's a sad story though," he replied.

"Yeah, it is."

"At least the wife was able to safely land the plane, so it does have a semi-sweet ending."

(You better kill yourself. I may not be able to touch you—otherwise I would—but if you don't start killing yourself, I'm going to start killing those close to you. Don't believe me? How about I start with your bitch-whore girlfriend?)

2

When Derrick waltzed into the living room, Bruce was passed out on the couch. A bottle of Captain Morgan was positioned between his legs.

(Go ahead and do it. You know you want to kill him, then yourself.)

[I'm not going to kill myself.]

(Take the baseball bat behind the couch and hammer his nose into his skull. Then you'll have a reason to kill yourself.)

[Before I pop another three pills to make you STFU, why don't tell me why you insist on taunting me.]

Derrick walked to the couch and looked behind it. Sure enough there was a baseball bat—an aluminum one—resting on the floor. He pulled the bat out and clutched it in his hands, maneuvering it as if he were at bat.

(You don't listen, do you? Your soul belongs to me. It's mine. Give it to me.)

[And if I don't?]

(Things will get worse for you.)

[If you need my soul so bad, why don't you kill me?]

(That's not how I operate unless absolutely necessary.)

Standing in front of the arm rest of the couch on top of which Bruce's head rested, Derrick stared at him for several seconds, as Bruce's chest rose and fell, lightly snoring.

If Derrick did take his dad out at this time, it would be a great way to go. Bruce was dreaming about making sweet love to the woman of his dreams—whom he wanted to marry—but who would never have him in that way.

(If you're not going to kill him, then kill yourself. I'm warning you. Things are going to get worse from here. I'm done fucking around with you.)

[What is about my soul that is so attractive to you?]

(Nothing. It's just another soul—one of many. But you said that words that let me in; you're the reason I'm in your ear. You should already be dead, but then someone cheated me out of what's rightfully mine.)

[My soul doesn't belong to you; it belongs to me. Go find yourself another soul if there isn't anything special about mine.]

(You know you want to bash your dad's skull in. Go ahead. Cave his face in. Pummel it to dust. Think about all the times he's abused you, neglected you, and fucked you.)

Derrick positioned the aluminum alloy baseball slightly above Bruce's nose—roughly a centimeter or two gap of space was between the bridge of Bruce's nose and the tip of the bat.

But then Derrick thought about the mess it would generate. The blood splatter across the ceilings and the walls, the damage to his dad's face, the blood, brain, and bone matter that would land on himself.

In spite of these things, Derrick still felt some sort of attraction to stamping out the life of his dad. He thought about the release of anger that would happen after the deed was done.

(I'll make you a deal, but it's also more like a dare, dick. You kill your so-called dad, you get to live. I'll take his soul over yours. All you have to do is flog his face into fragments. What do ya say? Do we have a deal?)

But now Derrick's mind shifted to the consequences. Arrest. Trial. Jail. Potential execution. The thought of being shower bait for the established convict residents of the prison pierced every bone in Derrick's body, causing him to shudder. Being passed around the prison shower like a doobie at a bong party didn't seem all that appealing to Derrick.

And then there was the loss of opportunity. If he was imprisoned, he wouldn't be able to get married and start a family.

(I've proposed a sweet deal. His soul goes, yours stays. You've got twenty-four minutes—that's one-sixtieth of a day—to start pounding his nose like a nail. Otherwise, get ready for me to drive you mad, make you crazy—so crazy you'll be begging for a swift death. Time starts…now.)

A digital countdown timer appeared on Bruce's forehead and started to countdown. 24:00, 23:59, 23:58, 23:57, 23:56…

Staring with wide eyes at the timer descend a second at time, Derrick questioned his sanity more so now than he ever did before. He wondered if he needed to return to the BAU for a more thorough neurological evaluation. MRI, CT scan. The works. *What if I have a brain tumor?*

[Do I have brain cancer?]

But the once-garrulous voice Derrick heard in his head clammed up.

Derrick leaned in closer to his dad's forehead. He placed his hand above his dad's forehead, expecting the timer to be blocked out of sight, and hoping when he moved his hand to reveal his dad's forehead, the timer would be gone.

But that didn't happen. When Derrick's hand was above his dad's forehead, the timer appeared on the top of Derrick's hand. When he moved his hand to see his dad's forehead again, the timer was back on his dad's forehead.

When Derrick placed his arm above his dad's forehead, the timer appeared on it. 21:47, 21:46, 21:45, 21:44,…

This can't be, Derrick thought as his heart raced like a runaway steam engine, the beats per minute increasing with each passing second.

3

Nobody believed Karla. She was now a suspect in the alleged murder of her best friend Marcy. Her outlandish story made headlines around the world. Scores and scores of people created their own personal videos vocalizing their opinions about Karla's assertion she didn't killer her friend nor did Marcy commit suicide.

But Karla did see *what* murdered her friend and she shared her description of it. A shadow figure. No face. No eyes. No nose.

Esteban stepped into the private room within in the jail, set his attaché case on the table, and slid the lock releases in opposite directions. The lock latches slung up, producing a sound thwack sound when they hit the top lid of the attache case.

"How are you this morning?" Esteban asked Karla.

"I've seen better days," she replied. She was wearing an orange jumpsuit with a white T-shirt underneath it.

"I understand." He set a legal pad on top of the table and fountain pen on top of it.

"Do you?" she asked, her tone sardonic.

He uncapped the fountain pen, jotted down her name and the date and time, and with a singular stroke created a line underneath these particulars. She sat across from him with her arms folded.

"I think our best shot is to enter an insanity plea," he said.

"No fucking way. I'd rather be put to death than claim insanity."

"I'm trying to throw you a lifeline here. I mean seriously, Karla. A shadow man strangled your friend. No jury is going to believe that."

"Do you believe me?" When he didn't answer after a few seconds, she asked: "Do you?"

Esteban sighed. "It doesn't matter whether I believe you or not. It's the jury we've got to convince."

"I'm not making this up."

"We need evidence to prove a shadow figure murdered your friend. What evidence is there? None. I can't go into court and make a claim without any evidence to back it."

Flipping through a different legal pad, Esteban stopped when he found the page he needed. He reviewed it while biting on the end of his fountain pen.

Marcy drooped he head back over the backrest of the chair and sighed. She wanted this nightmare to be over. Death was a welcomed friend to her at this point.

But then she chided herself. Death would be the easy way out. She tried to make vindication her focal point.

"Isn't it true Marcy stole your fiancé?" Esteban asked.

Karla scoffed with a confused expression on her face. "No."

Esteban gave her a look as if to say you're full of shit.

Marcy looked into his eyes and without so much as blinking once said: "What? No. She didn't steal my fiancé."

"I want you to keep in mind I often ask questions I already know the answers to, so please, give it to me straight."

"My fiancé and I broke up. A few months later, Marcy and my fiancé hooked up."

"And that's when you started to plan your revenge, right?"

Karla folder her arms, broke eye contact with him, and sighed. "I never once plotted revenge. I was happy for Marcy and Dan."

But Esteban wasn't entirely convinced. He flipped through pages of his legal pad and reviewed some of his notes. She uncapped her bottle of Pepsi and took a swig, all the while trying to keep her cool.

Some of the notes on Esteban's legal pad had asterisks next to them and were also highlighted in pink. These were important notes he needed to discuss with Marcy.

"Some of your friends and family I and my dad have interviewed indicated there were times you did express your dissatisfaction with their romance," he said. "I spoke with at least two people who told me you even went so far as to proclaim you hoped they both would die a tragic death. What do you have to say about that?"

She pushed her hair out of her eyes and closed her eyes. When she opened them, she said: "Yes, it's true. Okay? At first I was hurt, crushed, and jealous. But I got over it." She massaged her temples for a few seconds. "I didn't kill Marcy. An entity did."

Esteban slightly shook his head. "What about the fistfight you and Marcy got into a few weeks after you found out they were secretly an item? When were you going to tell me about that?"

"I was—"

He put a hand up. "Don't. Just don't. I'm trying to save you. Please understand this. However, if you withhold information from me, it's going to make my job increasingly difficult. Do you understand me?"

After a few seconds of hesitation, Karla nodded. "I do."

"Good," he said, smiling. He readied his pen for her to open her Pandora's box of secrets. "I'm all ears."

As she opened like a book and shared her story, Esteban jotted down notes, nodding occasionally.

4

Jimmy—who was sitting in a chair near Roberta's couch—removed his reading glasses and placed one of the earpieces in his mouth. Roberta—who was sitting on the couch—stared at him, waiting for him to say something now that she shared with him the notion Madison was communicating with a spirit.

Madison was asleep, laying with her head on her mother's leg.

"I do believe she can see and hear a little boy spirit," he said. "I don't believe it's an imaginary friend."

"What can we do to help her?" she asked. "This spirit is dangerous. He keeps trying to get her to kill herself."

"Are you a religious person?"

"Agnostic."

Jimmy nodded. "I'd recommend a medium be brought in and try to make contact with the boy spirit. Maybe the medium can help the boy cross over."

"What am I to do in the meantime? I can't have her out of my sight for any amount of time, but I also have to go to work."

Over the past few weeks, Madison's behavior became increasingly erratic and dangerous. Last Tuesday, Roberta heard a ruckus, awaking her in the middle of the night, and got up to check out what was happening. When she lumbered out of her bedroom with squinted eyes due to the hallway light being left on, she noticed the bathroom light was on and walked in it. Madison was gulping cough syrup. When Roberta confronted Madison about it, Madison explained her friend—the boy spirit—told her to do it. Another one of his dangerous games.

And, most recently, Roberta discovered Madison in her bedroom lightly dragging a knife across one of her wrists.

"I'll take off work for a few days," he said. "I've got some personal business days I can use."

"I can't have you do that. This isn't your responsibility," Roberta said.

"I'm happy to do it. It's no trouble."

"I don't know. I feel like it's having you do too much."

"It's not. You can still go to work, I'll keep an eye on Madison. I'll also try to find a medium. I think my sister has a friend who is a medium or has a friend who knows a medium. I'll give my sister a call and find out."

Shortly after Jimmy walked outside to make his call, Madison awoke. She rubbed her eyes and asked where her mom placed her Happy Meal. Roberta told Madison it was in the kitchen on the counter.

"Can I go get it? Me so hungry," she said, rubbing her tummy.

Roberta smiled. "Sure, let's go get it."

"No, Mommy. I do it all by myself. You stay here. You've had a hard day today."

"It's okay. I'll come with you."

Madison jumped several times as she shouted: "No! I said I can do it all by my fucking self! Goddamn it!"

"Excuse me, young lady? You don't use that language, and you certainly don't talk to me like that either. Now, what do you say?"

"I'm sorry." Then she cupped her mouth and whispered: "No, I will not tell my mom to die and burn in Hell."

Roberta accepted Madison's apology, but was still in a state of shock Madison would use profanity.

Together, Madison and Roberta walked into the kitchen, as Madison leading the way. Roberta handed Madison her Happy Meal box, and then Madison climbed onto a chair and removed the items from it: three chicken nuggets, a handful of fries, and a pre-packaged chocolate chip cookie—not her favorite kind of cookie, but she didn't mind a chocolate chip cookie every once in a while.

With the push of her foot, the chair pulled out and Madison invited her spirit friend to sit.

"Your friend is in this room with us?" Roberta asked.

Madison turned her head towards her mother and stared at her with hard eyes. Then she turned away from her.

Roberta walked over to Madison. "Why did you give me that look?"

"He doesn't like you, Mommy. He wants to do bad stuff to you," Madison responded.

"Then he needs to leave."

About five seconds later, Roberta clutched her left arm and wailed in pain. Her arm had long welted scratches running down the top of her arm—from where the arm bent down to the top of her wrist. On the back of her arm, three welted scratches running laterally started to form on her arm, and ironically, though these were smaller in size compared to those on the top of her arm, their pain was ten times greater.

Madison chuckled. "Yeah, Mommy does look funny when she's crying in pain."

The sound of the front door opening stifled Madison's laughter. Jimmy stepped into the kitchen and immediately rendered aid to Roberta, ripping a long stretch of paper towel off of the roll.

"What happened?" he asked.

"If I wasn't a believer Madison's friend was a ghost before, I am now."

"The spirit did that to you?" Jimmy asked, not entirely surprised.

Roberta nodded.

"What's your name?" Jimmy asked. "I demand for you to tell me your name."

A cabinet door silently swung open behind Jimmy, nearly striking him on the back of his head. A second later, it slammed shut, and Madison cackled as she pointed at Jimmy, who was clutching his chest.

"Not funny," he said to Madison. "I've got a heart condition."

"I want you the hell out of my house!" Roberta shouted. "I'm tired of telling you!"

Madison's laughter stopped on a dime. "What? You tried to kick my friend out?"

"He's not your friend, Madison," Roberta said. "He's evil, and he can't be around you anymore."

"But, Mom, he's my friend!" Madison said, swiping her arm across the table, knocking her food and drink onto the floor, which hit her mother.

"I'm your mother! Don't you care about me? Don't you love me? I'm trying to protect you," Roberta said.

"He said you would try to tell me that and I shouldn't listen," Madison said.

"Please tell me his name," Roberta pleaded. "Who is he?"

"I can't tell you his name, but I can tell you he was killed in his bathtub. His dad's name is Mike and his mom's name is Heather."

"Is that why he wants you to kill yourself?" Roberta asked. "Because someone killed him he now wants to take other people down with him?"

Madison put a finger to her chin. Jimmy dabbed the puddle of Pepsi on the floor while Roberta cleaned up the food mess.

"He didn't want to die, Mommy," Madison said. "But The Umbra killed him."

"The who?" Jimmy asked.

"Umbra, dumbass," Madison responded.

Roberta stomped her foot. "Madison! What did I say about using bad words?" The pain from the scratches dissipated, though only a little.

"Sorry, Mommy." And to Jimmy: "I'm sorry I called you a bad word to your face."

"I accept your apology," Jimmy said. "Will you tell us more about this Umbra?"

"I don't know anything else. That's all Dylan has told— Oh, shit! No, don't go, Dylan! Please!"

"Dylan? Your spirit friend's name is Dylan? What is his last name?"

"I don't know," Madison said, "but he's super-pissed—I mean mad—at me now."

Roberta placed her hands on Madison's shoulders and looked into her eyes, her big brown eyes. "I understand why your ghost friend is angry now."

"Because I squealed. That's why," Madison said.

"Well, yeah, but I didn't mean that. What I am talking about is someone murdered him. That's a terrible way to leave this world. We're going to help him. Okay?"

Madison nodded and hugged her mom. Jimmy tossed the food and soaked paper towels—some with soda and others with blood from Roberta's scratches—into the trash.

5

As Derrick and Aaron finished raking up the fallen leaves in the front yard of Derrick's house, Bruce swerved into the driveway and honked several times, but not in the car he had left with a few hour ago. This was a 2018 Lexus—a silver one.

Derrick rushed over to the car. Bruce rolled down the tinted window and handed him his cellphone.

"Talk," Bruce said, his tone stoic. "You'll find out."

Derrick pressed the MUTE button on the screen. "Who is it?" he asked.

"Your mother. I've decided you have a right to know who your mother is and have an opportunity to get to know who she is."

"Really?"

Bruce smiled. "Yeah."

The fact Bruce had a new car was completely pushed out of Derrick's mind with the news his mother was on the phone waiting to speak to him. Now that the moment for the two to speak to one another was here, his mind became a blank slate. After a few seconds of hesitation, he started to panic. *Should I say hello, Mom?* he thought to himself. *Should I simply say hello? Or would it be better to begin with a formal introduction.*

Still seated in his brand-spanking new car, Bruce pushed the phone to Derrick's ear and told Derrick to talk.

"Hi, there," Derrick said, his tone deflated.

"My baby boy!" a woman with a mousy voice exclaim. "How are you?"

"I'm decent. You know, doing what I can. How are you?"

"I'm doing wonderful, actually, but I don't want to talk about me. Let's talk about you. Tell me about yourself. Give me the 411."

As Derrick spoke to the lady—the stranger that was his mom—Aaron walked over to his house and shot some free throws, waiting for Derrick to finish his call.

Bruce stepped out of his car, pulled out a package of dusty clothes from a bag in his back seat, and buffed his car.

After Derrick finished his introduction of himself, he asked: "Can you tell me your first name?"

"Mom," she said, her tone motherly.

Derrick lightly chuckled. "I know that, but what's your first name."

"Mom. That's my first name to you. Do I make myself clear?"

The assertive position she took was refreshing to him. Unlike Bruce—who essentially let Derrick do as he pleased—so long as he took care of the cooking and cleaning around the house, having some structure and constraints was a nice change. Part of Derrick wished Bruce set stricter parameters and participated in his life more like most parents did with their children.

"Yes, Ma'am—mom," Derrick said. *That is weird calling this stranger Mom all of a sudden.* "I wanted to ask you something, and this isn't easy."

"Lay it on me."

"Why did you leave me and Dad?"

She breathed a few times into the phone before speaking. Nearly fifteen seconds went by before she said: "I was wrong to do that. I regret it. I wasn't ready to commit to being a parent or a spouse. I didn't want to settle down."

"Did you think about aborting me?"

"Never. But I wasn't ready to be a mom either. I asked your dad throughout my pregnancy what would happen to you if something happened me, if I died, for instance. Your dad said that would never happen but I pressed him for an answer based on the hypothetical. He told me he would do the right thing and take care of you if something happened to me."

"So that was you getting a read on him and his intentions. You wanted to make sure if you did leave, I would be cared for? Is that it?"

"Bruce was right. You are smart and perceptive."

"He said that about me?"

"He did."

"Cool."

As she asked Derrick to tell her more about his interests, hobbies, and aspirations, Derrick quickly glanced at the phone number from which she called. The area code was 417. He answered her by sharing he enjoyed strength training, aspired to be an engineer, and was dating his future wife. She advised him not to be so possessive with her, and recommended he not say to Danielle he wanted to marry her this early in their relationship.

"But I want her to know she's the only one for me. Besides, if anyone is possessive, it's her," Derrick said. He looked up which state the 417 area code corresponded to, and that was Missouri. "She won't even let me see a female doctor."

"Well, I can see why. You don't need a female doctor. Your plumbing is different."

Derrick rolled his eyes and sighed. "Not that kind of female doctor. I mean a doctor who is female."

(How about I kill the bitch on the phone? You want to hear her scream? Listen closely and you'll hear the snap of her neck!)

[Leave my mom alone!]

(If only you knew what I know.)

"Oh. I see," she said, tittering. "Well, maybe she does want to be with and only you then. Good for you."

"It's too bad we didn't start this conversation a few weeks ago. I could have made a trip to Missouri and visited."

"Who said I live in Missouri?"

"Well, I mean your area code is 417, so I figured—"

"You're not too bright, you are? Bruce was right—you aren't exactly the sharpest bulb in the box, are you?"

Derrick's heart sank to his stomach and he nearly fell over from disorientation. He sat on Bruce's front fender, but immediately jumped off of it when Bruce admonished him.

"Excuse me?" Derrick asked, confused.

"Now listen! Because I'm not repeating myself for your stupid never-going-to-any-Ivy-League-school ass! I have no interest in wanting to get to know you—over the phone or in person. I only talked to you as a favor to that cradle-robbing asshole father of yours. Move on with your life! You're crazy to have thought after all these years I would want to all of a sudden want to make up for lost time. Stop obsessing about me. I've moved on, and so should you."

The line went dead but the pain in Derrick's heart was all too alive and well. *What the hell happened here?* Derrick thought as he sat on the back fender of Bruce's car. *We were having such a good conversation.* He held the phone in his hand, staring at it and pondering whether he should call her back.

He pressed her number and the phone rang seven times before it cut to the voicemail. The automated message indicated the number Derrick had reached was of a TextForFree subscriber. Derrick left a message for her and afterwards tried calling her once more. This time, the phone didn't ring seven times, but only one full ring and then a partial ring, at which point Derrick was sent to voicemail.

Aaron wandered back over and asked Derrick how he believed the conversation with his mom went, and Derrick held nothing back.

"She told me she wants nothing to do with me," Derrick said. "She only gave me the time of day to tell me to fuck off."

"I'm sorry," Bruce said before Aaron could. "I tried to tell you she's dead to me." *Fuck that dead bitch.*

Aaron said: "At least you now know she isn't interested in reconnecting. Now you can focus your energies on your studies."

(Listen to that smug asshole! Go ahead! Put his fucking head through the window of your so-called dad's new car! Kill them, Der-limp-dick! Then slice your wrists like that little fucker Dylan! He was so much fun to kill when he didn't take of business himself! Nobody wants you! Nobody loves you! Kill yourself, you worthless waste of human space!)

"Yeah, I guess you're right—both of you," Derrick said. He pulled out his Ice Breakers container and placed one in his mouth. "What's funny is even though she wants nothing to do with me, it makes me want to try harder to convince her otherwise."

Bruce almost slammed his fist on the hood of his brand-new car. "Goddamn it! Do you know how to take a hint? That dead bitch mom—I mean brain-dead bitch mom of yours—just told you you're dead to her. Leave her alone. Leave it alone."

"But, Dad, I don't think that's the right thing to do," Derrick contended. "I think she regrets leaving us and it's hard for her to talk to me, so she is taking the easy way out."

"What the hell are you talking about?" Bruce asked.

"I'm a constant reminder of the bad thing she did, and that was leaving us," Derrick said. "But deep down I think she wants to get to know me as the son she hardly knew."

Aaron shook his head. "I'm telling you, man. I don't think she's remorseful at all based on what you told me. I think she's telling her true feelings. I would listen to your dad and forget her."

"I can't," Derrick said. "At least not until she tells me *why* she wants nothing to do with me."

Bruce stuck a finger in Derrick's chest. "Look—I'm warning you. Leave this alone. I already went above and beyond against my better judgment and gave you an opportunity to talk to your mother. I'm not fucking around anymore. Drop it."

(Punch that drunk asshole in the throat!)

"Dad, stop!"

"Little bastard! I wish you were never fucking born!" Bruce shouted. Then he stormed off into the house.

"Wow. And I thought my dad was nuts," Aaron said.

"I don't know what to think right now," Derrick said.

"What do you mean?"

"I'm flooded with emotions right now. Anger. Sadness. Hatred. When my dad was poking my chest I wanted to punch his fucking nose into his brain. I was so close to socking him, and that scares me."

Aaron assured Derrick there was nothing to worry about, that his feelings in the heat of the moment were perfectly natural, but then again Aaron wasn't privy to the voices Derrick heard— especially the inhuman one. Rage surged through Derrick's body like electricity in a circuit.

But Derrick wasn't convinced. The inhuman voice he heard in his mind wasn't something he experienced up until after his attempted suicide—at least as far as he could recall.

The battle wasn't over though. Derrick was determined to get an explanation from his mother as to why she didn't want anything to do with him.

"I got to get to my dad's cellphone and text myself the number," Derrick said. "I need to call my mom back and find out why she loathes me."

"Let it go, man," Aaron pleaded. "All you're going to do is open yourself up to more hurt."

(He's right, ese. She'll hurt your feelings and crush your spirits. Call her. Then you'll slip into a dark place, say the words, and then you'll have to kill yourself!)

[Fuck you!]

Aaron and Derrick fistbumped before parting ways. When Derrick stepped into the house, Bruce was seated on the couch with a bottle of Jim Beam in one hand and a partially-eaten roast beef sub sandwich in the other.

"You come to your senses?" Bruce asked. "Or do you still have a hard-on for your mom?"

"You're disgusting," Derrick snapped back.

"No—I'm just keeping it real with you. I've told countless times that bitch who is dead to me wanted nothing to do with you or me, but you didn't want to listen to reason."

"But why doesn't she? That's what I want to know."

"Because she's a fucked-in-the-head brain-dead bitch. She's psychotic. She hears voices. It's a wonder she's not in a mental institution. She's not somebody you would want to know. I'm trying to protect you."

Derrick lightly sighed. "I can see your point. I don't want to try strike up a mother-son relationship with her after the way she talked to me, but I still want to hear from her why she feels this way."

"Does it matter? Like the Beatles song, let it be." He took a lengthy swig of his Jim Beam. No shot glass. Straight from the bottle.

Before opening his mouth to speak, Derrick gave pause and considered what Bruce said rather than responding in a knee-jerk reaction fashion.

"Maybe you're right," Derrick said. "Maybe it is better to leave it alone."

"I'll drink to that!" Bruce said, his tone exuberant, smiling.

"Will you tell me her name though?"

"Heidi was her name. No, that's not right. Catrina. Wait, no-"

"Dad, what the hell is wrong with you? Didn't you speak to before giving me the phone? How can you not know her name?"

Bruce slammed down another swig of the whiskey. "Because she had some many fucking personalities and names—like that Sybil broad—I couldn't keep track of what her name was. She changed it from one day to the next."

"Seriously?"

"Yeah. I wouldn't joke about something like that. I think today she told me her name was… What was the last name I told you?"

"Catrina, I think."

As Bruce mumbled he counted on his fingers: "Heidi, Catrina, Tabitha." Then with a resonant voice, he said: "Tabitha is what she told me her name was today. If we called her back tomorrow, she'd probably tell us her name is Ingrid. And the day after that, Bethany. She talks to thin air. She hears voices like she's fucking Joan of Arc or someone. She also suffers from different inner voices speaking to her to do bad things to herself and to others. It's ridiculous."

I guess that explains why I'm hearing voices then, Derrick said. *Thanks, Mom.*

(He's lying to you, Derrick. Kill him. Then yourself.)

Derrick wanted to tell Bruce about the voices he was hearing, but before he could, Bruce ranted for several minutes, and this deterred Derrick from coming forth with disclosing the disturbing inner voices he had been hearing since his suicide attempt.

"Did she ever try to hurt you?" Derrick asked.

"Try? She did hurt me. She up and left with another man and left me to raise you all by myself," Bruce answered.

"Did she ever try to *physically* hurt you?"

"A few times, but I took care of her good and proper."

"You hit a lady?"

"Of course not. I'm simply saying I didn't allow myself to be pushed around." *Fuck that dead bitch. That bitch is dead to me. That's how she'll always be to me.*

"Why wouldn't you get her help if you knew these things about her?"

The Jim Beam satiated his bloodstream. Bruce slurred: "I did get her help. She was on a host of meds, which she refused to take on a regular basis." He took another drink of his Jim Beam, but spat it out. "There's that fucker again!"

"What fucker? What are you talking about?"

Bruce rolled his eyes. He scratched his chevron mustache. "Who do you think?"

"That shadow figure?"

"Yep. It darted into my room."

Unafraid, Derrick sauntered into Bruce's room. No ghosts. No goblins. No shadow figure. But for some reason, the words *shadow figure* sparked something within Derrick. *Shadow figure,* he thought. *Why do I feel like I had an encounter with a shadow figure before?*

"Why don't you show yourself to me?" Derrick asked. "Too much of a pussy?"

Bruce called from the living room, slurring his words more so than last time. "Don't provoke it, Derrick! I don't want an angry spirit in the house."

I'm an idiot, Derrick thought. *He's all shitfaced and seeing things. I haven't once seen this shadow figure. Why is that? They're crazy.*

(Do you honestly believe that?)

[Yes.]

(Good. Now go to Mike's house, retrieve a shotgun from his gun cabinet, and blow your head off your shoulders in Dylan's room.)

[I hate you! Leave me alone!] "Please leave me alone," Derrick whispered with a firmness in his voice.

When Derrick returned to the living room, Bruce was passed out on the couch, the bottle of Jim Beam still clutched in his hand. Every seven seconds or so, a snoring sound would emanate from Bruce.

With his dad knocked out from the happy tonic, Derrick made his move. Partially sticking out of Bruce's pocket was his cellphone, which to Derrick was like a diamond shimmering in the sun. Creeping towards his dad with a nefarious smile on his face as he thought about the victorious feeling he would soon experience after he retrieved his mom's number.

(Just kill yourself. He hates you. You're worthless.)

[Shut up!]

(I'm going to find a way to kill you. I promise. I'll drive you mad until you throw yourself off a tall building.)

[Die! I don't want to hear you right now.]

(Your dad isn't even a dad to you. Maybe if you weren't such a burden on him, he'd be happier. Hey! Wanna see your mom? You want to get to know her better? Here's a little preview of where you you'll be able to find her!)

An image of a graveyard flashed into Derrick's mind, stopping Derrick in his tracks. As if he was in a movie, his mind's eye traveled towards a gravestone. WENDI RICE was the name on it though, not Wendi Price, which confused Derrick. *Why is my mind changing my mom's name?* he wondered.

(Let's fertilize your mom's resting site.)

A massively-sized buttocks—and only a buttocks— appeared about fifteen feet above the grave with its cheeks pointing towards the grave. A stream of liquid feces squirted out, somewhat like a soft serve ice cream machine—just like the one at the Burger King he and his friends so often enjoyed a meal. An endless flow of runny shit doused the grave, eventually flooding the ground.

As if walking up a flight of stairs, a woman exited the grave wearing a shit-covered white dress. Feces freckled her face. She sloshed through the shit-saturated ground towards Derrick.

"Come join me, Derrick," she said. Her voice was pleasant as pie, soothing as the scent of sage, smooth as silk. She reached out her hand. "Let's go downstairs and I'll let you pummel my love tunnel." Then she flicked her tongue out a few times at him.

Derrick screamed at the top of his lungs, which awoke Bruce, who chewed his ass out and sent him to his room.

Her voice sounded nothing like my mom's though, Derrick thought.

6

Waking up to the sounds of Bruce and some chick moaning, Derrick stumbled out of bed and made his way downstairs to get himself a small something to snack on and a glass of juice.

When he reached the foot of the stairs, the inhuman-sounding voice in his head spoke.

(Look out the front window of the living room. There's a surprise there for you.)

And he did. In the driveway was Danielle's car. He disabled the home alarm and walked outside to her car, but she wasn't in it. He rushed upstairs to his room and sent her a quick text message.

He texted her: *Are you here? I see your car in the driveway.*

She replied via text: *Yes. I'm on the back porch.*

But he didn't reply back. He scurried to the back door, which led to the back porch. He turned the porch light on and peeked through the spyhole, but he didn't see her on the back porch.

He walked outside to look for her, searching the backyard, and then the front. She wasn't anywhere to be seen, but her car was still in the driveway. He walked to the backyard once more and checked the back porch, but still no Danielle.

Before entering the house again through the back door, he called her, but terminated the call when he heard her phone ringing within the house.

"How did you get in the house?" Derrick asked when he walked into the living room.

"The front door," she answered.

"But I locked the front door when I came back inside."

"I let her in," Bruce said, half awake, as he walked down the hallway. "Take a pill."

"Sorry," Derrick said to Danielle. "Is everything okay?"

"No. I had the strangest feeling you were going to do something bad—either to yourself or Bruce."

Derrick paused before speaking. "Why didn't you call me and let me know you were coming over?"

"I didn't want to wake you. I mean I thought about waking you—that's what I was doing on the back porch. I was torn between waking you or letting you sleep. You must think I'm crazy."

Derrick slightly smiled. "No, I don't think that at all." He turned his head towards the hallway leading to his dad's room. Then he turned back to Danielle and place a finger to his lips. "I'll be right back."

"Where are you going?" she asked.

"I gotta check something," he whispered.

He discreetly walked down the hallway and peeked in his dad's bedroom. Nobody was laying in the bed though. He stood there in the doorway for a few seconds when out of nowhere a hand was placed on his shoulder, which caused him to scream.

"What's going on out there?" Bruce demanded to know.

"Nothing, Dad. Sorry," Derrick said. And to Danielle: "You scared me half to death."

(Half isn't good enough, you little fucker! Be dead all the way!)

Derrick ignored the inhuman-sounding inner voice this time. He didn't really cancel his appointment with the female doctor Dr. Pritchard, but the good doctor did have an emergency the day of his appointment, and the office rescheduled his appointment, which was six days away.

Derrick and Danielle took a seat on the couch. She pulled out a brush from her purse and ran it through the length of her long brunette hair, which she had been growing out for since summer. She wanted to donate her hair to St. Baldrick's.

"She left his room already," Danielle said.

"Gayle?" Derrick asked.

"No. Someone else. Gayle left for Virginia weeks ago. I thought I told you that."

"Oh, yeah. I forgot. Who then is in Bruce's room getting the treatment?"

Danielle shrugged her shoulders. "Beats me." She took out a scrunchie from her purse and tied her hair into a ponytail. "How is Gayle anyway?"

Derrick shrugged his shoulders. "I haven't really seen or talked to her lately. She's been busy with work. Besides, she wasn't happy when I spilled the beans about my dad banging another woman to her, but I believed she needed to know."

"But your dad and Gayle aren't even dating, so what would it matter?"

"She loved him—probably still does."

It was an accident. Derrick didn't intend for Gayle to find out his dad was sleeping another woman. He presumed the woman his dad was with that one night he stormed into his dad's bedroom was Gayle. The next day he sent Gayle a text, apologizing for barging in on her and his dad during their get-freaky session.

But Gayle contended it wasn't her, and ever since kept her distance from Derrick's dad. She never, however, confronted Bruce about his sexual encounter with the other woman since it wasn't any of her business.

Flashing red lights coupled with the sound of sirens put the brakes on their conversation. Derrick lunged off the couch and approached one of the living room windows when the flashing red lights didn't vanish.

An ambulance was parked in front of Aaron's house. Derrick disarmed the home alarm system and stepped outside to watch the show. Aaron's front door was wide open and Derrick could see into the house. There wasn't any activity though.

About five minutes passed before paramedics rushed outside, one of whom was carrying Emily. One paramedic jumped into the driver's seat of the ambulance while the other—the one holding Emily—climbed into the back of the ambulance. Seconds later, it sped off into the dead of night.

7

"Don't you think it's time you learned how to drive?" Mike asked. "You aren't going to be able to rely on people to chauffeur you around the rest of your life."

"I'm growing more comfortable to learn, but I'm still too afraid to drive," Derrick responded, raking leaves into a pile on Mike's front yard.

"Why?"

"About two years ago, my dad and I were in a major car accident. He wanted me to drive on the expressway to get practice. We were driving on Cline Avenue when a snowplow for the city hurled a shitload of snow onto our windshield. I panicked and ended up striking the truck's plow twice before colliding with the median guard, which caused us to flip over several times."

As Mike bagged the pile of leaves Derrick had just raked, he said: "I can understand why you might be afraid to drive. That sounds like a traumatic experience. Have you talked to a therapist to get over your fear of driving?"

"No. I'm not sure I want to drive anyway. There are other alternatives to driving a vehicle. Bus. Train. Bike. Roller blades. I've got options."

Mike chuckled and bagged another pile of leaves. Derrick continued to rake the front yard. An icy cold breeze skidded across Derrick's face. It pierced his skin. He looked into the direction the wind traveled. A little boy stood in front of him, who held up his wrists, from which blood squirted out of them, before disappearing in an instant.

Derrick looked over at Mike who was thumbing a text message. A few seconds later, Mike felt eyes on him and turned to Derrick.

"What's wrong?" Mike asked.

"I just saw Dylan's spirit," Derrick responded. "He said you killed him."

Mike stumbled backwards as if an invisible force had slammed into his stomach. He fell to the ground and began to sob. Derrick dropped the rake and approached him.

"I don't know why he thinks I killed him," Mike said. "I didn't. He committed suicide."

(Dylan is wrong and so is Mike. I killed that finicky little shit Dylan. It was a glorious sight—his blood squirting all over the walls and tub.)

Now Dylan appeared in back of Mike but in front of Derrick. Dylan shook his head with his facial muscles tense. He pointed at the back of his dad's head.

Why am I seeing ghosts all of a sudden? Derrick thought.

"Because I want you to see me," Dylan whispered in his ear, even though he wasn't near Derrick's ear.

The inhuman-sounding inner voice with Derrick's head spoke. *(Hi, Dylan. How's death? Enjoying it? Sorry I had to kill you, but you wouldn't do it yourself like you were expected to do. You were a ripe little peach I enjoyed slicing.)* Then the inhuman voice cackled. *(I do appreciate you serving me though. You're one of the few spirits who I do not torture since you serve me.)*

Why am I thinking these thoughts?

"They're not your thoughts," Dylan said. "It's The Umbra speaking."

The Umbra?

"Yes. The Umbra. It's an—"

(Now, Dylan. Let me warn you as a courtesy if you share details about what I am, I can kill your spirit, and then you'll be nothing more than dispersed matter within the universe. Do you want me to kill you all over again? Enjoy eternity as a spirit. Don't make me have to murder your spirit. Go persuade Madison to kill herself. She's not too far from cracking.)

"Fuck you!" Dylan shouted at The Umbra. And to Derrick: "The Umbra is an omni—"

A white mass whisked Dylan's spirit away and vanished an instant later.

(Rescued by the Soul Savior, and just in time, too. I was about to turn Dylan into nothing more than scattered atoms—kind of like breaking at the start of a pool game.)

Is this real? I must be losing my mind. "What do you want with me?" Derrick whispered.

(How long are we going ride this Merry-Go-Round, Der-Dick. I want your soul released from its vessel. It belongs to me, just as Dylan's does. You should be dead, and you know that. I tried once to kill you when you failed to do it yourself—time was up—and I had to intervene, which I honestly dislike doing. I prefer it when people kill themselves. It's such a fun sight to see. At least Dylan had the balls to puncture his wrist, at least he made a valiant effort to kill himself. The electric knife was my favorite.)

[How were you cheated out of killing me?]

As The Umbra answered, Derrick placed a hand on Mike's shoulder and asked if he was okay. Mike nodded, stood, and plodded into his house.

[Your dad speared me with the Sacred Sword—my only weakness, though he missed the sweet spot to destroy me. He thinks he's hunting me, but I'm hunting him, also. I'm going to turn your dad's spirit into fragments of items. I've got to go now. Watch your back, jack!]

This doesn't make sense, Derrick said. *My dad isn't a spirit.*

Though it was difficult to force himself to do, Derrick got back to work raking up the leaves into neat piles. While doing this, his mind processed different pieces of information, all of which seemed to contradict one another. Several questions ran through his mind, and he tried his best to resolve the contradictions. *How could my dad have saved me if it was the police officer who found me at the baseball field? Why does Dylan claim his dad murdered him yet at the same time The Umbra takes credit for his murder? And who the fuck is this Umbra entity? Does it really exist or is it my mind constructing it?*

Though he expended considerable energy searching for answers to the questions he posed himself. But then he remembered something The Umbra—whoever or whatever the hell it was—said, and that was a remark to Dylan about Madison.

Oh my god! Dylan is the boy spirit Madison has been playing with, and he's the reason she's been trying to kill herself.

Derrick promptly whipped out his phone and within ten seconds, Roberta was greeting him in his ear. He replied back in kind before getting down the brass tacks.

"Listen—you're probably going to think I'm crazy, but I do believe Madison is interacting with a ghost, and I know specifically who that ghost is," Derrick said.

"I believe you," Roberta said. "Who is the ghost?"

"His name is Dylan. He was the son of one of my customers. He slit his wrists in the bathtub. When was the last time Madison encountered Dylan? Can you ask her, please?"

Creeping into Derrick's ear were the sound of footsteps and light breathing. Meanwhile, Derrick knocked on Mike's front door, but entered before Mike had a chance to invite him inside.

Mike was inside the bathroom, laying in the bathtub with his clothes still on his back. The once-white tub was tinged with a light red color from the blood Dylan shed that fateful night. Though Mike had tried numerous times to remove the stains, it was no use, and he feared how Heather would react to them when she saw them upon her return. Mike considered replacing the bathtub for his wife's sake.

Roberta knocked on Madison's door and then tried to open the door by turning the knob, but it was locked. "Madison. Derrick wants to know when was the last time Dylan spoke to you," she said. "Open the door right now. We talked about you locking your door, and you're going to be in more trouble if you don't open it right now." She pressed her ear against her door and could hear faint talking between two people: a girl and a boy, and this was a first.

"Did she open the door?" Derrick asked.

"No, not yet." Roberta pounded on Madison's door with an open palm. With an assertive tone, she demanded: "Open the door this instant, young lady." She pressed her ear to the door again, but this time she didn't hear any talking. "I'm breaking the door down."

And she did with one swift kick near the doorknob, slightly above it. Too bad she dropped out of the police academy before finishing due to becoming pregnant with Madison. She was a natural.

The sight that greeted Roberta when she gained entry to the room was Madison hanging from her ceiling fan. Roberta quickly lifted Madison up to minimize the death grip of the bedsheet noose wrapped around her neck.

Though Madison's eyes were nearly closed, she was still alive—though just barely. She coughed a few times, much to Roberta's relief.

Without saying anything to Derrick, she hung up on him to call 911. He tried calling her back a few times, but she was too busy tending to Madison.

Derrick stepped into the bathroom and sat on the closed-lid toilet. His face was droopy and his eyes watery. He wasn't sure how to initiate the conversation with Mike, but he figured starting anywhere is better than sitting on the toilet in silence with Mike laying in the bathtub. There was more than enough awkward going on in there.

"What's on your mind?" Mike asked sheepishly.

Derrick was relieved Mike said something, and truth be told, Mike could have said anything and it would have been warmly received.

"Has Dylan visited you recently?" Derrick asked.

"A few days ago. Why?"

"Just curious. Has he ever mentioned a little girl named Madison?"

"He never talks to me about anything other than his persistent belief I killed him. Sometimes he doesn't say anything at all. Sometimes he just stares at me with his black eyes, those menacing eyes. I sometimes wonder if it really is Dylan or if its an evil spirit masquerading as Dylan."

"Like a demon?"

Mike nodded. Then he sat up and turned the bath water on, but just slightly. A thin stream of water fell perpendicular to the drain. Mike closed eyes and imagined being at Niagara Falls—where he and Heather spent their honeymoon. He worked so many hours of overtime—a time when it was available before the economy took a massive shit—to save enough to take Heather to the one place she dreamed of visiting since she was a seven-year-old and saw Niagara Falls in *Canadian Bacon*—which became one of her favorite movies. In fact, Heather was a huge John Candy fan, and had nearly every movie in which he starred.

"Why would a demon want to pose as Dylan, especially if it is accusing you of murder? If anything, wouldn't the demon want to befriend you to then make its move to harm you? Or why wouldn't it just harm you outright?"

Mike shrugged his shoulders and increased the water pressure of the bathtub faucet. Then he removed his socks and placed his feet underneath the water.

"I'll admit," Mike said. "I don't know if it's Dylan or not, but my gut tells me no. I can't imagine Dylan—or Dylan's spirit—accusing me of murder. I think it is a demon masquerading as him. Suicide opens the door to a lot of negative energy. Maybe his suicide let something in that shouldn't be here."

Uncertainty filled Derrick's mind at this point. He wondered if the spirit Madison had been encountering was really the spirit of Dylan or if the spirit was nothing more than a Trojan horse. It seemed more likely than not the spirit was not that of Dylan but a demon who wanted to use Dylan's image to taunt Mike.

And if it were true, where was this situation headed? Did the demon want to eventually kill Mike?

Another question pressing on Derrick's mind was the inhuman inner voice. Dylan's spirit—if that was in fact what it was—told Derrick the inner voice was The Umbra. But could Dylan's spirit be relied upon? How credible was the information it supplied?

"I saw Dylan," Derrick said.

"Where?" Mike asked, genuinely interested.

"Outside."

"And what happened?"

"He spoke to me."

Mike sat up in tub and asked for more details. Derrick wasn't sure how much he should share with him nor how much of what Dylan told him he should believe.

"He said he was murdered."

"Let me guess. He said I did it, right?"

"No, actually he didn't. He said The Umbra murdered him."

Mike contorted his face in such a way it conveyed he was confused. "What the fuck is The Umbra? Is this some sort of prank you're pulling on me? Are you making this up to make me feel better?"

"I'm giving it to you straight, man."

Mike shook his head. "Well, it's ridiculous, goddamn it. My son killed himself. He slit his wrists in this bathtub. No fucking Umbra—whatever the hell that is—killed him."

With information available to be accessed at Derrick's fingertips, he typed in THE UMBRA DEMON into the Google search field and executed the search. To Derrick's amazement, only a handful of search results were returned, and nothing of value.

But just because there wasn't any useful information available on the Internet, did that mean The Umbra didn't exist?

8

The aroma of garlic from the slow cooker on the kitchen counter next to the sink permeated the air. The flaky biscuits were baking in the oven. Dinner was nearly finished.

Lauren removed four plates from the cabinet and handed them to Nikki, then followed by placing silverware on top of them. As Nikki walked away, Lauren grabbed four glasses and followed Nikki into the dining room.

Nikki started to distribute the plates around the rectangular table. One at each end of the longer dimension of the table, the other two on the shorter dimension rather than across from each other. Ashlee liked sitting next to her older sister.

"I know that smell," Nikki said. "That's pot roast, isn't it?"

"You shall see. It's a surprise," Lauren responded. *Wow! She's got the nose of a bloodhound.*

"Smells kind of like the way my mom's pot roast smelled."

"Maybe it's not pot roast. In any event, you'll find out soon enough." Lauren now switched subjects. "Your dad told me one of the assistant principals of your school called and left him a message," Lauren said. "What's that about?"

"I fell asleep in class again. The teacher woke me up by dropping a textbook onto the floor right by my desk. When she did that, I cursed at her," Nikki said.

"Was that wise?"

"No, but she wasn't right when she did what she did either. I mean she could have lightly tapped my desk and asked if I was sick."

"Perhaps, but you shouldn't be falling asleep in class either," Lauren said as she placed the final glass in front of a plate. "Why are you falling asleep in class?"

Nikki shrugged her shoulders, but Lauren wasn't buying it. Just last night when Lauren was passing the girls' bedroom, Nikki's moans caught Lauren's ear, just as they did the night before.

"Tell me about the nightmares," Lauren said. "Maybe I can help."

"How did you know?"

"Lucky guess."

Nikki smiled and her face loosened a little. "Well, you're sort of right. They aren't nightmares."

"Go on."

"I'm awake. I see my mom in front of my bed. She is clutching a gun—the same gun she used to shoot herself."

Lauren nodded, acknowledging she was listening to Nikki. They walked into the kitchen, Nikki following Lauren. The garlic scent once again smacked the both of them in their faces. Though the scent was noticeable in the dining room, their brains blocked it out of their minds.

When Lauren lifted the lid off of the slow cooker, Nikki pierced the meat with the stainless-steel basting fork. She pulled off a piece of the rump roast and sampled it.

"How is it?" Lauren asked.

"Good. It takes almost the same way my mom used to make it," Nikki said.

"Is that a good thing?"

Nikki nodded. "Yes, definitely. It's one way I can remember her. Every time I'll eat pot roast, I'll be thinking of her."

"I'm glad I was able to make it the same way she did," Lauren said. "Are you surprised?"

"I am surprised. Thank you."

A win for Lauren it seemed. She made the pot roast as a special surprise for Nikki and Ashlee—who was still at school. Lauren had found a stack of three-by-five index cards, each with a recipe on it. Meatloaf. Fried chicken. Jambalaya.

But it wasn't only main courses though. Some of the index cards contained recipes for desserts—one of Thomas' weaknesses, given his penchant for sweets. When he and Sharon were married, she often had a different dessert prepared for him each night as part of the night's dinner and dessert combination. This lasted for the first three years of their marriage. Thomas would arrive home at the same time, every day. It wasn't until he was promoted to Supervising Psychiatrist when his hours drastically shifted and he no longer arrived home at his usual time, which at first this didn't bother Sharon.

Soon, though, she became starved for attention and affection. Thomas seemed to put work first and family second, all the while thinking he was doing the right thing, yet not realizing money meant nothing to her and the children. To this day he still didn't understand how he was wrong for doing what he did.

"I'm going to go pick up Ashlee now," Nikki said.

"Why don't I tag along? The pot roast could use a little more time in the slow cooker anyway."

Boy could it. I'm still chewing it. "Okay. Fine, I guess."

"Great. Let me grab my windbreaker."

The fact was Nikki wanted to be alone. She wanted some time to clear her thoughts. The pot roast induced a flood of memories to surge through her brain.

The duo headed out the door. Lauren was wearing her pink and blue windbreaker.

"So, tell me," Lauren said. "What happens in the visions you've been having about your mom? You said she's clutching the gun, but we didn't get past that part yet."

"She stands with it and presses it to the side of head, but then lowers it. She glances at her left wrist and then raises the gun back to her temple. Back and forth, back and forth. Occasionally, she paces from spot to the next, sometimes with the gun still kissing her temple."

Lauren's heart skipped a beat upon hearing this information. "Her wrist?"

"Uh-huh."

"Can you show me which part of the wrist?"

"Why?"

"A story is about details. I'd like the complete picture, that's all."

"Seems sort of creepy you'd want to know that level of detail."

Lauren slightly grinned. "It's okay if you don't want to tell me."

And Nikki didn't. She carried on with the rest of her story, but this incited Lauren, who wanted to know which part of the wrist, even though she believed she already knew the answer.

They turned onto Primrose Avenue and would remain walking on this street until they reached the next intersection. Primrose Avenue was the street on which Thomas lived when he was a child.

As Nikki continued to divulge bits and pieces of her story, her eyes welled up with tears. Clearly, the story was reaching a climax, a breaking point, a kicker.

"So, my mom glances at her wrist on last time, and whispers, 'Time's almost up. I love you, Nikki, and Ashlee. Know Mommy's sorry.' And then she places the gun to her temple and she starts to pull the trigger back, but then stops. She whispers again, but this time, saying: 'I can't do it."

"Then what happens?"

"She vanishes followed by a gunshot."

"Wait. She vanishes first? That doesn't make sense. Wouldn't the gun go off first, then she vanishes?"

"I was there. I'm telling you what I saw."

"You mean you witnessed your mom shoot herself?"

"No, I was upstairs with my sister. I told you earlier these visions I have happen when I'm wide awake, as if I'm watching a movie. And now, come to think of it, I think my mom vanishing and the gunshot happen almost simultaneously… No, it's she vanishes, and a split second later, BANG!"

Lauren stopped and turned to Nikki. "The second before your mom vanishes, is the gun to her temple?"

"Why are asking me such graphic questions?"

"I'm sorry. I'm a psychologist. It's part of my training to ask probing questions, to ask things that go beyond a superficial level."

"Yeah, well, I'm not one of your whacko patients, so lay off."

Filled with sadness, anger, and frustration, Nikki stormed off. Lauren followed behind, but let Nikki have her space, not wanting to damage their already-fragile relationship. Lauren made a mental note to herself to talk with Nikki about referring to her patients as whackos, which was a terrible misconception, and one Lauren didn't want Nikki carrying around in her head for too long.

9

The police station lobby was like a ghost town, and this was a relief to Usha. She wanted to get in and get out. She approached one of the windows of the front desk. Not only was the lobby a ghost town, but so was the front desk. Nobody was back there.

In between the windows was a button that resembled a doorbell. A pink sign—no larger than the size of a business card—

with small print had on it: PUSH TO RING BELL FOR SERVICE.

She pushed it a few times and in the background bells chimed similar to those she heard from a nearby church she lived near while growing up in Hamming—a smallish city in Northwest Indiana and a neighboring city of Chesterville.

Moments later, a police officer walked to the window Usha stood in front of and greeted her.

"Is Detective Benito Monteleone available?" Usha asked. "I need to talk to him. It's urgent."

"One moment," Officer Hutchins responded. He picked up the phone, chicken pecked a few buttons, and seconds later was talking to someone. Once the call ended, he said: "Benito is in the middle of something at the moment. Can I take a message?"

"Damn it," she muttered. "How long do you think he will be tied up? Like I mentioned before, it is important I speak to him."

Officer Hutchins slurped a sip of his steaming coffee, which was inside a Styrofoam cup. "It's hard to say. But I can have him give you a call. What is a good number he can call you when he is available?"

Usha paused for a few moments, contemplating what to do. *Stay or wait, stay or wait*, she thought. She ultimately took a seat in the lobby area and thumbed through some of the magazines scattered across the coffee table that was centered within the U-shaped configuration of chairs. People. Cosmopolitan. Good Housekeeping. Parenting Today.

In the chair next to Usha was the lockbox Alejandro had instructed her to take to Esteban, the attorney Alejandro consulted yet never retained, and this was unfortunate. Had Alejandro retained Esteban to handle the formalities of his will—or at least did some legal research on wills—he would have learned in order for a will to be legal, it must be signed by witnesses. Since the will was signed only by Alejandro, it wasn't valid, and this meant all of his worldly possessions belonged to the state—not to Usha, who was the sole beneficiary.

About fifteen minutes passed before Officer Hutchins called her up to the front desk. He advised her he had called Ben's office once more but received no response. She insisted she would wait for him, and he had no qualms with that.

Usha sat back down in the same seat she sat in before and opened the lockbox. She shuffled through the stack of papers inside the lockbox, glancing at each document for a few seconds before moving to the next. As she did this, she hoped Ben would listen to her and ultimately help her.

Another fifteen minutes passed, at which time the sound of a door opening shifted Usha's focus away from the lockbox. She turned towards the source of the sound and standing of the doorway was Ben, with the sleeves of his dress shirt rolled up just before his elbow joint and his blue parallelogram-patterned tie loosened.

"Ben," Usha said, not knowing what else to say.

"I understand you wanted to see me," Ben said. "What can I do for you?"

Usha closed the lockbox with a delicate hand before walking to Ben. With each step Usha towards took towards Ben, his heart increased incrementally.

"Is there somewhere we can go to talk?" she asked. "Somewhere private?"

"Yeah. There's a conference room we can use," he replied.

He led the way to the conference room, which was down a lengthy hallway. Along the way he asked her how she had been holding up and she held nothing back, sharing with him she was still grieving, still trying to make sense of Alejandro's death.

The conference room was bland, the walls painted with a neutral color: gray. An eight-foot boat-shaped wooden conference table took up the majority of the space in the room, which had the capacity to seat ten people, four on each side and one person at each end of the table.

There were no pictures of anything on the wall. Only one of the walls had something on it, and that was a standard-sized marker board, and nothing was written on it.

Usha took a seat in one of the chairs along the longer side of the table while Ben sat at the head of the table with steepled fingers.

"I wouldn't blame you if you thought of me as crazy, but I need you to keep an open mind and avoid passing judgment too quickly," Usha said. "Do you think you can do that?"

Ben slightly nodded his head. "I can't make any promises."

Usha sighed. *He nods yes but basically says no. Men. They never know up from down.* "Well, please try, because I think Karla is innocent and what's more…"

About ten seconds passed before Ben folded his arms and said: "You were saying?"

"Maybe I should present to you some things. Let's see if you can connect the dots."

"A test of sorts?"

"Sort of."

"I'm game. Bring it," he said, smiling, with a cocky tone.

Usha opened the lockbox and pulled out the contents of it—several sheets of typing paper neatly folded into thirds, one stack on top of the other. She sorted through them, ordering them as she saw fit.

"This is Alejandro's suicide note," Usha said. "But it's not exactly that either."

"Sounds like the case of Schrödinger's cat. A paradox. It's a suicide not, but it isn't," he said, with a smirk of superiority showing.

"He says he didn't want to kill himself but a force beyond his control forced him to do so."

"That could mean anything. It's open to interpretation." *Damn. I was hoping she would have asked me about Schrödinger's cat.*

"But, wait. There's more." She handed him a new document after unfolding it. "Check this out."

The piece of paper had the number 24 written numerous times, hundreds of times, in fact, and on both sides of the paper.

Ben analyzed the paper, noticing the multitude of different ways the same number was written. Sometimes the four was written as an open four; others as a closed four. And the sizes of the numbers were just as varied, some small while others tall.

In Usha's purse was a bottle of water, which she pulled out and drank a bit of it while waiting for Ben's response.

He would fixate on one side of the paper for thirty to forty-five seconds before flipping to the other side for another thirty to forty-five seconds only to flip back to the other side. Over and over again. At times he would rub his chin or pinch his nose.

"I don't get it," Ben said nearly five minutes after being handed the piece of paper. "What's the significance of this?"

"Well, how many hours are in a day?" Usha asked, smug.

Ben caressed his chin as if in pensive thought for a few seconds. "Twenty-four."

"You're an ass."

"What?"

She pointed a finger at him. "I'm being serious here, goddamn it, and I don't appreciate you making a joke of it."

He wringed his hands. "I apologize. I'm not seeing what it is you want me to see."

"Alejandro called me around 11 in the evening. Twelve forty-two to be exact. Look at this piece of paper."

And Ben did, and the paper had a timestamp—11:36 to be exact along with a date of 07/16/18—written numerous times, and in different sizes, all over both sides of the page.

Usha unfolded another document and skimmed over it. It was Alejandro's autopsy report. She had the information on the report memorized, but she wanted to do something to keep her mind doing something while waiting for Ben to say something, which he did a few minutes later.

"We've got twenty-four hours and a date of 07/16/18," Ben said. "What are you trying to get me to see?"

"Look at this," she said.

After a few seconds, he said: "Holy shit. He died on July 17, a day after—but…"

"Look—I think Alejandro was murdered. I think someone was after him, someone who warned him he had twenty-four hours to live."

"If that's the case, why wouldn't Alejandro call the police or flee or arm himself with a fucking Uzi and defend himself?"

"I don't know," Usha admitted. "But he left behind all sorts of clues to help us understand his story."

Ben shook his head. "I understand it is difficult to accept someone you loved and cared about committed suicide. Shit—I have a hard enough time digesting it when I read about it in the paper or hear about it in the news. But you have to come to terms with the reality. Alejandro committed suicide. He wasn't murdered."

"He didn't commit suicide. He was murdered, and I'm going to find a way a prove it to you." She started to pack the lockbox back up with the documents. "He didn't have any terminal illness after all like I thought. He planned to propose to me."

"Propose?"

She held out her hand. "This ring was also in this lockbox. He had every reason to live. He didn't commit suicide."

With the documents safely tucked away in the lockbox, Usha stormed out of the conference room, sobbing, without saying goodbye.

10

The chimes of one of the psychiatrist's cellphone coupled with idle chatter in the hallway outside Madison's hospital room within at St, Margaret's Hospital were the only noises Roberta heard for the past few minutes after she awoke from a brief nap.

Roberta rubbed Madison's forehead. A few seconds later, Madison opened her eyes. Roberta smiled at her.

Madison's lip curled. "Are you mad at me, Mommy?"

"No, baby," Roberta said. "I'm not mad at you."

"I didn't want to do it, Mommy."

"Then why did you?"

"I didn't," Madison said, crying.

Roberta shushed her while caressing her forehead. All Roberta wanted right in that moment was for Madison to understand she loved her all the same. She climbed into the bed with Madison and hugged her.

"Everything is going to be okay," Roberta said.

"I want Dylan to leave me alone. He's bad. He's not my friend," Madison said.

"Did Dylan tell you to do that to yourself? To hang yourself from your fan?"

Madison nodded. "I hate myself for listening to him."

"Why would you want to kill yourself?"

"I don't, Mommy. I swear I don't." *I do wonder about killing myself though. Like that man who blew his brains out on TV.*

Roberta smiled at her. "That makes me happy to hear."

"Dylan tricked me, Mommy. He made me think we were playing a game, like we were acting in a play."

Roberta swallowed hard. "What was the name of the play?"

"He called it Texas Justice," Madison said, squinting her eyes.

Roberta asked Madison to share as many details as she felt comfortable sharing. Madison explained Dylan said he would serve as executioner and she would be the prisoner.

"What did he tell you to do?" Roberta asked.

"He told me to push my bed so it would be underneath the fan, but I wasn't strong enough," Madison said. "So, we decided to use my step stool."

"Then what?"

"Then he told me how to make a hangman's knot."

But that wasn't all Dylan shared with Madison. He went into a lengthy historical lesson about ropes used to hang people. He discussed the boiling of the rope, the stretching of the rope. The military table created to correlate height and weight with rope length.

Roberta covered her mouth as Madison revealed Dylan's teachings. It chilled her to the bone. Madison was like a continuous fountain of information.

"How can a boy your age know so much about executing by hanging?" Roberta asked.

Madison shrugged her shoulders. "I don't know, Mommy. Sorry."

"It's okay." She ran her fingers through her hair, fighting not to show her true emotions. "So, you made the noose and then what?"

"I looped it around the fan."

Roberta stood and walked to the wall in front of Madison's bed. Her back was to Madison. Roberta didn't want Madison to read the horror and sadness in her eyes.

"Are you okay, Mommy?" Madison asked after a few seconds.

"Yes, baby, I'm fine. I thought I was going to sneeze—that's all." She sat on the bed. "Keep going. What happened next?"

"Dylan stood on the chair with me and told me to place the rope around my neck. And I did. Then said something about me being sentenced to die for my crimes. He talked for the longest time."

Actually, it wasn't that long. It was for a couple of minutes. Dylan orated a death warrant and asked Madison if she had any last words. She didn't know what he meant, so he explained she had the chance to say whatever she wanted to say if she were going to die and never come back to see her mom again. Madison took the opportunity to say her last words, and in an ironic twist between the two of them was the long-winded one. Her last words lasted about four minutes, and Madison remembered almost verbatim what she said, which she shared with her mother.

The emotional turmoil Roberta was going through drained her of energy. And the fear she was experiencing as Madison shared the story with her was all too palpable.

Madison continued the recantation of the events leading up to her being suspended in midair, dangling from the ceiling fan.

"Dylan stepped off the stool and announced the sentence would now be carried out," Madison said.

"Dear god," Roberta whispered. She took a breath. "Keep going, please. I know this is tough, but I need you to tell me."

Madison slightly nodded. "I got a bad feeling about the game. I told Dylan I didn't want to play the game anymore and I started to take the rope off. That's when he immediately disappeared from in front of me. A second later I felt the noose tighten around my neck again. I tried to pull it off, but I couldn't. That's why I couldn't answer you, Mommy—when you were calling from outside my room. Then Dylan yanked the stool from behind me and I was hanging like a piñata from a tall tree at a birthday party."

"It's going to be okay. I'm not going to let Dylan hurt you anymore. He's not going to bother you anymore."

"But, Mommy. He is in the room with us right now."

Roberta stood and looked around the room. The cadence of her heart was all out of whack at this point.

"I want you to leave my daughter alone," Roberta said. Then she shouted: "You hear me? You leave my daughter the fuck alone!"

A few seconds later, nurses and a doctor rushed into the room. Roberta explained the situation and they all gave her a look of concern, but Madison confirmed what her mother told them.

Shortly after the medical professionals left Madison's room, Derrick knocked on the door and asked if it was okay if he visited for a bit. Roberta agreed, and Madison was tickled with delight Derrick was there to see her.

11

Fortunately, Emily survived. Doctors and nurses were baffled. They couldn't figure out what was causing Emily to have spells where she couldn't breathe, which always led to her to being rendered unconscious.

Scott and Karen stood over Emily—who was asleep in her crib—and gazed upon their precious daughter.

"Thank god you were in the room when she started to struggle to breath," Karen said. "It's amazing that you always seem to be in the right place at the right time."

Scott slightly smiled. "It must be divine intervention. I just hope the doctors can figure out what the hell is happening with our daughter."

Karen shot him a derisive look. "You shouldn't swear in front of the baby."

"But she's asleep."

"Even still."

"Sorry."

After Scott kissed Karen on the cheek, she stepped out of Emily's room to take a shower. Soon after, Aaron walked into Emily's room and put his hand on his dad's shoulder.

Scott gasped. "Jesus fucking Christ, son," he muttered. "You scared the shit out of me."

"How's she doing?" Aaron asked.

"Much better, thank the good Lord."

"Have the doctors pinpointed a cause yet?"

"Of course not," he said as he pulled out a chamois cloth from his pants pocket. "What a waste of space they are. How can they not know? They're doctors, for fuck's sake."

Aaron chuckled. "I don't know, dad. It baffles me, too, but guess what? I'm going to start my own investigation."

"Investigation?" Scott snapped. "Who the fuck you investigating? Your mother and I haven't done anything wrong."

"Dad, I'm talking about my own *medical* investigation. Relax," he said, backing away from his dad a few steps. "I want my baby sister to get better. It seems each time she has one of her spells, they get worse and worse. I don't want anything bad to happen to her. Could it be COPD? Maybe asthma?"

"If the doctors don't know, what would make you think I know?"

Aaron caressed Emily's hand, then covered her up with her bear-patterned blanket.

12

Mike wandered out of his living room and returned about a minute later. In his hand was a white bed sheet, but it wasn't translucent; it was opaque.

"I want to thank you again," Mike said, unfurling a sheet. "I think that's a wise idea to cover up Dylan's shrine and do an unveiling for Heather when she comes home tomorrow and is ready to see the shrine."

"You're welcome," Derrick responded. "And let me thank you once again for getting me my mother's name."

(Fuck your dead bitch mother. Bruce did a few times, but someone else's seed conceived you.)

[Stop it. Fuck you. You're a pussy. Show yourself.]

(In due time, mon ami.)

Mike nodded. "How's the search going?"

"Not good."

As Mike covered the shrine he made for Dylan with the sheet, Derrick provided him an update about the situation with locating his mother. So far, nothing but dead ends, but Derrick was determined to find her.

"I think you need to get over your fear of driving," Mike suggested. "I'd like to teach how to drive."

"I don't think that is a good idea."

(Yes, it is. Get behind the wheel and drive off the Rickety-Racket Bridge. Plummet to your death. I'm going to kill you. I have the power to do so—if you don't do it yourself.)

"Goddamn it! Shut up!" Derrick shouted.

"Whoa. What's that about?" Mike asked, genuinely concerned.

Derrick lowered his head as he shook it. "I've been hearing this voice in my head, this ungodly evil voice taunting me over and over to kill myself."

"That's fucked up. Not even gonna sugarcoat it for you."

"I agree, but don't worry. I've seen a doctor about it and the test results do show a slight abnormality with the part of the brain that controls hearing and speech. I also have a brain contusion."

Lies. All lies. His neurologist Dr. Pritchard found nothing wrong with Derrick's brain. She gave Derrick's brain a clean bill of health. He didn't want to admit an evil entity—The Umbra—was heckling him.

"What are they going to do to treat it?" Mike asked.

"The contusion will work itself out," Derrick replied. "The abnormality will be treated after a few more tests are run."

"I hope everything works out well for you."

"Can we talk about Dylan for a bit?"

"As long as it doesn't involve you trying to get me to believe my son was murdered by an umbrella."

Derrick rolled his eyes, but Mike didn't see it since his back was turned to him.

"The *Umbra*, not an umbrella," Derrick responded, mildly agitated. "And why can't we debate this issue? If someone murdered your son, wouldn't you want justice to be served?"

"We've been over this ground again and again. You're coming up with all sorts of crazy theories about my son and his spirit. You think he was murdered without any evidence, and the reason there is no evidence is because he killed himself, he wasn't murdered."

"I've got something else to tell you about Dylan."

"What now?"

"He tried to kill a little girl, and nearly did. That Madison girl I babysit every now and again."

Mike stood from of the couch and opened the front door. He said nothing, but he didn't need to either. His eyes said it all.

But Derrick was convinced the spirit masquerading as Dylan was a demonic entity, not the real spirit of Dylan. He also convinced the same demon masquerading as Dylan was also the source of the voices in his head.

"Please don't throw me out," Derrick pleaded. "If you don't want to talk about this, we don't have to. I'm trying to help. This demon's intentions—"

A humanoid-shaped translucent shadow appeared behind Mike. No facial features whatsoever.

(Peek-a-boo, Der-Little-Dick!)

[You're the—] "You're the demon who is masquerading as Dylan," Derrick said.

"What are you talking about?" Mike asked.

Derrick gestured for Mike to look behind him, which he did, but the figure vanished before Mike could see it. As Derrick walked towards the front door, he stopped and gasped. He had a flashback to the night he and Bruce had their big fight—the biggest fight they had ever had.

"I remember you," Derrick whispered, referring to the shadow figure. "You revealed yourself to me that night my dad and I had the fight over him spending my college savings... But why did you show yourself to me?"

"Come back tomorrow, man," Mike said. "I need your help cleaning the gutters."

Derrick nodded as he exited through the front door, his mind fixating on trying to recall why the shadow figure appeared to him that night.

"Bye," Mike said, expecting Derrick to respond.

But he didn't. As if being controlled like a doll with strings, he continued to walk while in deep contemplation. He vowed to find out what this shadow figure was—The Umbra, and then find a way to eradicate it—if that was even possible.

13

(The spirit that looked like Dylan was right about one thing: I am The Umbra)

[What do you want with me? Why are you taunting me?]

Reaching underneath his bed, Derrick pulled out a bottle of Disaronno and poured himself a glass, but one wasn't enough, so he had one more.

(I've told you so many times what I want. You ask and I answer. If this were a court proceeding, you'd be dead in the water.)

[Tell me again.]

(Your soul, if possible.)

"Well you can't have it," Derrick said, faintly. "It's not yours."

The Umbra appeared near Derrick's bed, causing Derrick to frantically back away in his bed, cracking the back of his head on the wall.

A flash of bright lightning illuminated his room. A few seconds later—maybe six tops—a boom of thunder sounded.

Though The Umbra had no mouth, he still spoke, and this time not within Derrick's mind.

"You're wrong," The Umbra said. "And I will have your soul. But if I can't have that, you dead is still good enough for me, because that's what you should be. You're currently out of order."

"If you want my soul so bad, then kill me," Derrick said. "I'm right here. Go ahead. Kill me."

"No. It's not that simple."

"Why not?"

"I can only have your soul if you kill yourself by you saying the words to let me set you up for death."

"That's never going to happen. I would never want to kill myself, and there's no way you're going to set me up for death. So why don't you go find someone else to mess with other than me?"

Derrick's cellphone was on the nightstand next to his bed. He feared reaching for it, unsure what The Umbra was capable of doing to him if he made any sudden moves.

The air in the room was thick and statically charged.

The Umbra took a moved closer to Derrick, but not by taking a step. Instead, The Umbra seemed to float forward. It said: "I almost had your soul once. You're not completely out of the woods yet. All you need to do is say those fateful words that opened the door, those words that gave me permission to compel you to try and kill yourself, which you were too much of a sissy boy to do anyhow. I started the job, but was thwarted."

"Why don't you possess my dad and get him to kill me then?"

"Because watching you commit suicide would be infinitely more satisfying than me killing you myself. Besides, I'm going to let you in on a little secret. I *did* murder Dylan. That little shit didn't have the courage to do it himself, but I have to give him credit. He was a lot more tenacious than you were. He tried so hard to off himself."

"Am I hallucinating? Is this real?"

The Umbra laughed wickedly and maniacally, even though he had no visible mouth—at least not visible to Derrick.

Derrick swallowed hard as his heart slammed against his chest.

"No, you're not hallucinating," The Umbra said. "But then again maybe you are." A few seconds later, it said: "Another one bit the dust. What a rush."

"What do you mean by that?"

"A man jumped into a blast furnace at Mittal Steel Mill. He didn't even wait for his watch to reach absolute zero."

"His watch?"

"He'd been on suicide watch for…seven hours, nineteen minutes, and forty-one seconds before he did the right thing and killed himself before I had to kill him myself."

Derrick paused for a moment to collect his thoughts. "Are you saying you give people a certain amount of time to kill themselves and if they don't, then you kill them?"

"Do I really need to answer that? Aren't you a master of deduction? Do the math. Connect the dots. I already know you're doing that anyway."

"Are you Satan?"

"Let me end this conversation by giving you one last chance to kill yourself. Otherwise, I'm going to start to snuff out the people you care most about in your life. That cheating-whore-slut Danielle. Your so-called dad. You've got—"

Before The Umbra could finish his warning to Derrick, the man who sported the fedora and trench coat appeared seemingly out of thin air behind The Umbra. He unsheathed a sword and stabbed The Umbra through its chest from behind. The Umbra wailed in pain as it faded to nothing.

"I love you, son," the fedora-sporting man said. "I always have."

That's a little creepy. "Is The Umbra dead?"

"Probably not, but I'll keep trying to kill it. I must be going now. The Umbra can return at any moment and kill me. The sword cuts both ways, so to speak. I shouldn't even be talking to you, but it's hard not to, and I wish I could stay longer. I love you, son."

The fedora-sporting man vanished just as quickly as he appeared. Derrick stayed positioned in his bed with his back against the wall, his mind racing.

He regretted not asking the fedora-wearing man if there was a way he could block The Umbra from his mind, if there was a way he could prevent The Umbra from bothering him any further.

He poured himself a shot of Disaronno. Down the hatch. No second round this time though. He walked down the stairs, still trying to make sense of the events that had unfolded.

When he reached the fourth step from the foot of the stairs, he stopped and turned around. His mind flashed back to the time he first encountered The Umbra. It was on that stairwell not too long before the Chesterville officer found Derrick sprawled out near the fence in the outfield of one of the baseball fields.

You revealed yourself to me the night my dad and I had that big fight, Derrick thought. *But why then?*

The sounds of the springs of a bed bouncing along with light moaning caught Derrick's ear. He decided to levitate his mood a little at his dad's expense.

Derrick tiptoed down the hallway and stood in front of his dad's door for a several seconds, stifling his laughter as he listened to his dad say things such as that's the spot and keep doing that.

Now it was time to go in for the kill. Derrick pushed the test button on the smoke detector. An ear-piercing, high-pitched alarm sounded. Derrick bolted as discreetly as he could into the hallway closet, waiting for his dad and whomever he was smashing in his room to come out, naked and disgruntled.

Bruce stepped out of the bedroom and did a quick inspection of the house. His inspection was half-ass at best. Once the search was finished, he returned to his bedroom and he and his lover picked up where they had left off before the smoke detector interrupted their love-making session.

But once wasn't enough for Derrick. He crept out of the closet and once again pushed the smoke detector test button, snickering as he retreated back into the closet.

This time Bruce released a torrent of expletives as his balls began to ache. Clutching his shriveled sack as he limped out of his bedroom, he silenced the alarm and did a quick cursory inspection of the house, investigating most probable sources of smoke: the kitchen.

"I swear to god if this happens again I'll kill myself," Bruce muttered as he passed the closet in which Derrick was hiding. He entered his bedroom and as he closed the door, he said: "Alright, baby. Daddy's ready for you again."

"Gross," Derrick said aloud, and afterwards slapped his hand over his mouth, fearing his dad heard him.

But fortunately Bruce didn't. He was too busy getting his chicken chafed, among other things.

"Third time's a charm," Derrick whispered. *But this time let's up the ante.*

He placed a shoe on top of his dad's bedroom doorknob and pressed the smoke detector button again.

"Goddamn it!" Bruce shouted. "I'm gonna fix that smoke detector real good." He threw open his door and the shoe fell onto his foot. "Ow! God fucking damn it!" He swung with a baseball bat at the smoke detector, knocking it off the ceiling. Then he performed a good old-fashioned Mafia-style beating on it all while cursing at it. Once the hospital job on the smoke detector was complete, Bruce spit on it and tossed the aluminum baseball bat into the closet, striking Derrick on top of his head. Then he returned to his bedroom, feeling like he had just slayed a dragon and saved a princess from certain death.

"That fucking shadow ghost is playing games with us," Bruce said to his lover. "I'm about ready to call some ghost hunters to rid this house of that asshole."

"Come here, Daddy," his female companion said.

"Forget it. My shrimp has gone limp."

"I can make it rise again."

That voice sounds familiar, Derrick thought. *That's not Gayle.*

And Derrick was unequivocally correct. The owner of the voice was someone he knew, though not as well as he thought.

"Hey, Derrick," The Umbra whispered whilst Derrick started to crawl out of the closet. "Your so-called dad is fucking her good. I dare you to sneak a peek."

"No. Fuck off."

"Awww, come on, sport. I think you'll slip into a state of rage, kill both your dad and his fuck buddy, then yourself."

Derrick started to hit himself in head with a closed fist. *Leave me the fuck alone! Leave me the fuck alone!*

"Then kill yourself and I will," The Umbra whispered, his tone calm.

"If you want me dead, you'll have to kill me," Derrick replied.

A second or two after Derrick finished that sentence, The Umbra screamed in pain when a sword came through his chest again. The Umbra vanished. Bruce came running out of his room, opened the closet, and grabbed the baseball bat, which by this point, Derrick was creeping up the stairs, trying to avoid making any noise, but then stampeded down them.

Bruce turned around and nearly struck Derrick (again, but this time purposefully) with the baseball bat.

"What's going on?" Derrick asked, squinting his eyes.

"There's someone in the house," Bruce said, naked. "Here. Take this bat and find out who's in the house. Cave their face in. I gotta bitch to fuck right now."

"Okay, Dad. Fuck her good."

Bruce turned around and fired two finger pistols at Derrick before retreating back to his room to finish his smash session, hopefully without any further interruptions.

When Derrick turned around to head back upstairs, the fedora-wearing man was in front of him, almost nose to nose.

"I love you, son," the fedora-sporting man said. "The Umbra will likely be back soon."

"How can I block him from—"

"It—not a him."

"Sorry. How can I block *it* from my mind, prevent it from further harassing me?"

"Until it's dead, you probably can't. You just need to find a way to tune him out your—"

"It, you mean."

The fedora-sporting man smiled. "Yes. It. Fight like hell to tune it out. It can't physically hurt you, that is not unless you say the words that invited it in to being with, and if you think I'm going to tell you what those words are, you can forget it. I can't. I shouldn't even be here right now speaking to you, and on that note, I must go. Remember, son: I love you."

"Why do you keep calling me son?"

But Derrick didn't get a response. The man wearing the fedora disappeared before he even finished his sentence.

14

The sound of sirens wailing as they sped down Derrick's street and approached his house from his slumber on a crisp November Saturday morn, and Bruce, too. Derrick rushed down the stairs and glanced out the living room window. An ambulance and fire truck were parked in front of Aaron's house. Two paramedics were opening the doors of the ambulance. They pulled out a stretcher and tossed a medical bag on top of it.

Aaron ran towards the paramedics, clutching Emily in his hands. "She's dead! She's dead!"

One of the paramedics pulled Emily's lifeless body away from Aaron and laid her on the stretcher. The other paramedic placed a ventilation bag over Emily's mouth and began pumping it.

Hunched over on the lawn, Aaron relentlessly cried. Bruce and Derrick's eyes were glued to the events unfolding next door.

The first paramedic checked Emily's heartbeat using a stethoscope. After a several seconds, he shook his head at the other paramedic.

Derrick covered his mouth.

"Get over it," Bruce said. "People die all the time."

"How can you say something so callous? Aaron's sister is dead," Derrick snapped.

Bruce stepped out of the kitchen grasping a bottle of tequila. "I'm not saying anything that isn't true. We're born, we live, we die."

Disgusted at his dad's unsympathetic remarks, Derrick didn't even dignify them with a response. Instead, he slipped his bare feet into his tennis shoes and sprinted over to Aaron.

"I'm sorry about your sister," Derrick said, placing his hand on Aaron's shoulder.

"It's my fault. I should have been keeping a better eye on her," Aaron replied, sobbing. He sniffled. "Now she's dead, and it's all because of me."

Derrick lightly exhaled. "What do you mean it's your fault?"

Before Aaron responded, he stood. "I was supposed to be watching her. My mom got a job to help with the bills. With both my parents working now, I've become the de facto babysitter."

It was true. About a week ago, Karen did start a job at Mittal, the steel mill located nearly twenty-five miles northwest of Chesterville, and the same one at which the man The Umbra mentioned jumped to his death into a blast furnace just a few days ago.

"I still don't see how it's your fault," Derrick said.

"My dad woke me up around six, telling me to get my ass up. I was supposed to check on Emily every thirty minutes and provide updates to both my mom and dad. I fell back asleep shortly after my dad hounded me to wake up." He started to sob again. "I…I didn't mean to. I've been so tired lately from all of the studying I've been doing."

This was true, also. In order to ensure his timely graduation, Aaron took a full schedule of classes plus four credit recovery classes. He worked diligently in his classes during the school day, came home and did his homework, then chores, followed by spending the rest of evening hours working on his credit recovery classes.

He hadn't had any leisure time since the school year started, and only had a few more weeks before Thanksgiving holiday started—which consisted of an entire week off from school.

A police officer asked Aaron for the number to either his mom or dad's work or their cell numbers, and Aaron relinquished his cellphone after unlocking it and commanding Siri to call his mom. Once the phone started to ring, Aaron handed it to the officer, who then walked a few paces away.

Derrick tilted his head. "I don't understand how you killed your sister though."

"My dad woke me up once before he had to leave for work," Aaron said. "His words to me were: Emily is dead to the world. No need to get out of bed or anything."

"Wow. That was somewhat prophetic. What is it you did that caused her death?"

"I didn't get out of bed even after my dad came back to my room and woke me up a second time. Maybe if I would have, I could have saved her life. God, I hate me! I should kill myself! I want to kill myself! I wish I were dead!"

The Umbra appeared in front of Aaron—though this time Derrick couldn't see The Umbra nor could anyone else except Aaron—and spoke to him. Aaron listened wide-eyed with a slacked jaw as it said: "And in twenty-four hours, you will be. That's exactly how much time you have to kill yourself. Congratulations, Aaron—you're one of the chosen ones. At the end of the twenty-four hours, if you haven't killed yourself, I will kill you myself. If you do kill yourself, your spirit will live eternally in unbridled ecstasy. If you don't, however, I will own your soul and torture it until the end of time. And, speaking of time, a countdown watch located on the back of your wrist will show you how much time remains for you to kill yourself. Only you can see the countdown timer. Go ahead. Take a look."

And Aaron did. It read: 24:00:00.

The Umbra continued: "Once I finish my little spiel, the countdown timer will begin. It won't do any good to tell anyone about the countdown watch—which only you can see—and if you do I may kill you on the spot. I'm everywhere and anywhere all at the same time. Do the right thing and kill yourself. Get creative with your suicide. Grandstand. The more gore, the higher score, as I like to say. Make your choice: die or be killed." The Umbra faded to invisibility.

During The Umbra's little speech—sounding like a car salesman—Derrick raised and lowered his hand a few times in front of Aaron's eyes, but Aaron showed no response to this. Aaron's eyes remained open, fixed on the back of his left wrist, and his mouth was open wider than it was initially.

The instant The Umbra out of sight—though not necessarily gone—the countdown timer started to count down from 24:00:00. A second at a time, it decreased. 24:00:00, 23:59:59, 23:59:58, 23:59:57,…

"This can't be real," Aaron whispered. "I'm losing my mind."

The Umbra spoke from within Aaron's mind. *(No, you're not, Caring Aaron. This is real—all too real. Face facts and mangle your face. You'll be able to see Emily again.)*

The sound of Emily giggling reverberated in Aaron's mind.

"Dude, I know this is difficult, but you've got to face facts," Derrick said. "I'll help you deal with this."

Aaron held up his arm with his wrist facing outward. "Do you see it?"

(I warned you! But go ahead and show that little faggot Derrick your wrist. It'll be nothing but a freshly-cleaned chalkboard to him. A newly-painted wall. A clean slate. All flesh.)

"See what?" Derrick asked, confused. "All I see are some of your old track marks on your arm from when you used to shoot up with heroin."

"Look at my wrist. Do you see the numbers?" *23:54:19, 23:54:18, 23:54:17,...*

Derrick shook his head. "Your sister's death is getting the better of you. Why don't we go inside and wait for your mom to get here?"

"No! I'm a marked man. I have to kill myself. I deserve to die."

(Then go ahead and do it already. Emily misses you.)

"Time is the ultimate healer, man."

"Time? So, you can see the countdown timer on my wrist?" He presented the back of his wrist to Derrick again.

"Countdown timer? No. Sorry. I don't."

(Told you, you fucking stoned loser. I told you he wouldn't see it! Only you can see it. You let me in, and now death is your only way out, your saving grace.)

Aaron ran to the garage and slammed the door closed. He paced back and forth for several seconds, all the while staring at his wrist, watching the numbers change, one second at a time.

"How about a trade? Someone else's life for mine. I'll kill anyone you want," Aaron whispered, his voice trembling. "Just let me live."

The Umbra appeared in front of Aaron. "If only it were that easy. It doesn't work like that, unfortunately for you," it whispered back. "But if you convince Derrick to kill himself and then you kill yourself, when you and I reunite in the hereafter, you'll be handsomely rewarded."

"But I don't want to—" Aaron started to say, but was interrupted when someone knocked on the door.

"Aaron?" Derrick asked. "Please unlock the door. Let me in."

"Now is your chance," The Umbra said. "Let that piece of shit in and convince him the two of you should kill yourselves together."

"No! I won't do it!" Aaron shouted. He turned the table saw on to drowned out The Umbra.

Derrick knocked on the door again, though this time a bit more forceful. He threatened to break the door down if Aaron didn't open it.

But Aaron didn't respond. He was too busy climbing up a ladder to retrieve a rope from atop the rafters. His master plan was to hang himself from a tree in the local park. If he had to kill himself, he didn't want to do it at his house where his younger brother or his parents would find his body.

The table saw did no good to silence The Umbra's taunts. Aaron frantically sifted through boxes on top of the plank of thin wood that served as a makeshift floor on top of the rafters.

One of the boxes he turned on its side and opened had several bobblehead figures in it. These were handed down to Scott after his dad passed away. The bobbleheads were largely sports-themed, and the primary sport represented was baseball. Cubs.

Mariners. White Sox. Red Sox. Indians. One bobblehead was of Sammy Davis Jr. and another was of Marilyn Monroe.

Frustrated with Aaron—desperately wanting to help him—Derrick pounded on the door several times. When Aaron didn't open it, Derrick rushed towards the door and collided into it with his shoulder. The door swung open and the bobbleheads fell, one of which onto the table saw's blade, slicing its face straight down the middle. Several of the other bobbleheads hit the table saw, but not the blade.

"Now look what you made me do!" Aaron shouted. "These are my dad's cherished possessions of his dad—the only thing my dad has left to remember my grandpa by, and now a bunch of them are busted." He turned off the table saw.

"I'm sorry, man," Derrick said, "but you wouldn't open the door. I was worried about you. Right now, you shouldn't be alone."

Aaron glanced at the countdown timer on his wrist. "What's it matter? I've got less than twenty-four hours to live at this point."

"Stop talking like that. There's been enough tragedy today. Your parents don't need to lose another child. They need you, man."

Before Aaron could answer, a police officer stepped into the garage. He informed Aaron his mom would be at the house soon and he should go inside and wait for her there.

And he did along with Derrick, who kept a close watch on Aaron—similar to the watch he himself was under when he was at the BAU—a suicide watch.

But it wasn't only Derrick who was watching Aaron's every move. The Umbra watched him, also, eagerly awaiting him to snuff his life out like a spent cigarette.

Brandon zombie-walked out of his mom and dad's bedroom and into the living room where Derrick and Aaron sat on the couch in silence.

"Does he know?" Derrick whispered to Aaron.

Aaron shook his head.

"Are you going to tell him?"

Aaron shook his head again. He glanced at the back of his wrist displaying how much time remained before he had to kill himself. He swallowed hard.

"Who's upstairs?" Brandon asked as he rubbed one of his eyes.

"Nobody," Aaron said, his lip trembling. "Come with me."

Aaron took Brandon by the hand and escorted him back into their parents' bedroom. Derrick followed close behind. Aaron flipped the TV on and switched the channel to Brandon's favorite Saturday morning cartoons: Looney Tunes.

The gravity of the situation hit Derrick head-on. The reality that Emily was dead tore into Derrick's heart.

"I need you to stay right here," Aaron said. "Will you do that for me?"

"But I want to go visit with Emily for a little bit," Brandon said.

"Not right now, little man," Aaron responded, his voice quivering. "Okay?"

"What's wrong? You sound so sad," Brandon said.

"I'll be fine."

The same inhuman voice—The Umbra's voice—that spoke within Derrick's mind was now inside of Aaron's.

(Real fine once you're stiff as a flagpole.) The Umbra made tongue-clicking noises several times, each one roughly a second apart, mimicking a clock ticking. *(Twenty-three hours, six minutes, and twenty-four seconds left before I get to kill you. Do*

you want your soul tortured for all of eternity? Don't let the timer hit absolute zero. Remember: die or be killed.)

15

After the police finished investigating the death of Emily—combing over her crib and bedroom for any clues—Scott and Karen drove to Crown Crematory, located in King Point, Indiana.

Though neither Karen nor Scott was in a proper frame of mind to drive, Scott's state was worse. He was experiencing difficulty forming coherent sentences. He constantly drooled on himself. When asked a question—no matter how simplistic it was—it took him an inordinate amount of time to answer, and often times he didn't vocalize his answers. For example, when Karen asked if he wanted cream for his coffee before they left for the crematorium, he shrugged his shoulders.

In the backseat of the car were Aaron, Derrick, and Brandon. Though Karen initially declined Derrick be a part of their family's planning of Emily's final arrangements—and truth be told Derrick tried to tell Aaron he had no business being involved—she ultimately relented for Aaron's sake, who clearly was in a state of severe distress.

Karen swung the car into a parking space in front of the building.

Scott exited the vehicle with one of Emily's shirts slung over his forearm. He staggered to the entrance and waited for everyone else to join him. They stepped inside the building. The lobby was small, and had no chairs or couches for people to sit. A room immediately to the left had a small rectangular table with chairs situated around it. Next to the room was a hallway where bathrooms were located. And next to the hallway was an office where someone was inside shuffling papers.

"Go ahead on in the meeting room there," a man said from the office. "I'll be right out. My name is Rich, by the way."

"Okay. Thank you," Karen said.

The meeting room had a few pictures on the blue-painted walls, mostly those of a religious nature. A picture of Jesus. Another of Michael the Archangel. Another of the Virgin Mary.

But not all of the pictures had religious connotations. One picture displayed the sun burning through the clouds. In the bottom right corner of it was the artist's name: Bryan Dupree.

A burly man with a mustache coupled with five o'clock shadow waddled into the office. "My name is Rich Dupree. I'm the proprietor of Crown Crematorium. Nice to meet you all. Sorry for your loss." He shook everyone's hand as each person introduced him or herself before taking a seat at the head of the table. "I truly can't begin to tell you how much pain I feel for you and your family, Mister and Mrs. Gaines."

Scott slightly nodded. "Thank you," he said, faintly.

"How did it happen?" Rich asked.

"Emily had been having issues breathing at times," Karen said, wiping tears from her eyes. "Each time she had one of these spells, Scott was there to the rescue. This time, however, she slipped away before anyone could have saved her."

"That's a shame," Rich said. "Again, I'm sorry for this tragic loss." He opened a padfolio and wrote down some basic information. The name of Emily's parents, the name of the deceased, and the date. "The first thing we'll need to do is pick out an urn." His cellphone rang and he glanced at the watch on his wrist—and then Aaron checked his. "Would you all excuse me a second, please? Look through this here binder of urns in the meantime. I won't be long."

While Rich was out handling whatever business it was, Scott and Karen shuffled through the binder of urns. Each page was encased in a plastic casing to prevent wear and tear on it.

I'm hallucinating this watch, Aaron thought. *Trauma is powerful. It can mess with your mind.*

Rich returned to the meeting room, apologized for having to step out, and resumed servicing his newest clients.

Rich scratched the back of his wrist. "Have we picked out an urn?"

Scott nodded. He placed the book in front of Rich and pointed to one. It was a rectangular-shaped black marble urn with a gold name plate on the front of it.

"Excellent choice. That's one of my favorites," Rich said. He jotted down the item number. "Let me give you a rundown of how this process will work. I will pick up the body from the medical examiner's office once the autopsy is completed and released. I'll run the body through the crematorium oven, and that takes about one to two hours. I'll finish handling the cremation remains before placing them in a blessed plastic bag—is that okay with y'all? Is it okay if I bless the plastic bag for your daughter's remains?"

"Yes," Karen snapped, not meaning to though. She took a breath. "That's fine. You're Christian?"

"No. Catholic," Rich responded. "Is that a problem."

"It's fine," Karen said. "Then what happens?"

"I'll place the plastic bag of Emily's fragments into the urn. Then you can come and pick the urn up for the service. Are y'all doing a service for her?" He erratically tapped his foot on the floor.

"Are you alright?" Derrick asked, genuinely concerned. "You're sweating."

Rich scratched the front and back of wrist and smiled. "Never better."

Scott raised his hand. He mumbled: "Is there a bathroom. I may use?" Drool from his chin dripped onto his shirt. "I'll be quick."

"Take all the time you need," Rich said. "The bathroom is in the hallway right next to this room."

Scott stood with Emily's shirt still slung over his arm. He lumbered out of the meeting room, leaving a trail of drool behind him.

While Scott was out of the meeting room, Aaron stared pensively at the back of his wrist. The timer continued to count down. 17:42:21, 17:42:20, 17:42:19, 17:42:18… *That's all this is, a hallucination brought on by years of drug use, withdrawal, and the trauma from the death of my baby sister.*

"When Mr. Gaines gets back, I'll need to use the restroom," Derrick announced.

"That's fine, young man," Rich said. "Time is on our side. Right, Aaron?"

Aaron swallowed hard. Rich rubbed the nape of his neck. Brandon laid his head on the table and Karen rubbed his head.

The sound of a toilet flushing alerted everyone Scott finished his business. Karen hoped this time he would wash his hands, especially after she had shown him a recent research study that quantified the number of bacteria contained in public bathrooms.

"So, Brandon, what do you want to be when you grow up?" Rich asked. *He reminds me so much of my son.*

"I think a cop. Then I can arrest the people who pick on me," Brandon said. "Fu—screw those haters."

Rich smiled. "Do you know how to shoot a gun?"

Brandon shook his head. "Do you?"

"I do," Rich said. "I've got a gun on my hip right now." He pulled it out and displayed it to the crowd at the table.

Derrick leaned over and whispered in Aaron's ear: "He must use that when business is slow."

Aaron sputtered a snicker, but silenced it almost as fast as it started. Rich looked in their direction after Aaron stifled his laugh, but didn't hear exactly what was said.

The gun Rich brandished was a Smith & Wesson 9 mm. It had a black finish with a stainless-steel slide and barrel. He stared at it, admiring its beauty, and reminisced about the days he and his father would go the shooting range together. It was Rich's father who first taught him to use a gun, and then Rich taught his sons and daughters how to fire a gun, often taking them to the shooting range a few times a week, even the youngest, who was around Brandon's age, approximately a year older.

Rich pulled a tissue from the box in front of him and wiped the sweat accumulating on his brow. Scott shambled into the room. Emily's shirt was still draped over his arm, and he never once took it off from the time he placed it there.

As he wiped the sweat that fell from his brow onto his gun, Rich said: "My life wasn't supposed to turn out like this. I had everything. A wife. Four beautiful children." He glanced at his wrists. "Now, it's all over for me. I caught my wife in bed with another man a few days ago. I almost killed the both of them as their naked bodies melded together like two molten metals forming an alloy. But I'm the one who has to die. Time is almost up."

"I'm sorry to hear about your problems, but don't you think you need to maybe share that information with a friend or a family member, not your customers?" Karen asked.

"I apologize, Mrs. Gaines," Rich said. "How inconsiderate of me." He placed the barrel of the gun under his chin and pulled the trigger.

Brain and bone matter shot upward with extreme velocity, striking the ceiling and walls—and blood, so much blood, which not only struck the wall but flowed from the Rich's nose onto his shirt and the table.

Everyone in the room screamed and shrieked. Brandon projectile vomited onto the table while Derrick and Aaron choked and gagged.

Karen called 911 and soon after an assortment of emergency personnel swarmed the building.

16

Thomas removed his glasses and chewed on the earpiece for a few seconds. His patient—Holly Pinkerton—lay in her bed, wanting to share with Thomas the information she was forbidden to share.

Holly was a thirty-six-year old mother of three. She had luscious blond hair that ran slightly past her shoulders and the bluest eyes, like a Caribbean sea.

"Why is it you can't tell me?" Thomas asked. He pushed his glasses up the bridge of his nose.

"Because he'll kill me if I do," Holly answered, sitting up in her bed. "He told me he would."

"But you're perfectly safe, and he doesn't even know where you are, right?"

Holly shook her head. "He's always with me."

After jotting a few notes down on his legal pad, he removed his glasses once again and gnawed a bit on the earpiece, but this time the opposite one from before.

As she sat biting her nails, numerous thoughts raced through her mind. How would she do it? And with what? If she didn't do it, could he really harm her?

"How long has your husband Marco abused you?" Thomas asked.

"Over the course of our entire relationship—ever since we started dating," Holly said.

"Did you ever file any charges against him?"

"No. I was too afraid to do that."

"And so you thought suicide was the only way out, am I right?"

Holly nodded. "The perfect and ultimate escape. He'd be happier because he doesn't have to see my ugly face anymore. I'd be happier because I wouldn't have to endure his constant abuse, and he covers the entire gamut."

"You mean he doesn't just physically abuse you."

"That's right. There's the emotional abuse. The sexual abuse."

"Sexual?"

"He's raped me more times than I can count on my fingers and toes," she said, sniffling. "It's just like when I was growing up… He once raped me when I was pregnant with our second child."

After Thomas scribbled some notes down, he pulled out a Twix bar from his breast pocket. He unwrapped it, pulled one of the bars out, and started to nibble away the caramel layer. He offered Holly the other one and she accepted.

As she devoured the sweet treat, her heart raced, thinking about the future, along with the lack thereof.

With his hand armed with his ballpoint pen, Thomas was ready to scribble some more notes down onto his pad which he'd struggle to read later.

Thomas cleared his throat. "You said like when you were growing up."

She nodded, but didn't speak since she still had a mouthful of Twix in her mouth.

"So your father abused you sexually. Is that correct?"

"Yes, but not only him. My mother, too."

After giving her a silent pat on the back, Thomas suggested they explore that topic in greater detail, but Holly didn't want to, and Thomas didn't force it. He never forced his patients to delve into something they didn't wish to discuss, instead letting them gradually develop the courage and strength to face the unresolved issues negatively affecting their lives in due time.

Thomas pulled out another Twix from his breast pocket and not breaking precedent, asked Holly if she wanted one of them. This time she politely declined. She feared eating too many sweets—something she never did while married to Marco— would lead to her gaining weight, and the last time her weight exceeded one-hundred-ten pounds, Marco wailed on her, and after the beating was over, he warned her if she ever exceeded one-hundred-ten pounds again, he would kill her.

At least three times a week, Marco checked Holly's weight. A few times it crept near one-hundred-ten pounds, and though he said he would kill her if it exceeded that value, he gave a good slug to the jaw as a reminder.

Her fear of gaining weight affected her food consumption, often only eating just enough to sustain herself, but never out of indulgence.

When the session was over, Thomas thanked her for her time. As he opened the door to walk out of her room, she called him back.

"There's someone other than my husband who wants me dead," she said, sobbing. "But it's not—"

Holly grasped her throat as she gasped for air for several seconds. Thomas yelled from her room for help and nurses swarmed into the room to render aid.

That fateful night, Holly entered The Umbra's Paradise of Pain, where her soul was *continuously*—not constantly— tormented.

17

When Derrick walked through the front door, Bruce grabbed him by the shirt and demanded answers. The scent of burped-up alcohol made Derrick's stomach churn.

"Why the fuck did you do it?" Bruce shouted.

"Do what?"

"Scratch the shit out of my car!"

Derrick tilted his head. "I didn't scratch your car, Dad. I swear, I didn't."

"Bullshit! Don't lie to me! Ever since you've been stroking that hard-on for your mom you've gone out of your way to find ways to retaliate against me! Leaving messes around the house. Not cutting the grass. Sneaking into my room to try and steal money. I guess you've decided to escalate your tactics to a criminal level now, huh?" He burped in Derrick's face.

Stifling his gag reflex, Derrick said: "How could I have scratched your car? I've been gone all day."

Bruce released Derrick's shirt from his hands and stepped into the bathroom to make room for more booze to fill up his bladder and fuck up his liver.

Now was Derrick's opportunity. Bruce left his cellphone on the living room table. No password required. A YouTube video was playing about how to commit the perfect murder. Derrick quickly scrolled through Bruce's call log, searching for his mother's number. When he found it, he placed the phone down onto the coffee table and snapped a picture of his mother's number.

But a second or two later, Bruce's phone launched off of the table and crashed through the living room's picture window, shattering it.

"What the hell!" Bruce screamed. He stumbled out of the bathroom while trying to pull up his boxers and shorts. "Are you kidding me? Now you're busting my windows up?"

"I didn't do it, Dad!" Derrick asserted. "Your phone took off like a magic carpet and struck the window."

"Don't lie to me, damn it!" He stuck his head through the window frame and surveyed the damage. *There's hardly any glass left in the frame.*

"I'm not. I didn't break the window."

(Yeah, Bruce. Der-prickless didn't do it. It was the one-armed man.)

[I'm so sick of you causing problems for me. You need to leave before you get sword fucked again.]

(Your dad can only stab me if I make myself visible. That's how he was able to save you that one night at the baseball field. That's the only reason you're alive. Your dad saved your life.)

"You're lying," Bruce snapped.

"I swear I didn't do this! God! Why don't you believe me? Sometimes I want to ki—"

"Get a fucking broom and dustpan and get that mess cleaned up," Bruce demanded. "I'm about ready to pack your shit and toss you out of here. I can't wait to see what you bust up next."

(Damn that Bruce! You almost said the words I needed to hear!)

No sense in arguing. How could Derrick pick a fight with his dad after being reminded again it was his dad who saved his life?

But why should Derrick believe anything The Umbra told him? How trustworthy was this entity anyway?

Derrick began sweeping up the innumerable pieces of glass that littered the porch and walkway. Bruce was sitting on the couch pouring himself a shot of Glenlivet 12.

"Hey, Dad," Derrick said, "what did you do to stop me from dying that night at the baseball field?"

Bruce slammed the show down and poured himself a new one. "I've told you several times. I wasn't there that night. I was on this couch marinating my brain in booze."

Why does he keep denying it? "But someone told me you saved my life that night."

"Well, they're a goddamn liar then. I was here." Down the hatch another shot went. "Besides, use your fucking brain. If I saved your life, why would I leave you lying on the ground on the baseball field like a hot dog wrapper from the concession stand?"

A valid point, and one Derrick gave pause to ponder. The only person he recalled having any sort of interaction with at the baseball field was the Chesterville police officer, but the police officer wasn't his dad.

For the first time, Derrick took the initiative to reach out to The Umbra for answers.

[Why do you keep lying to me? My dad wasn't at the baseball field.]

(But he was. I don't lie.)

18

Carrying the paper bag of broken glass, Derrick stopped when he saw Aaron standing in his garage staring at the back of his wrist. Derrick shouted Aaron's name four or five times, competing with the table saw running, but Aaron didn't seem to hear him—or if he did, he had no interest in responding.

Still gazing at the back of his wrist, Aaron placed his hand over it, but it didn't do any good. The countdown timer appeared on the top of his hand, still continuing to count down. 12:43:18, 12:43:17, 12:43:16,…

"What are you doing?" Derrick asked.

Aaron shuddered and lightly screamed. After he caught his breath, he said: "No. I'm not okay. My sister is dead, and I'm next. I can't lie to myself anymore."

"Are you still blaming yourself? It's not your fault what happened to your sister."

"It is my fault. I can't help but wonder how my family would look at me now if I had gotten up and saved my sister—just like my dad was able to do each and every time. I've become an enemy of the state. My family blames me," *Wait a minute…*

Without giving Derrick a chance to respond, Aaron rushed out of the garage—leaving the table saw running—and stormed into his house through the back door.

Derrick hoped the fence and walked into Aaron's garage. He approached the table saw. Out of nowhere an unseen force pushed his head towards the rotating blade, which was nothing more than a blur. Plenty of revolutions per second.

(I'm about to show you a whole new meaning to splitting headache!)

Derrick screamed. "Let me go! Don't!" He fought against the force, but the force had the upper hand.

(You're going to be dead one way or the other.)

"You said you can't hurt me though. You said you can't kill me."

The Umbra pushed Derrick's face closer to the blade, his nose an inch or two from the spinning circular blade.

(I'll risk being executed—converted into scattered matter for your soul. It's worth it. Are you ready to die?)

"How can you be executed if you are a spirit?"

(Get ready! You're about to have one hell of a nosebleed!)

"No!" Derrick shouted. "You can't kill me!"

The Umbra pulled Derrick up from the table saw. The two were now face to face, and though Derrick thought The Umbra had no definitive facial features, this was now no longer the case.

"I've been cheated out of your soul," The Umbra said. "I must have it. I'll get you to kill yourself one way or the other."

"I'm not going to kill myself," Derrick responded. "I'll never kill myself."

The Umbra released its grip from Derrick's shirt and vanished. Derrick flipped off the table saw. When he walked around the other side of the table saw, he stepped on a doll's hand—the Kool Kids doll whose face was mangled—and picked it up. From the top of its head to the top of its lip was a gash from when it made contact with the blade.

Derrick placed the Kool Kids doll on a chair near the table saw, which the doll faced. Ironically, the doll looked sad from its wound.

Sunset was near, and this meant Derrick needed to get home and start dinner for his dad.

19

Sitting in his room at his desk studying for an upcoming advanced engineering exam, Derrick took a break and tried calling Aaron back. It had been nearly eighteen hours since he found his sister dead at this point.

But Aaron didn't answer—just as he hadn't the last twenty-two times Derrick tried calling him. This didn't surprise Derrick though, considering he had just lost his only sister. *He's probably too busy grieving,* Derrick thought. *Just give him some space.*

Back to the books. Derrick was rereading the chapter on trusses along with various load calculations.

Soon his study session was interrupted when his phone jangled. The number on the screen indicated it was the same number he tried calling throughout the evening—his mother's number.

"Mom?" Derrick said.

"Excuse me? I think you have the wrong number," the woman said. "Goodbye."

"Wait, don't—"

But she terminated the call. He called her back and she answered.

"Listen, asshole. I don't have any kids, never did. You're mistaken," she snapped. "Quit fucking call me!"

"You spoke to me a few weeks ago," Derrick responded. "Bruce is my dad. Do you remember now?"

"No, I don't. Don't call me back or I'm going to call the police and file harassment charges on your juvie ass."

She ended the call again. He didn't dare call her using his number. He didn't want any trouble with the law. Instead, he downloaded a texting app that assigned him a different number.

Her sent her a text message: *Wendi?*

She texted back: *You have the wrong number.*

Derrick sipped his protein shake and sent her in a text: *No, I don't. Why won't you talk to me?*

I don't know you or anyone with this number. Now I'm blocking you, she sent him back.

He sent her a few more texts, but she didn't respond to them. She didn't lie; she did block the number.

But Derrick was persistent and decided to change the number within the texting app, switching it to an area code matching hers: 417.

This time he sent her in a text message a veiled text message, claiming he had to get a new number and she wanted him to delete his old number but save this new one.

She didn't respond back to the text. Instead, she called. When Derrick answered he lowered his voice an octave and spoke in a lethargic manner—as if he had just woken up sleeping—and to top it off, in a Southern drawl.

"Who is this?" she asked.

"Yeah, little lady, this is Jimbo. How are y'all doin' down yonder?" Derrick answered.

She snickered. "Okay. Is this a joke? Who is this?"

"I done told ya, little lady. This is Not-So-Slimbo Jimbo, also known as Big Jimbo."

"I don't know a Jimbo. You have the wrong person."

"Wait, now hold on there a tiny second. According to my contacts, this is Wendi's number. You are Wendi, aren't you?"

She sighed. "No, this is not fucking Wendi. You're the second person tonight who has called asking me that."

"Well, shucks and fucks. May I ask then who I'm speaking to, please?"

She cleared her throat. "You can ask, but I'm not answering."

"But I told you who I am. Now don't you think it would good and proper to tell me your name?"

"You contacted me, not the other way around. I don't know you. You have the wrong number. I'm hanging up now."

And she did. Derrick questioned why she denied her name was Wendi, even when she thought she was talking to a complete stranger. He concluded she must have known it was him all along and didn't fall for his ruse—a mother always knows. In his mind, that's why she continued to refute her name was Wendi.

But in spite of this, Derrick intended to continue his pursuit of his mother. He wouldn't stop trying to reach out to her until one or the other was dead.

Tomorrow was Emily's wake, so Derrick decided to get some sleep.

20

A little rumble of thunder greeted Derrick immediately after he stepped onto his front porch to bring in the paper for his dad. Sirens faintly cried in the distance, but then they grew louder and louder.

The intuition within Derrick was on high alert.

(I wonder where those sirens are traveling.)

"You son of a bitch," Derrick muttered. "What the hell did you do now? You kill somebody else?"

The Umbra appeared in front of Derrick and said: "Not this time," The Umbra said. "He did it all by himself. And now his soul belongs to me, and I'll torture it for all eternity. Gotta go—I think your dad is on his way to pierce me again." The Umbra began to become more and more translucent, but then returned to its original shade. "Before I go, give your dad a message. If you see him, tell him I'm going to kill him very soon—and you, too, of course."

What a jerk, Derrick thought. *He's implying my dad is dead—a spirit.*

The source of the sirens—an ambulance and a police cruiser sped down Derrick's street, passed his house, and slammed on their brakes in front of Aaron's.

Two paramedics jumped out of the cabin of the ambulance and opened the back doors. They yanked out the stretcher. One of the paramedics—the driver whose name was Greg—pulled out a medical bag from the back of the ambulance He tossed it at his partner—Paul—who wasn't expecting it to be tossed at him.

"Dumbass!" Paul—who was struck in the face with the medical bag—which nearly knocked his glasses off—said. "What have I told you about throwing stuff at me without giving a warning first?"

"Chill out," Greg said. "Or I won't massage your neck after dinner tonight."

"Well, then I won't cook dinner at all."

Greg stopped pulling the stretcher and turned to Paul. He apologized and Paul accepted. Derrick snickered a little at the banter between the paramedics—who were somewhat like a married couple, playfully arguing every now and again.

With amends made—for the time being, at least—they hightailed it the backyard. Derrick ran inside his house to the kitchen and look out the window towards Aaron's garage, but by that point paramedics had already entered it and closed the door. Whatever was going on in there couldn't be good.

Clodhopping into the kitchen, Bruce yawned while scratching his backside.

"Where's my breakfast?" Bruce said, surly and hoarse. "I gotta go to work this morning."

"I'll start making it right now," Derrick said. He pulled a pan out of the cabinet. "Something is going down at Aaron's again. You didn't hear the sirens?"

"I'm dead to the world. Just cook." Bruce grabbed a bottle of bourbon out of his liquor stash and took a little drink to wet his whistle. "I've got a hangover that won't quit."

Derrick cracked some eggs into a bowl and whisked them with a fork, which produced a clinky-clangy sound. Bruce took his seat at the kitchen table and admonished Derrick for whisking too loudly. Derrick tried to explain if he didn't vigorously whisk the eggs, they wouldn't be fluffy—the way Bruce liked them— and the only way he would eat them.

About ten seconds after their exchange ended, Bruce shot up from his seat and vomited in the sink. As Bruce retched after his stomach contents slowly drained out of the sink, Derrick helped his dad back to his seat, then poured him a glass of water.

More sirens grew in volume. Bruce ripped open the loaf of bread sitting in front of him on the table, yanked out several slices in each hand, and squashed them against his ears.

Derrick stifled his snickers. "What's wrong, Dad? You want me to open the doors and windows so you can hear a little better?"

"No! Cook goddamn it!" Bruce paused for a second or two. Then he said: "I've got to leave for work soon."

"Shit. You're right. I've got to get packed."

"Packed? What are you talking about?"

"Mike is taking me to Missouri. With exuberance, Derrick said: "Road trip!"

Bruce tossed the bread onto the table in front of him. "What's in Missouri?"

"Dad, come on, cut the crap. You know."

"I don't. I haven't any idea why you'd be traveling to Missouri. What's there? You visiting a college or something?"

Something didn't sit right with Derrick at this point. How could Bruce not know he was traveling to Missouri to reconnect with his mother? Derrick reconciled this confusion though, chalking it up to denial.

"Yeah, Dad. I'm going to check out University of Missouri," Derrick said, pouring the eggs into the pan. "I read they have a great engineering school there."

Bruce placed his head onto the kitchen table. "Yeah, well, I don't think you should be missing school to go check out a school."

"Since when do you care when I miss school?"

"Well, you don't really miss, so I haven't had to show I care. Don't you think you should be visiting colleges on vacation?"

"I will be, Dad. I plan to spend Thanksgiving in Missouri."

"Excuse me? What made you think you could up and leave without consulting me? Have you forgotten I'm your dad? I guess that boner you've got for your mom has gone to your head," Bruce said, snickering at his own stupid grouping of words. Boner. Head. "You can't go."

Derrick slammed the spatula onto the counter. "You just want me to stay here so I can slave over the stove for you to cook you a fancy Thanksgiving dinner."

"That's not true, young man. I don't like the idea of you driving hundreds of miles with some strange man and staying down there for umpteen days. Where are you getting all of this money to pay for lodging?" *I should start charging his freeloading ass rent. I've hardly any money.*

"We're not staying in a hotel. We're staying with a family member of Mike's—his mother."

Derrick dumped the eggs onto a plate, scraped the remainder out of the pan, and smacked the spatula onto the plate a few times, much to Bruce's irritation.

"Eat up," Derrick said, dropping the plate in front of his dad.

"These fucking eggs aren't fluffy!" Bruce shouted. "But I'll eat them anyway. I need to get something inside of me, speaking of which, how's Danielle doing?"

"Busy—just like me. School. Work. Why?"

Bruce shrugged his shoulders. "I don't know. Just wondering why your bitch hasn't been around to see you much. That's all."

"Speaking of bitches, who was the bitch you were smashing with last night?" He covered his mouth with wide eyes. "I'm sorry, Dad. I didn't mean to blurt that out."

Bruce gestured with his hand as if to say not to worry about. He scarfed down the eggs and handed Derrick his plate. When Derrick placed the plate in the sink, his eyes widened again. He couldn't believe the sight he saw: a man entering Aaron's garage wearing a black jacket with white capital letters strewn across the back of it. The letters: CORONER.

21

The sounds of children next door giggling as they played on the swing set brought back a flood of memories Thomas had of his girls before the separation, divorce, and move.

Nikki handed her dad a cup of hot cocoa. Then she took a seat next to him on the back-porch swing. They swayed back and forth, their movements in sync.

The sun was setting and the temperature was dropping. A winter chill was in the air.

"I want to talk to you about something," Nikki said.

"Great. I want to talk to you about something, also," Thomas responded. He sipped his cocoa.

"When are we moving into our own house again?"

"When the time is right. Besides, we've got a good thing going here, don't we? Lauren's house is much better than the one I was living in."

Nikki rolled her eyes. "It is a nice house, but it isn't *our* house. I thought I would have my own room by now. I moved up here with the understanding I would have my own room."

"And you will have your own room. I'm not breaking that promise. It's just we've had one thing after another happen that has prevented you from getting your own room. I am pleased you've straightened yourself out in school. You're not falling asleep in class anymore."

This was true, but that's because she pocketed her lunch and retreated to a bathroom stall where she ate in the bathroom stall and took a catnap afterwards.

The visions—the horrific visions of her mother committing suicide—seemed as though they would never die. Even as she sat right there with her dad the visions played in her mind.

Nikki sighed. "When Dad? When?"

"Soon. I've been looking at houses. Actually, Lauren and I have been looking at houses together. That's what I wanted to talk to you about."

"What? You mean you and she are going to get married?"

"Heavens, no. Well—not right away at least."

"So you and she are boyfriend and girlfriend."

Thomas smiled. "Sort of. Yes. We've been keeping that under wraps though."

Nikki made a grand exit, stomping on the porch into the house, declaring she should kill herself and she wanted to die.

22

Five days passed since Aaron's corpse was discovered in the garage with the table saw running. Today was his burial. He would be laid to rest next to his sister.

Derrick and Danielle parked behind Scott and Karen's car along the concrete path near the gravesite of Aaron. A few seconds later, a car parked behind Danielle's. Soon, a row of cars were lined up behind them.

With her arm around his, they walked to the site where Aaron's urn would be interned. It was resting on a table in the same make and model as his sister's, but a different color. White.

Scott, Karen, and Brandon were already seated in the front row of white folding chairs under the canopy. Scott shook hands with the people who took time out of their day to pay their respects to Aaron, mostly family members, but also several of his friends—the better of the lot. Not the fellow druggies and thieves he banned from his life not more than a few months ago when he turned his life around for the better.

After Danielle pulled down her black skirt, she sat in the second row of chairs on the end. Derrick placed his hand on Aaron's urn and spoke silently some words to his now-departed friend.

Other people congregated towards the back of the canopy where they hugged and conversed.

Brandon had his face in his hands, holding back tears, still shocked at the sight he saw when he walked in on his brother's corpse—its face split nearly in half from the table saw.

"I know, buddy," Derrick said. "It's awful."

"Why did he do it? Why did he kill himself?" Brandon asked, choking up.

"I think he was filled with guilt and grief because of what happened to Emily. He blamed himself."

"But he didn't do anything to her. He didn't kill her."

"I know, buddy, but in his mind, he thought it was his fault."

Scott announced the memorial service was about to start and everyone took their seats. After Scott said an introductory benediction, he explained how the memorial service would proceed. Anyone who had some last words they wished to share with the crowd was welcome to do so.

Sobs and sniffles ensued, but the show needed to continue.

Scott wiped his eyes with his tie. "Aaron and I had our differences. We had good times, bad times—as family members have over the years. He struggled for years with drugs and alcohol, but that didn't change the love I had for my firstborn. After today, I want to encourage all of you to tuck this memory away underneath a floorboard of your brain and keep it there. Let's remember the good times we had with him. Let's remember the good qualities about him."

Everyone nodded in agreement. Some said amen.

"Mom? Dad?" Brandon asked.

"Yes?" Karen said.

"Can I go now?"

"It's okay with me if it's okay with your dad, but I thought you wanted to go last."

"No. I changed my mind. I want to go now. It's my time."

Karen looked up at Scott and he slightly nodded. Brandon approached his brother's urn and looked at the picture on each side of the urn. One of Aaron lifting weights with Derrick; the other was of Aaron laying on the couch after Brandon had pulled a shaving-cream prank on him.

The crowd stood silent as Brandon readied himself to deliver his oration. The majority of people in the gallery grieved not only for Aaron's death, but also for Brandon and his parents, who had just recently lost their daughter.

After releasing an exhale, Brandon reached at first into his jacket's inner left pocket, but then corrected himself and pulled from right—an index card—a five by eight one—which had his oration spelled out.

Brandon said: "I still can't believe you're no longer here with us, but I know you're up in Heaven with Emily now. Maybe that's the best place for you, considering how much of a fuck-up you were while your useless ass was alive." He momentarily stopped when several members of the gallery gasped. "Emily's death was hard, but yours was harder, only because we had spent more time together. And now you're gone. Rest in peace, brother."

"Amen," several people within the crowd said.

But Brandon wasn't finished. He turned to the crowd and placed a finger to his chin and the crowd complied. Many were excited to hear what he had say next while a few were on tenterhooks.

He holstered the index card back into the right inside pocket of his black suit jacket, then reached into the left side and kept his hand there.

"I'm mad you selfishly killed yourself. You hurt us when you were alive, and you continue to hurt us now that you are dead. You're dead and Emily is dead. Now I have no brother or sister," Brandon said.

Rapidly, like a contract killer who spotted his target, Brandon pulled out a Glock from his inner jacket pocket and fired several times in rapid succession at the urn, shattering it into pieces.

Scott ran towards him until Brandon placed the barrel of the gun under his chin. "Stay back!" Brandon ordered. "I want to go be with Emily and Aaron!"

"Brandon," Derrick said, "please don't do this. It's not the answer. Suicide is never the answer.

The Umbra appeared next to Brandon. "I like his style."

[Get the hell out of here! Leave Brandon alone!]

"Make me," The Umbra said. Then it vanished

"I'm mad as hell!" Brandon screamed.

"It's okay to be upset," Karen said. "We are all upset. But Derrick is right. Suicide is never the answer. Please put the gun down."

And Brandon did.

CHAPTER 7

1

Against Bruce's wishes, Derrick made plans to travel to Missouri and find his mom, though Bruce was still under the impression Derrick was going down there to visit a college campus.

Three beeps blared from Derrick's driveway. Derrick locked the front door behind him and sauntered to Mike's truck. Mike stepped out of the truck and told Derrick he would drive the first leg of the journey, and Derrick didn't mind. In fact, he embraced the challenge.

For the past two weeks, Mike gave Derrick driving lessons nearly every day. First, they started off in parking lots, where Derrick developed confidence behind the wheel. Within a few days, Derrick then drove up around his residential area. And a few days after that, Derrick was driving on the highways and expressways. A fast learner he was.

"Morning, Heather," Derrick said as he hopped into the car. "That's a nice blouse you're wearing."

"Thanks," she responded. "Dylan picked it out for me one time when we were at a department store."

"Good choice." Derrick started the truck. "Have you seen or heard him lately?"

Mike obnoxiously coughed. "Remember to check your mirrors." He gestured to Derrick to shut his mouth about Dylan's spirit—or the demon masquerading as Dylan. "Let's hit it. Missouri—here we come."

The road and weather conditions were ideal. Dry pavement and nothing but sunshine. But this wouldn't last the entire day. Freezing rain was on its way, but nobody in the truck was aware of this.

To Derrick, it was a pleasant sight to see Mike and Heather together again. Dylan's death—be it the result of a suicide or murder—nearly destroyed their marriage.

Fortunately, Heather saw the light and no longer blamed Mike for Dylan's death. She now blamed herself for not persisting with Mike to restrain Dylan to prevent him from killing himself. The only thing that gave her solace at this point was knowing one day she would reunite with Dylan.

Aside from this, Mike and Heather had something big planned, something that gave them a glimmer of hope and encouraged them to find the strength to carry on even when it seemed like no hope was in sight.

Ten minutes passed, at which point they merged onto 80-94, or as many folk called it around those parts, the Borman.

Mike turned on the radio and tuned it to a country station. "What's your mom's address again?" he asked, queuing a Maps app on his cellphone.

"According to the one she gave me it is 6279 Kansas Avenue," Derrick said. "The city is Hannibal."

(You're a dumbass. Driving down there for no reason.)

[Fuck off, Umbra. I want to see my mom and she wants to see me.]

(If you want to see your mom, crash that eyesore of a truck. Accelerate to over one-hundred miles per hour, then jerk the wheel violently to the left.)

Oddly enough, Derrick did accelerate, but unknowingly. The Umbra would not leave him alone, and this was irritating Derrick beyond belief.

He wanted The Umbra to go away, but The Umbra made it clear the only way Derrick could rid himself of his presence is to kill himself.

"Slow down," Heather suggested.

Mike glanced over at the gauges. "Your speed is fine."

"Mike—no it's not. He's going almost twenty miles over."

Mike glanced at his phone, which had the Maps app running, showing their current location. The Maps app also indicated if they were traveling at a speed beyond the posted speed limit by showing a fraction: current speed/posted speed. When traveling above the posted speed limit, the box containing this information flashed in red, and the greater above the speed limit traveled, the faster the flashing.

The box within the speed information was flashing red. Mike observed this and nodded his head, but it indicated Derrick was exceeding the speed limit by seven miles per hour. About a minute ago, it was over twice that.

"Actually, you could speed up a little," Mike said, grinning.

Heather swatted his arm from the backseat and Mike bellowed a chuckle. She advised him not to teach Derrick poor or dangerous driving habits. He assured her he was only joking. Then he instructed Derrick to decelerate a little.

The once-clear sky started to show signs of cloud formation. Mike changed the station to WHAM, an AM news station that focused on earth-shattering news sound bites, some shockingly serious and others shockingly outlandish.

A commercial was wrapping up when Mike tuned in to the station.

The narrator for the commercial said: "…special taking place for the next week. Three whoppers for eight dollar."

"This is WHAM 980—that's W-H-A-M 9-8-0," the broadcaster said. "Current time is seven sixteen. And here's Joyce Fey bringing you up-to-date weather."

"Thanks, Mark," Joyce said. "Expect the high today to be in the mid-thirties. Current temperature is twenty-seven degrees. Expect to see some freezing rain within the next hour, at times moderate to heavy. Drivers are encouraged to…"

As Joyce read her weather report, drops of rain began to strike the windshield. Out of an abundance of caution, Derrick decelerated, but Mike directed him to maintain his previous speed since the roads were not yet wet.

This time, Heather didn't disagree. The roads weren't bad, and decelerating may create a traffic hazard rather than prevent one.

Derrick's cellphone chirped like a baby bird, and that ringtone was all too familiar to him. It was his dad—calling from the house's landline. He quickly answered the call and placed it on speaker, but nearly slid out of control when the truck's right wheels hydroplaned slightly through a puddle he didn't see. Fortunately, he didn't panic, which may have led him to overcorrect and crash.

"Dad? What is it?" Derrick asked.

"Where are you?" Bruce asked, irritated.

"On the road—driving to Missouri. I left you a note on your bed."

Bruce sighed. "I've told you to stay out of my room. Besides, I haven't been in my room yet."

"Well, I left another note taped to the liquor cabinet. I figured that would be the first place you'd look. This would all be so much easier if you would get your phone replaced. Then I could send you text messages like a normal person."

"First off, screw you for accusing me of being an alcoholic. Secondly, I don't have enough money to replace my phone. Thirdly, back in my day, we didn't have cellphones, so there."

"What do you want?"

"Get home. You're not going to Missouri right now."

"Dad, yes I am. I waited until vacation time came. I cooked your damn Thanksgiving dinner with all the fucking trimmings and fixins. My work is done. Now it's time for me to do what I want to do. You're not going to crash the party for me—not this time."

Bruce sighed. "Fine. I'll tell you what. Good luck trying to get into the house when you get back. Good-fucking-bye!"

A loud slam followed by silence. Bruce ended the call. Neither Mike nor Heather needed to ask how that conversation went.

"You okay?" Mike asked.

"I'm fine. My dad can be a total asshole sometimes," Derrick said. "He will do anything he can to stop me from seeing my mom. Now he's threatened to lock me out of the house if I don't turn back now."

"Don't do it, Derrick," Heather said. "If you need a place to stay, you can stay with us."

Mike nodded.

"I appreciate that," Derrick said.

Heather cleared her throat. "Besides, we may be needing a babysitter soon." She rubbed her belly when Derrick looked in the rearview mirror.

Derrick smiled. "Are you serious?"

They both smiled and nodded. Their eyes said it all. Though they lost a child, they now gained. Heather leaned forward to give Mike a kiss. Derrick turned to watch the moment, thinking about him and Danielle. How one day the two of them would start a family of their own.

The truck hit a patch of black ice and several times before cutting across traffic. The back part of the truck was struck by a big rig—who was speeding and momentarily distracted looking at gay porn on his phone while servicing his member—and the pick-up truck flipped over an innumerable number of times.

2

With a car loaded with Thanksgiving food she prepared, Gayle pulled into Bruce's driveway. She did a quick makeup check, wanting to look her best for him. It had been several months since they last saw each other and she wanted to make this first impression since then as best as it could be.

She stood at the front door and almost knocked, but stopped herself. She opened the front door. The coffee table had empty booze bottles and plates of uneaten food strewn across it.

Moaning and panting trickled from Bruce's bedroom. Gayle tiptoed down the hallway. When she reached the door, she closed her fist to knock on the door, but stopped herself. She paused for several seconds, listening to the sounds and pondering whether she should open the door.

But then the voice of the female in the room sent a chill up Gayle's spine. She stormed into the bedroom, startling Bruce and the vixen in the bed with him.

That was the second to last memory Gayle had before leaving.

3

A scream radiated through the entire house, and it was a scream Thomas never heard before in his life, a scream that induced chills and caused him to shudder.

The scream continued, but in tandem with loud footsteps as Thomas rushed to see what was happening.

"What are you screaming about, Ashlee?" Thomas said.

Ashlee pointed towards the living room. "In there, Daddy. A shadow person was standing by the fireplace. It was scary."

Thomas looked at Lauren. "I'll go check it out."

Lauren nodded and grabbed Ashlee by the hand. They walked to the back porch and waited for Thomas report back.

At a snail's pace, Thomas crept to the living room, finding it impossible not to remember the incident that happened in his living room with his ex-wife's urn where the shadow figure created an erupting and exploding volcano from the cremation ashes.

Thomas swallowed hard. He stood near the egress of the living room, but not the point where he could see within it. The fear coursed throughout his body like the blood in his veins.

"Is someone in there?" Thomas said.

"Yeeeeesss," a voice whispered.

His heart rate nearly doubled after hearing that voice. His muscle tissue stretched like a rubber band. But he wasn't entirely certain if what he heard was real or imagined.

"Who is in there?" Thomas asked.

In a drawn-out whisper, it said: "Nooooot aaaaa whooooo." A brief second passed. "But a what. Remember me?"

In Thomas' mind, there was no denying it now, and the verdict was in: the voice wasn't imagined. "*What* are you?"

"The Umbra," it shouted, appearing at the egress of the living room—in front of Thomas. "I want you to know something, Tommy-the-Tank-Ass-Engine."

"Get out of here. You're not welcome here."

The Umbra took a step forward and slightly cocked its head. "I enjoyed every second of watching your wife blow the top of her skull off her head."

Thomas covered his mouth, horrified, now that he was able to see *within* the shadow's figure. Though it had no discernible features from a distance, up close it did. Its face wasn't a skull—at least not a human one—but it was skull-like. Its mouth was a triangular orifice. Its eye sockets were hollowed out.

"Why are you saying such horrible things?" Thomas asked, his fists clenched. "Why would you use my wife's suicide as a way to get at me?"

"Because I *was* there. I had to be there to watch her go out with a bang. Couldn't miss that."

"What do you want?"

"She pulled the trigger with so much time to spare. She was much braver than my other victims."

"Victims? She killed herself."

"Because of me, Thomas. Because of me. But she opened the door that allowed me to walk into her life and present her with two options: die or be killed."

Thomas shook his head in disbelief. "What the hell are you?"

The Umbra stepped forward—only slightly though. "I'm the essence of evil. Like subatomic particles to an atom which then forms molecules. I am perfect evil in its purest form. I thrive on watching people off themselves, Tom-Tom. And if they don't, I kill them myself."

Though this entity—The Umbra—had a mouth, it never moved.

"I want you out of this house," Thomas said, clenching his teeth. "How do I get you out of this house? A blessing? A sage cleansing? How?"

The Umbra laughed, which was dark and strange. Its laugh alone gave Thomas the shivers. "There's nothing *you* can do to stop me, and if that fedora-wearing fucker tries to stab me again, I'll be ready to kill his spirit."

"How can you destroy a spirit?"

"I don't have time to give you a physics lesson. I've got some more killing to do. Toodles, Thomas. I'll be sure to kill—I mean kiss—your daughters goodnight each night."

The papa bear within in Thomas was in high gear. "You stay the fuck—"

The Umbra faded out. Thomas all of a sudden felt lightheaded—as if he had stood too quickly—and heel-toed it to the couch. The lightheadedness lasted nearly five minutes before he was able to stand and walk normally.

Now he was sitting at the patio table on the back porch, laughing and chatting with Lauren and Ashlee.

4

After the moving truck was dropped off at a U-Haul location, Roberta and Madison hopped into Jimmy's car and they drove back to their new apartment.

"This is stupid," Madison said, crossing her arms. "I miss our old house."

"I know, baby, but that house was too expensive for us to stay there," Roberta said.

"I thought you liked the new apartment," Jimmy said, smiling in the rearview mirror.

Madison exhaled. The air released blew her bangs upward. "It's okay."

"Here's an idea," Jimmy said. "How about when we get back home we change into our trunks and hit the indoor pool? How's that sound, Maddy? Do you wanna go swimmin'?"

"Pool? What pool?" Madison asked.

"He's lying to you," Dylan whispered in her ear. "There is no pool."

Roberta whipped her head around. She looked from side to side. Jimmy glanced at her, but then resumed keeping his eyes on the road while maintaining his cool-guy steering wheel grip, which consisted of his left arm stretched across the window sill door and his right hand gripping the steering wheel at the twelve o'clock position.

"Did you hear that?" Roberta asked Jimmy.

Jimmy shook his head. "Did you?"

"Yeah. It was a faint whispering," Roberta said. She turned back to Madison and asked: "Did you hear whispering?"

Madison put her finger to her chin and squinted her eyes. A little girl in deep thought. "No, Mommy. I don't know what you're talking about," she said, her hands in front of her.

They ended up getting stuck at a stop light. Jimmy chided himself audibly yet unintelligibly for wimping out on punching the accelerator when the green light switched to yellow.

The faint whispering crept into Roberta's ear again, but before Roberta could turn around to get a better listen, the whispering ceased. And, before Roberta could say anything, Madison beat her to the punch.

"Quit your bitchin', Jimmy," Madison said.

"Maddy, that's not nice to say to me," Jimmy said. "I've never said bad language around you—or your mom for that matter."

Madison rolled her eyes. Roberta lightly chuckled, confused. Jimmy released an exaggerated sigh. He didn't mind waiting at red lights—a believer everyone needs to share the road. This light, however, had been red for the past four minutes.

When Roberta rubbed the back of Jimmy's neck, a smile slithered on his face and his tension melted away.

"What made you say that?" Roberta asked.

Madison shrugged her shoulders.

"Was that you who was whispering?" Roberta asked.

And, once again, Madison shrugged her shoulders and whispered: "I don't know what you're talking about."

"Now, Madison, we talked about this. You promised me you would tell me if Dylan is still talking to you. Has he talked to you?"

A few seconds passed. Madison winced and lightly grunted. Then she rubbed her arm.

"What's wrong with your arm?" Roberta asked.

"Nothing, Mommy," Madison replied. "And, no, Dylan doesn't talk to me anymore. I promise. It was me who whispered, I swear."

Roberta smiled. "I'm glad he's gone, but if he comes back, do you promise me you'll tell me?"

Madison nodded, albeit unconvincingly.

After a few minutes passed, Jimmy approached another stop light. It switched from green to yellow, and this time he wasn't going to let the light get the better of him. He punched the accelerator, but then slammed the brakes. He placed his arm across Roberta's chest. She smacked him.

"Why'd you hit me?" Jimmy asked, rubbing his arm.

"You touched my boobs," Roberta snapped back.

Madison giggled. "Yeah, Mommy. You've got a nice set," she said.

Roberta gasped. "Madison. I'm—"

"Mommy, if you say the right words, The Umbra might visit you," Madison said.

"The Umbra?" Jimmy asked, confused. "What's an umbra?"

"The Umbra is an evil thing that likes to watch people kill themselves," Madison said. "And if they don't kill themselves, The Umbra does it for them."

Jimmy smiled, looking at Roberta. "Kids and their imaginations."

"I'm not imagining this," Madison contested. "The Umbra has visited me before."

Roberta felt her blood run cold hearing these things from Madison, but Jimmy chalked it up to nothing more than Madison making things up as a way to compete for the attention of her mother.

5

Two uniformed sheriff deputies—Markle and Ginsberg—knocked on Bruce's front door even though the doorbell was perfectly functional. They waited a several seconds with their arms folding, facing each other, talking about nothing earth-shattering. Last night's hockey game—Blackhawks versus Capitals. The final score was two to four—Capitals won and Deputy Ginsberg lost, financially that is, but fortunately not too much money this time.

Deputy Markle knocked on the door this time—not Deputy Ginsberg—and resumed his arms crossed position.

Deputy Ginsberg was a recent hire of the Portake County Sheriff's Department, assigned to Deputy Markle's command.

"How's your divorce going?" Deputy Markle asked, looking down at Deputy Ginsberg. Markle once played the role of the Jolly Green Giant for a commercial shoot.

"Great. It's almost final," Deputy Ginsberg responded. "I can't wait to be rid of that vicious two-timing skank. It's been a long journey—this divorce. I thank the heavens above Jacqueline and I didn't have any children." He turned away from his partner and burst out with laughter.

"What's so funny?"

"Nothing, boss. Nothing." He chuckled softly for a few seconds, then stopped.

But Deputy Ginsberg was lying. What he found so amusing was Deputy Markle's constant head nods as someone spoke to him. Nod-nod-nod (brief pause), nod-nod-nod (brief pause),…

Then again, though, Deputy Ginsberg found humor in the most trivial of circumstances. For instance, he laughed at the way his dog—Barksicle—would sniff anything placed in front of its nose. To pass time, Ginsberg would find random things to put in his dog's face just to watch him sniff.

"This is ridiculous," Deputy Markle announced. He pounded on the door and waited several seconds. "Maybe nobody is home. Come on. Let's leave a card with a message on the back. We'll grab a bite, then come back if Mr. Bruce Johns doesn't call us back."

"I heard footsteps inside though," Deputy Ginsberg said. "You didn't?"

"No, I didn't hear anything except your hyena-like laugh."

"I'll knock once more. That's it. If we don't get an answer, we're bailing." With the bottom of his fist, he pummeled the door. A brief period of waiting. "See—he's not home."

Deputy Ginsberg rang the doorbell. A few seconds later, Bruce answered the door, with his hair disheveled, in his bathrobe.

"Dear god. How'd you figure it out so quickly?" Bruce asked, his speech slurred.

"We're well-trained," Deputy Ginsberg touted, his smile a smug one.

Deputy Markle tapped Ginsberg's arm. "Sir, may we step inside?" he asked. "We need to talk."

"About what?" Bruce asked. He swallowed hard. "Whatever it is you think I did, I didn't."

"We're not accusing you of doing anything, sir," Ginsberg said. "You have a few too many last night?"

Bruce lightly chuckled, shaking his head. "This morning. Anyhow, I'm sorry. Please come inside. The place is a mess. I've been trying to clean-up. Please forgive me for that. My live-in maid absconded to Missouri."

The two deputies perched themselves on the couch, leaving Bruce to have to get a chair from the kitchen. A Rug Doctor machine was plugged into the wall. The white carpet had a large purplish stain where the hallway to Bruce's bedroom and the living room met.

Bruce staggered out of the kitchen with a chair in his hands. He offered them something to drink.

"We can't drink," Deputy Ginsberg said. "We're on duty."

Deputy Markle hit Ginsberg in his arm again.

"Okay, then. I'll have a beer," Deputy Ginsberg said.

Again, Deputy Markle nudged his partner in the arm. "We're not thirsty. We're going to be heading to—Sweet Jesus!"

"What? Bruce asked.

"A shadow figure just walked out of one bedroom and crossed into another, but both doors were closed," Markle said. "You have a ghost in your house?"

Bruce nodded. Deputies Markle and Ginsberg were surprised to learn the ghost in Bruce's house didn't bother Bruce in the least. In fact, Bruce divulged to them he and the shadow man—The Umbra—recently started communicating with each other.

"Let's get down to the nit and grit," Deputy Markle said. "We're here to inform you—"

"Of my rights? Am I going to jail?" Bruce asked.

"No, you're not. Please listen. This is about your son, Derrick," Deputy Markle said.

"Is he okay?" Bruce asked.

"No."

From that point forward, Bruce was quiet. The deputies shared with the Bruce the accident and Derrick's condition along with which hospital Derrick was receiving treatment at.

Panic-stricken, Bruce frantically changed into some clothes. When he reached for his keys off of the coffee table—in between a vodka and scotch bottle, Deputy Markle snatched them up.

"What the hell are you doing?" Bruce asked, slurring his words. "I gotta get to my son."

"You need to find a ride," Deputy Ginsberg said.

"Exactly. You're in no condition to be driving at this point," Deputy Markle added. "Is there someone you can call? A family member? A friend?"

"I don't have any family or friends. They're all dead," Bruce said. "I guess I could call Danielle. That's Derrick's skanky girlfriend."

And he did call her. While Bruce made his calls, the deputies wandered the living room, perplexed Bruce didn't have any pictures of Derrick on the walls or on one of the sofa's end tables.

Bruce kept an eagle-eye on the two deputies roaming his living room. He wouldn't dare let them go beyond that room—at least not without a warrant.

"What do you want now?" Danielle said as her greeting. "Haven't I helped you out enough?"

"Derrick is in the hospital," Bruce responded.

"I don't care."

"I need a ride to the hospital. I'm too fucked to drive."

"What? Did he try to kill himself again? What a loser. And so are you."

"I know he is, but I need to get to the hospital. Please—will you take me there? And, just so you know, it was a car accident, not that he tried to kill himself again."

Danielle initiated a longwinded tirade about how much she hated Derrick and him. He let her vent—hearing her, yet not entirely listening. As long as she agreed to drive him to the hospital, she could call him every name in the book and say whatever she wanted.

Deputy Markle attempted to walk down the hallway, but Bruce intercepted his path. The deputy explained he needed to use the restroom. Bruce led the way, leaving Deputy Ginsberg temporarily unattended in the living room. Bruce apologized for the floaters he left in the unflushed toilet not more than forty minutes ago.

When Bruce returned to the living room, Deputy Ginsberg was nowhere to be seen. A ruckus shifted Bruce's attention from the living room to the kitchen.

"I'm sorry. My throat is slightly parched," Deputy Ginsberg said. "Just getting myself some of water."

"Fine," Bruce said.

Deputy Ginsberg didn't use a glass though. He turned the faucet on and stuck his lips into the stream of water.

Now Bruce was keeping one eye on Deputy Ginsberg and the other on the hallway—waiting for Deputy Markle to finish his deposit.

"…So what do you have to say about what I just said?" Danielle asked, her tone agitated.

"You're right about everything," Bruce said. "But I need your help. I've got nobody else."

Danielle breathed heavily into the phone a few times. Then she said: "Fine. I'll take you. But I want you to hear me and hear me well. This is the last favor I do for you. And this is the end for me and Derrick, too. The two of you can die for all I care."

"That's sweet of you. Thank you. I'll get dressed as soon as I get rid of these two nuisances."

A few minutes after their call ended, Bruce knocked on the bathroom door. Deputy Markle was startled and screamed a little, then flushed the toilet, sending his feces and Bruce's to their next destination.

The deputies left and soon after Danielle arrived in her mom's Buick Enclave and beeped the horn twice. Bruce staggered out with a Dos Equis bottle in his hand, which he finished off and tossed onto Scott's yard.

Off to the hospital—located nearly eighty miles away—they went.

6

The correctional officer escorted Karla—wearing an orange prison jumpsuit—into the visitor's area. He sat her at Booth Seven.

Karla picked up the telephone. "Who are you?"

"My name is Usha, and I want you to know I believe your story," Usha said.

"Really? Why do you choose to believe me when nobody else does?"

"Because I think it was that shadow figure you saw murder your friend that also murdered my…boyfriend."

Karla's eyes welled up with tears, but she shed none, forcing herself to appear strong.

Usha placed a sheet of printer paper to the glass window. It was a picture Alejandro had drawn which was left in the lockbox. The picture was a tracing of his own hand with an arrow pointing at the wrist area. An inscription next to the arrow read: My time was up.

A RACE AGAINST TIME

CHAPTER 8

1

Lying in a medically-induced coma, Derrick heard the Umbra speak within his mind.

(You will kill yourself. You will enjoy it. You will declare to anyone and everyone you wish to kill yourself... You will think of different creative and flamboyant ways to execute yourself.)

Like an iTunes song on repeat, The Umbra started at the beginning and carried on.

2

Sitting in Aaron's bedroom, Karen reminisced about her firstborn along with many firsts associated with him. First word, first step. First Christmas, first birthday.

The shirt Scott had slung over his arm—an Aeropostale sweatshirt—when he and Karen traveled to the temporary location of Crown Crematory (the original location was being cleaned and remodeled after Rich's departure) laid on the bed just underneath the pillows with its sleeves spread outward.

"Dad is a killer," Aaron whispered in her ear.

She lunged off the bed. "Aaron? Was that you?" She paused for a few seconds waiting for a response, but received none. "Aaron—if you're here, please give me a sign."

But none surfaced.

3

Though the hospital room contained a ghastly sight, Bruce had seen worse, so he gritted his off-white teeth and bore it. Derrick was on a breathing machine with a tube down his throat. Several wires extended from his chest and headed to different machines.

A few sounds stood out in the foreground to Bruce. The breathing machine pumped several times, then would hiss. The beeping of the heart machine. The recalibrating of the IV machine. To a lesser extent, idle chatter in the hallway.

A man wearing a shortened lab coat with a completely shaved head—which he ducked as he entered the hospital room with his hand extended. He towered over Bruce—like a doll house to a skyscraper. Bruce shook his hand.

"I'm Dr. Jeff Mills, but please call me Jeff," the doctor said. "And you must be—"

"Bruce Johns. I'm Derrick's father," Bruce said, his voice groggy. *This hangover is a bitch.*

Their hands released from each other and Jeff wiped his hand on his lab coat. Bruce's hand was sweatier than the backside of an all-star NBA player during the last thirty seconds of a tied game in the fourth quarter.

"It's nice to meet you," Jeff said. Bruce concurred. "I'm sure you'd like to know about Derrick's diagnosis and prognosis. Am I right?"

Bruce rolled his eyes. "Yes. Of course. That's why I'm here."

"Very good. Very *very* good." *Damn that Dr. Ivy—I've got to quit doing that.* He had Thomas as a professor in medical school during the psychiatry clinical rotation, and every once in a while, he exhibited characteristics of Dr. Ivy through himself. "He has several fractured ribs, a broken arm, and a broken leg. The majority of the damage was to the brain though. We've managed to get the hemorrhage under control."

"How soon will he be able to come home?"

"It's difficult to say. We need to ensure he can breathe properly on his own first. That's why he is in the medically-induced coma—so we can regulate his breathing for him."

As Bruce took a seat in one of the two chairs positioned along the wall near Derrick's bed, Jeff shuffled to the EEG machine. He reviewed the strip of paper showing the different waves Derrick's brain exhibited. Now his attention was on the EEG machine screen. He shook his head and clicked his tongue a few times.

"What's wrong?" Bruce asked, slumped in the chair.

"It's fascinating how active his brain is even though he's in a coma," Jeff said, "and especially the occipital region of the brain."

"What's so special about that region?"

"It controls—part and parcel—speech and hearing."

Bruce yawned. "What does that suggest?"

"Well, I can't say for certain, but to me I interpret these results as Derrick having a conversation with someone."

Bruce swallowed hard. "Could he be communicating with spirits. I mean he does look as though he's near death."

"Looks can be deceiving, Mr. Johns. Derrick is likely to make a full recovery. But, yes, it is possible he may be communicating with spirits. Or he could be conversing with his inner voice. Another possibility is he thinks he's talking to someone—could be anyone—a relative or a stranger. There isn't any way to definitely ascertain what's going on in that magnificent brain of his. I just hope the brain damage will repair itself."

Running through Bruce's mind was what spirit or spirits may be communicating with him. There were a select few he hoped wouldn't bother Derrick.

Bruce stood next to Derrick's bedside, looking at his face, thinking about the best course of action. Jeff logged some notes into Derrick's electronic file using a computer mounted to an arm attached to the wall, which swung outward.

"DNR," Bruce said, his tone sharp and bitter.

Jeff spun around, his lab coat looking like a dress with a draft blowing upward into it. "Excuse me?"

"If it comes down to it, DNR—*do not* revive."

"Resuscitate, you mean. And I don't think it's going to come down to that."

"I said if it does come down to it, damn it. Do not resuscitate his ass. Let his ass go."

Jeff's eyes bulged out of their sockets. He was at a loss of words. Never in his fifteen years of serving as a critical-care physician did he hear the parent of a child speak callously in the way Bruce did.

After Jeff finished entering the notes into Derrick's medical file, he brought up another issue.

"If you don't mind, Mr. Johns—" But before Jeff could finish his sentence, Bruce interrupted, instructing Jeff to call him Bruce, and Jeff assured him he would from now on. "What I wanted to ask you is presuming your blood type is compatible with Derrick's if you'd be willing to donate some blood for us to have on reserve in the event it's needed. What do you say?"

"I don't know about that," Bruce said. "I have a fear of needles and being stabbed. I'd probably faint at the mere sight of the needle."

Jeff lightly snickered when Bruce exaggerated the length of the needle using his hands. "It won't hurt. I promise. I'll have our best phlebotomist do it. I had her draw some blood from me for a donation and I didn't feel a thing."

"I don't understand why you need my blood anyway. I said not to resuscitate his ass."

"In the event he is in the situation where a decision needs to be made to either resuscitate or not, we will not per your wishes. We'll need to have you sign some papers." He cleared his throat. "Now, the blood is on hand if we need to perform surgery of some kind."

Bruce rolled his eyes. "Fine. I'll donate some of my blood. Can I get paid for it?"

"No—that's why it's a donation, and this *is* your son, right? Your biological son, correct?"

After a brief pause, Bruce said: "Yes, Derrick is my son and I am his father."

Normally, Jeff shook hands before leaving with the people he met for the first time, but this time he didn't.

4

Sitting in front of the vanity, Ashlee brushed her hair while Nikki laid in bed with the covers over her head.

"Why are you so mad and sad?" Ashlee asked.

Nikki heaved a sigh like a fierce wind. "I've told you before. Because Dad and that mom-wanna-be are boyfriend and girlfriend. They're going to end up getting married. Lauren is your new mom."

Ashlee somewhat shrugged her shoulders. "It doesn't bother me dad has a new girlfriend. And Lauren is nice."

"Whatever," she said, the covers still over her face.

"Why won't you give Lauren a chance?"

"Because she's not Mom. I feel like she's trying to take her place, and I'm mad at Dad for letting her do it. Let's just drop it. It's bad enough I've been stuck in the same room with you ever since we moved up here from Florida. I'm sick of things not going my way. I've had it!"

Nikki didn't see it, but Ashlee's lip quivered as her heart shattered. Ashlee sat for a several seconds, clutching the brush and wavering between sadness and anger—an emotional tug of war. Finally, anger won the match.

With a foghorn-like voice, Ashlee announced: "Fine! You know what? You want your own room? You can have this one all to yourself!" She pulled the covers off of Nikki and stormed out of the room.

When Ashlee reached the downstairs, Lauren was sitting on Thomas, facing him. Fortunately, most of their clothes were on. Lauren lunged off Thomas and fixed her rat's nest hair while Thomas straightened his glasses on his face.

"Hey, angel, what was all the yelling up there about?" Thomas asked, placing a pillow on his lap.

"It's Nikki. She's selfish. She wants her own room, so I'm letting her have ours," Ashlee said. "And I don't even care if she says she's sorry. I'm not gonna go back in there with her, because she's a big doody head."

Thomas and Lauren both chuckled. Then Lauren said: "I'm sure she didn't mean the things she said, but tell me, where are you going to sleep from now on?"

"On this couch," Ashlee said. "So, you've got ten minutes to finish up whatever game you two were playing, because I'm exhausted and wanna get to bed."

Thomas looked over at Lauren. "I can be finished in three."

Lauren—unamused—smacked his arm.

"What game were you two playing?" A second—two at the most—passed before Ashlee added: "Can I play with you guys?"

Though Lauren didn't find Thomas' remark funny, for some reason, she found Ashlee's delightful—probably due to the innocent naiveness Ashlee possessed, not knowing yet what she and Thomas were actually doing.

Thomas cleared his throat. "Tell you what, angel. Why don't you and I go into the kitchen and share my famous Twix double chocolate sundaes?"

"Yeah!" Ashlee said, her tone exuberant.

"Sweetheart—your diet though," Lauren said. "You've been doing so well."

"That's why I said *share*. I'll make one bowl. I'll only have a little wee-bit. I promise," Thomas said.

Lauren crossed her arms. "Once you get a taste of it, you won't be able to stop yourself. I strongly feel you should not eat any of that sundae. Maybe I need to come in there and supervise."

"It'll be fine, I promise," Thomas said, walking to the kitchen. He stopped before entering it, double-backed, and said: "If you prefer, I won't have any. And, I tell you what. I'll make it for her with extra scoops to buy us some more time." He wiggled his eyebrows.

She glared at him with a motherly look. "That ship has sailed."

Thomas prepped the sundae for Ashlee. Three scoops of ice cream—two vanilla and one chocolate—which ran contrary to Thomas' preferred two chocolate and one vanilla MO—topped with Twix pieces, drizzled with hot fudge and caramel, with four whipped cream puffs—which resembled White Silk Hydrangea Kissing Balls—equidistant around the circumference of the bowl.

But that wasn't all. Thomas ground up some of the cookie layer from several Twix bars in the food processor, but before he could sprinkle some of this onto the sundae, Ashlee wrapped her arms around and covered the top with her torso. A health-conscience choice.

"What's the verdict?" Thomas asked.

"It's good," Ashlee said, caramel sauce stuck to her chin.

Thomas grabbed a spoon and took a big helping—as much as he could fit on his spoon. At that same moment, Lauren walked into the kitchen.

"Stop right there," Lauren demanded. "Put it down."

"I was bringing a bite. I thought you'd like to try it," Thomas said.

"Yeah. Okay," Lauren said. She gave a wink.

Before Thomas could respond, Ashlee shook her head. "There goes the shadow man again. I don't like him. He makes me feel weird."

"Where?" Thomas asked, concerned.

"It walked past the kitchen door towards the stairs," Ashlee said.

For fear of how Lauren would react, he never shared with her the entity that she and the two girls saw in the house was the same one he had encountered at his house. He didn't want to be accused of bringing something into her home.

He also never told his daughters about the entity because he didn't want to scare them. Besides, they had enough to contend with, grieving over the suicide of their mother.

5

The indoor swimming pool at the apartment complex was the only selling point to Madison. Every day, after school, she was in the pool, and not just idly swimming. Far from it. She was practicing all sorts of swimming techniques: the front-crawl stroke, the backstroke, the breaststroke, among others.

Today was no exception—it was the Wednesday before Thanksgiving, and just as she had done the previous four days—starting on Saturday—she did this day, also. She awoke at six in the morning, ate a light breakfast, and stretched before heading down to the pool with Jimmy, who was coaching her for the time being until he and Roberta found her a permanent swimming coach.

Without skipping a beat, Madison dipped her right foot into the pool to test its temperature—sort of a little warning for her body to get ready. After a few wiggles of the foot in the water, she dived in and began her laps from one end of the pool to the other—lengthwise.

"That's it," Jimmy said. "Remember your form."

Madison corrected herself, which improved her efficiency in the water. Jimmy gave her some praise and encouragement. After a few laps at a relatively moderate pace, Jimmy started crack the figurative whip while rapidly clapping his hands. "Alright! Let's pick it up, let's pick it up! Faster! Faster! Schneller! Schneller!"

Right—like saying faster in German would have any effect on her speed. He said it only because he liked the way it sounded.

As Madison kept herself afloat in the middle of the deep end of the pool, Jimmy gave her some suggestions on her to improve her speed. He took out a stopwatch. As he supplied her with instructions, she kicked her feet in uniform motion, keeping herself afloat.

When he finished his spiel, she asked: "Do you really think I can beat my own time?"

"Of course you can," he answered. "You're improving by leaps and bounds. Now I think if—"

In a flash, Madison's head and shoulders were no longer above the surface of the water. Jimmy jumped into the water— shoes and all—and grabbed her around her waist. He tried to swam upward with all his might, but it was as if cinderblocks were tied around her ankles. And, then, out of nowhere, an unseen force pulled both of them down deeper into the water with ease—like a boulder off a cliff. Both Jimmy and Madison kicked and squirmed against the force pulling them down, fighting like hell for their lives.

Their lungs felt as though an elephant was standing on them. It wouldn't be much longer now before both Madison and Jimmy were incapacitated.

But then both of them swam to the surface. When the heads broke through the water, they both coughed, choked, and gagged. Jimmy looked down in the water. Standing on the pool's floor was a young boy—around Madison's age—with a head of black hair and a pale white face who pointed at Madison and Jimmy and then dragged his finger across his wrists.

Jimmy lifted Madison out of the water and then he himself climbed out of the water. Other than being shaken up, they were fine.

"Did you see that boy?" Jimmy asked.

"Yeah! That was Dylan!" Madison shrieked. "He tried to kill us!"

"That was Dylan? The boy spirit?"

Madison nodded. "Uh-huh." She lunged at Jimmy, wrapping her arms around his neck. "What am I going to do? He wants me dead… He wants me dead so he and I can play together in The Umbra's lair." She started to cry. "Please don't let him kill me."

"I don't understand. What does he want with you? Why you—and not someone else?"

Nor did Madison.

6

Unable to stomach the sight of Derrick laying in his hospital bed, Bruce was leaning against the wall near the ingress of Derrick's hospital room door.

Derrick's primary care physician—Jeff—was walking up the hallway with a file folder clutched in his hand.

"Hiya, Doc," Bruce said, his tone stoic.

Jeff flashed a closed smile. "Hi." He nodded his head a few times. "So, you're Derrick's father, right?"

"Yeah, I'm Derrick's father." *Lucky me.*

"His biological father, yes?"

Bruce swallowed hard. The atmosphere around him seemed to change. He looked at Jeff. "Yes. That's right."

"You're not Derrick's father. Can you explain to me what is going on here?"

"I don't know what you're talking about. I am Derrick's father."

Jeff sighed. Both men remained silent for about ten seconds. Then Jeff said: "Mr. Johns—I *know* you're not Derrick's father. I can prove it."

"How?"

"The blood results."

Bruce's eyes widened. A few seconds passed. Then his face returned to normal. "This is ridiculous—"

With a stern tone, Jeff said: "Mr. Johns. You are *not* Derrick's biological father. Given his blood type, his mother's blood type, and yours, you couldn't possibly be the father."

That first day Bruce visited Derrick and met Jeff, they had a brief conversation on the way to the Phlebotomy Department. Jeff asked Bruce about the mother and Bruce told some more half-truths. Bruce told him Derrick's mother was unavailable and that she had an interesting blood type—Type O. Bruce even disclosed her name—her *real* name—to Jeff, unlike what he had been doing to Derrick—giving all sorts of false names. Bruce even shared with Jeff the hospital at which Derrick was born and if Jeff needed to get any medical information about Derrick's mom, he could contact that particular hospital. Bruce knew Derrick's mom wouldn't have anything to offer, and having that knowledge, gave Jeff his blessing to do whatever he wanted to make contact with Derrick's mom.

And that's just what Jeff did. He called the hospital asking for any contact information that may be on file for Derrick's mom. He also asked the nurse reviewing the file of Derrick's mom what her blood type was—hoping she could potentially donate, if need be, but the nurse said she couldn't divulge that information to him because it violate HIPPA. Fortunately, Jeff had low friends in high places who could get him information he wanted when he wanted. Normally, Jeff wouldn't violate medical ethics in the way he did, but there was something about Bruce that seemed off, and this prompted Jeff to probe deeper.

Jeff's patience were wearing thin though, and he wanted answers.

Bruce released an exaggerated sigh. "Okay. I'll level with you. I'm not Derrick's biological father. I am his legal guardian, and therefore, his father, in a loose sense."

"I specifically asked you if you were his biological father though, and you said yes," Jeff said. "Quite frankly, I'm a little concerned about you altogether."

"Let me explain. Derrick's real mother abandoned him. I took Derrick in and raised him as my own son. It really was his mother's wishes. What do I need to do to prove to you I'm his legal guardian?"

"Do you have any paperwork I could see?"

"Yeah. I can have it faxed here. I mean—if that's what it's going to take."

"It would put my mind at ease."

"Alright."

"Thanks."

Jeff placed his hand on the latch to open the room to Derrick's hospital room, but before he could push down, Bruce said: "Wait a second."

"Yes?"

"Would you do me a favor and not tell Derrick I'm not his biological father? He's suffered enough emotional turmoil and him hearing from someone other than me I'm not his biological father would crush his spirit."

Jeff smiled—slightly an open smile this time—and said: "Of course." He entered Derrick's room.

But Bruce didn't move an inch.

7

The time was three-sixteen in the morning. Derrick was still in a medically-induced coma, but was now showing signs of improvement.

As he laid in his bed, The Umbra continued to speak to Derrick from within his mind.

(You will soon kill yourself. You will do it in a flamboyant, memorable, violent, and slow way. You will do it publicly. You will kill yourself. You will enjoy it.)

Derrick's inner voice replied back. It said: *[I will kill myself soon. I will do it in a flamboyant, memorable way. I will kill myself violently and slowly for many to see and enjoy with me.]*

The Umbra repeated himself once again, and afterwards Derrick's inner voice responded, affirming The Umbra's commands.

The Umbra was using a form of autosuggestive technique, similar to the way Dr. Nikolai Dahl—a notable psychiatrist and novice musician—helped Sergei Rachmaninoff cure his depression though having Rachmaninoff repeat statements over and over again.

8

There didn't appear to be any other choice. Moving into the apartment didn't seem to have any impact on keeping Dylan away from Madison.

The incident in the pool was the final straw for Roberta. She wasn't going to risk it anymore. She called in a medium to communicate with the spirit of Dylan—and hopefully to release him to the other side where he belonged.

But then the question still needed to be asked: Was this spirit really Dylan or something far more sinister cloaked in Dylan's appearance?

Madison was sitting on the living room couch next to Roberta sipping from a juice box. Roberta—who rarely ate empty-caloried sweets—unwrapped a Milky Way—not a Twix liked Thomas loved so much but was now forbidden from eating due to his strict diet he so often cheated on—and bit into it.

"Dylan talked to me this morning, Mommy," Madison said. She took a drink of her juice and swallowed. "He's angry at me."

"Before we talk any further about that. I want you to tell me the truth," Roberta said. "Did he hurt you?"

Madison's lip jutted out, and that said it all.

"What did he do?"

"He's mad at me because I didn't kill myself in twenty-four hours like he had to do."

"What are you saying to me? I don't understand."

Madison sighed. "He told me I had twenty-four hours to kill myself. If I didn't, he would kill me. That's why he pulled me under the water—to punish me for not killing myself."

"My god. How do we stop him?"

Madison slurped on her juice box, fighting like a tiger to get every drop out. Roberta finished her Milky Way, chewing the final piece of the candy bar slowly, savoring it—and not wanting it to end, like passionate love making.

A chime sounded from the intercom system, which alerted Roberta someone was in the main entrance requesting to be let inside the main complex.

As Roberta walked to the intercom system, Madison said: "Dylan said The Umbra is brainwashing Derrick to kill himself."

"Okay, Madison," Roberta said, somewhat dismissively. "I need to answer this."

"Okay, Mommy. But The Umbra is evil."

Roberta pushed the button labeled TALK. The lady who Roberta was expecting identified herself. Roberta then pushed the button labeled UNLOCK—though still not feeling any sense of relief even though some form of help was there.

But who could blame Roberta for being apprehensive? It seemed nowhere was safe.

Knocks on the door mimicked the rhythmical pattern to *Shave and a Haircut*. A second—maybe two—later, the *Two Bits* was knocked—and this gave Roberta a sense of closure, for had the pattern not finished, Roberta would have patted her thigh to complete it. She only hoped the closure she experienced from the pattern being patted out completely would be what she experienced with this entity; in fact, she predicted if this medium could rid her apartment of Dylan, the feeling would be a thousand-and-a-one times better—in essence, pure euphoria.

"How do you do," the medium said in a proper English accent—kind of like Mrs. Doubtfire. "Permit me the pleasure of introducing myself, dear. My name is Gertrude Smythe. I specialize in chasing those angry and overly-attached spirits out of your home."

"Pleasure," Roberta said, shaking Gertrude's hand. "May I take your coat?"

"Oh, thank you, dear, yes, my coat, please do take it."

And the full-length coat came off. Gertrude was wearing a pair of black slacks and a red blouse with a broach. She scanned her surroundings, taking in all the information in waves—and at times, tidal waves.

At the same time Gertrude did her cursory inspection, Madison and Jimmy left the apartment to walk to the local diner—Northside Diner—for some food.

"There's something not quite right," Gertrude said.

"Exactly. That's why I asked you to come," Roberta said, not impressed so far. But Roberta took a moment to reflect. "I trust it is going to take a lot longer than a few minutes to fix this, right?"

In her English accent, waving a finger, she said: "Yes, dear. Definitely. We must be patient."

Roberta shook her head. "Where are my manners? Would you like something to drink?"

And Gertrude did. She requested tea in a standard-sized teacup with two sugar cubes and precisely a half teaspoon—measured—of cream.

While Roberta tended to the tea, Gertrude continued her inspection. When she reached Madison's closed bedroom door, the environment changed instantly. She clutched her heart, pressed her back against the wall, and sank to the floor. She took a few seconds to catch her breath, then stood and placed her hand on the doorknob. This wasn't the first time an angry spirit or evil entity tried to harm her—as a way to scare her away to prevent her from banishing it—and it wouldn't be the last either, no doubt.

"Something wrong?" Roberta asked.

Gertrude gasped.

"Sorry. I didn't mean to frighten you."

"Quite alright, dear. I like to be frightened. It reminds me I'm alive."

Roberta handed Gertrude a cup of tea. "I hope I made it right."

"Thank you, dear. How lovely. I'm sure it will be delicious." Gertrude sipped the tea. Though it tasted like Old English furniture polish—and Gertrude knew that taste all too well—she drank it anyway. "Your home definitely has a spirit in it. It's the spirit of a young boy. I'm getting the sense his first name starts with a D."

"Is that right?" Roberta said. She didn't confirm or refute anything, not wanting to skew Gertrude's senses. She wanted to see if Gertrude was the real deal or just blowing smoke up her ass. "Is there anything else you can tell me?"

Gertrude sipped her tea again, set it on the saucer, and closed her eyes. "The boy died in a tragic way—a horrific way. He killed himself. Slit his wrists in the bathtub… Before he slit his wrists, he had this constant obsession with the back of his left wrist for some reason—perhaps thinking about what it would be like to slice into it—like a ripe orange."

"Let's head into your daughter's bedroom."

"I'll lead the way—"

"No bother, dear," Gertrude said. "I know right where it is, and I must do this alone."

"How? You're a medium, not a psychic."

Gertrude didn't answer Roberta though. She walked down the hallway and flung the door open to Madison's bedroom without a smidgen of hesitation. Roberta remained in the living room, drinking some tea herself, slurping it down at a furious rate.

Fifteen minutes passed before Gertrude exited Madison's room and returned to the living room.

"Anything?" Roberta asked.

"Yes," Gertrude said, sitting on the sofa next to Roberta. "And it's not good."

"Tell me. I can handle it."

9

The food was cold but it still tasted good. Derrick was no longer in his medically-induced coma and the rest of his injuries were healing nicely.

Derrick thought: *I must think of a creative way... I must be flagrant about it...*

"I'm glad you're feeling better," Bruce said. He was sitting in a chair against the wall. "Are you looking forward to leaving soon?"

"I am. I can't wait to get home to Danielle," Derrick said, cutting a sausage link.

Bruce nodded. "Yeah—about her. I have some bad news."

"Oh? What?"

The words were in queue, but Bruce struggled to say them. He knew he had to though. After all, Derrick had a right to know.

"She's gone missing," Bruce said.

Derrick spat out his scrambled eggs onto his covers. "What?"

"It's unbelievable. She drove me down here and left. Apparently she never made it home."

Derrick started to cry. "When?"

"Four days ago."

The Umbra crept into Derrick's mind and put its two cents in—trying to keep Derrick on the straight and narrow—in terms of The Umbra's goal.

(What do you care about that bitch? You're going to kill yourself, remember?)

[Did you kill my girlfriend?]

(I didn't, but I can't speak for others.)

[I don't want to kill myself. I want to find Danielle. She's my everything.]

The Umbra laughed. *(She was your everything. And now she's nothing more than a meal to the wildlife.)*

Derrick's heart plummeted to the bowels of his stomach and like a spanked toddler cried for several minutes. Bruce kept quiet.

10

Not surprisingly, Derrick refused to sit idly by in a hospital bed. He wanted to get out and find the love of his life—even if she wasn't any longer alive. He felt it was his duty, his obligation as her boyfriend, to find her and bring her home.

"Where's my cellphone?" Derrick asked, getting out of bed.

"What are you doing?" Jeff said. "You stay in that bed."

"You can't force me to stay in the hospital. That's kidnapping."

Bruce interjected before Jeff could respond to Derrick. "I think it's best for you to say in the bed."

"But, Dad, I need to—"

"No buts, Derrick," Bruce said, his tone stern. "Now get your ass back into the bed and rest. That's what you're here for."

This was different, and Derrick wasn't all used to this new nurturing side to Bruce. Maybe it was Bruce's lack of access to alcohol—since he was sleeping in Derrick's hospital room since arriving.

Derrick complied, albeit begrudgingly.

"I understand you're upset and angry about not knowing what is going with your girlfriend, but you must stay in bed," Jeff said. He typed a few notes into Derrick's medical chart.

Bruce chimed in. "Besides, it's the police's job to find where her body is, not yours."

Surely enough, this incited Derrick. He didn't appreciate the cop-out remark.

"Excuse me, but I love her," Derrick said. "I want to find her, hopefully alive."

"I'll keep the fingers crossed on both hands," Jeff replied, smiling.

To Derrick, Bruce said: "Keep a stiff upper lip." *Stiff. Haha. That's funny. Kind of like that bitch Derrick's mom is. I hate that dead bitch. She's dead to me, and always will be.* "Just lie there and shut the hell up."

There it was—the old Bruce—he was back.

"Where's my cellphone?" Derrick asked.

"Are you kidding me? You want to go to an Ivy League school but you can't even put two and two together?" Bruce asked.

"Just give it to me."

"I can't. It was damaged in the accident. It was found smashed to bits. Car after car ran over it."

Derrick lowered his chin to his chest. He desperately wanted to send Danielle a quick text saying he loved her, missed her, and hoped for her safe return.

"Dad? Let me use your phone, please," Derrick said. "I want to text Danielle."

"What phone? You broke mine, too. Remember?"

"That wasn't me, Dad. I told you. That was The Umbra."

"The what?"

"The Umbra? That's the black mass we've been seeing around our house."

This boy is fucking insane. Oh, yes, he is. Loony-fucking-tunes. Psycho. "Listen—even if I had my cellphone, I wouldn't let you use it."

"Why not?"

Bruce rolled his eyes. He couldn't understand how Derrick could be smart in innumerable ways but clueless when it came to common sense. He stood and stretched, then sat again. Derrick slumped down in the bed and covered his head.

"Because I don't want you breaking that phone either—that's one," Bruce said. "And, secondly, I don't think it's a good idea for you to be texting Danielle from my phone anyway. I don't want to police sniffing me out any more than I want them doing to you."

Derrick pounded his bed with clenched fists. Though he wasn't restrained in the strictest sense of the word, he felt that way.

After several moments passed by, Derrick pondered what Bruce had said. Meanwhile, Bruce pulled out a mini-alcohol bottle—one he had finessed from one of the rooms from inside the hotel near the hospital. Plenty of minibars that were ripe for the picking.

"Why would the police think I had anything to do with it?" Derrick asked, sitting up in his bed. "That doesn't make sense. I have an ironclad alibi."

Bruce sneered. "Yeah, well, I'm just saying it doesn't make sense for you to be sending text messages that make no sense. Where are you? Are you okay? You're going to attract unwanted attention."

"I don't understand."

"Look—you don't text a dead person. It's dangerous."

How could Bruce be so callous and refer to Danielle as a dead person? Clearly, using tact wasn't his strong suit.

11

Nikki sliced her turkey-and-Swiss sandwich she made in half, creating two triangle wedges, then sat at the kitchen table to eat as well as to work on her science homework: a fill-in-the-blank worksheet. The topic of the unit was matter and energy.

"When am I ever going to use this shit?" Nikki muttered, scribing an answer in one of the blanks.

"Nikki—you really need to stop swearing," Lauren said as she chopped up some celery. "We've talked about this before."

"And we've also talked about how you're not my mom, so stop acting like you are."

Lauren shook her head and continued to chop the celery. She was smart to not let her anger cloud her actions. A part of her wanted to place the tip of the knife blade to Nikki's jugular and say: I dare you to sass me once more.

After adding the celery to the skillet, Lauren said: "Why don't you read the chapter first, then fill out the worksheet rather than simply scan the chapter for the answers? That's not a good learning strategy you're using."

Nikki sighed. "I swear—sometimes I wish I were dead. I want to kill myself."

"Excuse me?"

"I want to kill myself. This class sucks."

"Why don't you at least try my suggestion? If it doesn't work, you can always go back to the way you're doing it."

"Because reading the chapter takes too long. I like to find the answers and get my work done."

To Lauren, that sounded like a challenge—something worth researching. What would take longer and be less efficient? Searching for the answers to complete the worksheet or read the chapter first and then complete the worksheet.

12

The news articles published on the Internet sent a chill down Derrick's spine. Hearing about Danielle's disappearance was one thing; seeing it on the Internet coupled with the details was quite another.

Yet there was hope. While Bruce referred to Danielle as dead, the reports online seemed more optimistic. Her vehicle was found toppled over in a field of corn. The driver's side door was opened, and her purse and cellphone were missing.

Additionally, her cellphone showed movement according to the GPS data detectives investigating her disappearance received. She never answered her calls though—no matter what time of day the call was placed.

But though there was some hope Danielle was still alive, some things didn't make a lot of sense either. The damage to her car wasn't exactly a fender-bender. The chances of her walking away from the accident unscathed were slim to none. Yet there were no reports of Danielle checking into any nearby hospital for treatment.

As Bruce and Derrick rode in the train back to Chesterville, a big part of Derrick wanted to abscond and search for Danielle.

"Will you quit reading about her?" Bruce asked. "All it's going to do is make you crazy."

Before Derrick could reply to Bruce, The Umbra piped into the conversation, speaking from within Derrick's mind.

(You wanna see your beloved Danielle? Throw yourself in front of a train—not on one.)

[I'm not going to kill myself—at least not until I find Danielle.]

(I hope you do find her. I think it'll be the nail in the coffin.)

But now another voice crept into Derrick's brain, though this one wasn't malevolent-sounding—far from it. This one was silky smooth, kind of like the first G below middle C on a cello.

<*Leave my son alone.*>

(Your son. What a joke.)

[What's happening to me?]

The two voices didn't utter another word perceptible to Derrick. He took a few moments to analyze the brief exchange. *But my dad isn't dead.*

(Sorry about that. I had to take care of that annoying spirit. Little did he know I have the power to banish—well at least temporarily.)

[What are you?]

(The Umbra. Death in disguise. I'm as powerful as God.)

[Obviously you like talking to me. Otherwise you wouldn't be, so why don't you tell me what happened that night I tried to kill myself.]

(No.)

[I'm protected. You can't hurt me. The voice claiming to be my dad told me since he defeated you to an extent, I'm protected. Isn't that so? You can't hurt me.]

(You're not immune to me. If you utter the right combination of words, your fate is sealed. I'll bide my time—kind of the way the Wicked Witch of the West did.)

[Where did you come from? How do you operate?]

The Umbra wasn't heard from after that.

13

Laying on her bed with her face in her pillow crying, Daisy—a fourteen-year-old—sent her mom a text. As she wailed from the sting of the emotional pain, the sound of two cars colliding shifted her attention. She lunged off of her bed to check out what transpired.

Outside of her window were two cars in the middle of the intersection. One crashed into the other at a ninety-degree angle.

A few seconds later, there was another crashing sound, but this was of Daisy's mom, Hailey, kicking in her door.

"Mom!" Daisy shouted. "What did you do that for?"

Hailey pointed to the text message she had received from Daisy a few moment ago. "You shouldn't ever say something like this unless you mean it, and that includes in texts. Do you really want to kill yourself?"

Daisy's head sunk to her chest. In a sheepish voice, she said: "I feel like I want to kill myself."

The two of them sat on the foot of the bed, and Daisy wore her heart on her sleeve.

14

The Umbra once again spoke to Derrick in his mind as he slept, but the difference Derrick was no longer in a medically-induced coma.

(You will kill yourself. You will enjoy it. You will declare to anyone and everyone you wish to kill yourself... You will think of different creative and flamboyant ways to execute yourself.)

[I will do it. I need to do it. I miss Danielle too much. I want to see her again. Killing myself is the only way.]

<Don't listen to him, son. Also, test out the stain in the living room.>

(You again? I'm going to find you and slay your spirit.)

<Good luck finding me. I could be anywhere in the universe—just the same as you can. Leave my son alone. If you leave him alone, I won't pursue you anymore. I promise I won't kill you. You can continue to force people to kill themselves and I

can return to my grave and rest, metaphorically speaking, of course.>

(*That's okay. I'll take my chances.*) And to Derrick: (*You will kill yourself. You will enjoy it. You will declare to anyone and everyone you wish to kill yourself... You will think of different creative and flamboyant ways to execute yourself.*)

[Are you the devil?]

(*I'm anything and everything evil.*)

<Don't talk to it, Derrick. Don't try to reason with it.>

(*And who are you?*)

<Your father, son.>

But this made no sense to Derrick. How could this spirit be Derrick's father if Bruce told Jeff his real father was living in Memphis and that he had spoken to Derrick's biological father not more than a few days ago?

While The Umbra and this other spirit claiming to be Derrick's dad conversed, Derrick listened closely.

(*You know as well as I do we're beacons for one another. I'm getting closer to you. You better tuck tail and skedaddle before I find you.*)

<I'm not running away from you; I'm moving towards you. Here I come. You're the one who needs to skedaddle.>

The Umbra hesitated to speak for a few minutes. Then it said: (*The Sacred Sword. You have it, don't you? I can sense it.*)

<Why don't hunker down where you are and you'll find out.>

The Umbra offered no reply. He fled the scene.

15

The stain in the living room bothered Derrick more so now than it ever did—thanks to the other inner voice that spoke to Derrick claiming to be his dad. The stain looked as though someone had poured wine on top of some other stain rather the stain being originated from wine itself.

Derrick rubbed a cotton swab into the stain after treating a section of it with a sodium chloride solution. Next, he pulled out a bottle of phenolphthalein and squirted a few drops over the cotton swab.

The color change spoke volumes. The cotton swab tip changed to a purplish color—a presumptive test for the presence of blood.

He stood, shaking his head. *How did blood get on the carpet?* he wondered. *Whose blood is this?*

16

Gertrude entered the apartment after Roberta opened the door for her. Roberta took Gertrude's coat—the same one she wore the last time she visited—and took a seat on the couch.

Without uttering a sound, Roberta pointed to the kitchen and mimicked sipping tea. Gertrude nodded, then Roberta sought to accomplish the task.

"How are you doing today, Dylan?" Gertrude asked, with her sweet, silky English accent.

"A little better," he said.

"What would you like to talk about today?"

Dylan shrugged his shoulders.

"Why don't you tell me about why it is you wanted Madison to kill herself. I mean—why would you want her to do a thing like that?"

Dylan shook his head, and that is all he did. Gertrude paused for a few seconds, given Dylan the opportunity to change his mind.

In the meantime, Roberta carried out a tray, which held some teacups, a tea kettle, and a small bowl containing sugar cubes.

Roberta served Gertrude some tea, and it was at that point she realized she forgot the cream. She journeyed back the kitchen for it.

"Dylan, why don't you want to tell me?" Gertrude asked, stirring her tea.

"It'll kill me," Dylan replied.

(Damn right, I will, Killing Dillinger. I admire your work with what you're doing with Madison. I may make you my protege.)

"Who will kill you?"

"The Umbra."

"The Um… What's The Umbra?"

"I can't tell you that either. The Umbra will kill me."

Gertrude gave pause for a few seconds. She took a sip of her tea—now that it was no longer sans creamer—and then set the cup back onto the coaster it had once rested.

"Is it The Umbra that keeps you here?" Gertrude asked. "Can you tell me that?"

"Yes. I am one of The Umbra's children now."

"One of his children," Gertrude repeated, confused.

"I can never ascend into Heaven, if such a place even exists," Dylan said. He lowered his head and closed his eyes.

"Heaven does exist, Dylan, and it's a wonderful place. Would you like to see it?"

"Even if it does exist, I can't leave The Umbra. I'm his slave and he is my master."

Gertrude was unsure what The Umbra was, but one thing she was certain of: Dylan wasn't bound by The Umbra's will.

"Think again, Dylan," Gertrude said. "How can he have control over your spirit?"

"Because I didn't kill myself in time," Dylan said. "He had to do it for me. He made it look like I killed myself though."

"Don't you see the light? Step into the light. Go to where you belong."

"What light?"

"The bright white light."

But Dylan didn't see any bright white light.

17

With a bottle of Jack Daniel's in his hand, Bruce was sitting on the couch watching some TV—The Hugh Hefner Show. A few knocks on the door interrupted Bruce's happy-time session.

As Bruce stumbled to the door, Derrick crept out of his room and stood near the stairwell to get a listen. After Bruce was finished taking care of whoever was at the door, Derrick wanted to have a heart-to-heart with Bruce.

"May I help you?" Bruce slurred, after he opened the front door.

"Hi. Yes. I'm Samantha. Is the missus of the house available? I have some AVON products I wanted to present to her," Samantha said. *Damn. He is two kinds of fine.*

"No, there is no missus here, but you can still show me what products you're selling. Maybe I try some of them."

(My—your dad is quite the ladykiller, isn't he?)

[I swear. I wish you would die.]

(And I wish you would, too—via suicide.)

Samantha and Bruce chatted for nearly thirty minutes. After she left, Derrick made his move. He stepped into the living room and interrupted Bruce's happy-time session.

"Damn it, Derrick," Bruce snapped. "You scared me. I was just checking my junk out for any weird spotting. Can't be too careful when you get to be my age."

"You're not my dad," Derrick said, his tone confrontational. "So, who is?"

Goddamn that Jeff. I'll kill him, too. "You're talking out of your ass, Derrick. Of course I'm your dad."

"You're lying. I want the truth." *Please let this work.*

"The truth is I'm your dad, now quit blocking the TV. I wanna see those juicy jugs bounce and bounce."

Bruce sighed. "Who told you I'm not your dad?"

"Someone. That's all you need to know."

Bruce stormed out of the room into his bedroom and slammed the door. Derrick sat on the couch and enjoyed the rest of The Hugh Hefner Show.

But Derrick wasn't about to let Bruce off that easily. Derrick also had another bone to pick with him, also.

When Derrick reached Bruce's door, he tried to push the handle down, but it was locked. Derrick knocked on the door a few times.

"Dad?" Derrick asked. "Whose blood is that on the living room floor?"

"What are you talking about?" Bruce shouted.

"The big stain on the living room carpet. There's wine and blood mixed together. Whose blood is it?"

The sound of heavy footsteps from within Bruce's room sounded. His bedroom flung open. Bruce lunged at Derrick, slamming him against the wall.

Derrick swallowed hard and did his best to relax. His fists lightly clenched though.

"Where do you get off accusing me of murder?" Bruce asked, pointing his finger at Derrick's face. "I didn't murder anyone!"

"I never said you did, Dad," Derrick said, his tone calm. "I was asking if you knew where the blood came from?"

"And that's something else. What proof do you have there is even blood within in that big ass wine stain?"

"I did a test for the presumption of blood. The chemical reaction undeniably showed there is blood in that stain."

Bruce's facial muscles tensed up. "Listen to me. The blood is mine. Okay? I tripped and landed on the wine bottle. Wine spilled every which way. I cut my hand on a broken piece of glass while cleaning the mess up. That's where the blood came from. Anything else, detective? Want to arrest me and book me in jail now?"

"No, Dad. Everything you said makes sense," Derrick said, walking away from Bruce. "I don't understand why you had to be so secretive about it."

Derrick sauntered upstairs to his room where he resumed working on ascertaining where his mother was.

On a sheet of paper, he had all of the names Bruce claimed his mom's name was: Heidi, Tabitha, Catrina, Ingrid, Bethany, Donna, Allison, Erika, Deborah. Not a single Wendi though. Bruce was a liar all along.

Now Derrick wondered: *If he's willing to lie about my mom's name, what else has he lied to me about?*

18

Two plain-clothes detectives knocked on the front door of Derrick's house. One was short and pencil-thin; the other was tall and rotund.

The short-and-slender detective—named Hodges—said: "Do you think he'll be able to help us?"

"I would think so," the gargantuan giant detective—named Benson—replied. "He was one of the most recent individuals to converse with the doctor."

The front door opened and Bruce asked the detectives to state their business before they even had a chance to sputter out a single syllable.

"We had some questions for you," Detective Hodges said. "May we come in?"

"Not without a warrant," Bruce snapped back.

The two detectives glanced at each other, then back at Bruce. Their radars were pinging alright. Bruce quickly went into damage-control mode and explained he didn't like the idea of law enforcement officials being in his home without a court order. He stepped outside and closed the front door behind him. The pings on the radar diminished and now the two detectives got down to brass tacks.

"What do you know about Dr. Jeff Mills?" Detective Benson asked before puckering up with a freshly-lit cigar.

"He's a doctor. His first name is Jeff and his last name is Mills," Bruce replied, "and, yeah, that's about it."

"Very funny, wise ass," Detective Hodges sneered.

"What? I don't know him that well. He treated my son Derrick for his injuries. And he seems to be a charmer with the ladies."

"Bingo," Detective Benson shot back. "He was one of the last individuals to see Danielle alive."

"Oh?" Bruce said, perplexed. *That bitch lied to me. Too bad she can't be killed again.*

"Did Jeff mention anything to you about Danielle?" Detective Hodges asked. "Anything at all?"

"Nope, nothing," Bruce said.

Detective Benson pulled out a business card and handed it Bruce, who accepted it, placing it in his trifold. Bruce and the detectives shook hands and parted ways.

As the two detectives walked down the walkway, Bruce looked on at them. Detective Hodges turned around and said:

"Remember, Mr. Johns. If you think of anything that can help us in this investigation, give us a call."

Bruce nodded, turned around, and walked through the front door of his house.

19

Thomas, Lauren, and Ashlee walked up the stairs to Nikki's bedroom. For several weeks Ashlee was sleeping on the couch, letting Nikki have the bedroom all to herself.

The plan was to hopefully have Nikki invite Ashlee to come back into the bedroom, but this never came to be. The implicit guilt trip was useless.

Now the time came for Ashlee to start sleeping in her bedroom again.

Nikki sat up on her bed when the front door swung open. Ashlee ran to her bed and leapt onto it, excited.

"What's going on?" Nikki asked, thoroughly confused.

"Well, Ashlee needs to start sleeping in her own bed again," Thomas told her.

"But, wait. This is *my* room."

Thomas pulled out a mini-Twix bar, unwrapped it, and nibbled off some of the caramel layer. Then he sat on Nikki's bed. Meanwhile, Ashlee climbed out of her bed and exited the room to go downstairs and get a snack from the kitchen.

After he bit into the cookie layer of the Twix, he said: "I'm sorry, but this was never your room. We were hoping you would have said something to your sister, something that would invite her back in the room."

Nikki sighed. "This is total BS, Dad. You and Lauren— that mom-wanna-be—made it out like this is my room. Ashlee told me she liked sleeping in the living room alone every night, even when that shadow thing was near her."

"Has that shadow person ever come by you?"

"Yes, but I'm not afraid of it. I try and talk to it, but it doesn't answer me."

For a few seconds, Thomas pondered about what to do about this shadow person—unbeknownst to him, it was The Umbra.

But why was it lurking around his house? What did it want?

Thomas unwrapped another Twix mini candy bar and nibbled at the caramel layer. Lauren passed by, then double-backed. She approached Thomas with fire in her eyes.

"What are you doing eating chocolate?" Lauren demanded to know. "You're supposed to be dieting. We are going to be getting married in a year."

"I'm entitled to a little reward every once in a while," Thomas replied. He nibbled at some more of the caramel layer. "And I've lost seven pounds in the past few weeks. I'm doing pretty good."

Lauren rolled her eyes. "Yeah—I suppose. Give me one, will you?"

And he did. She unfurled the wrapper and chomped into the chocolate bar. By this point, Thomas was almost finished with his candy bar.

Nikki was sitting on her bed, sulking, as Ashlee walked in and climbed into bed. Ashlee let out a beast-like yawn, and before falling asleep, she told everyone good night.

Nikki folded her arms. "I'm not happy about this," she said. "This is my room."

"I'm sorry, angel, but this room is your sister's, also," Thomas said.

"Dad, you are nothing but a breaker of promises. You really are the reason mom killed herself, aren't you? I wish I were dead, too. I should kill myself!"

Lauren pointed a finger at Nikki and said: "I thought we talked about saying that when we don't mean it. And, honestly, that was a little rough to say to your dad, wouldn't you agree?"

Nikki stomped to the bedroom door. "I don't care. I wish I were dead. I want to kill myself."

And, at that moment, The Umbra appeared in front of Nikki. Nobody else could see it but her.

It said: "And in twenty-four hours, you do just that—kill yourself. That's exactly how much time you have to kill yourself. Congratulations, Nikki, my dear—you're one of the chosen ones. At the end of the twenty-four hours, if you haven't killed yourself, I will kill you myself. If you do kill yourself, your spirit will live eternally in unbridled ecstasy. If you don't, however, I will own your soul and torture it until the end of time. And, speaking of time, a countdown watch located on the back of your wrist will show you how much time remains for you to kill yourself. Only you can see the countdown timer. Go ahead. Take a look."

And sure enough, on the back of her left wrist was a countdown timer fixed at 24:00:00. Nikki's jaw was resting on her feet.

The Umbra continued: "Once I finish my little spiel, the countdown timer will begin. It won't do any good to tell anyone about the countdown watch—which only you can see—and if you do I may kill you on the spot. I'm everywhere and anywhere all at the same time. Do the right thing and kill yourself. Get creative with your suicide. Grandstand. The more gore, the higher score, as I like to say. Make your choice: die or be killed." The Umbra faded to invisibility and the countdown began. 24:00:00, 23:59:59, 23:59:58, 23:59:57,...

Nikki swallowed hard and ran to the bathroom, seeing— yet not believing—the countdown timer function as flawless as any other. She flipped the faucet on and grasped the bar of soap.

She scoured the back of her wrist with a Brillo pad, but it didn't do anything except rough up her skin and turn it an awful red.

(The only way out is to kill yourself. Remember: Die or be killed.)

20

Though most people were convinced Danielle was dead, Derrick thought otherwise. He never gave up hope the love of his—the one and only true love of his life, to be exact—was dead.

But this wasn't the only issue weighing heavy on Derrick's mind. He still couldn't get it out of his head the spirit who referred to him as son. *Why would he call me son?* Derrick wondered several times day after day.

His cellphone vibrated a few times in his pocket. It was Mike. Derrick answered. "How are you?" Derrick asked.

"Better. Much better. The physical therapy is helping—as is the psychological," Mike replied.

"I still can't believe Heather passed. Again, my condolences."

"Thank you. I'm actually at peace in a sense. I think she's watching over Dylan now. I haven't seen his spirit since she passed."

But Mike was wrong—dead wrong. Dylan was still caught in the clutches of The Umbra. Heather was actively searching for Dylan though, wanting to be reunited with him once again, but this wouldn't be possible unless The Umbra released Dylan or The Umbra was destroyed.

"I think that's a good perspective to have," Derrick said. "I do hope Dylan's spirit is at rest."

(You'll soon be joining Dylan, you worthless shit.)

<Leave my son alone. Last warning. Then no more Mr. Nice Guy.>

[Who are you, sir?]

<Your dad. Your biological dad.>

Mike called for Derrick a few times, but Derrick's brain didn't register the sounds. He was too fixated on the inner voices within his mind.

[What's your name?]

(Keep talking. I'm coming after you.)

<My name is Brian Rice. Your mom's name was We—>

Derrick waited a few seconds, but was interrupted when Mike started to call his name once again.

"Sorry about that," Derrick said. "I was momentarily distracted."

"Everything alright?" Mike asked, genuinely concerned.

"Yeah. I'll be fine."

"I hope the police find Danielle safe and sound—and soon."

"Me, too."

The two ended their conversation ten minutes later, at which point Derrick sat gobsmacked on the couch. The name Rice sounded familiar to him. He had heard that name before—sometime, someplace. But where? And when?

Another question looming over Derrick's head was why was his last name Johns if his biological dad's last name was Rice.

21

Crying her eyes out while laying on her bed in a fetal position, Nikki stared at the digital watch counting down the amount of time she had left to end her life. 11:44:17, 11:44:16, 11:44:15, 11:44:14,…

She no longer doubted the veracity of the situation. She knew what had to be done. What ran through her mind like a gerbil on an exercise wheel was *how* to do it.

The Umbra tried to remain a source of encouragement—just like he did with all of his potential victims.

(Mommy misses you, Nikki. Come visit with her. The sooner you send yourself to your grave, the sooner you'll feel more alive than ever before!)

"It's okay, Nikki," Sharon said after she appeared standing at the side of Nikki's bed. "Embrace death like a loved one—like me. Do you need some help coming up with ideas to propel yourself into the afterlife?"

Nikki sprang up. "Mom? Is that you really you?"

The apparition of Sharon turned her head about ten degrees to her left. The entry wound from the gunshot was still there—and looked just as fresh the moment the bullet pierced her skin and skull.

Nikki swallowed hard with extreme difficulty and remained silent for several seconds as Sharon stared on at her.

"I understand you're afraid, but let's work together. I want you to score some high points with The Umbra," Sharon said, sitting on Nikki's bed.

"Can't you stop him since you're on the other side?" Nikki asked.

"I'm sorry. The Umbra is much too powerful for me, and aside from that, he owns my soul. I'm afraid killing yourself is your only escape—and you must do it before your time runs out."

"What happens if I don't kill myself before the timer runs out?"

"The Umbra will kill you itself, and it will make your death appear like a suicide, even though it's really a murder. Then, when he acquires your soul, he'll torture it until he runs tired of it—which would be never."

Nikki started to cry again. It was ironic to her. A mom is supposed to make her child feel better, not worse. The fact that

Sharon could do nothing to keep Nikki alive was a daunting prospect.

22

Jimmy and Madison ventured back to the pool after several days had passed from their encounter with Dylan. He—for some reason—stopped bothering Madison, no longer enticing her to kill herself.

"Are you ready?" Jimmy asked.

"Ready!" she exclaimed, eager to dive into the pool. "I missed this pool."

"Let's see what you've got."

Madison ascended the stairs as Jimmy followed behind her as a safeguard in case she slipped. Once they reached the top, Madison walked to the edge of the diving board, closed her eyes, and envisioned the dive she intended to perform.

After Jimmy sneezed and blew his nose, he said: "I'm going to head back down. I'll watch you from there. Okay?"

Madison signaled the okay symbol, but he made mental note to advise her that symbol also meant asshole.

Standing on the opposite side of where the diving board was located, Jimmy whistled and waved to Madison. He started to cheer her on, but she grimaced at him, which quickly extinguished his fiery exuberance.

Madison rocked the diving board a few times and dove off. As her head accelerated towards the surface of the water, she released an ear-deafening scream.

A big splash. A lengthy applause from Jimmy followed. When Madison broke through the surface of the water, she choked and gasped for air. Jimmy dove in and swam towards her.

"Are you okay?" he asked her, swimming her to safety.

She nodded. "I'll be okay, but that was so scary."

"What was? Did Dylan try to hurt you again? Is he here?"

That was one of Jimmy's biggest fears—Dylan would be waiting for Madison in the pool.

Another nod. "He was standing at the bottom of the pool, looking up at me as I was falling. Then he pushed his arms out to the side. The water moved out of the way—leaving me with no water to crash into. My head was going to hit the bottom of the pool." She started to bawl.

Jimmy rubbed the back of your head. "It's alright now. That was in your mind. That's all. I watched you dive into the pool and the water never moved the way you said it did."

"I want him to leave me alone."

"But he wasn't here this time," Jimmy assured her. "It was all in your imagination."

Jimmy suggested they leave the pool area for the day and maybe come back tomorrow, but Madison collected herself and insisted they stay.

23

Now he remembered where he heard the name Rice before. It was in one of the newspaper clippings Danielle stumbled across when she and him were searching for his birth certificate in Bruce's bedroom.

Derrick thrust open the sliding glass mirror door and began removing boxes from the closet, searching for that one particular box that contained the newspaper clippings.

When he found it, he tossed it on the bed, and placed the other boxes back into the closet.

Derrick rushed upstairs to his bedroom and ripped open the box, not caring it was now destroyed.

He located the news article with the headline: 2 FOUND DEAD IN HOUSE FIRE. There were two victims: Harold and Gertrude Rice—ages 43 and 44, respectively.

But neither of those names was a Brian. He sifted through the other newspaper articles. Some about local historic events, such as mayoral wins and the annexation of certain areas of Northwest Indiana. Others were obituaries.

Nestled at the bottom of the box was a newspaper article detailing a tragic car accident on the Borman Expression.

(Go ahead, Derrick. Read it. You'll be pleased to know your dear Mommy and Daddy are safe and dead.) Now The Umbra laughed. *(Come join them.)*

TWO DEAD AFTER DRIVER LOSES CONTROL

Two people were killed after the driver of the vehicle lost control of it and tumbled in front of the path of a semi-truck. The driver, Brian Rice, 22, was killed, along with his passenger, Wendi Rice, 23.

According to Bruce Rice—Brian's older brother—who was following the couple to help them inspect a house they wanted to purchase—Brian lost control of his vehicle—a 1996 Pontiac Grand Am—and appeared to jerk the steering wheel abruptly to the left.

Brian and Wendi were scheduled to get married in August. They are survived by their three-month-old son, Derrick, who escaped the accident with minimal injuries, which is nothing short of a miracle.

(What do you think? Aren't you happy you finally know the truth about your parents? They were killed in an accident thanks to Bruce, your uncle.)

[What do you mean thanks to Bruce?]

But The Umbra didn't respond.

CHAPTER 9

1

After stretching, Lauren stumbled down the stairs to the kitchen to start the coffee and prepare breakfast for Thomas and the children.

When she stepped into the kitchen, a horrific sight greeted her.

"What are you doing?" Lauren squealed. "Don't do it!" She lunged after Nikki.

"Stand back!" Nikki warned.

And Lauren did. *I can tell by her eyes she's determined,* Lauren thought.

The Umbra spoke to Nikki, though not from within her mind. Instead, he spoke to her externally.

The Umbra said: "Do it now! She's watching! It'll be perfect! Remember what I told you! Grandstand! Get flamboyant with your fatality! Get showy with your suicide! The more gore, the higher the score!"

Nikki stood still and silent with a kitchen knife to her throat—the blade kissing her jugular vein. Lauren herself found herself in a situation she had never been in before. Sure, she had dealt with suicidal patients, but that was after they had been admitted to the BAU and were devoid of any weapons they could use to harm themselves.

Lauren swallowed hard and took a breath, forcing herself into a different frame of mind. "Whatever it is, whatever is wrong, we can fix it."

Nikki shook her head. "Not this time, you can't. Nobody can."

(Would you make like Nike and just do it already?)

"Put the knife down," Lauren pleaded. "Let's talk about it. I'm sure there's a solution to the problem you feel can't be solved." A few seconds passed, but they felt like a millennium to Lauren. "Is it school?"

Using all the breath within her lungs, Nikki screamed: "You can't fucking help me! Nobody can!" She drew out the short-a sound in can, kind of like an opera singer would hold a long note.

Ashlee strolled into the kitchen rubbing her eyes. Lauren pulled her back, not wanting her to approach Nikki. Good thinking, too, as Nikki was highly unpredictable.

"What's wrong?" Ashlee asked Nikki.

Nikki glanced at the back of her left wrist. 2:14:54, 2:14:53, 2:14:52,… She looked on at Lauren and her sister and started to weep. A few seconds later, she dropped the knife as she fell to the floor.

Lauren rushed over to her and embraced her. Nikki wailed from the emotional pain she felt as The Umbra taunted her.

(You weak-ass child. Time is running out. In a little over two hour's time, you'll be dead, either by your own hand or mine.)

Lauren looked at Ashlee and said: "Get your shoes on. We've got to take Nikki to a safe place."

Ashlee complied. Meanwhile, Lauren picked Nikki up and carried her to the car, placing her in the backseat.

2

The landline telephone rang a few times. Derrick rushed to it and answered the call.

"Johns residence," Derrick said.

"Derrick? Is that you?" a woman with a melodic voice asked. "This is Cindy."

"Cindy?" He paused for a second or two. "Gayle's sister?"

"Yes. Can I speak to Gayle? I needed to ask her a few questions."

Derrick slightly grimaced, confused. "She's not here."

Cindy sneezed. "I don't understand. She texted me a few moments ago saying she was staying there a few more days, extending her vacation."

Derrick slightly shook his head in confusion. He remembered from past conversation with Gayle when she and Bruce dated the love-hate relationship she had with her sister Cindy. Derrick didn't want to blow Gayle's cover.

"Let me check," Derrick said. "I've been in and out of the house so much with problems of my own that maybe I didn't see her today."

"Okay. Thanks," Cindy responded.

"Yeah. Not a problem… So, how have you been?"

As Cindy answered Derrick's question, he went from room to room, searching for Gayle, knowing full-well she wasn't there, but figured he would check anyway just on the slight off chance she was there. *Gotta play the part,* he thought.

He didn't find Gayle, but refused to say she wasn't there. He knocked on the ajar bathroom door. "Gayle?" He paused. "Cindy is on the phone for you." Another pause, though this one a few seconds longer. And now to Cindy, he said: "She's in the shower. Can she call you back?"

"Yeah. That would be fine," she replied. "By the way, I hope they find Danielle. I know how close you two are."

That's right—Danielle's body still was not recovered, so most people leaned towards the idea she could still be alive. But authorities were more realistic and openly announced they had their doubts.

Derrick stepped into the living room, and when he did, The Umbra was in his mind chatting him up once again.

(Look at that blood stain, Sir Der-dick-less. Isn't it a beaut? The way the baseball bat came crashing down onto the skull was a thing of sheer beauty.)

[Go fuck yourself. That's a wine stain mixed with blood, Dumbra.]

(Oh, you wish to start a battle of wits, do you?)

But Derrick clammed up, not wanting to give into these conversations anymore. Enough was enough. Besides—he wanted to focus his energies on finding Danielle and obtaining more information on his biological mother and father, Brian and Wendi, as for he was now convinced Bruce was his uncle, not his dad.

And now some other questions popped into his brain. Why was Bruce lying all this time about being Derrick's dad? Why did he persistently lie about his mom being alive but not wanting Derrick to have any contact with her when in reality she was dead? Finally, what about all the names Bruce would spew when asked about his mother's name?

3

The winter chill in the air pierced Derrick's exposed skin like a bed of needles, but he didn't care. He wanted to get the driveway shoveled before Bruce got home. The last snowfall finished around ten in the morning, and Derrick struck while the iron was hot.

As he shoveled up and down the driveway, Mr. Brink walked over with fear consuming his eyes.

"Can you come check on me tomorrow at seven-thirty in the morning?" Mr. Brink asked.

"Sure. I can do that. Are you feeling alright?" Derrick asked.

"No. I'm near death, I think. I'm going to go home and lay down." He retreated.

(Isn't he the face of health? He better take care of the matter himself.)

[Go to Hell!]

(Been there, done that, got the T-shirt. Now fucking kill yourself already!)

Derrick finished the driveway and returned to the garage to put the shovel back. He wanted to get a shovel that met at a point to break some ice that was on the walkway, but he couldn't find any in the garage, so he walked to the shed.

Denied entry. It had a padlock on it. He didn't give up though, knowing where Bruce kept all of his keys. Though none of the keys in Bruce's top dresser drawer seemed to match the key slot for the padlock, something else caught Derrick's attention, but it wasn't a key at all. It was an envelope with a large capital G on it—written in purple marker, and inside of it was a key—one that looked as though it would fit inside a padlock key slot.

Weird, Derrick thought. *What's the G mean? Garage?*

A good guess, but ultimately incorrect. The letter G meant something else.

Derrick trudged through the snow across the backyard to the shed. His intuition was right; the key in the envelope marked G did match the padlock on the shed door. He removed the lock and swung open the shed doors. Not much to see inside. Garden tools, lawnmower, weed whacker, some shovels.

But there was one item that stood out to Derrick, and that was a rusty and battered oil drum—also marked with a G—on the top. What the hell was that doing in there? And what was inside of it?

4

Madison sat on the pool steps, wading in the water. Standing next to her was Dylan. She turned and looked up at him. He already had his finger to his lips. She didn't scream.

And now he sat next to her with his knees to his chest.

"You tried to kill me and my mom's boyfriend," Madison said. "And that wasn't at all nice of you."

"I'm sorry. I shouldn't have done that," Dylan admitted.

"Then why did you?"

"I was pretending to be The Umbra. I wanted the same power it had. I wanted to control people's lives the same way it controlled mine. I wanted to convince people to kill themselves the same way The Umbra got me to do so, even though I wasn't able to go through with it."

Madison shook her head. "You're a bad spirit."

"Not anymore. I came to tell you I'm going to Heaven. You won't see me again."

Dylan stood and held out his hand for Madison to grasp, which she did. Now they were eye to eye.

"Before you go, I have one question for you," Madison said. Dylan nodded and she continued. She said: "Why did you pick me and not someone else?"

A tear exited Dylan's eye and started to stream down his cheek, but he rubbed it away. Madison grabbed Dylan's hand and assured him he could tell her and that she wouldn't get upset.

"Thank you," Dylan said. "The reason I'm sad is because I should have left you alone. I saw you in Burger King the day The Umbra warned me I needed to kill myself. You never saw me though—or if you did—you didn't remember me."

"You're right. I don't remember."

And that was the reason. Nothing more than a brief encounter with one another.

Madison kissed Dylan on his cheek and he did the same to her. A resilient warmth enveloped Madison's body—as if kissed by an angel—a loving angel whose intention was to do nothing more but to bring love and inner peace to people.

Dylan walked out of the pool and into the light. The Umbra granted him freedom after he delivered the goods.

5

To the BAU in Lauren's SUV Nikki went with Ashlee seated in the passenger seat in the front and Nikki in the back—all to herself.

Nikki glanced at the back of her wrist. Time was dwindling. The Umbra crept into Nikki's mind and once again made a valiant attempt to persuade her to do the deed herself or risk eternal torture on his watch.

(Don't be scared, Nikki. Once it's done, you'll feel more alive than ever before. Death is sort of like a rebirth... Now get on with it!)

"How are you doing back there?" Lauren asked, looking in the rearview mirror at Nikki. "We'll be at the hospital soon. They'll help make you feel all better."

Lauren didn't like to take the expressway to drive to work, because of all of the crazies on the road, but in this case she felt it necessary given the dire circumstances.

(The sand continues to fall, the seconds continue to pass, stop the stall and become a carcass.)

Nikki knew if she reached the hospital and was admitted, she would be quarantined, rendering her powerless to kill herself, and that was not something she wanted to let happen. Now, even though there was more time remaining for her to off herself, the trip to the BAU would be less than twenty minutes from the time they left the house.

About three minutes passed, during which time Nikki weighed her options.

"Alright. Make sure your seatbelt is on tight," Lauren said to Ashlee. "Lots of nuts on the expressway."

They merged onto I-94 and headed west towards Chicago. Lauren punched the gas, accelerating, not wanting the eighteen-wheeler behind her to kiss her back bumper.

But Lauren didn't accelerate fast enough. The big-rig truck driver honked his horn. He wanted to merge into the middle lane, but there was traffic to his left, so blaring the horn like a madman seemed like the only logical recourse.

"I'm going as fast as I can," Lauren lamented, pushing the accelerator even further. "Golly. These drivers out here sure are insane… Insane in the membrane."

Ashlee chuckled at the remark.

The semi-truck driver blared the horn once more. Lauren checked her gauges and chided herself for slowing down unknowingly.

But it was no matter to the truck driver. He swerved into the middle lane and accelerated. And, the timing was just right. Nikki opened the back door and threw herself in front of the truck driver's path. Her body exploded on impact, and fragments of it struck the sides, back, and top of Lauren's SUV, among other vehicles.

Chalk up another win for The Umbra.

6

What is in that oil drum? Derrick tried with all of his might to loosen the lid, but it didn't budge. It was as if the lid had been welded onto the barrel—and it was.

The steaks in the skillet sizzled as Derrick tossed in some sliced onion for flavor. Bruce was sitting at the kitchen table sipping on an Angry Orchard. He was starting light and building up.

"Who was Brian Rice?" Derrick asked out of the blue.

Bruce choked on his beer. "Who? I don't know anyone by that name."

"Bullshit." Derrick swirled around to face Bruce. "Why would you lie about your own brother?"

"I'm not lying. I don't know anyone by that name."

Derrick shook his head in disgust. He wondered what reasons Bruce would have to pretend he didn't know his own brother's name.

And something else bothering Derrick was the ever-pressing question: Why did Bruce changed his last name from Rice to Johns? Why do that?

The only answer Derrick could arrive at was Bruce changed his last name to break away from his past—to start anew.

"Cindy called for Gayle," Derrick said. "Gayle is using our house as a front. Any reason why she is doing that?"

"You know how it is between her and her sister. Don't worry about it," Bruce responded. "It's okay if Gayle does that. I know all about it." He wanted to switch topics, so he chose something that would hit Derrick like a ton of bricks. "Would you like to hold a memorial service for Danielle in our backyard after dinner tonight?"

That stung. Derrick's bottom lip jutted out, much to Bruce's amusement, though he did a great job keeping those feelings below the surface.

"She's still alive," Derrick said. "I will not hold any sort of memorial for her until her body is found. Until then, I will continue to believe she is alive and well."

"Suit yourself," Bruce said. "Live in denial." He lightly snickered. *If you only knew what I knew.*

Derrick turned the stove off, removed the skillet, and opened the back door.

"What are you doing with my dinner?" Bruce demanded to know.

Derrick threw the skillet out the back door. The steaks twirled in the air like damaged airplanes tailspinning out of the sky. "Oops. Clumsy me. I dropped it."

Bruce stood—his eyes widened and his jaw dropped—and contemplated what to do next. His first instinct was to bash Derrick's skull in using the meat hammer resting on the counter, but Derrick was closer to it. Besides—Derrick saw Bruce glancing at the hammer, and he was prepared to defend himself.

"What the hell did you do that for?" Bruce shouted. "Now I don't have any damn dinner."

"Make yourself something. I'm done being your slave," Derrick said.

"Don't you talk to your father like that!"

"You're not my dad! You're my uncle! Brian Rice was my dad, and he died. He died in a tragic car accident along with my mom, Wendi."

Bruce swallowed hard and sat back down. "How do you know these things?"

"What's it matter?" Derrick shot back with a furrowed brow.

"Where the hell are you going?"

"I've got more important things to do than to stay here and listen to your lies."

(Exactly. He's got a date with death. Can't be late for that!)

[I'm not going to kill myself. I'm going to go search for Danielle.]

(With no car? You're a dumbass. Just kill your fucking worthless self. Then you'll see your Mommy and Daddy.)

Like an arc flash, an idea lit brightly in Derrick's brain. The man—the other voice—was his dad speaking to him. That was Brian.

[Dad? Are you with me?]

<Yes, Derrick. I'm with you, but I can't always be. Stop engaging The Umbra. The more you interact with it, the more power and influence it can have over you. I'm going to kill The Umbra once and for all. I have the tool needed to do the job.>

The Umbra laughed at Brian's threat. *(I'm shaking in my boots. I'll kill you before you kill me. Bring it on. Let's do this. Let's dance to the death.)*

<Derrick. Stay away from Bruce, also. He's not the man you think he is.>

[I've already picked up on that.]

No additional conversation took place.

7

Around two-sixteen in the morning, Derrick awoke to the sound of tree branches scratching the outside of his window. He sat up in bed, yawned, and flipped on his light.

A few seconds later, a new clatter caught his ear. It sounded as though someone was rooting around in the shed in the backyard.

Derrick hopped out of bed in his T-shirt and boxers and scurried down the stairs to the kitchen. His senses didn't mislead him. Someone was rooting around in the shed, but it wasn't a prowler or burglar; it was Bruce. He had just parked a dolly in front of the shed.

Interested to find out what Bruce was doing, Derrick opened the back door and flipped on the security lights and porch light.

Bruce rushed up to Derrick. "What the hell are you doing?" he stammered faintly. "You nearly gave me a heart attack."

"I could ask you the same thing," Derrick snapped back.

"I'm doing work. I couldn't sleep, so I'm taking care of some loose ends. Now, please, go back to bed."

Derrick shook his head. "I can't sleep either. Maybe I can help you."

"Why would you want to help me? According to you, I'm not even your dad."

Though Derrick had a desire to go toe to toe with Bruce about the veracity of him being his dad or not, he squashed that idea. Bruce, on the other hand, wouldn't have argued anyway.

"Come on," Derrick said. "It will be good for us to do something together."

Bruce smiled, but it was a Machiavellian smile. "Okay. Sure. You can help me. Get some warm clothes on, bundle up, and meet me out here in five minutes. I'll wait for you. In the meantime, I'll have myself a little drink to melt the icy chill running through my body."

<Derrick! What are you doing? I told you to stay away from him! He's evil! He's dangerous! He'll do whatever it—>. Brian wailed in pain, which faded to a deadly silent.

Derrick's intent was to reestablish a rapport with Bruce, hoping to extract pertinent information about why he lied to him all of these years about being his dad, though truth be told, he had a hunch.

Also weighing on Derrick's mind was the whereabouts of Danielle. He prayed for her safe return each waking moment he thought of her.

Now, Bruce finished his shot of rum and waited outside for Derrick.

Nearly seven minutes passed before Derrick approached Bruce, but this didn't bother Bruce that Derrick was a few minutes late. Bruce was none the wiser anyway. He didn't even remember how much time he gave Derrick to return.

Derrick fitted a hand with a glove. "So, what are we doing?"

Gloves. Smart. No prints. "We've got to move this oil drum out of the shed and dump it somewhere."

"Where?"

"The further away, the better."

Derrick snickered. "What do you have in there? A dead body?"

Bruce got all up in Derrick's grill. "Don't make jokes like that now! Especially since you've got your girlfriend still missing. What's wrong with you? Are you suggesting Danielle is in this oil drum?"

"I'm not suggesting—"

A fire erupted in Bruce's eyes like never before. "You want to see what's in the oil drum? I'll show you. Let me get a fucking crowbar and show you there's no goddamn fucking dead body in that fucking oil drum!"

Bruce retreated to the shed and started to hurl objects around. Derrick didn't stand around and watch though. He walked into the house and stepped into the garage. After about fifteen seconds of searching, he found the crowbar Bruce so desperately wanted in order to open the oil drum.

"Here you go," Derrick announced. "You stop your temper tantrum. I found the crowbar."

Bruce spun around. "Well, isn't that just great. You found the crowbar. Now I guess I have to show you what's in here, huh?"

(Go ahead. Jab that crowbar straight into that killer's heart. You know you wanna. Do it! Then kill yourself. Murder-suicide. Beautiful. They're my favorite.)

Dad told me not to engage The Umbra. Ignore it. Ignore what it says.

(I'll be with you until you're dead. And, then, guess what? I'll own your soul like Park Place in Monopoly.)

Derrick dismissed The Umbra's idle threats. He knew good and well The Umbra had no power over him—believing if The Umbra could do something to make him kill himself, it would have already done it.

"Look, I don't care what's in the oil drum," Derrick said, throwing the crowbar into the shed. "I never thought you had a body in there. But if we're going to move this thing, then let's do it."

Bruce nodded. "You sure? I have no qualms showing you what's inside of it."

"Really, it's fine."

"Alright. Help me lift the oil drum onto the dolly. We'll need to create a makeshift ramp and load it into the van."

"What van?"

"The van I'm borrowing from Mr. Hutchins. Shit. I gotta move it down here. You stay here with the oil drum. Do not open it. Understand?"

Derrick nodded, but now his interest in the oil drum was even greater than it was before. Now he *wanted* to know what was inside of it. The crowbar was in the shed along with the oil drum. Why not take a peek while Bruce was away? He'd never be the wiser. And it would put any fears to rest that Bruce was housing a corpse in there, not that Derrick seriously thought he was, but a small part of him wondered.

He picked up the crowbar and contemplated where to begin to pry open the lid. But then his inner voice crept in and advised him not to violate Bruce's trust.

But Derrick questioned this. Bruce had done nothing but lie to him his entire life. Why can't he to him?

Fortunately, the needle of Derrick's moral compass landed in the section DO NOT DISOBEY BRUCE.

About ten minutes later, Bruce approached Derrick and the two of them rolled the oil drum on its bottom edge onto the dolly. They both could have lifted it, but Derrick suggested rolling it would require less energy and would likely be more efficient.

"I'll get a board so we can pull the dolly up it," Derrick said. "We might want to wrap some rope or something around the oil drum and dolly."

"Why?" Bruce asked.

"Because it will make the oil drum more secure on the dolly that way."

Bruce dismissively waved his hand. "It'll be fine. We don't need to get super technical here." He hiccupped, and the pervasive scent of booze float into Derrick's nostrils.

"Suit yourself."

Once Derrick had the board, he positioned it near the edge of the back of the van's floor and then he and Bruce carried the dolly up it and placed the oil drum in the back of the van, laying it longways—not upright.

"Alright, you little worthless piece of shit, get in the van," Bruce snapped. "We got to get this oil drum to the shipyard. I've got a pal of mine waiting."

"I'm not a worthless piece of shit, you dick," Derrick fired back. "I just helped you in more ways than you realize."

"Whatever, whatever. Just shut the hell up and get in the van! This is a critical situation!"

"Okay!"

Through traffic was light, Bruce maintained the speed limit on every street he traveled, including the expressway, and this resulted in the drive to the shipping yard lasting nearly forty-five minutes.

Along the drive, one had much to say to the other. Derrick did bring up some of his newly-favorite musicians: Paul Hester, Otis Redding, and Jill Janus. Bruce was familiar with the first two, but not the latter—at least not at first. Slowly but surely he remembered her and some of her songs.

The radio played hip hop and R & B tunes, and this was an eye-opening experience for Derrick, who really didn't listen to those sorts of tunes.

Once at the shipping yard, they unloaded the oil drum off of the van. Bruce ordered Derrick to stay by the van, which he did.

Meanwhile, Bruce wheeled the dolly to a man near a large shipping vessel—named VIRGIN MARY. The man was a short, portly gentleman with a balding head of gray hair wearing a blue collared dress shirt with black slacks. Sticking out of his mouth like a morning wood was a stogy, from which smoke emanated upward as he stood static listening to Bruce.

Derrick witnessed the older gentleman hand Bruce a wad of cash. Bruce placed it in his pocket and the older man wheeled the dolly towards the Virgin Mary. Just as the man was about to enter the cargo hold of the ship, Bruce called the man's name: Hank. Bruce sprinted to Hank and handed him the wad of money back to him. The two men shook hands before both went their separate ways.

When Bruce and Derrick were driving back home, Derrick asked: "Will you tell me what was in the oil drum? It must be something valuable if Hank gave you money for it."

"The oil drum had a carcass in it," Bruce said, his tone cold and sincere. "A deer."

"A deer?"

"Yes. You know, like the song, doe—a deer—a female deer." He took a swig of Jack Daniels from a small bottle—sort of the type you'd find in a hotel room's mini-fridge—then belched loud and proud.

Derrick grimaced at the sight and smell. "But why did he give you money?"

"Because he wanted the deer. I don't eat deer. Never have, never will. But Hank does. So, I called him, and he agreed to pay me for it."

Derrick nodded as he rubbed his peach-fuzz chin for maybe six seconds, but then stopped. "Then why is he shipping it?"

Bruce smacked his hand on the steering wheel. "What's with all of these questions, huh? Don't worry about it. He paid for it. He can do whatever he wants with the son of a bitch."

"Okay, okay. Calm down. Jesus."

For the remainder of the drive, it was dead silent. Not even the radio uttered a sound.

8

In her prison cell, Karla's lifeless body dangled from a bed sheet wrapped around her neck, but she hadn't committed suicide. She did run out of time to kill herself though, and The Umbra made good on its promise to take her out if she didn't tackle the task herself.

Frustrated with the way her life turned out—being accused and convicted of a crime she didn't do—she uttered the words that The Umbra gravitated towards one too many times.

Her soul now belonging to The Umbra was continuously—not constantly—tortured, and unless someone defeated The Umbra, this wouldn't cease.

9

The time was seven-twelve, and this meant Derrick had twenty-six minutes to get over to Mr. Brink's house to check on him—just as Mr. Brink had asked him to do last night as Derrick was shoveling more snow.

Normally, Mr. Brink would ask Derrick to check in on him at seven-thirty on the nose, but this time not. In fact, Mr. Brink insisted Derrick check on him at seven-thirty-eight—an awfully precise time.

Derrick showered, brushed his teeth, and ate a quick breakfast: a raisin bagel lightly buttered and sprinkled with cinnamon.

But this wasn't his usual breakfast. Normally he had eggs with Swiss cheese and tomato slices, regardless of what Bruce demanded for breakfast. The raisin bagel breakfast was Danielle's favorite, and ever since Derrick returned to the hospital after the car accident, the raisin bagel was his breakfast, and he wouldn't switch up until after Danielle's safe return.

After breakfast, he lumbered over to Mr. Brink's house, unlocked the front door using the key hidden under the planter pot, and entered the residence.

Dangling from the living room ceiling fan was Mr. Brink's frail body, his eyes devoid of any life.

Another victory chalked up to The Umbra.

Derrick called 911 to report the incident. After he ended the call, he stood staring at the dead body of Mr. Brink. As he did this, The Umbra spoke from within Derrick's mind.

(I will make sure all the people in your life you love and care about are destroyed until you kill yourself.)

[You killed Mr. Brink?]

(No. He had the balls—albeit shriveled—to do it himself, unlike someone I know. You've got people waiting to see you on the other side. Come join them.)

At the end of that sentence, Brian chimed in with a reminder for Derrick.

<*Stop engaging The Umbra,*> Brian said. <*Do not interact with it.*>

The Umbra shot back instantly. *(Shut up. I'm getting closer and closer to killing you once and for all.)*

Derrick was confused. He said: *[That doesn't make sense. How can you kill a spirit?]*

(It can be done... Tell you what. I think you need to see it rather than be told how.)

<*I'm going to kill you before you kill me, Umbra.*>

No additional exchange took place. Derrick sat on the porch, waiting for the authorities to arrive. Meanwhile, he thought constantly about Danielle.

10

Standing in front of his bookshelf, Derrick gazed at the pictures of Danielle located on the second shelf. He caressed each one, sometime picking it off the shelf and holding it in his hand.

I miss you and I want you to be returned safely home, Derrick thought. *But the reality seems to be you're in danger and I wish I could rescue you.*

In Derrick's mind, he was convinced Danielle was abducted, being held captive somewhere. He hoped and prayed the kidnapper would release his or her demands, and, if that happened, Derrick vowed to do whatever he could to make good on said demands.

After sulking for several minutes, he pulled out his Organic Chemistry textbook he was studying from before Danielle had gone missing. When he turned to where his bookmark was, something else greeted his eye: an envelope with a message written on it. The message said: CRITICALLY

IMPORTANT. DELIVER TO MY MOM PRIVATELY (NOT WHEN MY DAD IS AROUND).

The handwriting was a dead giveaway. The person who penned the message on the envelope was Aaron. The date on the envelope was one day before Aaron committed suicide, and Derrick took a few minutes to reflect on the last time he and Aaron spent time together—and it was in Derrick's room.

The day before Aaron's suicide, he and Derrick took a long walk, worked out together, and hung out in Derrick's room for a while, listening to music and talking life and their futures.

Aaron slipped the note inside Derrick's Organic Chemistry textbook, but didn't realize Derrick was finished with it. The book was closed on Derrick's desk. A butterfly-patterned bookmark stuck out of the textbook—in between the Advanced Problems for Chapter 10: Further Reactions of Alcohols and the start of Chapter 11: Using Nuclear Magnetic Resonance Spectroscopy, and it would be Chapter 11 Derrick would begin his study when he took Organic Chemistry B online through Indiana University's Distance Learning Program.

But this never came to be. Derrick became consumed and obsessed with locating his mother.

Derrick considered violating privacy and reading the letter inside the envelope before bringing it over to Karen to read.

But he didn't. Instead, he did the next best thing and tried to read what he could through the envelope itself. After his close inspection, he was no wiser than he was before.

He rushed downstairs, bundled up, and walked next door to Aaron's house. Fortunately, Karen is the one who answered the door, and she invited Derrick inside.

"It's been a long time since I've seen you," Karen said. "How have you been?"

"Horrible. With Danielle missing and all, but I'm sure she'll be found safe and sound," Derrick said, his tone confident. "Anyhow, I wanted to—"

"Derrick!" Brandon exclaimed, running towards him.

Derrick took a knee and gave Brandon a hug, patting him on the back. Brandon pulled away and sat on the couch. Karen joined him and invited Derrick to have a seat, also.

And he did, though Derrick chose to sit in the new vibrating chair Scott had recently purchased thanks to money he was able to save with two fewer mouths to feed and backs to cloth.

Just as Derrick was about to reveal the envelope, Karen corrected her manners and asked Derrick if he wanted something to drink. Not wanting to be rude, Derrick accepted and asked for a glass of water if they didn't have any bottled water. Brandon asked for Kool-Aid, and Karen said she would have to make some.

While Karen was in the kitchen preparing the Kool-Aid, Derrick and Brandon got to talking.

"Are you looking forward to Christmas?" Derrick asked.

"Not really. All I asked Santa for was my brother and sister back," Brandon replied, deflated.

Derrick slightly nodded. "That would be a wonderful gift, wouldn't it?"

"Yeah. I miss my brother and sister." He whipped his head towards the hallway leading to the bathroom. He shook his head. "There goes that shadow person again. He's scary."

"The Umbra," Derrick whispered to himself. And to Brandon: "What does it say to you?"

"Nothing much. He just visits me sometimes."

"Visits?"

"Yeah, like at night when I'm asleep. I'll feel these eyes on me. I wake up and there the shadow man is. And, you know something else? A few times, I slept in Aaron's room, and the shadow man sat on the bed as I slept."

Derrick's heart skipped a beat. He swallowed hard. "Do your mom and dad know about this shadow man?"

"Yeah. They've ordered him to leave a few times, but he doesn't listen," Brandon said, rolling his eyes.

"Brandon, whatever you do, don't interact with that shadow man. It's dangerous," Derrick replied.

Karen walked into the living room with a plastic serving tray. She handed Brandon a glass of Kool-Aid, Derrick a bottled water, and then placed the serving tray down on the coffee table in front of the couch before sitting on the couch near Brandon.

"So, what brings you over?" Karen asked as she reached for her glass, inside of which was a Pink Squirrel. "Something on your mind?"

"Yes, actually," Derrick said. He uncapped the bottle, downed a quick drink, and recapped the bottle. "Aaron left an envelope in one of my textbooks instructing me to give it to you. I didn't see until today, I swear."

She nodded. "I believe you. May I have the envelope?"

Derrick pulled the envelope out of his pocket and handed it to Karen, who hugged the envelope as if it were Aaron himself. Then she opened the envelope and removed the later from it. Her eyes moved from side to side as she scanned the letter. Karen was a speed reader—had been since elementary school.

As her eyes scanned the contents of the letter, they welled up with tears, some of which rolled down her cheeks. She placed the first page behind the second and continued to read. The tears began to flow like a mighty stream. A few moments later, she folded the letter back up and placed it into its envelope.

"Derrick, thank you for bringing this letter to me," Karen said. "This answered so many questions. It's also going to help put a killer where he belongs."

The Umbra? "I'm glad I was able to help," Derrick replied. "Thanks for the bottled water." And to Brandon: "Take care. If you need me for anything, you know where to find me."

Derrick left the house and returned home. On the way, The Umbra offered him some advice.

(I'm not as bad as you think I am. I don't force anyone to kill themselves. I don't pull the strings that way. Once they say the words to invite me in, I decide whether or not to enter.)

[You're an evil fuck, and you need to be destroyed.]

(So kill yourself and come and get me.)

[I will never kill myself. I've got to find Danielle.]

The Umbra didn't offer a response, and Derrick made no further attempts to contact it either.

11

Three forceful pounds on the front door awoke both Derrick and Bruce. Derrick rushed down the stairs, but Bruce beat him to the door.

"Wake up, Gayle," Cindy shouted.

"What the fuck is she doing here?" Bruce said, confused.

Five more forceful pounds, but this time even louder.

"I don't know, but why don't you answer the door before the neighbors call the police?" Derrick suggested. "She's making a scene."

"I can't let her inside," Bruce said, scratching his chevron mustache. "She'll know I've been playing her all this time."

"What are you talking about?"

Bruce rolled his eyes and sighed. "I've been—nevermind. Go back to bed. This is my problem, not yours. Now go."

"She said wake up Gayle. She really believes Gayle is here."

"I know. And Gayle was here, but not anymore."

Derrick pulled out his cellphone and glanced at his messages, none of which were from Danielle. "When was Gayle here? I don't remember seeing her."

"That's because you weren't here. Now would—"

Louder pounds on the door, coupled with kicks, startled Bruce.

"Answer the fucking door, Gayle!" Cindy shouted. "I'm tired of the games! I need to make sure you're okay! Bruce! Open the door and let me see my fucking sister!"

"You better—"

"Get your ass upstairs! Now!" Bruce bellowed.

"No. Not until Cindy's mind is put at ease."

Derrick stepped down the stairs and reached for the door, but Bruce pushed him down on the stairs. Derrick grasped his back. The pain wasn't too great, but still palpable.

(You're going to let that killer get away with putting his hands on you? Go to the kitchen, get a knife, and stab him over and over in the gut. Watch him suffer, watch him bleed out like a slaughtered animal—like venison. Then cut his throat. After you watch him die, kill yourself.)

Derrick bolted up the stairs, fearful if he stayed, he would follow The Umbra's advice.

When Derrick reached his room, the sound of more pounds on the front door radiated throughout the house. The final pound was followed by the door striking the wall. Then a gunshot sounded. A few seconds later, one more.

"Stay in your room, Derrick!" Bruce shouted from the living room. "Wait until I tell you otherwise to come out!"

(Another person dead by Bruce's hand. That man makes me so proud!)

<Hey, Umbra! You ready to be sword-fucked?>
(Showtime, Derrick! You ready?)

Now, playing in Derrick's mind was the interaction between his dad's spirit and The Umbra. Derrick's dad—Brian—was wearing a full-length coat and a fedora. In his right hand, he clutched a sword.

[Hey. I remember you, Dad. I saw you walking across the high school parking lot that day Mike drove me there. That was the day he pretended to be my dad and got—]

"Not now, Derrick," Brian said. "I'm about to fillet this Umbra. We'll chat later."

The Umbra said to Brian: "You've got the Sacred Sword, don't you?"

Brian nodded his head. "I'm afraid *your* time is up this time."

Brian lunged for The Umbra, stabbing through The Umbra, but it didn't have any effect. The Umbra laughed maniacally as Brian swatted his sword relentlessly at The Umbra, passing through it several times.

"Why isn't it working?" Brian asked.

"Because—you dumbass—you *don't* have the Sacred Sword anymore. That's a decoy my boy Dylan planted. He stole the real Sacred Sword right from under your nose."

Brian's eyes widened. "Oh, shit," he said, knowing he had made a fatal error. "Forgive me, Derrick."

In The Umbra's right hand appeared a sword nearly identical to Brian's, but it shimmered brightly. The Umbra now gripped the sword with both hands and brought it over his head. Then he followed through with his stroke, slicing through the top of Brian's head down to his crotch. The essence of Brian's spirit scattered into millions of particles, dispersing in all directions.

(Your Daddy is no longer able to protect you now, Derrick. His spirit is nothing more than scattered matter into the universe. He can't be brought back ever—at least not in his in-tact spirit form. Did you like what you saw? Wasn't it awesome to

watch your father's spirit die, to witness his energy radiate in all directions like an exploding bomb? Save your tears. They'll do you no good.)

The movie screen within Derrick's mind went blank. He fell to the floor and cried.

12

Ben knocked on Usha's apartment door. She answered and invited him inside. She led the way to the living room and encouraged him to have a seat while she prepared a fresh pot of coffee and plated some pastries.

She returned to the living room with a cup of coffee in one hand and a plate of pastries in the other. He grabbed one of the two cinnamon rolls on the plate along with the cup of coffee and smiled.

Usha sat and asked: "So, what is it that brings you by today?"

"I have something I think you need to see," Ben said. He bit into the cinnamon roll. Several crumbs fell onto his shirt. He scraped them off onto the floor. He removed a folded-up sheet of paper from his inner breast pocket of his jacket. "Take a look."

And she did. The sheet of paper displayed a picture of someone's X-rayed arm. A large red circle encompassed the person's wrist. Though faint, Usha could see some digits located on the wrist portion of the person's arm.

"You see it, don't you?" Ben asked, chewing his bite of cinnamon roll.

"I do. So, you believe me now, don't you?"

"I do believe you, yes. Clearly some supernatural entity persuaded Karla to kill herself. We are having Marcy's body exhumed to perform a similar test to see if she had any digits remaining on her wrist, too. Karla was likely innocent."

"She was innocent. She was a victim of circumstances. Now she's dead, needlessly and unnecessarily dead."

Ben sighed. "It is unfortunate. The more pressing issue is how can law enforcement stop this entity from harming other people?"

"You can't. Nobody can."

Usha walked out of the room without excusing herself. Meanwhile, Ben munched on his cinnamon roll, crumbs snow-falling from his chin with every bit and as he chewed.

About two minutes passed before Usha returned to the living room with a laptop. She sat next to Ben and showed him a webpage she had started asking people to share their experiences with people who committed suicide under strange circumstances. The majority of the commentators specified their loved one had an obsession with their wrist and were elusive with details about why. Also, the majority of the posts expressed their loved one's behavior changed after they announced they wanted to kill themselves.

"This entity operates on invite," Usha said. "Once someone utters the words they want to kill themselves or a close variation of that, this entity may or may not enter their life."

"How can you draw that conclusion?" Ben asked, genuinely interested. "I mean what evidence do you have?"

"That's a good question. I've spoken to these individual commentators. Each of their loved ones had uttered the works they wanted to kill themselves before, some more than others."

"So? What's that mean?"

"I think what can be inferred is it means this entity operates on a random-variable schedule, not fixed. One person may utter the words a thousand times and nothing happens. But on the one-thousand-and-one time, this entity may make its move. Another person may only say it twice and on the second utterance, the entity may make its play."

"Seems a little far-fetched," Ben admitted. "Are you certain there isn't some pattern?"

"I'm certain. I have commentators from all over the world who I've spoken to about this situation."

"Why don't any of them sound the alarm?"

"Because I haven't told them I believe there is an evil entity behind the suicides or murders. I've been using a ruse I'm conducting a psychological study of suicide. I don't comment on their responses. I document, and then afterwards I pool the data and make inferences."

Ben scratched his five o'clock shadow cheek and made sucking noises with his mouth. Usha placed her laptop on the table in front of her and excused herself (this time) to get herself a cup of coffee. She picked up his cup to refill it. There were cinnamon roll particles floating on the surface of the coffee. Backwasher.

While Usha took care of the refreshments, Ben bit at his nails, spitting the pieces he broke off across the room, off to his side. Before Usha reentered the room, he scratched deep within his crevice, wishing he had done that rewipe before leaving his office at the station—just as his conscience had told him to do so.

Fortunately for Usha's eyes, she didn't have the displeasure of seeing Ben scratch the fiery itch along the length of crack.

Usha sneezed. "Excuse me."

"Eww, gross, don't sneeze into your hand," Ben said, grimacing. "Sneeze into your arm." He dramatically shuddered.

"Sorry, I only had so much time to decide. Thanks for the tip though." *He finds me repulsive. I'll never get a shot with him now.*

"What do you think those numbers on the wrist mean?"

Usha took a deep breath followed by a sip of coffee. "I think it is a countdown timer of some sort. This entity gives the victim a window of time to off themselves. If they don't, it kills him or her itself."

"Are you sure it isn't a watch?"

"Well, it is a watch of some sort. A suicide watch to be precise." *Thanks, Alejandro, for tipping me off.*

Indeed, a few weeks ago, Alejandro's spirit visited Usha and they talked for nearly an hour about different things. She was sad to hear he wouldn't be able to have a conversation with her for as long as she lived, but he would check in on her from time to time. It brought her tremendous comfort to know he was now her guardian angel.

"So, you're suggesting this entity gives the person a limited window to kill themselves, a countdown timer is displayed on their wrist, and if the person doesn't take him or herself out, the entity will kill them?"

"Exactly. And you can confirm what I am saying makes sense by comparing the time of death of Karla to the numbers displayed on her wrist. They will not match."

Ben pulled out a pocket-sized stenopad and made a note of Usha's suggestion. He had one more cinnamon roll and two more cups of coffee before leaving, during which time he and Usha talked more about this evil entity, The Umbra.

"What are the origins of this entity?" Ben asked. "I mean if it truly exists."

"I wish I knew," Usha said as she brought her coffee mug to her lips.

But she did know—just wouldn't tell.

13

As Brandon and Derrick threw and caught pitches from each other, Derrick couldn't help but wonder if what he witnessed with the slaying of his dad by The Umbra with the Sacred Sword was fake or real. Sadly, he leaned toward real, mainly because since the demise of his dad's spirit, he did whatever he could to communicate with his dad, but never received a response like he used to, and this crystallized the notion his dad's spirit was nothing more than dispersed energy floating about within the universe.

"Has the shadow man been bothering you?" Derrick asked.

"Not really, but Aaron visits me sometimes," Brandon said. "Aaron tells me I should kill myself so he and I can be together again. He told me he and Emily miss me so much."

"I don't think that's really Aaron talking to you, buddy."

Brandon wound up a pitch and threw it to Derrick. "Then who is it?"

"The shadow man I bet has ways of fooling your mind. Killing yourself is never an answer. Your brother loved you, and he would never suggest you do something such as kill yourself."

Brandon caught Derrick's pitch, then threw the ball back to Derrick. Inside of the house, they could hear an argument ensuing.

After pitching to the ball back to Brandon, Derrick suggested they work on Brandon's batting swing, which needed some work.

But Brandon declined, insisting his swing was fine and needed no work. Brandon loved to pitch the ball, but despised working on anything else related to developing his baseball-playing skills.

Brandon released an irritated sigh. He shook his head, removed his glove, and tossed it towards the front of the house before walking inside without saying a proper goodbye to Derrick.

Uncertain if Brandon would be back out shortly, Derrick waited for few minutes before retreating back to his own house.

14

Scott stood in the kitchen fixing himself another tomato sandwich. As he sliced through the fleshy tomato, an object struck the back of his head and he fell to the ground, bumping his head on the counter along the way.

Standing over his motionless body, Karen stared at it for a few seconds. "It's time to play a game," she said. "Truth or Die."

Fortunately, Karen had made arrangements with Derrick for Brandon to sleep over at his house. She definitely didn't want Brandon to witness the bloodshed that may or may not occur during the night's interrogation.

The Umbra stood in the corner of the kitchen, watching. The hair on Karen's arms and neck stood on end. The air felt magnetized. Karen dragged Scott's body to the back spare bedroom of their home where she had been spending the past few days. Inside of it was a makeshift table with straps on it. In some ways, it looked like an execution table you would find in a death chamber of a state prison.

She lifted Scott over her shoulder and slammed his body onto the table. She tied him down to ensure he couldn't escape. His body was positioned like a cross, with his arms fanned out nearly ninety degrees relative to his torso with three straps on each arm holding them in place. Then there were six straps running across his torso. Finally, each leg had four straps—two above the kneecap and two below.

The Umbra stood in the corner of the room, invisible to Karen, though she still sensed its presence.

On top of a bottle, Karen placed a waded-up rag. Then she inverted the bottle and returned it to an upright position. And then again. Finally, once more. Her eyes watered from the powerful, noxious scent.

She waved the rag underneath Scott's nose. He shook his head and then lightly screamed, startled.

"Rise and shine, babe," Karen said with a sinister glean in her eyes.

He assessed his surroundings and the fact he was tied down to a makeshift execution table. "What the hell are you doing?" he asked, his tone agitated.

"Tonight, you will pay for your crimes."

"Crimes? What crimes? Have you lost your what little fucking mind you have? You untie me right now."

She shook her head. "You're an evil bastard. You killed our daughter."

He swallowed hard and closed his eyes. A moment later, he released a heavy sigh. "No, I didn't. You're wrong. What the fuck are you talking about? Untie me, you crazy bitch! Untie me this instant!"

Though he fought against the restraints, it did no good. She stood idly by and watched him wiggle and waddle around like a fish out of water. Soon—very soon—it would be filleting time, and by Karen's hand.

She walked over to a file cabinet and pulled out the envelope containing the letter Aaron penned. She unfurled the letter and held in front of Scott's face for him to read, and as he did, the color in his face changed, as if the blood from it drained to his feet.

"Why'd you do it, Scott?" Karen asked, her tone motherly.

He paused for a few seconds, licking his lips before speaking. "I didn't kill our daughter. Aaron is wrong. It wasn't like that."

She slightly nodded a few times. "I see. You can't admit your transgressions, can you? Maybe what you need is a little convincing."

"What are you going to do?"

"You'll feel it. Don't you worry."

To the file cabinet Karen walked, taking slow strides to get there. The silence of her socks striking the floor was ear-piercing. The anger in Scott's eyes from being tied to a makeshift gurney switched to fear, a fear he'd never experienced in his entire life.

She opened the top drawer of the three-drawer file cabinet and pulled out a straight razor—the same kind old-fashioned barbers used to shave a man—and a bottle rubbing alcohol.

Karen's stoic facial expression morphed into a devilish smile—and one Scott had never seen on Karen before. Also, her eyes sent a shiver up his spine. He knew he was in deep shit now.

At the head of the gurney was a smallish table—a TV tray table. She placed the straight razor and rubbing alcohol on the table and pulled it so the items were in Scott's eyesight. She wanted him to see the items, hoping his mind would wander and think the worst.

The Umbra standing in the corner of the room started to get excited. Even though this wasn't its handiwork, it still enjoyed a good torture session.

Karen used a pair of medical scissors to cut along the Scott's sleeve so his arm's skin was exposed. She placed her ear over his heart and listened to it beat, faster and faster with each passing second.

She opened the straight razor and said: "Are you ready to feel a pain like none other you've ever experienced before in your entire pathetic miserable life, you child killer?"

"I didn't kill Emily! I swear!" Scott shouted. "Don't do it!"

She swiped the straight razor across the meat of his arm and poured rubbing alcohol onto the wound. Scott thrashed about as he screamed in pain.

"Now are you going to tell me the truth or not?" she screamed. "I've got all night and all sorts of tools to fuck you up in more way than one."

Something in Karen had snapped after reading the letter several times over. She wanted to see Scott in pain; she wanted to see him bleed. She really wanted to torture him in the same way she saw a killer be tortured in the movie *Law Abiding Citizen*, but she didn't have the means or the testicular fortitude to do so.

"Jesus Christ! I didn't kill Emily! Aaron is making things up to get back at me!" Scott protested.

Karen swiped the straight razor across Scott's leg his time, cutting into the bone. "How dare you blame what you did to Emily on Aaron! How dare you accuse him of fabricating a story such as this!" She took a breath. "You better come clean or I'm going to bleed you out slowly. I don't care if I go to jail. I don't care if I get the death penalty. You deserve to be slowly tortured until you die."

"It's a mistake. I never intended anything bad to happen to Emily."

"But you did! And now Emily is dead!" she screamed, pouring rubbing alcohol onto the wound on Scott's leg. "You fucker! You fucking child killer!" She dragged the straight razor across his right cheek.

He wailed in pain. The warmth of the blood ran down his cheek. "You fucking bitch! If I get loose, you're dead!"

"Are you ready to admit your crimes and atone for them?"

He forcefully closed his eyes, the eyelids squashed against the cheekbones. Karen waited a few seconds for Scott to respond but the words never left his lips. She slammed the straight razor onto the table and walked to the file cabinet where she opened one of the drawers and pulled out an electric saw with a serrated blade.

As she unwound the cord and connected to an extension cord she spoke to Scott. She said: "You have a sickness, Scott. Do you know what your sickness is? Do you remember from Aaron's letter what disorder he claimed you have?"

But Scott didn't answer. He was too busy focusing on setting himself loose.

"Munchhausen Syndrome by Proxy," Karen said. She turned around and walked towards an outlet in the room. "Did the baby really deserve to be abused? Were you jealous of all the attention she was getting? Why'd you do it, Scott?"

Her back stayed toward Scott. He was as quiet and calm as a corpse.

The truth was Scott was jealous of all the attention Emily was receiving. When Karen and Scott had Aaron followed by Brandon, they always made time for each other. But for some reason—perhaps because Emily was the first girl—and Karen devoted nearly every waking moment to her daughter. The intimacy between Karen and Scott plummeted faster than a stone falling from the sky.

Scott missed Karen, and he missed being the center of attention. Karen used to laud him for always doing right by his family.

"You fucking bitch," Scott said. He gripped Karen's head back and slit her throat using the straight razor—which was also used to cut himself free from the gurney.

Karen mistakenly left the straight razor within Scott's grasp. He was able maneuver his wrist in such a way the blade contacted the rope and he was able to move his wrist just enough in order to create a back-and-forth motion to free his hand. From there, he was able to free his other hand and cut the other straps, also.

When Karen fell to the floor gripping her throat, hoping to contain the bleeding, Scott picked her up and slammed her onto the gurney. Moments later, she was tied down like a condemned inmate getting ready to be put down like a sick animal.

Scott held up the straight razor. "Are you ready to have some fun now, you stupid bitch?" he asked with a sinister, psychotic gleam in his eye. "I'm going cut you like a Christmas ham."

"Please…don't," she pleaded, blood oozing from her neck wound onto the gurney. "I was enraged at what you did to Emily."

He smiled. "It was such a pleasure to see the life leave her eyes, and now I'll get to see the life leave yours, too."

She shook her head. "Don't."

But he did.

15

Thomas loaded a box Ashlee carried to him into the back of the truck.

"Well," Thomas said, pulling his gloves further down, "that's the last of it. Time to get a move on. Are you ready?"

Ashlee nodded. "We're really moving to Florida?"

"You bet. That's where your mom and Nikki were their happiest and so that's where they belong, and I also think that's where I belong, also."

Ashlee smiled. "Yeah. I think so, too."

"Besides, I think the Floridians are going to be pretty stoked to see the new and improved me. What do you think?"

Ashlee laughed. "Daddy, what's stoked mean?"

Thomas chuckled. "Stoked means very excited."

"Oh," she said, after slightly curling her lip and pausing for a few seconds.

Lauren stepped from the front door carrying an urn—Nikki's urn. She walked to Thomas and handed it to him. He hugged the urn, then kissed Lauren on her forehead.

"I guess we better get moving, huh?" Lauren said.

Thomas rubbed her tummy. "Yeah, the four of us better get a move on. Right, angel?"

"Right!" Ashlee exclaimed.

Lauren and Ashlee hopped into Lauren's new vehicle—not an SUV this time though, but a mini-van.

Thomas closed the back of the truck, picked up Nikki's urn off of the driveway, and placed it in a box that was buckled in the passenger seat of the U-Haul moving truck. Next to Nikki's urn was her mother's—mother and daughter together again.

He started up the U-Haul, yanked the gear shifter down a notch, and backed out of the driveway. Before moving forward, he took one last look at Lauren's house and thought about the new future they were starting together in Florida.

16

The newspaper boy chucked the day's paper at the doorway to Bruce's house and it struck the front door with a force that caused Coreyann's new Doberman to start to bark.

Derrick opened the front door and picked up the paper, which was folded into thirds. The middle third had the letters DY OF MIS on it. He ripped off the rubber band and opened the paper. The full headline read: BODY OF MISSING TEEN FOUND.

Danielle's was found, but she was no longer of the physical world.

(Told you that bitch was dead. Now get on with it and kill yourself!)

Derrick's breathing became erratic. He tried to control it, but couldn't. His heart started to pound against his chest like a battering ram. He collapsed to the ground and sobbed.

(Quit being a baby and kill yourself! If you do it, you'll be welcomed into the afterlife where you will have everything you want. Now do it!)

"You killed Danielle?" Derrick asked The Umbra.

(No.)

"Who did?"

(It's not my place to tell you who, even though I know. My place is to watch you kill yourself. Now, be a good boy and do as your told!)

"Tell me."

(I hate you, do you know that? Ever since that night when I was so close to killing you—you know, since you were too much of a fucking limpwristed Nancy boy to do it yourself—but that fucking meddling asshole dad of yours had to save you, and he nearly killed me that night, too.)

"How did he do that?"

(He had something powerful enough to interfere with me killing you. He had a sword blessed by enough people to make it powerful enough to render me useless—only temporarily though.)

Derrick sniffled, then blew his nose on the inside neckline of his shirt. The Umbra appeared in front of Derrick and look down at him.

The Umbra no longer spoke within Derrick's mind, but instead outside of it—just like two people engaging in a conversation would do. The Umbra said: "You shouldn't be alive. Your dad interfered with your destiny. He broke one of the cardinal rules of the spiritual world. Don't shit in another spirit's backyard. You should be dead. You need to be dead. Go ahead, Derrick. Put an end to your misery. Your precious Danielle awaits."

"Is she really dead?" Derrick asked.

"Yes, she is dead," Danielle said. "She was murdered by the hand of someone. It was a delightful, orgasmic sight. I wish you could have been there to watch it."

"I want to kill you. I want you to be dead."

"That's is an impossibility. You don't have the means or the balls—for that matter—to take me on," The Umbra said, snidely.

"Someone has to destroy you," Derrick countered. "You killed my dad's spirit."

"It needed to be done. He was meddling where he didn't belong. He was going to kill me."

The notion a spirit could be killed still has a difficult concept to understand. A word he felt was a better choice was *destroyed*, not killed.

Derrick read the news article about the body recovered. Her body was discovered in an oil drum, charred. He started to cry once again.

The Umbra vanished.

17

Scott placed his hand on the glass pane separating him from Brandon, and smiled. Brandon placed his hand on the glass, overlapping his dad's.

"Did you kill Mommy?" Brandon asked.

Scott's sister, Belinda, chided Brandon for asking such a direct question, but it didn't matter. Scott had already pled guilty and was sentenced to life in prison without the possibility of parole, so he wouldn't be admitting to anything he didn't already. Even still, though,

Scott hesitated to answer. "Yes, I did," Scott said, "but it was out of anger. It was in the heat of the moment. And she tried to hurt me, too. I was afraid if I didn't do what I did, she would kill me."

"Our family is destroyed, Dad."

"I know, sport. I wish there is something I could do to change it, but I can't."

Brandon sighed. "Why did Mommy want to hurt you?"

Scott scratched his nose. "She blamed me for Emily dying."

"Why?"

Scott shrugged his shoulders and made a confused face. Brandon thought for a few moments and then looked back up at his dad, but he didn't say anything.

"What's wrong?" Scott asked.

Brandon turned away and thought for another ten seconds or so before looking up at his dad again.

"Tell me," Scott said. "What's wrong?"

"It just occurred to me every time Emily needed to go to the hospital, you were the one who was with her," Brandon said.

Scott swallowed hard. "I know it looks bad, but—"

Brandon stood and walked away.

"Brandon, come back here," Belinda ordered him.

"No," he said, continuing to walk away. "My dad killed my sister, and now I want to kill myself!"

"You shouldn't say things like that," Belinda said. "That's terrible."

Brandon whipped around. "But it's true! I do want to kill myself! Do you hear me! I want to kill myself!"

The Umbra appeared in front of Brandon—which he could see—but nobody else could. Brandon's eyes widened and his face turned pale. Belinda called Brandon's name several times, but he didn't respond to her.

The Umbra said: "And in twenty-four hours, you will do just that. That's exactly how much time you have to kill yourself. Congratulations, Brandon—you're one of the chosen ones—just like your brother was. At the end of the twenty-four hours, if you haven't killed yourself, I will kill you myself. If you do kill yourself, your spirit will live eternally in unbridled ecstasy. If you don't, however, and I have to kill you myself, I will own your soul and torture it until the end of time. And, speaking of time, a countdown watch located on the back of your wrist will show you how much time remains for you to kill yourself. Only you can see the countdown timer. Go ahead. Take a look."

And he did. Brandon stared in awe at the countdown timer that read 24:00:00, which was located on the back of his left wrist. His eyes welled up with tears and his body shuddered.

The Umbra slightly cocked its head. "Once I finish my little spiel, the countdown timer will begin. It won't do any good to tell anyone about the countdown watch—which only you can see—and if you do I may kill you on the spot. I'm everywhere and anywhere all at the same time. Do the right thing and kill yourself. Get creative with your suicide. Grandstand. The more gore, the higher score, as I like to say. Make your choice: die or be killed." The Umbra faded to invisibility and the countdown timer began to do its job. 23:59:59, 23:59:58, 23:59:57,…

The question was: Would Brandon do his?

18

A closed-casket service was provided for Danielle. After the final benediction was read by Father Verta, the guests attending the funeral scattered out the double doors to get to their vehicles for the funeral procession.

Father Verta—a tall, stout man with a goatee—placed his arm around Derrick's shoulder. Tears from Derrick's eyes poured out like water from a fountain. Father Verta embraced Derrick, which Derrick didn't refuse.

"I understand this is a tough situation," Father Verta said. "This is probably one of the toughest days you'll ever experience in your life."

"It is," Derrick said, sobbing. "I can't believe she was murdered, and in such a horrific way."

And this was true. According to the autopsy report, Danielle suffered a violent beating. She had several fractured and broken bones, her skull taking the brunt of the damage, but she was dead before being set afire.

"Put your faith in the Lord and take comfort in knowing Danielle is now in a better place," Father Verta said with a gleam in his eye.

"Better place," Derrick asked, stammering. "She's in a better place?"

"Well, of course, Derrick. She's in Heaven, sipping the finest wines and eating a bounty of food. She's in Paradise."

(Quit your fucking crying and do what you're supposed to do.)

Derrick looked up at Father Verta and asked: "Could I have a few minutes alone? I'd like to say some words to Danielle in private, please."

Father Verta nodded. "You bet. I'll close the doors on the way out. All I ask is you do not lift open the coffin lid and you keep your words to a few minutes. We've got to transport her to her final resting place."

"I'll be quick."

Once Father Verta closed the door, Derrick opened Danielle's casket and immediately retched at their sight. Then he examined her remains. They were charred, burnt beyond recognition.

He closed her casket lid and pulled out a 9 mm handgun, put it to his temple, and pulled the trigger.

The Umbra watched the entire scenario unfold. Watching Derrick's brains exit from his skull and spatter against Danielle's casket was music to its ears. The sight of the blood and brain matter was nothing short than a work of art to it, like the Sistine Chapel or the Mona Lisa. The aroma of the gun smoke and brain and blood matter put The Umbra into a state of euphoria.

About five more minutes passed before Father Verta opened the doors to where Danielle's casket was located. He immediately ran to Derrick's body and checked for any sign of life, but none existed.

Father Verta pulled out his cellphone and dialed 911, and as he did this, he rushed out of the funeral room and closed the doors.

19

"Johns!" a correctional officer—Tito—shouted from outside his cell. "Wake your ass up!"

"What?" Bruce asked, irritated.

"The chief wants to see you in his office," another correctional officer—Ernie—said.

Unbeknownst to Derrick, the same day he was attending Danielle's funeral, Bruce was arrested for the murder of Gayle's sister, Cindy. CCTV footage from the security camera located on Mr. Brink's house—which the new owners installed—discredited Bruce's story he opened fire on Cindy after she broke into his home, unlocking his front door using a key from underneath the doormat.

Bruce backed up to the cell door and Ernie secured handcuffs on Bruce's wrists. Tito then checked to ensure Ernie had the cuffs on tight enough.

Tito and Ernie escorted Bruce to the chief's office. They seated him in a chair across from the chief's desk and then they themselves took a seat on the ugly plaid sofa located near the entrance of the chief's office.

Bruce whistled randomly while the Tito and Ernie played thumb wars.

From the private bathroom located within the office, the warden sauntered to the L-shaped executive-style desk and took a seat.

"How are you, Mr. Johns?" the chief asked.

"Just fine, Chief Tharp, I guess," Bruce replied, his tone stoic. "What is it you wanted to see me about? Are you going to tell me I'm being charged with Danielle's murder now?"

Chief Tharp's eyes widened. "No, but I do have some distressing and saddening news to share with you. Are you ready?"

Bruce nodded. "Nothing is as bad as being told I'm being charged with murder, so go ahead and lay it on me." *Man, Chief Tharp has a nice ass. If I'm going to be executed, I'd like to make that ass my last meal.*

Tito and Ernie switched from Thumb Wars to Bloody Knuckles. Ernie accused Tito of being too rough, but Tito disagreed and mocked Ernie. As they went back and forth, their voices crescendoed.

Chief Tharp placed a box of Kleenex in front of Bruce. Then she said: "Hey! Beavis and Butthead! Take that action outside my office!" She shook her head in disbelief at Tito and Ernie for their immature behavior. And to Bruce: "Sorry for shouting in your face."

"It's fine." He removed a tissue from the box and blew his nose. "So, what did you want to tell me?"

Chief Tharp took a breath and then yanked a tissue from the box. After a few dabs to the eyes, it was time to spill the beans. "I'm sorry to tell you this news, Mr. Johns, but your son committed suicide earlier today at Danielle's funeral."

Bruce nodded and picked at his chevron mustache. She gave him a few moments to process the news she shared.

The only noises audible were the space heater on Chief Tharp's desk and the playful banter between Tito and Ernie arguing over who had the better cuticles.

Chief Tharp asked: "Mr. Johns? What are you feeling right now? Are you okay?"

"Oh, I'm fine," Bruce replied. "Things are going to be just fine." *I'm glad I'm rid of that fucking burden on my back.*

"Are you sure?"

"Yes. Thank you." *God, I want to pound that ass of Tharp's. It's so firm and sexy.*

Bruce yanked another tissue from the box and wiped his eyes. He thought he had Chief Tharp fooled, but he was wrong.

"Ernie! Tito!" Chief Tharp yelled.

"Yes, chief?" Ernie asked.

"Please take Mr. Johns back to his cell."

And they did. While Bruce laid on the bed, he relished in delight knowing he was going to be a free man—free from both jail and from his parental obligations—which he never really wanted in the first place.

As Chief Tharp sat at her desk, rubbing lotion into her hands, she couldn't help but think about how unresponsive Bruce was to the news his nephew had killed himself. Something else that stuck with her was his remark about being charged with Danielle's murder. What the hell was that about?

20

In an all-white marble room with a long—thirty feet if it was an inch—white table with comfy white executive-style chairs, Derrick waited patiently for whatever was to happen next. He didn't know where he was, yet wasn't scared or nervous. In fact, he was as at total peace.

The door—also white—to the room opened and a man wearing an all-white business suit sat across from Derrick at the table. The only non-white thing in the room was the red rose boutonniere on the man's suit.

"Derrick Rice, aka Derrick Johns," the man said. "How are you, my son?"

"Dad?" Derrick asked, confused. "I thought The Umbra slayed your spirit."

"I'm sorry to tell you that I am not your biological father, and, yes, you are correct, your dad's spirit was decimated, regretfully."

Derrick swallowed hard and look down at the table for a few moments. The man sitting across from him opened the file folder and began reviewing its contents.

"If you're not my dad, then who are you?"

The man didn't look up, but he did respond. "Just call me JC. Everyone does," the man said, smiling—his teeth as white as the marble in the room and sparkling, too.

"Where am I?"

"Paradise, my son. Heaven."

"Heaven? I died?"

"Yes. By your own hand."

"Am I going to be sent to Hell?"

JC looked up at Derrick. His face was like a blank slate, and stayed that way for several seconds. But then he cracked a smile. Derrick wasn't sure what to make of it.

"No, my son, you're not going to be sent to Hell," JC said. "Though killing yourself is a sin in the eyes of your Creator, it has already been forgiven. The stuff you read in the Bible and hear from Bible-thumpers about God outcasting people into Hell for this and that is nothing more than hokum. It's fear propaganda. In fact, to be perfectly blunt, it's bullshit."

Derrick snickered, but then pulled it back together. "I regret doing what I did. Honestly."

JC nodded. "I know, my son. You were deeply distraught over Danielle's murder. You loved her deeply. I regret to tell you she really didn't feel the same way about you though."

"Why not?"

"She just wasn't into you the way you were into her, and she really wanted you to get into her, if you catch my drift."

Derrick folded his arms and looked at the ceiling for a few seconds. JC shuffled through some more papers in Derrick's file.

The aroma of roses and lilacs tricked into Derrick's nostrils. He wondered if it was emanating from JC's flower on his suit.

"You mean she wanted us to have sex?" Derrick asked.

"Think about it, Derrick. You're a smart, young man. When you two first started dating, she tried every chance she got to lay you in the sack, but you always stifled her, and for good reason. You wanted sex to happen at the right time, the right moment. You wanted more than sex, didn't you? You wanted to make love to her, and on your wedding day, too."

"All true. Yes."

"She was quite the horndog. The number of times she banged your uncle is like a new Guinness World Record," JC said, snickering at his own quip.

Derrick grimaced. "Are you serious? She was having intercourse with Bruce?"

"Oh, yes. Plentiful amounts of it."

"Why him?"

"You wouldn't put out for her, so she decided to get it from somewhere else. She was especially attracted to Bruce's chevron mustache. Remember how she kept trying to get you to grow one."

"I wasn't able to for some reason. I'd only get some stubble. It's like my body hasn't hit puberty yet or something."

JC busted out laughing, and then Derrick joined in. After their laughing subsided, JC rifled through some more of the papers as Derrick bit his nails, waiting patiently for JC to speak.

A few minutes passed during which time JC strummed the air off to the side. Beautiful, angelic harp music sounded.

"So, what would you like to do now?" JC asked.

"Do? What do you mean? Don't I just get to kick back and relax now that I am in Paradise?"

JC laughed, but it was more of a snide laugh. "That's not how Heaven operates. You have to do something productive, something that benefits other people."

"I could be a guardian angel, I guess. Sort of like that one off of *It's a Wonderful Life*. Do I have to earn my wings first though?"

"No, it doesn't quite work the way it is portrayed in the movie. Angels really don't have wings. They're spiritual beings, so they don't need wings. Another fallacy portrayed to the human population."

"Alright then. So, no wings. That's fine. What do I do next?"

"You'll need to choose someone who you'd like to oversee."

Derrick scratched the back of his head and leaned back in his chair. He thought for several minutes. Meanwhile, JC strummed the air off to his right again and glorious harp music once again sounded.

Someone knocked on the door to the room. JC stood and opened the door. A young, beautiful woman—in her twenties—stepped inside and placed a serving tray on the table. On the serving tray was a bottle of red wine and three glasses.

She smiled at Derrick and said: "How are you feeling?"

"I'm feeling great," Derrick replied, smiling back.

"That's good. I'm glad to finally see you again."

Again? "I don't think we've met before. Are you sure you have the right person?"

"Positive. You wouldn't remember me though. You were just a pup, an infant, probably no more than four months old."

Though this woman was a stranger to Derrick, he felt as though he had known her his entire life. There was an innate, primal connection between the two of them. And, to be honest, the woman was experiencing the same feelings Derrick was.

As she poured wine into the three glasses, Derrick couldn't help but fixate on the letter W embroidered on her dress, located just below her left shoulder.

She placed a glass of wine in front of JC and Derrick, then picked up the last glass for herself. No toast was made, but JC and she started to drink their wine. Derrick never touched his glass.

JC peeked over his glass as he poured more wine into his mouth. After swallowing, he said: "Well, go ahead, Derrick. Drink up. That's one of our finest-aged wines. Drink, drink, drink."

"I'm good. Thanks," Derrick responded. And to the woman: "I'm curious. What's the W stand for?"

She shifted her eyes downward to view the W on her dress. Then she said: "The W is the first initial of my first name. My name is Wendi—and that's with an i, not a y." She finished her glass of wine.

JC politely offered some reassurance to Derrick. He said: "This isn't a test. We're not trying to see what sort of restraint you have. You're no longer bound by the rules of the physical world. You can drink as much wine as you like." JC poured himself another glass, much fuller than what Wendi poured for him. "And, here's the perk: you'll never get shitfaced, unless you want to be, then you can do that."

But Derrick still hesitated to drink the wine, even though he so much wanted to do so. Wendi pushed the glass a little closer to him.

"This has to be a dream or something," Derrick muttered. "This can't be reality."

Wendi smiled. "You are really in Heaven. You really are dead. You shot yourself in the head with Bruce's gun."

"You know Bruce?" Derrick asked, genuinely interested in knowing the answer.

"Yes, I do. He and I dated at one time. But he loved to drink too much, so I had to dump his always-inebriated ass," Wendi shared.

The gears were turning in Derrick's head now—full steam ahead. He now knew who he was talking to, and now he felt even closer to this woman named Wendi.

"You're my mom, aren't you?" Derrick asked.

She smiled and nodded. "I was wondering when you'd pick up on that."

"But you look so young," Derrick said. "You look as though you haven't aged over the years."

"Another perk of Heaven: you can look however you want. There are no limits, no bounds. If I wanted to look like a ninety-year old man right now, I could. You, too, Derrick, can alter your physical appearance, if you want."

Derrick wiped tears from his eyes, stood, and extended his arms. He and Wendi embraced for several moments. JC played his air harp again, adding atmosphere to the Kodak moment, and with his other hand he snapped a picture using his cellphone of mother and son hugging for the first time in approximately sixteen years.

After they embraced, Derrick took his seat, and she sat next to him. He finally mustered up the courage to drink the wine JC so eagerly encouraged him to drink, but he didn't gulp it down like he would his protein shake or a bottle of Dasani. He took slow sips, drinking it as if he were a seasoned wine taste tester.

After JC poured himself another glass of wine—this would be his fourth—he took a quick gulp. "So, Derrick, have you decided who you would like to oversee?"

"Yes, I have," Derrick said. "I'd like to oversee Brandon— my next-door neighbor. He's only ten and he's basically lost his entire family. He needs someone to watch over him, to comfort him."

"I'm afraid Brandon isn't an option," JC said with downcast eyes. "He's in serious trouble. He's in a grave situation, actually. You'll have to choose someone else."

The Umbra? No, I told Brandon not to engage that piece of shit. "Can you tell—"

"You were right, Derrick," JC said, after reading Derrick's mind in real time. "It is The Umbra. Brandon said the words that allowed The Umbra to be able to enter his life and snuff it out like a small grease fire."

"This doesn't make sense. Because Brandon is under suicide watch with The Umbra I can't help him? If anything, Brandon needs to be given priority. Can't he be spared in the same way I was? The way my dad was able to save my life from being murdered by The Umbra?"

JC rolled his eyes. He closed Derrick's file, placed his hands on the table, and interlaced his fingers. Wendi poured herself another glass of wine, and Derrick, too.

"We are spiritual beings aren't supposed to intervene and save anyone from anything," JC said, his tone stern, yet not rude or mean.

"Then what the hell does a guardian angel do?" Derrick asked, confused. "Sit back and watch the fireworks?"

"No, you little wiseass," JC said, his tone calm, "nothing of the sort. What a guardian angel does is—well, why don't you tell me why it is guardian angels are discouraged from intervening."

Derrick sipped his wine and thought about JC's question. He poured himself another glass of wine and took a swig. Wendi poured JC another glass once Derrick placed the bottle back on the tray. Then she exited the room after kissing Derrick on his cheek and excusing herself.

"Because life is about choices," Derrick said, unsure of his answer.

JC slammed his hand on the table. "You're goddamn right about that, son. It's about choices. That's why we can't help Brandon. He made a choice to say the words and now he has to suffer the consequences."

"I can't live with that," Derrick said.

"You don't have to since you're dead."

"Not funny, JC. This isn't a time for jokes, wouldn't you agree."

JC sighed. "If you decide to violate the rules and save Brandon, you can't be permitted back into Heaven. You'd be an earthbound spirit forever."

Derrick slammed his fist on the table. "This is total bullshit. How the fuck did this Umbra motherfucker even come into existence? How can God allow something that evil and wicked to walk among the human population?"

"You really want an answer to that?"

"Yes."

JC finished his glass of wine, then poured both himself and Derrick another glass. Oddly enough, Derrick just noticed no matter how much wine anyone poured from the bottle, the quantity of liquid in the bottle never changed. An endless supply of wine.

"The Umbra was an outcast from Hell," JC said. "Banished by Satan. The Umbra is now an eternal earthbound entity."

"Why did Satan banish it from Hell?" Derrick asked before taking another sip of wine. "I thought Satan would relish in The Umbra's work."

"Well, Satan does enjoy The Umbra's work, but Satan also has rules and boundaries for his people, also, and The Umbra attempted to overthrow Satan in order to take over Hell."

"The Umbra has to be stopped. It can't be allowed to continue to do what it's doing. It isn't right."

"I've told you the terms and conditions. If you intervene with Brandon's fate, you will no longer be permitted into Heaven."

"If I defeat The Umbra—wait, does it know we are talking about it?"

JC shook its head. "No. The Umbra is only omniscient in the physical world."

"Okay, good. That's a relief. No point in my plotting to kill it if it can hear all we're saying." He took another sip of wine. "Now, where does The Umbra reside?"

"Technically, I mislead you a little. So, The Umbra is earthbound, but it has the ability to create its own spiritual sector within the physical world. It has basically created its own version of Hell."

"The Umbra is a demon, right?"

JC shook his head and a finger in the air. "Not exactly. The Umbra is ten times worse than a demon. That's why it has to be destroyed using the Sacred Sword, and you must pierce it through its heart."

"The Umbra has a beating heart?"

"No, but you need to stab it through where its heart would be located, and it must be precise. The goal is get through the center of The Umbra's heart. One or more centimeters off could result in The Umbra living and then destroying your spirit, so that's something else you need to consider. Do you want to risk your spirit's life to save Brandon's human life?"

But Derrick needed some time to consider this. He could lose his spiritual essence. He would be nothing more than electrically-charged matter floating aimlessly throughout the Universe, sort of like bubbles at kid's birthday party.

JC pointed out to Derrick The Umbra was going to own and torture Brandon's spirit regardless if Brandon killed himself or if The Umbra murdered him, and this was the nail in the coffin for Derrick. The fact that The Umbra deceived its victims to believe if they killed themselves they would be in a better place crystallized Derrick's decision.

"I want to stop The Umbra," Derrick said, emphatically. "I don't care if I'll be eternally earthbound. I'm sure I can make a nice home for myself somewhere on Earth."

"It's a selfish act, but a foolish one, also," JC replied. "But I will give you as much information about The Umbra as I can to prepare you to battle it."

"Has anyone else ever tried to battle The Umbra other than my dad and me?"

JC nodded. "Three other people, all of whom lost their spiritual essence. And, I'm sorry about your dad, too. The Umbra is a powerful, malevolent, deceitful entity, and you really are placing yourself in mortal spiritual danger. I implore you not to go through with this, but ultimately it's your choice."

"My mind is made up, JC. I'm going to take on The Umbra and I'm going to do everything I can do destroy that evil bastard."

"Fine."

"One more question: Is there any possible way The Umbra could reform and transform and come back to wreak havoc on the Earth's people again?"

JC leaned back in his chair. A long beard—which dangled from his chin—instantly appeared and he caressed it. Meanwhile, Derrick helped himself to his ninth glass of wine.

"I don't believe so," JC said, his tone not entirely confident. Then emphatically he said: "No. Once The Umbra's essence is scattered by means of the Sacred Sword, it's gone for good."

JC and Derrick spent the next several minutes discussing The Umbra—more of its background, where its lair was, and the implications of what would happen if Derrick managed to defeat

The Umbra, JC stressing he would not be allowed back into Heaven.

But this didn't matter to Derrick. He wanted The Umbra dead.

21

Sitting on the floor, Brandon leaned up against his bedroom wall. He glanced at the back of his left wrist. 09:12:34, 09:12:33, 09:12:32, 09:12:31,…

The Umbra spoke within Brandon's mind.

(Don't be afraid, Brand-on, Brand-off. It's gonna be beautiful. I think you've chosen some magnificent ways to off your worthless, pathetic self.)

"Why are you doing this to me?" Brandon whispered, cowering in fear. "I don't deserve to die."

The Umbra appeared in front of Brandon, and Brandon looked up. Brandon could make out some facial features, but its face wasn't anything resembling that of a human. It almost looked as if The Umbra was wearing some sort of mask, even though The Umbra wasn't.

"Does anyone deserve to die?" The Umbra asked.

"Yes," Brandon said. "People like you. Murderers. You killed my brother, Aaron."

"No, I did not. He killed himself, and you will, too. Otherwise, I'll kill you myself, and make no mistake, Brandy-boy. If I have to kill you, the pain will be infinitely worse than if you do it on your own. Ask yourself this: Would you rather get stung by a single honeybee or a million hornets all at one time over and over again?"

Brandon cried as quietly as he could, not wanting to attract attention. He glanced at his wrist again, seeing but not believing entirely a countdown watch was staring him in his face, counting down the seconds, minutes, and hours remaining of his life. The Umbra chided him and encouraged him to stop acting like a little girl and take care of ending his life.

He pulled out a folded-up piece of paper out of his pocket, unfolded it, and scanned it. The top of it was titled SUICIDE PLANS. The paper had four rectangles, created by the folds. Each rectangle had a suicide plan mapped out with it. Plan A was to shoot himself in the head with the same gun—which he had taken from the house when his aunt brought him there to pick up his belongings after the house was no longer a crime scene—he used to shoot into his brother's urn. Plan B was to jump in front of a train—just like the woman he heard about on the news did a few days ago. Plan C was to climb the city's water tower and jump to his death. Plan D was to mimic how Derrick allegedly attempted to commit suicide and that was to strangle himself using his laces from his shoes at the local baseball field.

He carefully considered each option, ultimately placing a check next to the bottom-right rectangle titled: shoelaces method.

22

Wendi placed a silver crucifix necklace around Derrick's neck and clasped the two ends together.

"You be careful out there," she said.

"I will," he replied back. "I promise."

"I want you to come back, but as you know, you will not be able to do so."

Derrick nodded. "It's my hope I'll be allowed back inside. Maybe an exception can be made, but if not, I'll have to live with that."

As Derrick caressed the crucifix, he prayed he be given the strength to defeat The Umbra. He mediated for a few minutes, envisioning precisely where to stab The Umbra in order to render it destroyed.

After Derrick finished this, Wendi reviewed the directions and steps Derrick needed to take in order to reach The Umbra's lair.

He hugged his mom and walked towards the door with the EXIT TO PW sign above it. Before swiping his badge to unlock the door, he turned to his mom and looked at her for a few seconds.

"I believe in you," she said, "but will you please reconsider this? I don't want you to end up like your father."

"I have to do this, Mom," Derrick replied. "I wanted to ask you something though."

"What's that?"

"How did you and dad die—I mean from the physical world?"

She took a deep breath. "Brandon is running out of time. Are you sure you want to hear the story?"

"Give me the nickel-dime version."

She chuckled. "Your grandpa—my dad—used to say that to me all the time." She sharply exhaled. "I wish I could introduce you to him, but time is short, so let me get on with the story about how your dad and I died."

"Thank you. Please do."

"So, I first started dating Bruce—your uncle—at age eighteen and we were together for two-and-a-half years. At first, things were all roses and sunshine. He was a gentleman. But towards the end of our relationship, his parents died in a tragic house fire, which as it turns out, he started."

"Bruce murdered his parents?"

"Yes, he did. He is a murderer. He's killed a lot of people, including your beloved Danielle."

"What the hell? Are you serious right now?"

"As a heart attack, and I wouldn't joke about something like that."

"Who else?"

And in a motherly tone, she said: "Well, hold up now, let me finish telling you about my death. That is, after all, what you asked about, isn't it? One thing at a time now."

Derrick nodded, apologized, and hugged his mom. She accepted his apology.

"After Bruce murdered his parents, he started to drink heavily, pretending to grieve, but he acquired a continuous thirst for the booze. He started to steal money from me so he could buy his booze under the table, money I earned working at a Burger King, so I could put myself through college."

Derrick shook his head in disbelief, still processing the fact Wendi just shared with him Bruce murdered his girlfriend, Danielle.

"I understand this is a lot to take in," Wendi said, "but rest assured, this is only the tip of the iceberg." She poured herself a glass of wine, took a swig, and continued. "I fell in love with Brian, Bruce's younger brother. Brian and I started seeing other more and more behind Bruce's back. Yes, I cheated. I admit that."

"I don't fault you for it," Derrick said.

"Danielle was a cheater, too, by the way. I think you should know she and Bruce did the shiggety-diggety more than once, and often times right under your nose."

"What?" Derrick exclaimed. "Are you serious?"

She gave a look of derision.

"My bad, my bad," Derrick said. "So, he murdered Danielle, his parents. Who else?"

"Technically, me and your dad, too."

"Oh no. Because you were dating his brother on the sly?"

"Yes, but not exactly at the same time. Eventually, Brian and I came forth and told Bruce. He took it well, but that was all a façade. The day Brian and I were in that car accident, Bruce had given Brian an injection. Brian thought it was a B12 injection, but it wasn't."

"What business would Bruce have injecting anything into anyone?"

"He was an RN at that point. He took some of his medical classes while in high school to speed up his college years. Anyway, he really injected Brian with a non-traceable experimental sedative he had stolen from the university's medical lab. Brian and I both fainted at about the same time, and he lost control of the vehicle."

"So it was the car crash that caused your death?"

"Well, yes, but not exactly either. The amount of sedative Bruce injected your dad and me with was enough to kill us, so if the accident didn't, the sedative would have."

"He needs to pay for his crimes. He's a cold-blooded killer. Who else has he killed?"

Wendi hesitated to answer. She didn't want to hold Derrick up from accomplishing his mission as Brandon's suicide watch continued to count down. She suggested he text her after his mission was accomplished, at which point she indicated she would reveal more details.

Derrick agreed and hugged his mother. As they embraced, she tried one last time to dissuade him from leaving, but he was adamant about defeating The Umbra, not worried about the risk to his spirit.

Someone tapped Derrick on the shoulder. Derrick whipped around. "Gayle?"

She smiled. "Hi, Derrick," she said, then wrapped her arms around Derrick, hugging him.

"What are you doing here? You mean you're—"

"Dead?" Gayle interjected. "Yes, I'm dead. Bruce killed me, but let's not get into that right now. You've got a job to do."

"He killed you?" Derrick asked, shocked.

"Derrick," Wendi said, "you are running out of time. Brandon needs you to save him. This is a race against time."

"The alleged wine stain," Derrick said. "Was that your blood?"

Gayle nodded and hugged him. She then extended her arm and pointed at the door. Derrick reluctantly walked towards it, swiped his badge, and departed from the dearly departed he loved so much.

23

Following the instructions JC gave to him, Derrick approached The Umbra's lair with caution. The atmosphere of The Umbra's world crept Derrick out. The sky was a flaming orange with thick, black clouds, almost like locomotive smoke, scattered across it.

The Umbra's lair was a castle, much like a medieval one. Derrick approached the main entrance and knocked, but the door didn't open nor did anyone ask who was there.

Derrick pounded on the wooden castle door several times. This was a bad idea though. Six guards wearing metal armor— three on both sides of Derrick—charged at Derrick with their swords drawn and their shields out.

Derrick drew his sword and began to fight for his life. Two of the six guards ended up stabbing each other charging at Derrick, who moved out of the way just in time.

The remaining four guards were whittled down to two when Derrick used a singular thrust motion and beheaded two of them, and the matter making up their spirit scattered like a heap of balloons being released by a mob of people.

Now it was down to Derrick and two guards. Derrick drew his morning star and blocked the sword of the first guard—who was tall and stocky. The shorter guard tried to stab Derrick in the abdomen, but Derrick thrust his sword upward from under the guard's, effectively defending himself from certain spiritual death.

The shorter guard nearly stabbed himself in the face when Derrick blocked his shot. The guard stumbled backwards and fell over a boulder. Derrick charged after him, leapt off the boulder, and landed near the man's face. Derrick swiped his sword across the guard's neck, destroying his spirit, which scattered into the air like ashes in a fierce updraft.

It was down to one guard versus Derrick. The tall and stocky guard with his scruffy beard looked a lot like Bluto from Popeye. The smile on his face wasn't a friendly one. He taunted Derrick, pretending to lunge at him with his sword.

"Come on, you little pussy," the stock guard said.

"I am what I eat," Derrick said, lunging towards the stocky guard.

The stocky guard laughed. "You're pathetic. I'm doing the universe a favor by taking you out."

"Not going to happen. Not today, not ever."

The two of them shifted position, first one way, then the other, back and forth, enough to make the strongest of stomachs queasy.

"One stab is all it takes," the stocky guard said. "We are going to battle to the death. One of us isn't going to live."

"I'll give my condolences to your family," Derrick quipped. He lunged forward, but the stocky guard moved out of the way. Derrick tripped over the same boulder the shorter guard did. "Shit," he said, turning on his back.

The stocky guard charged at Derrick with his sword pointing downward, aiming for Derrick's neck.

Derrick rolled out of the way and jumped to his feet, still equipped with a sword in one hand and his morning star in the other.

"Come on, tough guy," the stock guard said. "Make your move."

"At least I can move with ease," Derrick snapped back. "Why don't eat a salad once in a while, tub-a-lub?"

The stocky guard mocked Derrick, who backed a few paces away, wanting to increase the distance between him and the stocky guard. Though it didn't do any good. With each step Derrick took backwards, the stocky guard took one or two forward.

"Hey! It's called Weight Watchers!" Derrick shouted, hoping to taunt the guard. "Try it sometime, blubber stuff!"

The stocky guard's maniacal smile disappeared, but even still he didn't appear angry.

"Hey, Fatty McFatty! Your ass is so huge it has its own zip code!" Derrick shouted, forcing himself not to snicker at his own joke. "I wonder what kind of wildlife frolics in your ass? I bet if we pried your cheeks apart, antelope and shit would come prancing out of it."

Guards on top of the roof of the castle raucously laughed at Derrick's hurl of insults. The stocky guard's face changed from an eggshell brown to a fiery red. The anger was coming through now.

The stocky guard tapped the ground a few times as if he were up to bat at home plate.

"Hey, tell me something, Not-So-Thin," Derrick said. "Do you miss seeing your dick when you take a leak? Oops, I'm sorry. You sit to take a leak. I can see your camel toe."

Like a fool, the stocky guard forgot he was wearing armor and looked down at his crotch. Derrick sputtered a snicker.

The guard's face was a stop-sign red. He swatted at Derrick with his sword several times, but Derrick managed to block them with the two weapons he clutched in his hands.

A voice inside Derrick's head—his mother's voice—spoke to him. *{Derrick. This is a race against time. Take the guard out. Stop playing games, finish him off, and get the Sacred Sword from The Umbra's secret chamber.}*

[Sorry, Mom! I will.]

Derrick regrouped his mind and decided to put an end to the shenanigans. The guard dropped his shield and pulled out a battle axe, which was located on the side of his waist. With both weapons over his head, he dragged the blade of his sword across the side of the axe blade.

"Bring it," the stocky guard said, nodding his head. "Bring it, you little shit."

"You first, Big Bertha," Derrick quipped. "I bet your mom has a really nice mangina."

The stocky guard's face turned red in an instant. "Hey! Nobody talks about my momma like that!" He charged at Derrick, screaming. "Aaaaaaaaaah…"

Derrick's sword clashed with the stocky guard's battle axe, as did the morning star gripped by Derrick's left hand and the sword in the guard's right hand.

The guard pulled back his weapons from Derrick's and swatted at Derrick as if chopping down wheat in a field during harvest time.

"I'm gonna kill you, pipsqueak," the stocky guard said. "You don't ever talk about my momma."

"Why not? She had plenty to say about you in bed last night," Derrick said.

The stocky guard screamed and lunged after Derrick, but Derrick fell to his belly and slid in between the stocky guard's legs. Then Derrick leapt to his feet and rocketed towards the stocky guard, stabbing him in the back.

But this didn't any good. Derrick hardly pierced the armor of the stocky guard. Derrick retracted his sword and retreated several feet away from the stocky guard, who in turn spun around and chucked his battle axe in Derrick's direction, though it landed behind Derrick. The guard charged at Derrick again, but this time Derrick fell to the ground and used his leg to trip the stocky guard, who fell face first to the ground.

Without hesitation, Derrick jumped over the man, with one foot landing on each side of the stocky guard. Derrick planted the sword through the stocky guard's armor, rendering him destroyed.

The guards watching from the towers and windows screamed and shouted at Derrick.

"Release the Kraken!" a guard with his head sticking out of a window shouted. "Send out the Kraken!"

"Sounds good," Derrick said, displaying a thumbs-up. "After all this soul slaying, I could use a drink."

Wendi's voice aired in Derrick's mind again, and this time her tone was slightly stern.

{Derrick! Brandon has less than four hours and sixteen minutes left before The Umbra will kill him. And, you have to remember, at any second Brandon could take his life away by his own hand, not wanting The Umbra to murder him. Get the Sacred Sword!}

Before Derrick could respond, the large metal gate surrounding a swamp near the castle's grounds opened and a tyke-sized Kraken with fiery red skin and stumpy tentacles squirted out of the muddy waters onto the shore and scanned its surroundings.

Derrick pointed at the Kraken and laughed as he approached it. When Derrick was about fifty feet or so from the Kraken, it instantly transformed, increasing its size by at least twentyfold.

Looking up at the Kraken, Derrick was suffocated by the smell of rotting flesh. The smoke emanating from the Kraken's nose also choked Derrick.

"How the hell am I going to defeat this beast?" Derrick muttered aloud to himself.

The Kraken extended one of its tentacles and wrapped it around Derrick's sword blade, and with another tentacle, wrapped it around the handle of Derrick's morning star. The Kraken yanked the morning star out of Derrick's hand while Derrick simultaneously pulled his sword downward with a sharp thrust, slicing the Kraken's tentacle, nearly severing part of it off. The Kraken shrieked and retreated back a few paces.

With his sword in his hand, Derrick readied it, waiting for the Kraken to make its next move. The Kraken eyed Derrick for several seconds as some of its other tentacles gyrated randomly about midair, up and down and laterally, including the one gripping the morning star.

The Kraken extended one of its tentacles towards Derrick, which shifted Derrick's attention. At about the same time, the Kraken also swung the morning star at Derrick, striking him on his right side. Fortunately, the armor Derrick was wearing was reinforced and galvanized. The spikes from the morning star dented the armor, but didn't puncture it.

The guards inside of and on top of the castle cheered the Kraken on while others whistled.

"Get him, Kraken," one guard on top of the castle said.

"Rip him apart! Use all your tentacles to overpower him!" another shouted.

"Kill him with pain!" a third guard said, peeking his head out of a window.

The Kraken rolled its eyes. *Shut the hell up and let me do it like Burger King! My way!*

"Let's dance," Derrick muttered, taking a few steps towards the Kraken, hoping to provoke it. *Shit. I got to remember that this is a race against time.*

The Kraken extended one of its tentacles towards Derrick's sword again as its skin illuminated and changed color—much like a cuttlefish attempting to mesmerize its prey—and Derrick fell for the trap, focusing his attention on the Kraken's light show rather than honing in on the Kraken as a whole. With one of its tentacles, the Kraken grabbed Derrick's leg and yanked with all its might, causing Derrick to tumble to the ground. With another tentacle, the Kraken wrapped it around Derrick's neck and hoisted him in the air.

But the Kraken was in for a rude awakening. Derrick sliced the tentacle around his neck. This, however, was a double-edge sword. Derrick fell several feet, injuring his left foot. He hobbled several feet away from the Kraken and repositioned itself to take the Kraken out.

The severed tentacle regenerated before Derrick's eyes and now the Kraken was furious, its nose like that of a locomotive chimney. The Kraken rushed towards Derrick, still clutching the morning star. As the Kraken approached Derrick, it threw the morning star, striking Derrick's chest. This time the armor was punctured, but the spike didn't enter Derrick's spiritual confines to destroy his spirit.

The Kraken grasped the morning star before Derrick could and pulled it from the armor with such force, it tore the armor from Derrick's body—kind of the way a horny lover would tear a bra from their partner. Now Derrick was in a highly vulnerable situation, and he knew it, too.

Derrick rushed from The Kraken, picked up the battle axe lying on the ground, and chucked it towards The Kraken's skull. A direct hit. The Kraken fell backwards into the swamp and perished.

The guards who once cheered The Kraken on swarmed to the foyer near the entrance of the castle, waiting for Derrick to breach the entry.

{Good work, son. Brandon has three hours and forty-two minutes left. He's contemplating ending his life soon. He's on his way to the baseball field.}

(He's going to mimic my attempted suicide?)

{Yes. So, hurry!}

And he did. Noticing the guards no longer gawked out the windows or from atop the castle, Derrick decided to scale the face of the building and gain entry though one of the windows—and specifically a window closest to The Umbra's secret chamber where the Sacred Sword was being stored.

Too bad Derrick wasn't able to float up to the window and enter. Had he been in the spiritual world, then he would have been able to, but because he was in the physical world—The Umbra's physical world to be exact—a lot of his spiritual perks were null and void.

Using specialized climbing tools JC had prepared for him, he scaled the building up to the window and climbed into it. Once inside, he was immediately taken by surprise when a guard hiding in the closet jumped out of it.

"Trespasser!" the guard said as Derrick unsheathed his sword. "And, now I'm going to *kill* you!"

"Bring it," Derrick said.

The guard made a hand gesture as if to say come over here by placing his palm towards the ground and bending his fingers as a unit inward from the third knuckles.

The guard lunged his sword forward at Derrick, but Derrick blocked it with his sword. When the two swords struck each other, a metallic clank sound was produced, and now the battle was on between the two of them.

Their swords struck each other several times. The guard got the upper hand when he rotated his sword as if swinging a baseball bat and knocked Derrick's sword from his grip. From there, the guard tried to stab Derrick directly into his chest, since there wasn't armor protecting it anymore, but Derrick maneuvered his body to prevent this, then rolled under the bed with this sword.

But this too was a mistake. The guard jumped on the bed. Derrick knew what was coming next. The guard stabbed his sword through the bed, just missing Derrick's neck. The guard's sword was stuck in the wood. Derrick rolled from underneath the bed and sliced off the guard's right leg. The guard lost his balance and fell off the bed and onto the floor. Derrick then stabbed the guard in the neck. The guard's body scattered into millions of particles, floating out of the window and into the atmosphere of The Umbra's world.

Derrick exited the room and rushed across the hall to The Umbra's secret chamber. He started to use a special cutting tool to break the combination lock and within ten minutes, the lock was off. He stepped into the chamber, grabbed the sword, and turned around. Standing before him were two guards.

"What the hell do you think you're doing?" the shorter and fatter guard asked.

"Do you two want to live or should I slay your soul, too?" Derrick asked.

The taller and skinnier guard said: "I dare you to try and slay our souls. We'll risk losing our spirits for The Umbra. He's our liege, our master, our God."

"Dumbass," Derrick said. "The Umbra caused you to either kill yourselves or it killed you itself, yet you worship him like he created the Heavens and the Earth."

"The Umbra treats us right, unlike the other spirits who refuse to serve it," the shorter guard said.

"Yeah," the taller guard said, "The Umbra doesn't torture our spirits as often as he does the others. The other spirits are in a continual state of torture and will stay that way until eternity ceases to exist."

"Fuck you both," Derrick said. "You've got thirty seconds to decide if you want to live or die."

Both guards nervously chuckled as Derrick drew his sword while holding the Sacred Sword in his other hand.

"The Umbra can't be defeated," the shorter guard said. "You must have a death wish thinking you can take on The Umbra."

"Five seconds," Derrick said. "Three, two, one. Time's up," then he lunged after both guards.

The two guards put their hands up and told Derrick they wouldn't stop him. They knew The Umbra had the upper hand and would take Derrick out anyway. Besides, The Umbra *wanted* Derrick to come after it. The Umbra looked forward to the satisfaction it would receive after it slayed Derrick's spirit and permanently destroyed him.

24

It was around one-sixteen in the afternoon on December 24. The temperatures were five below zero with the wind chill factored in and most people were at work.

Brandon shuffled down the sidewalk fully bundled up wearing multiple layers of clothes and a bulky winter coat. His hands he kept in his pockets of his coat since he didn't wear any gloves. He didn't care. He intended to not be able to feel anything not too long from now anyway.

While he walked with his hands in his pocket, he massaged the shoelaces inside the right one, imagining how the rope would feel coiled around his neck as it slowly strangled the life out of him. Then he thought about what would follow after his spirit left his body. The Umbra promised him a glorious afterlife where he would be able to see his brother and sister again, and this brought him some solace, though it was nothing more than smoke and mirrors, empty rhetoric.

"Brandon?" a lady standing outside of her home called out. "What are you doing out in this cold?"

Brandon stopped and glanced at the back of his wrist, really not wanting to get sucked into a lengthy conversation with the likes of Mrs. Newbury—the newest neighbor on the block who made it her job to be all up in everyone's business. "Exercising," he said. "I'm trying to keep the winter weight off."

She chuckled. "Well, why don't come over here and have some warm cocoa and a few chocolate chip cookies? You told me you loved my cookies a few days ago and that motivated me to make a motherload more earlier today."

"I'm pressed for time, but maybe later. I really must be going. The Umbra won't like it if I don't take care of this first."

"The what?"

But Brandon didn't answer. He continued to walk even though she called him back a few more times. All he did in response was wave without turning around to see her.

(Good work, Raisin Brandon! You tell that bitch the way it is. And, you're absolutely right. If you don't deliver the goods, there will be a severe penalty, so get your worthless self to the baseball field and strangle yourself.)

The reality set in again and Brandon started to cry. He really didn't want to kill himself. His knees began to shake and his heart rate increased. His fast-paced walk dissipated to a galumph.

(Check your suicide watch, Brandy! Time is running short. Do you really want to feel my wrath? Remember: die or be killed!)

"I'm going!" Brandon shouted. "Will you fuck off for like two seconds? All the time you're in my mind talking shit." *Aaron? Why can't you help me?*

(I know your thoughts, and you've been asking that same question over and over for the past twenty-two hours, forty minutes, and nineteen seconds. He can't help you because his spirit is trapped in my lair. Would you like to see your brother in real time? I can patch you through.)

"Go screw yourself," Brandon muttered.

The Umbra didn't care either way. It was going to show Brandon regardless, which it did. As Brandon walked down the sidewalk to get to the baseball field, the image of Aaron suspended in a cell—hanging from the ceiling with arm shackles—with flames engulfing the cell crept into his mind. A whip with nobody visible controlling it constantly took lashes at Aaron's backside. Scorpions traveled up and down Aaron's body, repeatedly stinging him. Aaron wailed in pain non-stop.

"Stop it!" Brandon shouted. "You're lying. You're trying to scare me is all."

Now, the image of Aaron in the cell said a few words of encouragement to Brandon. As Aaron spoke, he stopped for several seconds, unable to tolerate the excruciating pain he endured.

|No, he's not, Brandon. It's really me. My spirit… is being tortured. Kill yourself so we can be together. If you kill yourself, The Umbra will… release me and we can ascend into Heaven to be with Emily. Hurry!|

(Check your suicide watch. You've got just over an hour to kill yourself. Make this happen or I will. Die or be killed, Brandi-boy!)

Once at the baseball park, Brandon unlatched the fence and entered the same baseball field Derrick entered the night he attempted suicide, but failed, resulting in The Umbra intervening to do the deed Derrick couldn't do.

Near the fence in the outfield, Brandon pulled out the nylon shoelaces and tied each end to the fence. Out of his inside coat pocket, he pulled out a bottle of prescription sleeping pills his aunt had been prescribed a few weeks ago. He uncapped the bottle, placed on his mouth, and swallowed it. Then one more. He wanted to down as many as he could, but he found it difficult to swallow anymore. He didn't want to kill himself, but it looked like there wasn't any choice—in his eyes.

While mustering up the courage to swallow more sleeping pills—being fully aware eventually the pills would render him unconscious—he tested out his strangling apparatus. He looped his head through the shoelace and leaned his body forward so that his neck had pressure applied to it. He closed his eyes and envisioned what life on the other side would be like.

After about four minutes passed, Brandon uncapped the prescription bottle of sleeping pills and swallowed two more—both at the same time. He choked for a few seconds.

Given his heavy eyes and deflated affect implied the first two sleeping pills were starting to take effect.

The Umbra—though not visible to Brandon—watched Brandon's every move, eager to witness him extinguish his own life. The Umbra also was lying in wait for Derrick to show and attempt to spoil the party. Unfortunately, a leak from a corrupt designee of JC leaked the information about Derrick's plan to destroy The Umbra. The designee was banished from Heaven.

Even more remarkable was JC informed Derrick about the leak, but this didn't deter Derrick from following through with his mission to save Brandon and defeat The Umbra.

Brandon checked his suicide watch. 00:32:16, 00:32:15, 00:32:14,... His entire body shook, and not from the cold either. This was genuine primal fear.

(Hey, Brandy, you're a fine girl. Let me show you where you're headed if you don't kill yourself before you reach absolute zero.)

In Brandon's mind appeared The Umbra's castle—the basement of it—about one-hundred feet below ground. Several rows and columns of cells on both sides of the basement had spirits inside of them, shackled much in the same way Aaron was. Each spirit was being tortured with fire. Some spirits had hornets stinging their body while being whipped with a metal wire while others had their necks slashed, healed, only to be slashed again. The cacophonous discordance of the screams and howls terrified Brandon to death.

(You keep stalling. Get the job done or you're going to end up in the cell with the door swung open. Do you see it?)

Brandon nodded. The Umbra zoomed in on it for Brandon to see. Inside was a lion and a tiger, sitting patiently, waiting for Brandon.

(Now, aren't those some pretty pussies? They'll be your personal pets, ripping chunks of flesh from your body, which will then be healed in a matter of seconds, only for them to tear flesh again. Get your ass in gear.)

Aaron, please help me, Brandon pleaded. *Please break from your cell and help me.*

(He can't. Stop your whining and get on with it. You're going really be crying if I have to kill you myself.)

A realization crash into Brandon's brain like a drunk driver asleep at the wheel. He gave it some more thought before confronting The Umbra.

"Wait a second," Brandon said. "You're a liar. You told me Aaron carried out his own suicide yet he's being tortured. So, that means it doesn't matter if I kill myself or not. Either way, you're going to torture my spirit, so why should I kill myself?"

The Umbra showed itself in front of Brandon.

"Because technically he wasn't dead at 00:00:00," The Umbra said. "When his watch hit 00:00:00 and he saw me appear, he finally carried out his own death, but it was too little, too late.

He should have done it earlier. So, he deserves everything he is getting right now."

"Why don't you go back to Hell where you belong?"

"Hell? Why should I return to Hell when I've created a version of it myself?"

Brandon's lip quivered. He was somewhat in a state of disbelief that this was his reality.

The Umbra slightly cocked its head, gazing at Brandon. Then he said: "I'll let you in on a little secret since soon you'll be not of this world. Satan—my former liege—has invited me back to Hell several times, but I politely decline."

"Why did you leave Hell in the first place?"
"I was kicked out. I plotted to kill Satan so I could rule Hell myself. He's forgiven me though. He has a merciful side to him, and he's proud of my work."

"How long ago were you kicked out of Hell?"

"A few months ago, and that's when I started my own reign of terror. Satan gave me my props, lauding me for my creativity of both psychologically and physically torturing my victims."

Brandon shook his head. "I think you're in trouble."
"Why is that, Bran—"
A sword—The Sacred Sword—passed through The Umbra's chest, dead-on where it was supposed to hit. The Umbra scattered into several particles and vanished into thin air.

Derrick stood with a victorious smile on his face, clutching the bow he used to send The Sacred Sword plunging through The Umbra.

Brandon glanced at his wrist and smiled. There was nothing to see except a little Umbra residue from when The Sacred Sword stabbed The Umbra.

"You saved my life!" Brandon said, ecstatic. He ran to Derrick and hugged him around his waist.

"It was my pleasure, Brandon," Derrick replied. "Let's get you back to your aunt's."

"Yes! Let's!"

As the two walked and talked, Derrick couldn't help but wonder how The Umbra—being an omnipresence—had no clue he was behind it. This didn't make much sense to him, and the only way he was able to rationalize it was to conclude The Umbra *was* aware he was behind it and was planning its attack.

{Derrick, good news. All of the tortured souls under The Umbra's hand have ascended into Heaven. Job well done. JC and the Big Dog are both proud of you.}

[Thanks, Mom. I love you.]

{I love you, too. Gayle says hello, by the way.}

[Hi.]

Though Derrick was elated Brandon's life was spared and The Umbra was destroyed, part of him was deflated knowing he revoked his welcome into Heaven. He took comfort in knowing he would continue to keep a close eye on Brandon for a while and then make a home for himself in a dilapidated, abandoned house somewhere. He had no intentions of wanting to haunt the living anyway.

When Brandon and Derrick reached Brandon's aunt's house, Derrick got down on one knee. Brandon hugged him. They shook hands. Brandon walked up the walkway to the front door as Derrick watched on.

When Brandon entered the house, Belinda stood near the door with her arms folded and her eyes fixated on him.

"So, tell me, where did you go and why didn't you tell me?" Belinda asked.

"I'm sorry, Auntie," Brandon said, his tone sincere and remorseful, "but I promise I won't ever do that again. I was at the baseball field. I'm thinking about joining the team this season."

Belinda nodded. "What were you doing outside on the sidewalk? It looked like you were hugging someone. What was that about?"

"I was just saying goodbye to someone who saved my life."

Belinda's eyes widened. "Do you need to go to the BAU like that nine-year-old boy who was reported on the news last night? The one who tried to throw himself on a corn thrasher?"

"No, Auntie. Everything is fine. I promise." He hugged her.

She patted him on the head. "Your lunch is still sitting on the table. Why don't you go in there and eat it?"

"Yes, Auntie, and thank you for letting me stay here. I love you."

"I love you, too."

Belinda looked out the window once more. Standing on the sidewalk was Derrick—whom she could see. He waved at her, walked a few paces down the sidewalk, becoming more and more translucent with step, ultimately fading completely out of sight.

She gasped and covered her mouth before running into the kitchen to tell Brandon what she had witnessed.

EPILOGUE

SIX MONTHS LATER

1

Sitting in the kitchen of his dilapidated house he found on Fremont Road in South Haven, Derrick scrawled out another three-by-three grid for another suspenseful game of tic-tac-toe.

"Damn it," Derrick muttered. "Another cat's eye. I'd like to win just once."

Three knocks on Derrick's front door stopped him from facing off against himself in another game of tic-tac-toe. He opened the door and instantly smiled.

"Mom! JC!" he exclaimed, his voice exuberant. "What brings you two here?"

"How are you, my special boy?" Wendi asked, embracing him.

"Great, mom," Derrick replied, "but I wasn't expecting you guys. Had I have known I would have tidied and baked a cake."

JC and Wendi chuckled.

"Don't worry about the house, Derrick," JC said. "May we come in?"

Derrick silently chided himself. "Of course. Please do."

And they did. Once everyone was seated at the kitchen table, JC quickly drew a three-by-three grid and allowed Derrick to make the first move. Two minutes later, Derrick danced a jig, beating JC at a game of tic-tac-toe. Little did Derrick know JC did that purposefully, knowing Derrick wanted to win one game.

"Let's get down to business, shall we?" JC said. He waved his hand over the center of the table. A bottle of wine with three glasses appeared. "How would you like to come back to Heaven?"

Derrick spat out the wine in his mouth he was about to swallow. "Excuse me? Are you serious?"

"As flared-up hemorrhoids," JC said.

"I've been there," Wendi said, raising her hand. And to Derrick: "When I was pregnant with you."

"TMI, Mom, but I am sorry to hear that," Derrick said.

"What do you say?" JC asked. "Want to come back?"

"I thought I was banished for eternity."

JC nodded, sipped his wine, and pulled out a cigarette that looked hand-rolled. He placed the cigarette between his lips and lit it. After he exhaled the smoke that filled his lungs—much to his pleasure—he said: "The Big Dog decided you deserve to come back. You selflessly risked your own spiritual existence to save the life of another. You also successfully defeated The Umbra."

Derrick took a big sip of wine. "I'd love to come back."

"Good," JC said. "There's another surprise we have for you. Wait here—and no peeking."

JC finished his blunt, stood, and walked to the front door. Derrick heard faint chatter. A few moments later, JC and another man walked into the kitchen. The other man was wearing a long trench coat and a fedora.

"Dad?" Derrick said, awestruck. He stood and walked up to his dad. The two embraced and wept. "I can't believe my eyes. How did you—"

"The Big Dog—the Supreme Being—gave me a rebirth," Brian said.

Wendi, Brian, and Derrick embraced for several moments while JC snapped pics for his SnapChat and Facebook page (only visible to those in the spiritual world).

JC stomped his foot. "The Wi-Fi around here sucks," he said. "I may have to upload these pictures when we get back to Heaven. Our He-Fi is bunches better than Wi-Fi."

"He-Fi?" Derrick asked, confused.

"It's short for Heavenly Fidelity. Fastest damn bandwidth in the universe," JC answered.

After the lengthy hug broke up and the tears dried, everyone hopped in JC's convertible Corvette and drove to Heaven, passing through different dimensions to navigate there.

Along the drive, Derrick asked: "Hey, JC? How is it The Umbra didn't know I was behind him? Or did it?"

"It did," JC said. "The Umbra was a quasi-omniscient entity. It was waiting to make its move."

"But that doesn't make sense," Derrick countered. "It knew I had The Sacred Sword pointed at it and it was going to wait to make its move?"

JC lightly sighed as he lit another blunt. "Okay, you got me. I lied. The Big Dog scrambled and stymied The Umbra's senses for a few seconds to allow you to take the shot, but rest assured, even if The Big Dog didn't do that, you still would have defeated The Umbra, so don't go minimizing your achievement."

"Hey, The Umbra is gone for good, and that's all that matters," Derrick said.

JC passed the blunt to Derrick, who took a few hits off it. Meanwhile, Brian and Wendi got frisky with each other in the backseat.

Spiritual life was good all around.

2

Madison finished changing from her bathing suit to a pair of shorts and an Aeropostale tank top. She was meeting some friends at the park located on the street perpendicular to hers. The park was so close, Roberta or Jimmy could peek their heads out the front door and see it.

"I'm leaving now," Madison said.

"Okay. Have a fun time, but be home by four for dinner," Roberta said. "Do you have your phone with you?"

Madison sighed. "Of course I do, silly."

Roberta chuckled. "See you later."

Madison hopped on her bicycle and pedaled her way to the park. Once there, she locked up her front bike wheel using a bike lock.

Her new best friend, Kelli, was already there, sitting on a swing, swaying slightly back and forth. Kelli wasn't pumping her legs in order to gain momentum. Instead, she sat idly, with her eyes fixated on her phone.

Madison jumped on the swing next to her and began kicking her feet in and out in order to gain speed.

"How was your swimming lesson today?" Kelli asked.

"Great. My coach says I have a good chance of being in the Olympics," Madison replied.

"I bet. I've seen what you can do. I wish I were as good as you."

"Practice, and you will be."

The two girls talked for a few hours, and before Madison knew it, the time was eighteen minutes past four. A few seconds later, Madison received a text.

You need to come home now, Roberta texted.

Sorry, Mom. I'm coming, Madison replied back in a text.

That's good, but this is fourth time in six days, so you're grounded.

But, Mom! Don't be like that!

My mind is made up. I warned you twice this week already. You need to learn. Now get home for dinner. It's getting cold.

I swear! I want to kill myself! I want to die!

A text message from someone else was received. The sender's name didn't have any numbers associated with their message, only two letters: TU.

The text message from TU said: *And in twenty-four hours, you will be dead one way or the other. That's exactly how much time you have to kill yourself. Congratulations, Madison—you're one of the chosen ones. At the end of the twenty-four hours, if you haven't killed yourself, I will kill you myself. If you do kill yourself, your spirit will live eternally in unbridled ecstasy. If you don't, however, I will own your soul and torture it until the end of time. And, speaking of time, a countdown watch located on the back of your wrist will show you how much time remains for you to kill yourself. Only you can see the countdown timer. Go ahead. Take a look.*

Madison glanced at her wrist, and on it a timer appeared: 24:00:00. She swallowed hard and started to whimper.

"No, no, no, this can't be," she muttered, her tone frantic and fearful.

A new text message reached her phone.

This text from TU said: *Once I finish my little spiel, the countdown timer will begin. It won't do any good to tell anyone about the countdown watch—which only you can see—and if you do I may kill you on the spot. I'm everywhere and anywhere all at the same time. Do the right thing and kill yourself. Get creative with your suicide. Grandstand. The more gore, the higher score, as I like to say. Make your choice: die or be killed.*

The countdown timer began to lose one second at a time. Madison screamed: "NOOOOOOOOOOOOOO!"

3

As Derrick, Brian, and Wendi finished their dinner sitting around the dining room table in their little piece of Heaven, they relished in knowing Bruce had been sentenced to death for the murder of Gayle and Danielle and was now being investigated for the murder of his parents (who were also Brian's).

Five knocks on the door interrupted their rejoicing. Derrick answered the door.

"JC. Hey man, what's up?" Derrick asked, smiling. "Come to see my dad?"

"Yes, and you," JC said. "May I come in?"

"You seem upset about something. Are you alright?"

JC shook his head. "I fucked up in a big way. I made a mistake."

"What are you talking about?"

"The Umbra. It's back in the suicide business."

The color in Derrick's face turned white as a ghost. JC shed a few tears.

JC mistakenly forgot in the same way The Big Dog was able to rebirth Brian, Satan had the same power and capability to do for The Umbra, which Satan did, proud of The Umbra's work.

"Dad?" Derrick called from the living room. "You need to hear this."

Brian entered the living room with a drumstick in his hand. "What is it?"

JC and Derrick sat on the couch. Brian stood, waiting for an answer.

"Tell him, JC," Derrick said.

And JC did. Fifteen minutes later, Derrick and Brian suited up and began their travels to locate and destroy The Umbra once and for all.